Below Grass Roots

SWALLOW PRESS BOOKS BY FRANK WATERS

The Lizard Woman (1930, reprinted 1994)
Midas of the Rockies (1937)
People of the Valley (1941)
The Man Who Killed the Deer (1942)
The Colorado (1946)
The Yogi of Cockroach Court (1947, 1972)
Masked Gods: Navaho and Pueblo Ceremonialism (1950)
The Woman at Otowi Crossing (1966)
Pumpkin Seed Point (1969)
Pike's Peak (1971; reissued 2002 as individual volumes):
    The Wild Earth's Nobility
    Below Grass Roots
    The Dust within the Rock
To Possess the Land (1973)
Mexico Mystique: The Coming Sixth World of Consciousness (1975)
Mountain Dialogues (1981)
Flight from Fiesta (1987)
Brave Are My People (1998)
A Frank Waters Reader: A Southwestern Life in Writing (2000)

ALSO AVAILABLE

A Sunrise Brighter Still: The Visionary Novels of Frank Waters, by
    Alexander Blackburn (1991)
Frank Waters: Man and Mystic, ed. Vine Deloria, Jr. (1993)

Below Grass Roots

Book II of the Pikes Peak trilogy

Frank Waters

With a Foreword by Joe Gordon

SWALLOW PRESS/OHIO UNIVERSITY PRESS

ATHENS

Swallow Press/Ohio University Press, Athens, Ohio 45701
©1971 by Frank Waters
Foreword ©2002 by Joe Gordon
Printed in the United States of America
All rights reserved. Published 2002

Swallow Press/Ohio University Press books are printed on acid-free paper ∞ ™

10 09 08 07 06 05 04 03 02   5 4 3 2 1

This volume reproduces the text of *Below Grass Roots* as it appeared in Frank Waters's 1971 edition of *Pike's Peak*.

LIBRARY OF CONGRESS CATALOGING-IN-PUBLICATION DATA

Waters, Frank, 1902–
    Below grass roots / Frank Waters.
        p. cm. — (Book II of the Pikes Peak trilogy)
    ISBN 0-8040-1048-X (pbk.: alk. paper)
        1. Gold mines and mining—Fiction. 2. Colorado—Fiction. I. Title.

PS3545.A82 B45 2002
813'.52—dc21

                                                                2002021793

CONTENTS

Foreword

This is a story about the West, the day-to-day reality of the men and women who came to a frontier town to build homes and businesses and to raise families. It is not the formulaic, mythic West of cowboys and Indians, although Native American perspectives about the land are an important part of Waters's story. Such adventurous stories reside on the surface of Western experience, and are the stuff of the "western" as traditionally understood by outsiders. This is the story of the West as told from the inside by a writer who was born and raised in Colorado, who experienced first-hand its land and people. This insider's vision makes all the difference, and gives Frank Waters's story its realism, poignancy, and verisimilitude.

Joseph Dozier, Waters's grandfather, arrived in Colorado Springs, a frontier railroad town at the foot of Pikes Peak, "America's Mountain," in 1872, a year after the town was founded by General William Jackson Palmer. Dozier was a successful building contractor, and many of his buildings stand in Colorado Springs today, including the house at 435 East Bijou Street, where Waters was born July 25, 1902—the same year that Winfield Scott Stratton, the "Midas of the Rockies," died. Waters grew up in Colorado Springs, attended Central High School, and dropped out of Colorado College after his junior year in 1924. He left home shortly afterward. Real people, places, and dates are the historical-autobiographical basis of this story, the physical and imaginative places of Waters's story of the West. He didn't even change the names of people and places, except for his family—Dozier to Rogier—but there is no mistaking whom he is describing.

After leaving Colorado Springs, Waters worked at various jobs in Wyoming and California, traveled extensively in Mexico, and along the way became a writer. He visited the Pikes Peak region often in the mid-1930s. By that time he'd written two novels and published one, both set on the border between the United States and Mexico. He also was writing a new novel that would become the first of three in the Pikes (Waters used the possessive form—Pike's) Peak trilogy—*The Wild Earth's Nobility* (1935). The 1930s were important years in Waters's creative life. He was going back to his roots, rethinking his past, and formulating themes that he would develop more fully in his later work. He spent more than a year in the Pikes Peak region, in Colorado Springs and the mining towns of Victor and Cripple Creek, Colorado, where as a boy he'd worked in his grandfather's mines. His return is analogous to that of another Westerner, Mark Twain, who rediscovered his past, the deep pool of his imaginative center, in the small river town of Hannibal, Missouri. Pikes Peak, the mountain just west of Colorado Springs, became Waters's Mississippi River. His next three books focus on the "Matter of the Mountain." *Below Grass Roots* (1937) and *The Dust within the Rock* (1940) continue the story begun in *The Wild Earth's Nobility. Midas of the Rockies* (1937), while not directly a part of the Pikes Peak trilogy, is closely related. It is the biography of Winfield Scott Stratton, the richest and most spectacularly successful of all the miners in the Pikes Peak region, and a friend and sometime business partner of Waters's grandfather, Joseph Dozier.

The three novels that make up the Pikes Peak trilogy can be read individually, for each book is a complete story, each focusing on a different generation of Rogier family history; however, all are related by the central, tragic story of the rise and fall of Joseph Rogier, and the impact of his life on his family. Of growing interest in the story is the life of March Cable, Rogier's grandson, who is the semi-autobiographical representation of Frank Waters himself. Read successively, the books provide a panoramic overview of the history of the American West, especially of the mining industry during the late nineteenth and early twentieth centuries.

By 1960 all three books of the trilogy were out of print. Waters felt the story too important to be forgotten, and began an extensive redaction of the books, sharpening their focus, eliminating interesting but peripheral characters and scenes, and, in general, constricting the plot. In all he cut 800 pages. The result was a single volume, 743 pages long, divided into three sections that were titled after the original trilogy, but were more tightly structured, less rambling. *Pike's Peak: A Family Saga* was published in 1971. A reprint appeared in 1987, its title modified to *Pike's Peak: A Mining Saga*. Nothing else was changed, and the book remains in print today.

This new edition provides another interesting episode in the history of the publication of Waters's story, for it returns to the original three-volume format, but by replicating the redacted version that appeared in 1971. This allows the reader the benefit of Waters's own editorial judgment as found in the single-volume edition of 1971 without the awkwardness of balancing a 743-page book.

Central to all Frank Waters's writing is his understanding of and commitment to the land, what he calls his "sense-of-place." Pikes Peak, the 14,110-foot batholith rising west of Colorado Springs, dominates the geography of the region today much as it did when Waters was growing up. This explains why the mountain overshadows the three novels in the Pikes Peak trilogy. Joseph Rogier is mysteriously drawn to settle within its shadow. Its meaning and silent power haunt him throughout *The Wild Earth's Nobility,* even as he struggles to succeed in a frontier town still visited by roaming bands of Plains Indians. The mountain is always there "from the depths of dreamless sleep to the horizon of wakeful consciousness." Rogier builds a successful construction business, maintains a household full of relatives, and raises his children. Then gold is discovered in Cripple Creek, just over the mountain.

At first, Rogier resists the temptation to join the miners, to probe the mountain's depths. However, when *Below Grass Roots* opens he is deeply involved in mining; he is not interested in gold primarily, but in knowledge—a need to understand himself by unraveling the secret of Pikes Peak. On one level, this novel includes some of the most detailed and descriptive passages about hard-rock mining in Western literature. On the human level, it is the story, not often told, of those who failed. Rogier's mission to find the heart of the mountain becomes an obsession and ends in financial disaster. The family's dreams of wealth turn to dust in the dry holes drilled in the solid granite of Pikes Peak. Family members find an escape only at the Sweet Water Trading Post on the Navajo Reservation. At various times, Ona, Rogier's eldest daughter, her husband, Jonathan Cable, and her son, March, discover a new world: an environment, a way of life, totally different from that of Pikes Peak.

When *The Dust within the Rock* opens, the family is barely surviving. Rogier is a broken man, and though he lives until the end of the book, he is no longer central to the events of the novel. The story turns to his grandson March, a deeply troubled and alienated young man. March loves his grandfather, but is embarrassed by his failure, and resents the snobbishness of the millionaires who did strike it rich, and who abandoned Rogier and his family. Most important, March is struggling to find his own understanding of the mountain, his own sense-of-place. He drops out of college and leaves home. For several years he wanders the Southwest and Mexico, returning to Colorado Springs only after he learns of his grandfather's death. At the end of the novel, March, like his grandfather before him, stands contemplating Pikes Peak. "Toward it he began his long and resolute journey."

Frank Waters's story of the West is rich in history, the details of life of the people on the frontier. It is, as Waters tells us, the saga of a family and of the most important industry in the early West—mining. Pikes Peak, the great mountain to the west, becomes a symbol of all Western land. In the end the reader must stand with March contemplating that mountain and ask: What is my responsibility to the land? How shall I inhabit it?

JOE GORDON

BOOK TWO

Below Grass Roots

PART I

GRANITE

1

To glimpse again, after an absence of only months, that great Peak rising over the ears of his team; to watch it take shape above the forested slopes of pine and spruce and sparse aspen, above the frost-shattered granite of timberline; to see it stand at last an imperturbable sentinel on the crest of that Great Divide which separates earth and heaven as it does dreamless sleep and wakeful consciousness — to meet it thus, face to face, was to arouse in Rogier a resurgence of those inexpressible thoughts and conflicting emotions provoked always in a man who returns to a realm which destiny has marked for his own.

He drove steadily up the steep winding road, reins held loosely in his hands, the wind stirring gently the wisps of white hair sticking out from his hat. Ahead of him two men on foot were puffing up the grade. Rogier pulled up beside them. "Figurin' on a ride, boys?"

"We wasn't figurin' on it," spoke up one, stowing his blanket roll in back, "but we ain't objectin' any."

The two men climbed in beside him, both giants, middle-aged, red-faced, and dressed in corduroys and flannel shirts. For a time none of them spoke. "We're getting along," Rogier said at last. "You're just coming to the district?"

The two men looked him over again before replying: his black broadcloth coat stretched over his wide shoulders, the excellent but dust-covered hat, and beneath it the calm forceful face of a man with its graying mustache and white wisps of hair who looked as if he had long known the vagaries of men and mines alike.

"We had us a job in the mill in the Springs," said one. "To get it we had to take out a union card, and then the Standard let us out because we had one."

"What's the trouble?"

"Not enough pay. $1.80 a day less'n five cents insurance and one percent discount. So the Western Federation of Miners is organizin' the mill workers to get $2.50."

"Anyway we lost our jobs and have come up to Cripple to hunt for another. You got somethin'?" asked the other.

"Not a thing, sorry to say," answered Rogier.

"Saw an outfit in back, beggin' pardon," the other refuted calmly. "We ain't scabs or union men neither. Jes' two hungry men huntin' for bed and board."

For a moment the men were silent. Then one said, "I tell you, Colonel, if you're figurin' on somethin, we can keep our mouths shut and are tolerable hard-rock miners — leastways we get up our appetites. You might be keepin' us in mind. Zebbelin's the name. Jake here and me, Abe."

"I'll remember you, boys."

"And what do you call yourself, Colonel?"

"Rogier. Joseph Rogier. Plain Mister, boys."

"That's all right," spoke up Jake, drawing his finger under his woolen collar protruding an inch from his creased brown neck. "Somethin's liable to pop up any time. You can't ship scenery no more. You got to go down below grass roots. But mines are just like ladies. Stubborn as all get-out, not a welcomin' smile for months. And then first thing you know, like spring had got under their hides, there they be just beamin' at you all over! Take that old workin' we had once. Refusin' to show a color all winter. Then when Abe got mad and heaved his pick into her fer the last time — what do you reckon he saw! In a piece of quartz no bigger'n a fist, four leaders of wire gold you could pick out with a nail! Yes, sir! If you got a flighty workin' in mind, me and Abe's the men for you!"

Garrulous old men! Rogier shut his ears to their steady flow; and when they reached the Gold Coin shaft house on Diamond Avenue in Victor, he was glad to slip them a bill for eats and drive on alone. It was a steep cruel grade up to Altman on the high saddle between Bull Hill and Bull Cliffs. Putting up his team, he walked along the street and sat down on the rickety porch of Smith and Peters' saloon. Sam's highest city in the world was an eyrie of unpainted shacks overlooking the richest producing area in the district. Nearby rose the great shaft house Rogier had built for the American Eagles, and the Garnet and Fleur-de-Lis he had given up. Directly below him lay the Independence and Portland, and three other great producers — the Buena Vista, Victor, and Jones' Pharmacist. To the south lay Victor and Goldfield surrounded by the portals and gallows frames of a hundred more mines, thinning out toward Cable's New Moon on Big Bull. None of them mattered to Rogier. For to the north spread out his own garden of dreams pasturing the immemorial cow and her calf.

Directly below him, inclining west to east, stretched a grassy alpine valley watered by a meandering creek. From it now rose a small puff of smoke followed by the faint screech of a whistle. He watched a toy train emerge to view, running over a spindly straw trestle, chugging up Grassy Gulch and vanishing on its climb into the district. Across the meadow to the northeast rose Cow Mountain and her Calf, a thousand feet lower and sucking at a teat of granite protruding from her aspen covered flanks. Between them, entering this grassy trough from the north, lay a steeply rising gulch down which wound Beaver Creek and an old wagon road. Near its mouth Rogier could make out the shaft house of the Silver Heels and Reynolds' enlarged shanty. Above it, the right fork of the gulch narrowed and deepened, rising past a thin grove of aspens beyond which lay the Gloriana. Still it rose upward like a deep cleft in the granite cliffs. And above it, sheer and shaven, stood the pink face of the summit of the Peak itself. It looked, from where he sat at 11,000 feet, as close as a face in a mirror, one whose features he knew better than his own. But he could not see its deep gorges and rugged cliffs for the thing itself. As he stared back at it the sun sank with a livid blood red flare that deepened the pink of the granite hills and filled the shadowy gulches with pools of porphyry. Then suddenly it was dark. Worn out, he had a drink inside and a hearty supper before turning into bed.

Next morning at the Silver Heels he and Reynolds got down to business. Months before, when the vein began to splay out, Rogier had reminded Reynolds of his agreement to close the mine and move up the gulch to the Gloriana. Reynolds had bucked; he was sure they would pick up the vein again. But Rogier was obstinate and Reynolds had moved his crew to open the new working.

Everything had gone wrong from the start. The Gloriana ran into water. Cripple Creek from the beginning had been known as a wet mining district. Annual precipitation of from fifteen to eighteen inches accumulated water which had no outlet from this big granite bowl of porphyry. Hence the depth limit of all mines was restricted by the underground water that filled the shafts faster than it could be pumped out. As the average altitude of the top of the bowl was about 9,200 feet, and the average altitude of the mine portals was 10,000 feet, the depth limit of the shafts was 800 feet. But when Reynolds began to drill into clammy gangue below the first level he protested to Rogier with a common-sense observation. The Gloriana lay in a steep gulch that received the runoff of the snowpacks on the very summit of the Peak. There was no use going deeper.

Rogier was stubborn. He argued that its portal elevation was not too much higher than that of the Strong Mine on Battle Mountain at 9,756 feet, and the depth of the first water level would not be far short of the 700 feet of the Strong. "What if it's only half that?" he demanded. "Keep going down!"

They resumed drilling — at $36 a foot through hard granite. Two hundred feet down Reynolds struck water. Indomitably Rogier snaked in and installed pumps. Still the Gloriana, water-logged as an old ship weary for its inevitable grave, wallowed in a sea of eruptive porous rock that soaked up water like a sponge. The men, in slimy clothes that never dried out, began to grumble. Reynolds, who never swore, swore. Only Rogier kept silent. By day he would stand there, worrying about the huge sum he had sunk into the Garnet and Fleur-de-Lis for the benefit of Diggs and Handel, the loss of income from the abandoned Silver Heels and abandoned construction work in Little London, and watching pour out in a muddy stream one of his downtown store buildings and a house in town. In the evening after the crew had left he would still be there staring up the gulch. The clouds rolled in and all became a billowing sea of white upon which floated, high above, an iceberg of stainless purity, its smooth sides unscored by any mark of mortal earth. A little light-headed from the thin rarefied air perhaps, Rogier was discomfited by its metamorphosis from the intimately personal to the monstrously impersonal. It was as if that great living entity had withdrawn into a sheath of ice which it was melting, day and night, to flood his world with water.

The rains began, confirming the illusion. Water poured down the gulch in an angry flood. Patches of soggy earth on the hillsides gave way, carrying down trees and boulders. The few aspens, dripping rain, provided little firewood. The men, already slimy from manning the pumps, became soggy under the onslaught of water from above and below. Rogier could not break the spell cast upon him. Every time he went down the shaft, feeling the dank walls closing about him and hearing the gurgle of water below, he felt like a foetus still immersed in its prenatal fluid darkness, struggling vainly to be released to a world of air and earth.

"We'll empty her!" he kept insisting, reminding Reynolds that the new El Paso drainage tunnel, a mile long and built at a cost of $80,000, had lowered the water level to 8,800 feet.

Reynolds had become strangely quiet and solicitous. "But we're above that, Colonel," he said gently. "This ain't no mine. It's a well."

"Keep on pumping, man. I'll foot the bills."

Just how, Rogier did not know. But with great effort he tore himself away, and went down to Little London to find out. A week later when he returned, Rogier found the Gloriana boarded up and abandoned. Reynolds had taken the men back to the Silver Heels and was driving a new tunnel. It had saved him, despite his shocked amazement at the unspoken firmness of his uncouth partner. Not only had Reynolds immediately stopped his frightful expenditures, enabling him that winter to finish two construction jobs in Little London which restored his credit at the banks, but he had struck pay ore again.

But now again that mounting frantic urge had driven him to face Reynolds across the long kitchen table in his quarters at the Silver Heels. "Look, man!" He laid the results of the last assays before him. "Down to a half-ounce again. I told you at the beginning this was not a blanket vein or a chimney. Just gash veins always petering out. We've got to go down. Way down. And way up the gulch. There's where we'll strike the sheer wall of the granite dropping into the prophyry heart."

Mrs. Reynolds came in with a pot of coffee and two mugs. "Colonel, you hadn't ought to be movin' us again. Not when we're so comfortable like." She waved a hand toward the chinked walls plastered with the warm pink front pages of the *Denver Post,* the little bedroom adjoining, where they slept, the room beyond with bunks for the unmarried men of the crew who lived with them, and the opposite kitchen with its big wood stove and stocked shelves. "Why, this has been home for us nigh on ten years, Colonel! The boys and us are jes' one happy family!" She flounced out to her interminably dirty pots and pans.

"He's not movin' me!" Reynolds called to her departing footsteps with the voice of a new and unwarranted independence. "I'm rememberin' that day when I staked her out — the Silver Heels. And I reckon you ain't forgot the day you grubstaked me either, Colonel. There was gold here, like I told you. Not too much or too little, but enough. Sure we've had our ups and downs. But through thick and thin I've stuck by you. And so has the Silver Heels."

Yes, Rogier remembered it and more too — the humbleness and faithfulness of these two stout souls who had become like members of his own family. What could he have done without them? Still he knew how a man got attached to a mine, the great fallacy of every mining camp.

"That's true," he admitted. "But every mine, even the best one, has its day. Let's go on to a better one, Reynolds!"

"The Magpie, eh?"

Rogier grinned like a boy caught stealing cookies. "I did use that name when I filed papers on her," he confessed.

"Well, I don't know of a better one. The second bird in the bush worth less'n the one in hand!"

Rogier resumed his attack. "Look at its showin'. Here!"

Reynolds ignored the assays spread out before him, looking at Rogier as if he had heard all this an incalculable number of times. "We been all through this with the Gloriana. She's waterlogged, watersoaked, a bloomin' well."

Rogier leaned forward and as if imparting a great secret said solemnly, "But we're going above water."

Reynolds, so often childish, answered as if speaking to a still younger child. "Above water? Colonel, above gold."

"Why, man — " Rogier suddenly halted. There were some things he could not say to any man.

Reynolds' long narrow face with its walrus mustaches softened with the trace of a benign smile. "Now here's the Silver Heels. A producin' gold mine. Payin' the boys a livin' wage, providin' me and the Old Girl a mite against rheumatism and a rainy day, payin' your own bills, Colonel! And here you want to desert her again for a no-account claim outside the prophyry, way up the Peak itself! Partner, I believe in our mine. I'll stick by her!"

Nevertheless two weeks later men and mules began hauling the machinery salvaged from the Gloriana up the gulch to the Magpie, and cutting timber for a cabin to house Reynolds and his crew. Rogier was elated as he drove back to Little London. Not for a minute did he regret the money out of which he had been cheated by those mountebanks, Diggs and Handel. What if he had gained control of the Garnet and Fleur-de-Lis, or any of the big leases and million dollar producers with their splendid surface plants, the double-cage steam hoists, well timbered tunnels and tidy drifts, the ore blocked out and removed with mathematical precision? Then he would be facing the economics of illumination, transportation, and hoisting: estimating the tractive power of a burro on a two percent grade and deciding if the cars could be more cheaply trammed by hand, figuring the shipping and treatment cost of $30 ore — a mundane business like running a bank! But he had been saved from this by the Silver Heels and the Gloriana, each representing not only fundamentals in mining but elemental approaches to the elusive truth of his secret quest.

As he swung out of the steep-walled canyon the Peak rose to sight again. Once more it looked down upon him with a face calm and unperturbed as his own. He was free of the spell it had cast upon him. He felt born out of its gelid, watery womb into the light and air of the world outside. A deer stepped daintily across the road. A huge magpie, glistening white and blue-black, accompanied him from pine to pine. As it flew overhead one of its feathers settled on the seat beside him. An augury of good fortune! Rogier proudly fastened it in his coat lapel. The Magpie! That now was the step ahead and upward. And he was taking it resolutely, with a joyful quickening of his heart that convinced him he was nearing his goal.

2

Ona, in the last days of her pregnancy, left her little frame house to go home for confinement. Cable had wanted her to go to a hospital, but she refused. Home was home; she wouldn't think of having their baby born anywhere but in the great redwood bed in the master bedroom on the second floor. Cable's face was grim, but he said nothing. So this morning after he had gone to work, lest she hurt his feelings, she had laid out on the bed everything she wanted him to bring her and latched the door behind her.

The hour was almost nine o'clock. The sun was high in the summer sky, and she could feel its warm rays taking possession of her langorous big body as she walked slowly along the creek. It was July. The birds hopped busily through Mrs. Cullen's apple trees; the bees hummed their monotonous drone of summer; even the sand daisies and tall sunflowers in the patch of prairie beyond the Santa Fe underpass seemed to be smiling at the morning. A long block farther she reached Shook's Run and sat down weakly on the planks of the bridge, unmindful of the sun and dust.

Never in her life had she felt so secure and relaxed. It was as if her mind had been disjointed from her body, her thoughts wandering at random like clouds in the sky. Something mysterious was taking place within her body, so swollen now she could not recognize it as her own, but over it she had no control. She belonged to nature, something nebulous that had no time nor bounds but to which for the first time she felt intimately connected. As though she had never noticed them before, she watched the green leaves turning up with the breeze, their undersides coated gray with dust. Preternaturally alert, she noticed the sound of a woodpecker's hammering far up the lane of trees, the flicker of sunshine through willow branches, the murmurous undertone of Shook's Run below the iron-girded bridge. With difficulty she withdrew herself out of this vast anonymity, managed to get to her feet, and walked sedately to the tall gaunt house across the street.

Mrs. Rogier met her at the door with loud disapproval. "Of all things! Walking down alone! Jonathan come by and said he'd fetch you home 'round midday. What — you wasn't in a hurry, Ona?" she asked anxiously.

Ona laughed. "It was time to come and an awfully nice morning for a walk."

"You get up those stairs then. The room's all ready. We'll fetch the doctor just in case."

Soon the doctor came down in his buggy, joked, and said he'd look in again after supper. At noon Jonathan brought down her things. Then after a nap she put on her best nightgown and old robe, and sat resting in a big armchair drawn up in front of the windows. How wonderful to be home in this great room with its hand-burnished redwood bed, dresser, bureau, and panelling, its alcove and balcony! Methodically brushing her long hair and staring out upon the wall of mountains, cool blue in the dusty afternoon, she felt oddly detached from that complex world of the Rogiers bounded by Shook's Run and Bijou Hill. It was as if always she had been sitting here at life's window, watching like Sister Molly the intricate interplay of their human hopes and endeavors, forgiving with compassion the folly of those who lived courageously their thoughtless lives. Rogier and her mother, Sister Molly, Tom and Bob and Hiney, Mrs. White and Boné, Sally Lee and Mary Ann, Jonathan too! What a patternless fabric of continuity their lives wove, that neither ambition nor humility, nor hope and fear, courage and folly, could ever alter.

She dozed, slept. The doctor came and went. Mrs. Rogier poked her head in the door every whipstitch. "How do you feel now?" Sally Lee and Mary Ann came in. Lida brought bear soup and delicacies. Jonathan, sleeping in the alcove, was attentive. "Do you have everything you want?" She smiled. "Bring me that Two Gray Hills blanket from Shallow Water Bruce gave me. I miss it across the foot of the bed." One afternoon Rogier looked in the door. For a moment he stood motionless as if arrested by the specter of a woman wrapped in an old gray robe so like Sister Molly he stared transfixed.

"Well!" he said at last. "You're here."

Ona smiled. "It won't be long, Daddy. I'm glad that even the Kadles will be coming up the steps tonight. I wouldn't be anywhere else."

That night it happened. At five minutes till midnight. The doctor arrived in plenty of time. He could see the house blazing with lights from the top of Bijou Hill; and when he entered the house, satchel in hand, everybody in the household was crowded in the hall except Rogier who was still sitting in the shop. Yet he too came pounding up the steps when it was all over and the doctor, pen in hand, was bent over the birth certificate. "What name have you selected for this July baby, Mr. Cable?" he was inquiring.

Cable looked confused as all husbands, especially over forty, at such a time. Mrs. White, failing and irascible, stood at the foot of the bed, amazingly surprised and completely scandalized at the inevitable result of such a miscegenation of a Rogier and a De Vinney with a red niggah. Rogier flipped up the blanket, discovered that the infant had the Rogier twin toes. Yet even this apparently did not seem sufficient to allay a reasonable doubt engendered by Mrs. White's decidedly unforgiving stare.

"A July baby, nothing!" he said humorously. "The boy's going to be wild as a March wind! Eh, Cable?"

Cable's dark face set. Brushing back his straight black hair from a wet forehead, he took the pen from the Doctor with his slim brown hand, and swiftly inscribed on the certificate the name "March."

Important as a baby in the family was — and his own first grandchild — Rogier had his mind on other wild winds. There had been a fire at Altman. A block of cabins was wiped out, the gallows frames of the Pinto and Mercer mines just off the street were weakened, and all the timbering holding the dumps above the road had given way. It was necessary to clear the road for the steep climb up to the saddle and to reset the timber frames. Rogier was given the job. Hardly had he put a crew to work than he contracted to build a big mess hall and a dozen cabins on Bull Hill to house and feed those made homeless by the fire. The buildings were crude and cheap. and their construction gave him time to push work on the Magpie.

Then came another interruption far more serious. The trouble down in the ore reduction mills in Colorado City came to a sudden head early in August. The Western Federation of Miners called out all the mill workers in a general strike. Then, to make sure the mills could not receive ore shipments and reopen with scab labor, all the mines in Cripple Creek were ordered closed. Rogier could hardly believe it. The district was at its zenith with 475 shipping mines. In its ten towns and camps there was a floating population of some 43,000, with more than 6,000 men working in the mines. Yet within three days 3,500 men were out and the *Cripple Creek Times* ran the headline:

ALL THE MEN ARE NOW OUT
ALL THE FIRES ARE BANKED
GOD PROTECT THE DISTRICT!

The Mine Owners Association met and agreed to operate with scabs, opening several mines. The strikers retailiated with acts of violence. Governor Peabody ordered out the state militia with Brigadier Generals Chase and Bell in command. One thousand troopers arrived with 600,000 rounds of ammunition and a Gatling gun, establishing camp on Battle Mountain between the Portland and the Independence. The strikers derisively called it "Camp Peabody" or "Camp Goldfield," hooted at the soldiers, and on Labor Day marched throught the streets in a parade 5,000 strong. General Chase seized editor George Kyner and four members of the office force of the *Victor Record* for publishing editorials sympathetic to the strikers, and imprisoned them in a bull pen at the camp. The case brought up the question of *habeas corpus*.The prisoners asserted that as martial law had not been declared they could not be held. General Chase continued to hold them until the district judge ordered a hearing, whereupon Chase and his troop marched the prisoners to Cripple Creek. By the time they arrived at the court-house, Bennett Avenue was lined with cavalrymen and the Gatling gun was mounted on the corner at Fourth Street. Judge Seeds imperturbably ordered Kyner and his employees released. Then followed a court-martial of the officers. General Chase was found guilty of disobedience, but Governor Peabody remitted punishment.

Rogier in his eyrie on the saddle — a one-room cabin — looked down upon crowds gathering in the streets of the camps, groups outside portals and shaft houses being harangued by shouting speakers, men walking furtively as criminals past his own door. His work held up, he remained in the district despite Mrs. Rogier's frantic letters. A cold September rain made the camp miserable. Water ran in the door of the unfinished messhall, the roofs of the cabins leaked. He was threatened with a suit for defaulting on his contract, damned by Union and scab workers whenever he tried to resume work with either. At night he slept little, watching his material. By day he stewed and fretted.

Snow and cold set in. The miners began to feel the pinch of coming winter. The troopers, unable to stand the high altitude, came down with mountain sickness and were ordered to forego coffee. Eleven hundred men were now working. A hundred more were imported from Idaho.

Then late in November it happened just below Rogier. At mid-morning in the sixth level of the Vindicator an infernal machine containing twenty-five pounds of dynamite was exploded, killing Superintendent Charles McCormick and Shift Boss Melvin Beck.

The camp went wild. More troops were rushed in under General Bell, the mine owners agreeing to loan the state enough money to pay the militia's expenses. Martial law was proclaimed. Wholesale arrests were made and the bull pen filled with men. Rogier that evening, hurriedly walking through the crowd on Diamond Avenue in Victor, suddenly felt the grip of a huge iron paw on his shoulder. Spun about, he recognized one of the giant workers to whom he had given a lift months before.

"Colonel! It's me, Jake. We wasn't doin' a thing. Just walkin' down the street when they up and grabbed Abe. That quick he was down on the ground, bleedin' from a cut on the head, and they was measurin' his foot. Just because he looked like he wore a number eight. Dammit, Colonel! You know he don't wear no number eight." He stuck out his own muck-smeared eleven.

Rogier had no opportunity to listen further to his explanation. Both of them, like flotsam on a mounting tide, were shoved inside a saloon. The place was jammed with strikers listening to a derbied figure haranguing them from on top the bar.

"Brothers! Are we going to let our lives be dictated by a capitalistic slave in striped pants planted in an armchair down in Denver?Fathers! Are we going to take the bread from our children's mouths to fill the pork barrels of mine owners with their millions? See their little hands outstretched — not for pearls and diamonds, my fathers! Not for silks and satins. For bread, fathers! Dry crusts. Dry as snow crusts in winter!"

The speaker let down his arms, fumbled the watch chain slung across his vest, and waited for the yells and stamping to subside. Rogier, with a knee at his behind, was shoved closer to him. "Men!" the speaker began again. "Workers of the soil, workers in mill and factory, workers of hard rock. The best hard-rock miners in the greatest gold camp on earth — and the least paid, by God! Listen!"

He cursed mine owners — the dirty rich; Governor Peabody — the dirty capitalistic slave; General Bell — the dirty military; and the dirty scabs. Rogier could feel the dirt sifting through his clothes. He felt intolerably smirched with profanity, his common sense insulted, and his inborn aloofness unforgivably violated. He reached up and caught the speaker by the ankle, with one quick pull bringing him down off the bar, head over heels, into a spittoon. Then quite spryly for his sixty years, he scrambled on top the bar.

"Gentlemen! A little less noise and confusion! Let's don't lose our heads!"

Jake, awakened from the spell cast upon him by the grand-iloquent delivery of the moment before, stood, big and brawny, peering up at Rogier with a look of stunned amazement on his simple unlined face — like a child who had suddenly seen Cinderella jump off the page of a fairytale. The speaker on the floor beside him had just extricated his bony elbow from the brass spittoon; he got up, cursing and exhorting his companions to get that damned capitalistic spy off the bar. Jake reached out a long muscular arm and thrust him down again like a jack-in-the-box, and continued staring fixedly at Rogier. He had not even looked down. The room behind him shook with stamping and shouting. "You up front! Out with the old fool!" — "Give the Colonel a chance!" — "Look at that rock! Who said he was a scab?"

Rogier, meanwhile, looked like a man shouting at Niagra Falls. He gestured, leaned forward. His mouth opened, his lips moved. He had lost his hat; and his hair, reflecting the bar lights, shone like a silver halo. To all those figures below him, to their shouts and curses, their slow eyes burning upon him like the fires in their pipe-bowls, the wool-clad arms and stubby fingers that shot out to transfix him, he continued to deliver the unalterable convictions of an outraged man: flouting their follies with courageous sincerity, condoning their faults and condemning their injustices, and imploring their common sense. Of all this not a word was heard.

There was a sudden crash. Some troopers, riding to break up the crowd, had spurred up on the sidewalk to the door. One of the horses, rearing on its back legs, had kicked out the front window. The beast screamed, more from fright than cuts; and this shrill and frantic sound rose above the splintering of broken glass. The cavalrymen, dismounting, began to beat at the crowd. For a few moments a few lusty fellows resisted. Fists and boots beat against gun stocks, with stones, jiggers, and a bottle flying overhead. Then suddenly the trickle through the door became a cataract. In a jiffy the place was cleared. Jake, on his back in the gutter, looked back inside to see a trooper jerking Rogier to his feet from off the floor.

"Damn me! The old gent that was raisin' all the rumpus up on the bar!"

A stray missile had caught Rogier on the side of the head and a thin trickle of blood was seeping down his collar. He tried to raise his head and transfix his captor with an indignant stare. Instead it slumped down on his chest; his knees buckled. The trooper caught him by the back of the collar before he fell, cheerfully dragged him outside, and threw him over his horse.

Just outside of town Rogier was awakened by a volley of shots from behind. "By Jove, man! I won't be carted like this — a sack of meal!" It was a weak voice: the trooper could hardly catch it.

"Cheer up! Ain't I goin' easy as I can?"

As if to answer his question, the horse stumbled in the loose granite. " — fool — weight on her withers — " The trooper pulled up, catching a glimpse of his prisoner's white hair, the diamond collar button at his throat. "Can you sit up if I let you get in back? Put your arms around me. I ain't going to have you fall off and bust your head open!"

The transfer was made in silence. Reaching Camp Peabody at last, Rogier weakly slid off the rump into his captor's arms and was pushed inside the bull pen.

The inside of the tent to which he was taken was lit by a single guttering candle. On one side stretched a long plank bench. Four men were huddled on it, staring half asleep at the dying embers of a small fire on the earth floor. Beside it, on a mud-smirched blanket, lay a man who got up and stared at Rogier who had fallen to the ground. It was Abe. He knelt, lifted Rogier like a child, and laid him on the blanket. The night was bitterly cold. He turned up Rogier's coat collar against the gusts of wind blowing through the tent flap, and began to putter about the floor.

"Goddamn it!" came a voice from across the room. "You know they ain't no more sticks. Or any matches either."

Abe got up, peering out the flap at the sentry pacing by outside, and beyond him at the granite slope black against the night.

Down the draw sat Jake. He was staring at the few lights of the camp with a look of dull bewilderment. A coyote howled. And still he sat there, patient and enduring, completely bewildered by the night's happenings.

3

It was two days before Rogier received a hearing and was allowed to present his credentials and identification papers proving he was not a striker nor an agitator. But as a mine owner registered with the association, why was he continuing to employ union workers?

Rogier summoned what dignity he had left to explain that as a contractor and builder in the Springs, he hired without prejudice both union and non-union men, paying both the same scale — three dollars for an eight-hour day; that in Altman, with the present difficulty of meeting the terms of his contract, he was following the same procedure.

That was not the question, he was reminded. Rogier was employing miners at the Silver Heels who had not been issued work permits by the Mine Owners Association showing that they were not members of the Western Federation of Miners.

The statement hit Rogier like a blow in the belly. Reynolds and his men, as far as he knew, were not working at the Silver Heels but at the Magpie. He had sense enough to reply only that the greatest mine in the district, Jimmie Burn's Portland, had not closed a single day and was still working W.F.M. men.

"That is unfortunately true, Mr. Rogier," his military question-
er replied sharply. "If it continues steps will be taken to close the
mine. You may take the warning yourself."

Finally let out of the bull pen, Rogier trudged up to his cabin in
blood-stained linen, a suit that had been slept in for three nights, and
in a mood more black and somber than the cold winter night. That he
could have been taken for a cheap agitator, penned up like a
criminal, his very integrity questioned — these, the inexcusable,
rankled in his mind, pricked his self-assurance, made him out a fool.
Yet all this was nothing compared to the devouring suspicion that
Reynolds and his men had given up working on the Magpie.

It was dark when he reached his cabin on the saddle; the wind
was shrieking like a mountain cat. But through the window gleamed
the light of a lamp. He flung open the door. Jake was squatting
beside the stove, intently reading a newspaper line by line with a
stubby finger. Abe stood at the table, laying out plates and cups.

"Come in, Colonel!" Jake looked up and grinned.

"I see you found the place all right," Rogier said.

"You're just in time. Set and eat."

The three men ate in silence. Then Jake got up to wash the
dishes. Abe pulled off his coat and shirt, laid them carefully on a
chair. "Let's have your coat first, Colonel."

Rogier silently peeled off his coat and slumped down on a chair
by the stove. Abe spread it over the table and took up needle and
thread. The lamplight shimmered on his dead white arms and
shoulders; underneath, the great muscles crawled like snakes under
satin. His bald head never lifted as steadily, with a big coarse hand,
he plied needle and thread in small stitches that would have shamed
any woman's. When he had sewed up the tear, he gave the coat a
good brushing and handed it back to Rogier. "There, Colonel.
Reckon it will hold."

Rogier slipped it on. "Much obliged," he said gruffly, deeply
grateful.

"Well, we got a job!" Jake said cheerfully. "I knowed you'd find
us one, Colonel!"

Rogier sat there, cooked and sewed for, and protected by these
brawny giants who had moved in with him with never a word, feeling

as though he had adopted, with all his own worries, two helpless children. "I suppose you boys can finish those cabins. All the logs are there, and here's the keys to the tool house. You won't be troubled about work permits till you finish 'em anyway."

"We ain't carpenters. We're hard-rock miners," Abe said quietly.

"You can drive nails as well as I can while all this trouble's going on!" snapped Rogier. Worn out, he flung himself down on a cot and dropped into a troubled sleep.

Next morning he trudged to the Silver Heels. They were there as he expected: Mrs. Reynolds cooking pancakes for Reynolds and two of the men, comfy and cheerful as a family at Sunday breakfast. Rogier sat down to a high stack set out before him without asking questions. Reynolds as usual had obeyed the dictate of common sense. He and his crew had sunk the shaft of the Magpie into hard granite without a sign of paying ore. Their makeshift quarters would never do through winter, nor could they trudge back and forth through snow to the Silver Heels. So they had simply boarded up the mine and returned home here, where with a skeleton crew Reynolds intended to open up a new drift.

"Skeleton crew?" asked Rogier, peering in the empty bunkroom.

"Yep. Us three boys are all that's left."

"What about McGee and Carson?" asked Rogier, referring to the two married men who lived with their families in Altman.

Reynolds patiently explained. Rioting strikers had threatened both families unless the two men joined the W.F.M. and went on strike. Carson had joined and moved to Cripple Creek, hoping to pick up odd jobs to carry him through the strike. McGee was living with his family in a shack at Goldfield to protect them from possible harm. Reynolds and the two single men did not have work permits, but hell, they weren't workin', was they? They were simply wintering at a resort 10,000 feet high and fattening up on Mrs. Reynolds' pancakes. Money was not forthcoming too regularly, Reynolds added mildly, but when some did come in they might open up that drift. It wasn't likely they'd be bothered by any more nosey members of the military, W.F.M., M.W.A., or mine inspectors till spring.

"Money'll be coming! Haven't I always got it for you!" growled

Rogier. "But not one cent for timbering any more new cuts in this worked-out old mine! Come spring, we're going back down into the Magpie. I'll get McGee back. He's a good man with powder. You need him!"

A one-room, unpainted board shack on the outskirts of Goldfield held the McGees and their two small children. When Rogier arrived, McGee was covering the cracks in the wall with newspapers to keep out the cold. Mrs. McGee, who was taking in washing to support the family, was bent over a tub in the middle of the room. The two children were in school. McGee, who had worked at the Silver Heels for a long time, was embarrassed at having left but firm in his refusal to return to work. He could not join the W.F.M. because they couldn't give him a job to pay his dues and assessments. But neither could he scab for fear for his family. So like many hundreds of others he was trying to wait out the strike.

"I just can't figure it out," he said in a patiently suffering voice. "Gold worth a hundred million dollars or more comin' out of Cripple, and here we are with no more than a leaky roof over our heads. We're not standing in the bread line for something for the kids like hundreds of others around us. Alice takes care of that, washing all day and late into the night. But the strike's spread to the coal mines down south. Near Trinidad there's been a battle with thirty Italian strikers and two of them were killed. I can't see no reason for it at all."

Discouraged and balked at every turn, Rogier finally returned to Little London a week before Christmas. The holiday season always had been a big time for the family, and this year, despite an obvious turn in its fortune, everyone seemed to be heading into the stretch for a better one. The blue spruce tree in the front room just tipped the ceiling. Underneath it Sally Lee and Mary Ann kept piling more and more beautifully wrapped presents. Lida was busy all day in the kitchen. The fruit cake had to be prepared two weeks before New Year's Day and set aside to soak up the brandy. Then there were mince pies and chocolate cakes to bake, loaves of bread with crusts browned with butter. Two fifty-pound cans of honey arrived: one of strained honey, and one of hard sugared honey to spread on buckwheat cakes. Then there was cranberry sauce to make, jellies and jams and sauces to be brought up from the basement. And finally, as the tension mounted, the goose and the turkey to be bought and plucked. To all this confounded extravagance everyone in the family from Mrs. Rogier down had only one incontrovertible answer. What was Christmas for, except for children! Now there was a baby in the family, March, and this was his first Christmas!

Two days before Christmas, Cable, Ona, and March came down to stay in Sister Molly's big room upstairs. Cable looked glum. He had bought a tree for their own house, expecting to celebrate Christmas in his own home like any man. But this, he was finding out, was a false assumption. Home to Ona, who belonged with every entegument, ligament, and cell of her body to the Rogier tribal entity, was the big house down on Bijou. Here she had lived, been married, given birth to her son; and here, for every holiday, she had to return.

"Why of course, Jonathan! How could we sit here alone, when not a half-mile away everyone is waiting for us! It's your family too, Jonathan! Don't you realize that?"

The red niggah didn't. Familiarly acceptable to all the family as he was, one member still raised between her and him that strange and intangible barrier which in the South of her own girlhood had constituted an unbreakable color line. Nor could one impute to her an individual prejudice. Black niggers in the South, red niggers in the West, what was the difference? They both menaced by the color of their skins, which soaked through to their hearts and minds, the unstained purity of the superior white Anglo-Saxon race to which, by divine Providence, she had been born. Mrs. White, for all her outward vulgarity of speech, was a lady of breeding. Never by word of mouth had she ever insulted Cable in the presence of the family so devoted to him. She simply found it expedient to retire to her room. But since the night March had been born—that outright result of miscegenation between the Rogier and De Vinney aristocracy and a primitive race of savages condemned by the nation to extinction—Mrs. White had refused to speak to Cable. The rest of the family was at first embarrassed and then amused. They joked about it to Cable, a sure sign of their complete loyalty. But to Cable, a sensitive man, the hurt rankled. It made it more difficult for him to move down to the Rogiers' for Christmas. But of course he did.

The New Moon had been forced to close down by the strike, and Cable and both of his partners were making out in their haberdashery store. Coming home from work, he would go out to the shop to visit with Rogier. The older man was always tacking up clippings and quotations on the walls, the pillars, the window sills.

> The earth   neither lags   nor hastens, does not withhold, is generous enough, the truths of the earth   continually wait,   they are not   so con-cealed either, they   are calm,   subtle, untrans-missable by print.

> As the ox   ought he to   do; and his happiness should smell of the earth and not of contempt of the earth.

> The subterranean miner that works in us all, how can one tell whither leads his shaft by the ever shifting, muffled sound of his pick?

If to Cable they all seemed very much alike, they also reflected for Rogier the one dominating thought never out of his mind. He was worried by the prolonged strike. It was like a curtain upon which men and events moved dimly. He sat before it, striving to see the thing behind. Years before, when he had come West, it had been the familiar song of America he had tried to understand. The creak of canvas-topped wagons, the snap of flames burning off the prairie grass, the bite of double-bladed axes hewing down the thick sprawled forests, the rumble of buffalo driven over the last horizon, the whir of a million wings frightened from the drying water holes by gun blasts. It was the creak of ore trains crawling down the Pass, the sound of steel driven into granite, the steady beat of spikes as rail-ends crossed the plains and crept into the mountains. It was the voice of a hundred-tongued race of intruders stealing a continent with strong laughter and six-syllable Colts.

And now the song was sung. There was still a song of sorts, but it had a mechanical sound. It was no longer spontaneous, many-voiced, crude and strong. It was measured and metallic. You could hear in it the wheels go round. And the men who sang it sat in cushioned directors' chairs and counted every beat.

But the earth, the mute unresistant earth of a continent that had been burnt over, mutilated, dug into, disfigured, and reshaped, it too had a song, sung darkly like a rhythm in the blood.

> I am of today and heretofore, but something is in me that is of the morrow and the day after and the hereafter.

> To blaspheme the earth is now the dreadfullest sin, and to rate the heart of the unknowable higher than the meaning of the earth.

> The gold, however, and the laughter — these doth he take out of the heart of the earth: for, that thou mayest know it, the heart of the earth is of gold.

As if through a veil Rogier seemed now to glimpse a meaning in the blind, restless greed of men who had thought to rape and gut a continent without reckoning that the earth must have its due. They had creamed the top, had skimmed the grass roots. And now, down in granite, they were come up against the sterner stuff.

This was the new continent, this virgin America with rich long-grass prairies unmapped, and short-grass buffalo plains boundless as tawny seas; with dark, green forests primeval; a land of great slow rivers, brown and red, and countless white-water beaver streams; where one man's range would have made a royal realm overseas, his longhorn subjects more numerous than many a king's; it was a land watched over by great stone prophets lifting their white heads into the sky; a land where distance was measured in days; a vast unexplored treasure chest, halfburied, whose hinges a man's burro might accidentally kick off and reveal the hidden gold; an Ophir of mines thicker than prairie dog holes and scarcely deeper than topsoil. A land whose high snowy beacon was known from sea to sea. A land whose mother was the great mother of them all, the rain and the rivers, the thunder and the forests; the chief spokesman for every living stone and seed; the vessel of all life, the underworld womb of the unborn sun, the one great mother of the one great song. A scaly monstrous earth-mother of disillusionment, destruction, and death too, whom men had thought to bleed and carve and proportion in their bank ledgers. And now, unhurried, she was idly watching them grow mad over her mere surface wealth.

Rogier sat thinking of the hordes of strikers crowding the streets of camp, the women lined up with pennies for bread and soup, the troopers sick with fear yet riding up and down, dodging stones. He remembered a child walking barefoot in the snow and thumbing his nose at the sheriff, the bodies of McCormick and Beck too mutilated to be recognized at their funeral, a brick crashing through a restaurant window into his own soup. He thought of the inconceivable bitterness, the hopeless folly and fury of men fighting like mad dogs over a bone big enough for all.

The Peak, showing granite, had turned their picks and powder upon themselves. In the cry of Labor he heard the whine of machines dissonant with the forgotten earth.

"Daddy!" Mrs. Rogier pushed open the door. "Jonathan said he'd left you out here alone. Why, for goodness sakes, it's Christmas Eve! The candles on the tree are lit. Jonathan invited the Grimes down, and Mr. Denman's on the way. Professor Dearson's already here to play the carols the girls are going to sing. Land sakes alive! What can you be thinking of to be so late getting ready?"

It was never out of Rogier's mind, even during the confusion of Christmas morning with everyone tearing open packages, whooping and hollering, drinking egg nogs with every visiting neighbor, watching the baby. The big two o'clock dinner was no relief. He could hardly eat for thinking of Abe and Jake up in their cabin. Why, indeed, hadn't he brought them down if it was going to spoil his whole Christmas, asked Mrs. Rogier. Rogier abruptly gulped down his glass of after-dinner port, flung aside his lace-trimmed napkin, and called Mrs. Rogier into the kitchen.

That little frail woman no doubt had her faults, but she possessed that supreme virtue which permitted the girls to concede her to be what they called a "good sport." Within minutes she had commandeered the help and approbation of the whole family. While Mary Ann ran for a big striped box, she laid out plenty of turkey, cranberry sauce, rolls, mince pie, candy, nuts — "but Jake hasn't got teeth for" interrupted Rogier. Ona pulled him away. "Daddy, this is going to be a real Christmas box. We're not going to leave out a thing. And we're going to tie it with red and green ribbon!" Mary Ann came whooping in from the front room. She had heard of those two big raw-bones and had stolen off the tree two of March's trinkets to put in the box for them — a monkey on a stick and a small jack-in-the-box.

Rogier, elated, ran with many kisses to catch the late afternoon train. By nightfall he was trudging the steep trail up to Altman, the big box under his arm. The cabin was dark and cold. He lit a fire, adjusted the lamp, and sat down in his overcoat to wait for Abe and Jake.

They came in two hours later, both half-drunk and hilarious, too full to eat a bite. One of General Booth's "Blood and Fire Warriors" had squeezed them into a Salvation Army Christmas Dinner for destitute strikers.

Rogier felt so angry and ashamed that he pitched the box out the back door and went to bed in a huff. Rogier sentimentality! What a fool he had been to miss Christmas night at home with his family!

He was awakened by a stealthy whispering. He rolled over. Abe and Jake were bent over their bunk with lighted matches; they had crawled down the snowy draw and brought back the box. The bottle of port had not been broken, and they were trying to finish it without waking him.

"Hold on!" he cried, jumping out of bed and lighting the lamp. He had suddenly thought of the toys inside. "You two boys have had your Christmas dinner and so have I. But what about the McGees down below? What about them, hey?"

Abe with a shout had discovered the monkey on a stick inside and was trying to trade the jack-in-the-box to Jake for another swig of port. Good-natured and hilarious, they passed the bottle to Rogier and helped him into his boots. Then shortly before midnight, the three men left the cabin and set out. Abe, in front, held up a lantern and the little furred monkey on his stick. Jake, behind, carried the jack-in-the-box and a pick handle. In the middle, surreptitiously sipping port to keep warm, Rogier plunged through the drifts with the huge box.

The trail, greenish white in moonlight, dipped into the shadow of the cliffs. The stars hung low, cold, and brilliant as bottle glass. Down below glittered the few lights of Independence; at the bottom of the gulch on Wilson Creek loomed the larger splotch of Goldfield. The trail curved again. A thin wisp of smoke was rising out of McGee's chimney; the fire was not yet out.

Dom! It felt like Christmas night after all!

4

The second year of the strike began auspiciously. The mine owners had taken a resolute stand. A "vag" law was passed which in effect ordered every man in the district to work or get out. About 1,700 men were now working: imported scabs and workers who had given up their union cards. On the other side, the strikers were cheered by the news that their quarrel had been taken up by the United Mine Workers of America and a strike of coal miners was being called throughout Colorado. Las Animas County, following the battle at Trinidad, was declared to be in a state of insurrection; and militia had been sent into San Miguel County, where outbreaks had occurred in Telluride.

Late in January, after someone had greased the brakes, the big double-deck cage of the Independence failed to stop when coming up with a load of men. It shot up to the top of the frame, crashed against the timbers, and fell 1,400 feet back down the shaft, killing fifteen men. This was followed by a shooting affray at Anaconda in Squaw Gulch over the flag posted outside the Miners Union Store, setting off more outbreaks.

Rogier returned to Little London: he had been awarded a

contract for a new school, a fair-sized job whose proceeds he desperately needed. Leaving Rawlings, his construction foreman of many years, in charge, he hurried back to Altman. Abe and Jake were taking longer to put up a miserable log cabin with twenty bunks than would have been allowed him to construct a four-story hotel. The owners were in no hurry. Conditions were so bad and so many men out that the mess hall, built for over a hundred, was lucky to have a dozen men at meals. "Good God, Rogier!" they told him. "Why finish that last cabin? Haven't we paid off on the whole job, anyway? A pretty penny to spend in a hell-hole so torn up they ought to blow the whole thing to blazes and be done with it!" Still Rogier persisted in finishing it, not only to clear his contract, but to give Abe and Jake something to do.

Early that spring he drove Reynolds and his skeleton crew back to the Magpie. His whip was simple and effective. Money was coming in again, but he wouldn't spend one red cent to timber up any new cuts in the Silver Heels. If the men wanted to work and be paid for it, they could go to the Magpie. Like the earth, he would not lag nor hasten; strike or no strike, he was going down.

They had not gone very far down when they encountered trouble — bad air. Rogier went down the shaft with Reynolds and turned into a long tunnel. From habit he kept stopping to inspect the trapezoidal sections of timber sets, stamping on the sills, sounding the props and stulls, and peering up at the top lagging boards above him to see if any were bent, the first sign of pressure. Then Reynolds turned into a small crosscut leading off at right angles and stopped. Lighting a candle, he walked in a few feet. The candle went out.

"You see how it is," Reynolds explained. "It ain't got no color a man can see, and you can't taste it or smell it either. All you know is it's thick and wavy and lays down low. We always lower a bottle with water, empty it, and see if it fills up with gas. But it don't always work. One day it will be there and the next day it won't."

They returned to surface with a sample which Rogier took to have analyzed. The air of the Conundrum Mine, carefully analyzed by volume not long ago, had been found to contain 79.6% nitrogen with 10.2% oxygen and only .03% carbon dioxide. Yet Reynolds was encountering in the Magpie an air with 20% carbon dioxide — worse than ever the Elkton had, with over fifty times the amount of carbon dioxide than normal air.

"It's just a pocket. We'll ventilate," insisted Rogier.

So they connected the two levels with a winze driven through the orebody for ventilation. Then they encountered another gas pocket and another, driving more air shafts. It was expensive, and Rogier impatiently sold his remaining downtown store building in Little London to keep up the work. There was a showing of ore, of course. And he could not but believe that soon — soon! — they would exhaust all bad vapors. Yet every rock seemed to mechanically enclose gasses.

One bright spring morning Reynolds pointed toward one of the muckers sitting in the sunlight. His hat was off; his face was tinged greenish yellow from vomiting; he was rubbing his back. Rogier nodded. He knew the effects: first oppression and heaviness, perhaps a headache, then rapid pulse and breathing; the after-effects, nausea, vomiting, and pains in the back.

"This ain't no mine, Colonel," Reynolds said quietly. "You're spending all your money letting air in, not takin' ore out."

Rogier was not to be balked. Not here, high up on the shaft of that arrow pointed to his secret goal. Not yet!

"Keep at it, Reynolds, Once more is all I ask. Time and a half. And tell the men to take no chances."

He left them to go down to Little London in response to a telegram from Mrs. Rogier. She met him at the door and without preamble broke the news at once. Mary Ann had run off to Chicago with the Durgess boy and got married.

"That jackass? How can a man go through life pulling taffy and frosting doughnuts!"

"You forget Durgess Caterers is the best in town. But it does seem she might have had a dignified wedding in her own home!"

Rogier, as a matter of fact, was a little relieved; an expensive wedding now would have been impossible. "Well, what's the trouble you called me down here for?"

She looked at him with indignant amazement. "Trouble! Mary Ann! Daddy, what can we do about it?"

"Just stop worrying about bills from the caterers from now on!" He brushed past her and walked out to the shop.

There was trouble enough, although he did not know it. Ona,

now that March was big enough to trundle home in a baby carriage or little wagon, had resumed coming to the shop every day to help look after Rogier's work. Her absence had given Rogier plenty of time to thoroughly muddle his affairs. Property had been sold, money spent, mines opened and closed, construction jobs bid on and forgotten, accounts transferred — what a mess it was! Apparently he did nothing here in the shop but tack up clippings and quotations until the walls and pillars were covered. What in the world was happening to him, usually so methodical and constantly lecturing to her about figures? Figures!

Rawlings, his old construction foreman, had come down one afternoon soon after work on the new school had started. Rogier was in Cripple Creek. "You can sit awhile, can't you?" she asked. "It's been a long time since we used to eat ice cream up in Daddy's office."

"Don't mind if I do," he said, sliding into a chair. He was a small, blue-eyed man with a weak voice and shy manner that disguised, off the job, his knack of pushing things along. Rogier often declared that without him he'd have gone out of business. After awhile he undid a roll of blueprints. "I came down to see about this foundation, Miss Ona. He told me this ought to be twelve feet six. But look, the plans are marked twelve."

"You've scaled it?"

Rawlings looked embarrassed. "He added all them figures up according to numerology or something and they didn't fit in with the moon — something of the sort. So he said just to add the half all the way around. But that'll throw it off plumb. Do you reckon he was jokin'?"

"Of course, Mr. Rawlings. You just stick to the prints. Daddy doesn't go wrong on figures very often."

"That's the trouble." He hesitated. "Between you and me, Miss Ona, your Dad's got somethin' on his mind. He — "

Ona put her hand on his arm. "Mr. Rawlings, you were working for Daddy when I was in short dresses. He depends on you. You know what to do. Do it and don't let him bother you." For a moment she was silent and then courageously blurted out, "Rawlings, that spell of bad luck didn't do Daddy any good. He's having a hard time keeping in harness."

"Sure, oh sure," said Rawlings, rising. "I ain't criticizin' the likes of a man like Rogier. There's not another builder in town I wouldn't throw over to work for him. I'll push it along. Don't worry."

He had pushed it along, poured concrete, cut stone, and ordered brick. Rogier when he saw the work was pleased enough to slap him on the back. "Rawlings, when are you going to get off my back and stand on your own feet? I've been telling you for years you ought to get in business for yourself! You'd make us all hump!"

"I was just talking to Charlie about that," Rawlings said somberly. "Here he comes now." They were standing in front of the timekeeper's shanty when one of Rogier's rival contractors walked over from the new brick wall of the school.

"Charlie Geysling!" exclaimed Rogier, grabbing at the man's outstretched hand and looking into his worn, lined face. They stood exchanging the trivialities common to men of a kind and friends for many years. "I was just telling Rawlings he's too good a man to be working for another one. He ought to be making money on his own. Putting up something as tolerable looking as that new church of yours, eh?"

Geysling smiled a bit wanly, then let out a chuckle. "Between us and the gatepost, do you know what I got out of it?" He stepped aside and turned around. "This thirteen dollar suit of clothes! They figured me so close I was lucky to come out with a pair of pants!"

Rogier grinned; they understood each other. Yet the remark struck home. A suit of clothes for a good six months' work, and one that hardly covered his frayed shirt! And the man was actually getting old; his left leg had never dragged so noticeably before.

"Times are changing, Rogier," went on Geysling. "It isn't a clean-cut job of putting up a building anymore. There's a building permit, a heavy bond at the bank, a collateral assignment for material, union labor, everything else. A fellow has to figure down to the last piece of scrap lumber. You were always good at that, Joe."

"Yes. Figuring is the trick, not the building, eh Rawlings?" Rogier replied somberly. "Accurate figuring. Long hours. You've got to put your heart in it."

Rawlings bit off a chew without replying.

Back home in his shop, Rogier sat at his drawing board, chin in hand, staring out the window. He had looked forward to resuming business, to bidding on a couple of new jobs. Only to find himself caught in a boredom of unexpressive effort that left him no peace of mind. The school was taking shape under Rawlings' quiet and unassuming direction. All morning Rogier would spend with him on the ground, jacking up the men, turning back a load of brick, giving the assurance of a blunt and resolute man who knew what he wanted and expected it done without quibbling. Then all these details of construction would turn stale and unbearable. And he would return to his shop — to Ona working on his books, his ledgers, his cluttered files.

"Daddy!" Her voice was sharp. "You simply have to give me a full afternoon. Everything is in such a mess I can't make head or tail out of it. Take this invoice — "

"Now Ona!" he replied in a sharper voice. "If you haven't learned how to figure out those papers after all this time, there's nothing to be done about it now. Can't you see I'm too busy?"

Shortly afterward, on the fourth of June, he returned to Altman.

Strike violence spikes. Sally Lee takes up w/ Piano professor, then goes on tour.

5

That night the moon rode clear, shining through the open door of his cabin. He got up and closed the door. Still it glimmered through the window over his bunk, keeping him awake. Abe was snoring like an angry cougar caught in a trap. Restlessly, Rogier kept turning over and over. Then abruptly, about two o'clock, he found himself sitting upright, holding with both hands to the framework of the bunk. A dull resonant roar, like a clap of thunder, had almost shaken him to the floor and was dying away.

"God Almighty! Is it the Independence — or what?" shouted Abe, bounding from his bunk and throwing open the door.

Rogier, with Jake, leaped across the room and looked down. The hillsides were alive with twinkling lights as men hurried down the trails with lanterns and torches. The lights of Goldfield and Victor farther down flared up from every window. Rogier flung on his own clothes and with Abe and Jake hurried down the gulch. Flares were leaping from the hilltops. Every mine had put on its lights, showing men hurrying down the gulch. They were converging at the camp of Independence below Bull Hill.

The three men followed the crowd to the Florence and Cripple

Creek Railroad depot which stood near the Findley, Delmonico, Orpha May, and Lucky Cuss mines. Here they stopped: Rogier, with a stomach that suddenly turned over inside him, and Abe with a hoarse, "God A'mighty — they done it now!" The 2:15 A.M. train stood a hundred feet away, its headlights glaring upon an uprooted platform, lengths of rails sticking upright in the air, dead and mangled bodies, and directly in front of them a leg with the boot still on.

The explosion of the load of dynamite had been timed for the arrival of the train filled with non-union miners to replace the night crew of the Findley Mine waiting on the platform. It had gone off just before the train had stopped, killing thirteen of the men waiting to go home and blowing their bodies up the hillside as far as the Delmonico. Nobody knew how many others were injured. Miners were stretching them out beside the tracks, waiting for a switch engine to bring doctors and nurses from Cripple Creek. By daylight the place looked like the scene of the monstrous crime it was. People from every camp in the district milled around like mad cattle. Women weeping as they dug into the wreckage, and shrieking when they found a piece of flesh. Men hunting for a bit of wire, a contact plug, of the infernal machine.

No one knew who had set off the explosion. The Mine Owners Association blamed it on the Western Federation of Miners; it in turn condemned the crime as the work of a hired criminal and offered a reward for his arrest. The sheriff, marshal, and coroner were forced to resign. At Goldfield, six aldermen, the commissioners, and treasurer were placed under military arrest.

By three o'clock in the afternoon thousands were gathered for a mass meeting at Fourth and Victor Avenue in Victor. A special train had arrived with C. C. Hamlin, secretary of the Mine Owners Association, who faced the crowd as chief speaker. It was a time and situation which demanded a man of courage and coolness — above all, tact. Small, excitable Hamlin, justly outraged, was not the man. He shouted, flung up his arms, damning the strikers as murderers, exhorting every decent man to drive them from the district and stamp out unionism like a snake.

Rogier, standing in the crowd, let out a groan at the folly. He saw the accusing finger of the speaker sweeping over the crowd, pointing unintentionally at someone on his right as at hundreds of others. The someone's neighbor mumbled a word or two. There was a scuffle. Fists flew. Shots rang out. In less than a minute a riot was under way.

Rogier ducked and ran for cover, watching from a doorway the troopers clearing the lot and carrying off the two men killed and the five wounded. Then slowly he walked back up to his cabin. About midnight the Zebbelins arrived, telling him they had been among 1,300 men suspected and questioned, 200 being put under arrest.

At two o'clock next morning 200 men were assaulted at the Miners Union Hall and for three days violence was unabated. Union stores at Victor, Goldfield, Anaconda, and Cripple Creek were destroyed. The W.F.M. headquarters in Engineers Hall was broken into, flags and pictures torn down, furniture smashed. The *Victor Daily Record* plant was destroyed. James Murphy, superintendent of the Findley Mine, met a woman walking down the street whom he recognized as the wife of a union sympathizer. He tore her clothes off, kicked her until she was half-dead, and left her lying in the gutter.

General Bell, declaring martial law, issued a proclamation closing the Portland Mine for harboring dangerous and lawless men. Its entire force of 500 men were arrested because they were members of the Miners Union which had not taken out cards in the Mine Owners Association. The Portland directors then voted the mine's discoverer and president, Jimmie Burns, out of office. Deportation began of all men who refused to renounce the union.

Rogier's very entrails writhed in agony. The great Portland and Independence, King and Queen of the District, closed; hundreds of others. Production almost cut in half from its peak year—a gold camp that already had produced more than $126,000,000 and had three times that much more to give. The bloodshed. The savage violence. The corrosive bitterness that had preternaturally oozed in poisonous vapors from every stone in the Magpie! A raped and gutted earth that finally had turned on those who thought themselves its masters.

It was all there in the great Peak that loomed above him. Enveloped by black clouds through which protruded only its pale summit, it looked like a ghastly spider waiting in its web. Rather it looked like the bloodless face of a giant underwater squib spewing out its inkish black fluid to poison all it touched. Then fangs of lightning shot from it into a rainless June sky, and it took on the inimical aspect of the great devouring cosmic serpent itself.

There was no use going up to the Magpie. He knew that it already had succumbed to its poisonous vapors. Sick and shaken, he returned to Little London, leaving Abe and Jake to close the cabin and to find a room in Cripple Creek until things quieted down.

Sally Lee, slowly and unwittingly, had been caught in another kind of a web. Tall, big-breasted, with dark hair, she was by nature an energetic, outgoing girl whose one great love was horses. This activity had been denied her since Rogier unaccountably had lost his interest in them. It was as if in Aralee his strange mania for speed had been fulfilled. He had never raced her since, although he had let Denman take her on the Grand Western Circuit. Akeepee was still loved, but she was in foal again. So Sally Lee had given up going out to Denman's track and had resumed her music lessons with Professor Dearson.

This Master of Musicians was more of a chronic grouch, sarcastic and eccentric, than ever. He still drove around town in a rusty brown coat and leather puttees to match his reddish gray whiskers. Also he had picked up an Airdale dog, Dan, who accompanied him wherever he went, lying down under the piano while the old man played. Like many musicians, Dearson had the habit of humming while he played; and at a certain pitch in his voice, Dan would raise his nose and howl. The Professor's services at the College Conservatory had been abruptly terminated, and he had moved his specially built concert grand to his apartment; Rogier had been forced to tear out the two front windows to admit it. Here Sally Lee went to her lessons.

It soon became evident to Mrs. Rogier that she was at Dearson's every day on non-paying visits. "Of course!" Sally Lee replied. "He's helping us to arrange our program for the Trio. Oh, he's the gentlest, kindest, and most talented man in the world!"

The Freolich Trio, as Mrs. Rogier soon found out, was work the Devil had found for her idle hands. Sally Lee, oppressed by the dreary solidarity of the family and the big house so gloomy with a sense of impending change, wanted to get away from home. Her subterfuge was the Freolich Trio she was organizing to make a recital tour. Her willing accomplices were a German girl named Gussie who gave excellent humorous readings like a rags-bottles-and sacks man sing-songing through an alley, and a fair pianist named Alice. Sally Lee's voice, a deep contralto, they relied upon as the mainstay of the program. Before long Sally Lee showed her mother several letters from music clubs back east which expressed great interest in the coming recitals—letters which Gussie had composed and sent to friends to mail. Fortified by this sign of public encouragement, Sally Lee enlisted Professor Dearson's help in arranging a program and began going to his apartment daily.

Dearson's attitude toward his pupils was a mixture of hopeful patience, tenderness, and violently stimulating criticism. To sit through a lesson with him was an unforgettable experience. He had the magic of music. He became to Sally Lee no longer a cantankerous and uncouth old man, but a bright and luminous spirit that fanned into flame all the longings within her. She fell wholly, romantically, in love with him. Irascible as he was, there were depths in him that could be touched. And something about this big breasted, outgoing girl with a tragic innocence far beyond her years touched him. At least enough to let him bask without resistance in the warm halo of her homage.

It was only by chance that Mrs. Rogier stumbled into this compromising state of affairs when she stopped in at Professor Dearson's apartment. The afternoon was late, the window open. Pausing a moment on the front steps she peeked inside and gave one gasp of horror. Then, without a word, she swept inside, grabbed Sally Lee by one ear, and marched her home.

Now for a week Sally Lee had been weeping and pining in her room upstairs while Mrs. Rogier downstairs went about with a look of grim determination. When Rogier came down from Cripple Creek she explained things in no uncertain terms. Just exactly in what compromising situation she had discovered Sally Lee and that old reprobate she did not describe, but certainly the honor of the house was at stake. "And look at this!" She flaunted a paper in his face. "A bill from him for her music lessons! The effrontery! Wanting us to pay for his kisses! Daddy, there is only one thing for you to do."

"What's that?"

"Drive right up to Professor Dearson's. And take your horse-whip."

If Rogier was inclined to believe her zeal slightly excessive, he was mystified by Sally Lee's attitude. Through her tears she proclaimed her love for the Professor and talked wildly of running away with him. There had been considerable gossip of the sort about Dearson, as a matter of fact. Shortly after arriving in town, he had married a prominent widow named Mrs. Burke. They had left after the wedding for a tour around the world. On the second day from home they had had a lively quarrel. The Professor had torn up her ticket and continued his travels alone. While in Egypt he composed a piece while listening to a native orchestra. It was published and dedicated to his wife, he said, because the frantic antics and shouts of the dancers had reminded him of Mrs. Burke's quarreling.

That afternoon Rogier drove up to Dearson's apartment. The door was open and Dearson was stretched out on the couch. He jumped up and grabbed Rogier's hand warmly. "Well! You boys have certainly been orchestrating a symphony up there in the district! A Cripple Creek Suite for Gallow Strings! Sit down and have a glass of sherry and some biscuits!"

Rogier sat down stiffly and said in a quiet voice, "Dearson, I've come here on a deeply personal matter. Shall we speak frankly?"

Dearson rubbed his graying whiskers reflectively. "These damned women. They always cause trouble. But I must say that at your age you don't act the role of an avenging angel very convincingly. You should have a marriage license in one hand and a shotgun in the other. Eh? Is that the trouble?"

"You're an old fool yourself, Dearson. Far too old to let your back be scratched by a young girl."

"Oh Christ! What a mess you've got me into. Keeping all those girls penned up like animals in a zoo. While you go traipsing off to the mountains on a wild gold chase. Little wonder they all fall in love with the first thing in pants who shows them a little kindness."

Rogier relaxed and poured himself some sherry. "You got yourself into it, Dearson. How are you going to get yourself out?"

The Professor jumped up in his old scuffed puttees, took away Rogier's sherry, and poured them each a stiff drink of scotch. "I'll be damned if I know, Rogier, and I've been thinking about it a long time. She's a good girl. I'm too fond of her to hurt her — although I know that's the way to do it. Just get rid of her. Painful but quick."

Rogier was beginning to feel pleasantly amused. "What did you have in mind, cyanide or arsenic?"

"Well, if you insist on giving us a champagne wedding, a trip to Europe, and a dowry of a Cripple Creek gold mine, I suppose I can buckle down to it."

The two men stared at each other a long time, then both broke out into chuckles. Dearson jumped to the piano, rattled off a few bars of Chopin, then flung around. "I'll tell you what'll be cheaper, old man. Pack her off on that recital tour she's so anxious for. God knows, she needs to get away from that zoo down on Shook's Run as well as from me!" He paused. "I'm serious. Sally Lee's voice is not dependable enough for concert work. Nothing that grueling. But it's quite presentable for music clubs anywhere, perhaps small halls. They'll get along if you give them a chance."

The two men had another drink, shook hands, and as Rogier left he could hear Dearson pounding away at the piano his triumphant release from all worry. What an odd, kindly old man he was!

Sally Lee, upon hearing that the Trio was to be allowed to go on tour, showed immediate signs of recovering from the blow dealt her. She could see herself returning in triumph to kneel at the puttees of that grizzled knight who had refused her heart only that she might give it to an applauding world. Mrs. Rogier's assent was practical. From her cookie jar she miraculously withdrew enough money for two new frocks and a traveling suit.

Elated, the three girls who called themselves the Freolich Trio, unaware of the misspelled name, had some programs printed. Gussie, now named Augusta von Hering, was named the reader, with Sally Lee as soloist and Alice as pianist. Dearson fortunately never knew what they did to his carefully suggested program. It started out well enough with a Chopin prelude, followed by two vocal selections: "The Dawn" by D'Hardelot, and Fisher's "Noon and Night." Between them and the "Funeral March" was stuck, of all things, a reading by Gussie of "The Uncut Diamond" — that cowboy with a rough exterior and heart of gold. Sally Lee was to remove any lingering jocularity with her best group of songs: "The Bandolero," "The Prince," and Lalo's "L'Esclave." These did not ward off the inevitable "Dooley on the Grip" and "A Puzzled Dutchman," in which Gussie could not restrain an unaccountable emotion. After two short nursery songs by Geibel and Neidlinger, Alice appropriately ended the concert with Ethelbert Nevins' "Buono Notte."

Rogier drove them to the depot to catch the train. Amusing as the whole incident had been, there was a catch in his throat. Dearson's accusations had hurt. The girls had been penned up too strictly at home and he had never given enough attention to the family. Now all the children were gone except Sally Lee who was waving a last goodbye from the receding train. And where was she going — this last one, who from the time she was a gangling, freckle-faced youngster could sit a horse and handle the reins of a trotter or a pacer better than most men? He could feel again her skinny little arms around his neck, and shuddered as he thought of them lovingly entwined about the soiled, wrinkled collar of that damned weak-kneed piano professor. No harm had been done, but why had it happened? The heart of a young girl, who ever knew what it held? For a moment, as the train swung out of sight around the bend, it seemed as implacably mysterious and profound as that other golden heart imbedded in a cloud of granite rearing in the western sky.

Strike over - corporate mining takes over.
Silver Heels mine xplosion kills Reynolds,
Ona & Cable come to bring Rogier back.
He blows up Reynolds's cabin first.

6

The district had quieted down when Rogier returned. Nine-ty-seven members of the Western Federation of Miners had been rounded up for deportation. Some of them were bundled into trains under guard and carried across the state line into Kansas, others being carried south and dumped into New Mexico. Two hundred more names were now posted under the proclamation that every striker was to be driven out to the tune of Cripple Creek's "Liberty Anthem:"

> You can never come back, boys, never.
> The game's all up with you forever.
> We trusted you square, and the pay was fair,
> And all would be yours yet, but now you'll beware.
> The W.F.M. is fated, and you'll stay there, you bet!

Rogier like everyone else — mine owners, strikers, and non-combatants — knew that the disastrous strike and the power and right of union labor was ended. He knew too that the district was entering a new era. The days of independent mining development by men like Stratton, Burns, and a hundred lucky butchers, bakers, and candlestick makers were over. From now on mining was to be carried on by big business operators, syndicates, and boards of directors.

Abe and Jake had disappeared into the obscurity of a Cripple Creek rooming house out of fear of being deported. Reynolds, as Rogier had known, had deserted the Magpie and gone back to the Silver Heels. Rounding the curve of the road, he could see Mrs. Reynolds hanging out her wash outside the cabin. He did not go down to talk to her, but struck off to the mine and sat down on the slope in the bright June sunlight.

He could not blame Reynolds; the Magpie like the Gloriana had been too much for him, and for quite sensible reasons. Still Rogier was disturbed by an unaccountable feeling, almost of resentment, against the mine below him. The Silver Heels was very tidy indeed: a passably large shaft house containing a good hoist, a vertical shaft, levels well marked, dry tunnels needing little pumping, well ventilated, and easy to work in; and off to the right the enlarged cabin with its bunkhouse and well-stocked kitchen. A far cry from that first crude, inclined shaft into the original working, and the single-room log cabin Reynolds and his wife had lived in so long. They had not struck a rich chute of telluride. The ore lay in gash veins soon exhausted. It had not made them rich but through the years, by dint of Reynolds' persistence, it had been a paying proposition. The Silver Heels, in short, was a good working mine of which its discoverer was justly proud and to which he had prudently returned after successive and futile flings at fortune up the gulch.

If Rogier could admit its unspectacular and persistent virtues, like those of his partner, he also had to admit that the Silver Heels had served his purpose. That purpose was emphatically not to make a mint of money by grubbing for gold like any businessman! No! He had something else in mind that Reynolds wouldn't understand.

Two men came out of the old inclined shaft to the left with a small tram car of ore dragged by burros. They emptied it and began sorting the ore. Reynolds came out, and seeing Rogier came up to sit with him. They shook hands warmly as usual, neither man alluding to Reynold's abandonment of the Magpie. Reynolds briefly explained what he was doing. As there was no money available to go down another level in the Silver Heels, he had gone back into the original working on a hunch. He had broken into a cavernous chamber, encountering gash veins frozen to the wall but extending only a short distance until they gave out. Here in the stope he was bulldozing, exploding sticks of fifty per cent dynamite. Then, when the dust had settled, the two men helping him would tram out the ore for sorting.

Rogier nodded. It was the same old story. Gash veins. Low grade ore. Laborious work. And dangerous, for the timber sets in that old working were growing weak and wormy, the lagging boards arched with rock and gravel that trickled between them and rolled down into the darkness.

Reynolds did not request that new timbering be provided. Rogier did not suggest he continue development of the mine down the new vertical shaft. They simply sat there together, Reynolds biting off a wad from his plug, Rogier chewing on the end of a smoked out cigar. The silence held between them. What was there to say? It had all been said on the Gloriana and the Magpie, over and over again. Friends and partners for years, they knew each other beyond words.

Finally Reynolds got up. "I'll be goin' now. Got to keep the boys busy."

Rogier watched him saunter back down the inclined tunnel. The two men continued to sort ore. Mrs. Reynolds came out with another tub of washing. After a time he ground out his cigar, stiffly got to his feet, and walked down toward the road. Just as he reached the brow of the hill he slipped on the loose granite and fell forward with arms outspread. At that instant he had the momentary and peculiar sensation as of the earth lifting gently to meet him. Concurrently a faint rumble sounded from the ground. Before he could sit up, the muffled roar of an explosion reached him from the mouth of the shaft on the slope below. It was immediately followed by a faint but sharp crackling as of timbers, then the loud rumble of sliding, shattered rock.

His face paling gray as a piece of rock clenched in his hand, Rogier leaped to his feet and rushed wildly down the slope. The two ore sorters were wildly gesticulating as he plunged into the mouth of the shaft. One of them grabbed at his coat tail, was flung aside, and followed him with a carbide lamp.

The tunnel was so full of dust they could hardly see or breathe.

The top and side lagging boards were squeaking with sudden pressure. Then came the ominous splintering of props and stulls. A hand jerked Rogier back. A voice screamed in his ear. "It's comin' down! — On the magazine! — Back!" As they reached the crosscut the timber sets behind them gave way with a crash. They heard the beginning of a terrific roar of splintering rock, a sudden concussion that enwrapped them in a blast of sound. Rogier felt himself hurled against the wall. A sudden splatter of blood warmed his face. Then a hand got him by the collar, jerked him erect. Revived by a blast of air at the mouth of the shaft, he leaned against the cribbing, weakly clasping a big-bosomed woman who smelled of soap. With a face so covered with blood and rock dust that he seemed to be staring over her shoulder from a grotesque mask, he kept screaming back into the dusty chute, "Reynolds! Hey, Reynolds! Reynolds, come out!"

Reynolds never did.

From somewhere he raised $1,000 cash and took Reynolds' wife to her folks in Leadville, saying the money was a state compensation. From there he returned to the Silver Heels. The two men had been released, the burros set free to roam the gulch like dozens of others. He slept on a cot in the tool house, unable to enter the big cabin which had been the home of those two faithful cronies of many years. Occasionally he peeked in the window. The grimy blankets of their bed were thrown back as if they had just climbed out. One of the old man's trousers was hanging on a nail; one of her big hats lay on the floor. In the kitchen a pot of beans was molding on the stove. A tub of washed clothes sat on a bench. Cobwebs were beginning to form in the corners of the ceiling. It was impossible to believe that they had gone — so suddenly and without warning! — never to come back.

On the perimeter of his thoughts, like a wolf at the edge of firelight, there prowled the specter of an accusation that he might have replaced those old timber sets. Or better yet, raised money to sink the newer shaft still another level by organizing the mine as a company and selling shares in it on the exchange. Such a thought had never entered his head. He was a man who all his life owned outright whatever he owned and conducted his business as he saw fit. He could no more change now than Reynolds could have changed. With such rationalizations he drove back the guilt that kept haunting him, ignoring the greater specter that flooded his mind from depths deeper than the Silver Heels.

Mostly he puttered around the dump and the ore bins, selecting the best samples. These he ground with mortar and pestle, pouring the pulverized ore into a white saucer and adding three or four drops of sulphuric acid. Heating this over a lamp, he watched the tellurium in composition with the mineral slowly turn the acid purple. Or sometimes towards evening, building a fire in the blacksmith's forge to cook his beans and salt pork, he would roast a bit of the ore. The process was known as "sweating," the telluride passing off in white fumes and leaving a few tiny globules to muse over while the flames died and the moon rose full and golden as if beaten out from the specks in his palm.

Gold. The most treasured, valuable, and sought after of all metals, it occurred everywhere: in almost all rocks, in vegetation, in sea water. The most malleable, it could be hammered into a leaf so thin that one ounce of it could be spread over 150 square feet. The most ductile, it could be drawn into a wire so fragile that two miles of it would weigh but a single gram. The softest too, yet indestructible: permanent in water and air under all pressures and temperatures, indissoluble except by selenic acid. Like the spectrum it contained all colors, yellow, pink, red, blue, purple, and even black; and when beaten thin it was translucent, transmitting a greenish light. The first metal known to man, and still the strangest and most perfect. The one irreducible element in the earth. The standard of value, it was a synonym for purity, trueness, and generosity, as it was for selfishness, miserliness, and betrayal. The one great mystery of nature, equated since earliest times with the sun, the divinity Himself. Who knew what it really was?

Rogier stared time and again at the miniscule specks in his horny hand as if mesmerized. Whatever they were, they were drops of blood drawn from an arterial stream he had not yet tapped, from a heart he meant to find, come what may. Deep down in granite flesh it pulsed, giving forth life to plant and bird and beast. In the congealed tracery of the veins, the suppurating wounds of a pick, he read a life that gave heat to the walls. He could feel it when he walked into the sweaty darkness of the shaft, in the eagerness with which he climbed deeper and deeper until his very flesh seemed one with the granite that shut off his sight, constructed his breath, and enclosed him like a tomb in which he felt himself mysteriously living a life unknown.

Reaching the edge of the stope where Reynolds had been buried by an avalanche of rock, he would lift high his candle or one of the mucker's lamps and bend down into the darkness. By degrees the far rock wall emerged in the dim light. He could see the narrow contact vein arched like a broken rib above him, could turn and hold his light against the wall until every inch of rock seemed revealed with the clarity of a petrified instant of eternity. Sometimes he half-expected the Acheronic figure of old man Reynolds to climb tranquilly from the depths. Instead, there stared back at him with vague eternal features the face of Time itself. Then, standing as within a circum-vallation of precious metals, where even the granite walls held radioactive substances expending life for ages uncounted, he abhorently refuted death. For men, being part of universal life, do not die. Like a speck of radium they send out their vibrations to be caught and transmitted again from other dynamic bodies long after they themselves have expended their individual force.

Then he would blow out his light; and pressed hard against the hanging wall he stared down into a blackness blacker and more infinitely remote than interstellar space. Sometimes he believed he could hear, like the sound of water, the slow pulse of vein matter; could see lights like the recrudescence of stars when he emerged from the shaft. He heard his own breathing, the beat of his heart slowing, felt his body stealthily and infinitesimally sinking into the wall, as if it were the heart of the rock that pulsed rhythmically in the silence that enwrapped him —

Coming out of the shaft one morning he saw Ona and Cable standing on the dump, a suitcase at their feet. He walked up to them slowly, knowing why they were there.

"We've come after you, Daddy," Ona said as cheerfully as she could. "I've already packed your things."

Cable said nothing.

Rogier stared past him with a dull surfeited look at a couple of long-eared burros watching them. Suddenly, decisvely, he flung wide his arms to frighten them away, and then threw a piece of ore to hasten them up the hill. "Wait for me down the gulch."

Ona with a warning glance at Cable turned and walked down the trail.

"I'll wait," Cable said obstinately, a grim look on his face.

Rogier turned on him the full force of his unsheathed gaze. "Get off this property!"

Cable stalked away without a word. Rogier hurried to a shallow pit near the mouth of the shaft. With a short-handled shovel he dug up a box of dynamite that had been frozen and which Reynolds had been thawing out by imbedding it in burro manure. He worked quickly, wedging the sticks in the loose rock at the portal, the cribbing, and in the wall of the shaft house. Then he ran to place the last sticks under the door of Reynolds' cabin. Cable, rebuked by Ona and nervous at the delay, was running back up the trail. Rogier yelled, waved him back, and struck a match to the fuse. Deliberately he waited to be sure the breeze was not too strong, then turned and walked swiftly down the trail.

Cable, panting with exertion, met him and turned to walk at his side. Rogier did not turn his head. Nor did he lift his eyes to Ona, anxiously waiting at the turn. Head up and twisted slightly to one side, his right arm swinging rhythmically with his long stride, he walked past them without a word.

It was then Ona felt a slight and sudden jar. She looked up. The slope above the Silver Heels was expanding like an immense pie dough puffing up from inside. Suddenly it burst, rent with cracks, and throwing up puffs of dirt like flour. Concurrently Reynolds' cabin hopped up from its foundations. As it split apart in mid-air, there came the roar of a terrific explosion. For a single instant the shaft gaped open. Then an avalanche of rock swept over it, obliterating shaft, surface plant, corral, and the splinters of Reynolds' cabin.

Ona clung to Cable's arm, staring at the ruin. The roar subsided. The dust began to settle. Far up the slope the two burros stuck their heads inquisitively forward, ears up, and above them a hawk swooped leisurely out of its circle. And the hill, already immemorially old and disturbed but for that evanescent instant of one man's futile pecking at the enigmatic secret of its enduring strength, lay again supinely resistant to the wind and the rain, the glitter of the sun, and the ever-virginal snow that was soon to obliterate its trivial scar.

Rogier, almost out of sight, had never once looked back.

7

Mrs. Rogier for some weeks had been growing suspicious of Sally Lee's continued absence. The Freolich Trio's first stop had been Rogers, Arkansas where the girls appeared in the town hall and left on the midnight train for Springfield, Missouri. Here they performed at a cantata sponsored by a women's Christian association in return for their dinners and two nights lodging. Already short of money, Sally Lee telegraphed a kissing cousin in Memphis, Tennessee, whose name old Mrs. White had given her. A prompt and satisfactory reply was forthcoming; money for railroad fare and an invitation to visit the family, a branch of the De Vinneys.

In Tennessee, life for the Freolich Trio began to brighten, according to Sally Lee's letters. Under the auspices of the Confederate Veterans they gave programs at Ripley, Covington, and Lauderdale, with a trip to Fulton, Kentucky. To make the programs more palatable to their Southern audiences, Gussie's readings of "An Uncut Diamond" and "A Puzzled Dutchman" were eliminated, and the finger gymnastics of Alice on the piano were replaced by Dixie melodies. Apparently they were making innumerable friends and little money — a pleasant tour whose worry was borne by Mrs. Rogier and whose expenses were evidently footed by their Memphis hosts.

The phlegmatic Gussie returned home with Alice, dutifully reporting to Mrs. Rogier that Sally Lee was extending her visit with the De Vinneys, a most hospitable family. The information lacked specifics. And when Sally Lee's letters became more and more general, Mrs. Rogier's suspicions were aroused. A discreet phrase, a lady-like remark, a modest assurance — over and over Mrs. Rogier read them to Ona, wondering what lay behind them. Finally exasperated she had summoned Sally Lee home, emptying her sugar bowl for the necessary railroad fare.

Sally Lee arrived. Her trip had been the one episode during that dire period of the family's fortunes which attested, as if prophetically, that though the Rogiers had lost everything else, they still retained their capacity for propagating witless follies.

Her first evening home was something of a family reunion. Rogier had been brought back from Cripple Creek, and sat stolidly smoking. Mary Ann and her husband, Cecil Durgess, had returned home disillusioned. Young Durgess because Colonel Rogier's gold mines were not erupting a stream of wealth in everyone's lap. Mary Ann because the Durgess family expected her bridegroom to work for a living. Hence both of them were helping out in the catering shop. They were living in the North End, of course, but only in a cottage. They were an ill-matched pair but on this evening at least showed no marks of friction. Ona and Cable had brought down March as usual, and old Mrs. White sat in the corner gnawing at a wart. The focus of all their attention was Sally Lee singing beside Mary Ann who was accompanying her at the piano.

Mrs. Rogier, sitting erect on the sofa, watched her with the eyes of a mother hawk. The chick had hatched; there was no doubt of it. Tall, deep-chested, and full-throated, she sang with the aplomb of a professional just back from a successful tour. But at the end of a piece Mary Ann would whisper something to her with a giggle, and Sally Lee would smile back mysteriously. Something was in the wind. Then, when Sally Lee raised her left hand to brush back her dark brown hair, Mrs. Rogier caught the sparkle on her finger. That was enough. Waiting until everyone had risen to group around the piano for a family sing, she crooked her finger at Sally Lee and went upstairs.

Sally Lee obediently followed her to the bathroom. She closed and latched the door, then turned around to face her mother. Mrs. Rogier, as of old, was sitting on the closet seat, her left arm resting on the wash basin, and leaning forward. "Hasn't my girl something to tell me of her own free will before bedtime?"

A tremble of nervousness shook the girl. She took a deep breath, then suddenly burst into tears. Mrs. Rogier rose and put her arms around her; she was just short enough to support Sally Lee's head on her shoulder.

"I was going to tell you first off, Mother, before anybody. Really I was!"

"I know. I know," Mrs. Rogier said soothingly, raising the girl's head and wiping away her tears with a hanky.

"He's a wonderful man, Mother! Oh, he's the best man in the whole world — except Daddy, maybe," Sally Lee dutifully amended between sniffles.

Mrs. Rogier reseated herself to receive a full confession. "Now tell me about it," she said briskly.

Sally Lee sat down on the rim of the bathtub. "I didn't see him until that evening when he stepped out from behind that big cypress near the house. It was the very first time I ever saw him! He took off his hat, and with his hat off he looked just like —"

In twenty minutes she had come to the fox fur Mrs. Rogier had glimpsed in her bag. "But not until after — till I had my ring. Mother, really! I said a fur in Memphis! you know, but he said with the cold and snow here —"

"Nevertheless when he comes, if he does come, I think it should be mentioned. If only to assure him your father and I at least are aware of certain proprieties. But now I think you owe it to everyone to tell them too." She rose and unlatched the door, and Sally Lee dutifully followed her down the stairs to announce her engagement to Aurand De Vinney of Memphis, Tennessee.

He arrived one evening when they were all sitting on the porch, and presented his credentials by jumping out of the station hack and running up and kissing Sally Lee in front of all the family and neighbors — a courageous assault on Rogier undemonstrativeness that endeared him from the start. He was a big, black-haired, and goodnatured, with three suits of clothes and a careless manner of stuffing a wad of banknotes in Sally Lee's pocket whenever she went to town. Just where it came from the family did not learn, save that he ran a wholesale business of some sort and dealt in raw cotton. His parents had died, leaving him a rather large house looked after by an old maid aunt — a woman whom Mrs. White remembered vaguely as a charming debutante.

It was a trying week. Sally Lee spent most of the time upstairs with a dressmaker cutting corners on expenses at Mrs. Rogier's instruction. De Vinney took Mrs. Rogier to call on two New Orleans ladies visiting Mrs. James Slowe Puffer in the North End. Their visit had been prominently heralded on the society page of the *Gazette,* and Mrs. Rogier recalled their names instantly. The two ladies were in fact wilting flowers of the Old South, obscure relatives of Jeff Davis. Mrs. Rogier took for granted it was her duty as a Rogier and a De Vinney to reassure them that though the old mold of Southern aristocracy had been broken, its strength still ran true in every vein. In this high mood she was ushered with De Vinney into the drawing room of the Slowe Puffer mansion on Cascade Avenue she had stared at for years.

De Vinney was taken into the study for a drink with a few men. Mrs. Rogier was seated in the great drawing room on the edge of a circle of women whose names and backgrounds she knew well — women who had risen in grace to the exact level that their men folk had dug into Cripple Creek hillsides. In silk and lace and jewels they sat chattering with empty-headed abandon, giving sly looks at the little woman in black silk and black bonnet sipping her tea. The two guests of honor were decidedly not impressive. They were painted and overdressed, and looked sharp and cold. Mrs Rogier sat dumbfounded, listening to these gentlewomen of the Old South repudiating their birthright by talking of a New South — of the profit to be made by picking up old plantations at a song and splitting them up into small farms and land development areas, of cotton futures, of rising corn prices. One of them kept nudging the other to look at the pin on Mrs. Rogier's breast, a full-color enamel Confederate flag.

The climax came when one of them asked in a quite audible whisper, "Who's that Mrs. Rip Van Winkle? Doesn't she know the war's over?" At this moment Aurand De Vinney walked in and, hearing her, rose gallantly to the occasion. Flashing an engaging smile at the whisperer, he walked over and put his arm around Mrs. Rogier's shoulder, and led her straight across to the woman.

"Beggin' pahdon, Ma'am, I reckon you wasn't introduced properly. I have the honoh, Ma'am, of presenting my mothah-in-law of next Saturday mawnin'." Unbending his tall and handsome body from a slight bow, he then said in a direct and challenging voice, "All of us De Vinneys, my whole family Ma'am, will take it to heaht if you do not do us the honah of attending a De Vinney wedding,"

The hoyden! She *was* sharp! "And in what church will the wedding be held?"

Mrs. Rogier's heart sank in her boots and, as if grasping for support, she weakly reached up to finger her Confederate pin. Poor as the family was now, she had intended to have Sally Lee and De Vinney married in a simple ceremony in their own home. But now with this challenge flung back at her across the great room with its crystal chandelier and statuary, she too rose to the occasion. "The church which we have helped to establish and maintain for twenty years, whose pews my husband made at his own workbench, the only church we have ever and will ever attend! The Southern Methodist!"

A snicker went up and was suddenly stilled when De Vinney flung around a cold, appraising look. Then, with a bow, he offered his arm to Mrs. Rogier and they walked to their carriage.

Once inside, her fortitude gave way. She began to sniffle with shame and mortification. De Vinney gently laid his hand on her black silk glove. "They'll be theah! They know I'll blackball them from Natchez to New Orleans if they aren't. Yes Ma'am, they know which side theah cohn and cotton's buttahed on!"

"Oh, I knew you were a gentleman!"

"That, Mothah, is very neah the highest compliment evah paid me." He bent and kissed her glove.

Mrs. Rogier's sniffles were over before they reached home. She got out and in a cold fury began preparations to take over the little Southern Methodist Church and to transform it completely. Her extravagance knew no bounds; she never glanced at the florists' bills.

During all this hue and cry Rogier was nowhere to be seen.

What he thought of his coming new son-in-law no one knew; nor what De Vinney thought of the older man so dignified and so hazy of manner whom he had never talked to. Finally on the day before the wedding De Vinney walked out to the shop carrying a bottle of brandy. Rogier was seated at his drafting board staring out of the window, wisps of white hair sticking out from his hat. "Come in, sir! Yes! Come in!"

De Vinney for once had lost his casual ease. He set the bottle before Rogier and stepped back to watch him read the label. "From New Orleans, suh. I meant to get it out of my trunk for you before this."

"Humm. Reckon a nip would take the bad taste out of your mouth right now, wouldn't it? Supposin' you latch that door before you sit down."

Rogier wiped out two glasses with a handful of waste while De Vinney opened the bottle. Then, over their drinks, De Vinney began his efforts to get acquainted. "I don't know anything about gold, suh. Cohn, cotton, and maybe a lil' sugah, is my line. But youah gold mines, suh, must be a mighty fascinatin' business!"

Rogier did not reply.

De Vinney tried again. "Goin' to be a good day for a weddin'! My lucky day, suh! Why, I tumbled fo' that girl of youah's the fust time I laid eyes on her! I wondah what she was like when she was little."

This didn't work either. Desperately De Vinney launched into the background of the De Vinney family in an effort to convince this difficult old gentleman that his daughter would remain in a family distantly related to his own and highly respected still. Beginning with the appeal to the English government in 1629 by Antoine de Ridouet, Baron de Seance, in behalf of French Huguenots asking encouragement to settle in Virginia; the first settlement made near Appalachee Bay, on Nansemond River near Dismal Swamp; the influx of De Vinneys to Queen Anne County, and thence into Louisiana, Tennessee, and Kentucky; reviewing the De Vinney pedigree through General Marion, the Lee and Rogier ramifications; and ending with an ample discourse on everything that Robert E. Lee and Jeff Davis had fought and bled for, De Vinney left out nothing.

Rogier finished his glass and then another. He listened quietly without interrupting, staring a little dreamily out the window. When De Vinney finally finished, he remarked, "You've got it down pat, son. Good blood lines. A fine family. I'm proud Sally Lee's getting into it." He paused. "Fact is, my boy, I don't know of another pedigree that can quite match it — except maybe — "

De Vinney flashed him an engaging smile and leaned forward with anticipation. "I know, suh! That's one reason I'm marryin' her, suh. Not the main reason, bein' in love with huh. But I know the Rogiers — "

Rogier seemed not to hear him. Standing up on the rungs of his stool, he was pawing through his files of ledgers. From one he took out a thick sheaf of papers, the pedigree of the finest and purest bred lady —

"Amen, suh!" De Vinney loudly slapped his leg.

Rogier began reading through the pedigree of Akeepee —

The wedding next morning was quite satisfactory. The church was full of flowers. Cable had taken a day off to drive to the mountains with Ona and bring back a carriage full of wild flowers to shame those brought by the florist. The church was not so full of people, of course, but conspicuous in the front pew were Mrs. James Slowe Puffer and the ladies from New Orleans to whom De Vinney had extended such a cordial invitation.

At last all was ready. The preacher up front was waiting with his Bible. Mary Ann was at the organ beginning to play the wedding march. And Rogier, with a bleak look on his face, was standing in back with Sally Lee on his arm — When in the front door strode Professor Dearson in his greasy leggings, with Dan at his heels. Without greeting, he stopped Rogier by the arm and plucked a rose from Sally Lees' bouquet to put in his coat. Then he strode down the aisle to the organ.

"Get up, child. Ge-TUP!"

Mary Ann rose, walked back against the window. Professor Dearson threw back his long coat tails and sat down in her place, pulling up one of his leggings. Dan settled at his feet. At last, with a gentle smile, the old man reached out his hands to the keys. Rogier, still in a daze, did not stir. The Professor nodded at him, played more loudly, then began to hum. It was the pitch Dan knew as his cue. The dog rose deliberately, stretched, and let out a mournful howl. And with this prologue to Mendelssohn's march Rogier and Sally Lee walked down the aisle.

That night when it was all over — bride and bridegroom on the train, guests departed, Professor Dearson lurching home full of bourbon, brandy, and port, the family up in bed — Mrs. Rogier, worn out, slumped down on the sofa beside Rogier and clasped both his hands. When had they been like this before, alone, just they two, confronting a frightening future? "That's the last one, Daddy. The very last one of them all! Oh, what have we done for them? What'll we do now?" She had no tears now. Her anguish was deeper than that.

Rogier caressingly stroked the head on his shoulder, but as if to avoid a full demonstration of his own concern, answered in a gruff voice.

"Yes, Martha. And we got rid of her just in time, too!"

She knew what he meant behind the words. "It's not that bad, is it Daddy?"

"I'm broke. Busted, by gosh! There's no use beatin' around the bush."

Broke. Possible job building a
home for a North End man, Timothy.

8

The wedding bills kept comin in: from the florists, the dressmaker, the caterers; for food, liquor, and nonsense galore. To these
were added the normal household bills and feed bills for the horses
at Denman's ranch that had been accumulating. And yet all these
were but the last embroidery on the immense tapestry of Cripple
Creek debt Rogier had woven: pumping equipment for the Gloriana,
hoist machinery shipped to the Magpie, supplies drawn by Reynolds
from an Altman store, and an overdrawn account on a Victor bank.
Ona, ruthlessly meticulous, had unwound all the threads.

"I thought I'd paid all those," muttered Rogier.

"They're still coming in," Ona answered quietly. "It seems that
mining is an expensive business."

He fixed on her a level look without rancor. "What do you
know about it?"

There was only one thing to do and Rogier did it. He went out
to Denman's and told him to sell his entire stable. "I'm washing my
hands of the whole kabosh! I can't be buying any more bales of
hay."

There was something incongruously pathetic, revoltingly funny, about Tolar and Dorothy going to pay the milk man and the grocer, and that incorrigible chicken-killer Little Man being taken by the owner of the biggest women's clothing store. Aralee was something else. Rogier gave her to Denman in payment for the big feed bill due him, but Denman could not afford to race her. So she was sold to the owner of the hotel Rogier had built who got his money back by periodically racing her in Canada. There remained only Akeepee who had foaled her third and last colt.

"What are you going to call her?" asked Denman.

"Name her yourself. Here." Rogier passed him a bill of sale for both Akeepee and the colt.

The two men seemed suddenly abashed by each other's presence. Denman stood on one leg and then the other. "You better take her home, she's a good carriage horse," he said at last.

"The colt needs looking after. Keep her here."

Denman took his hands out of his pockets where they dangled helplessly as his tongue. "Look here, Joe!" he blurted. "I'll put that little filly in shape. But I reckon we know who Akeepee belongs to. She can't never belong to nobody else!"

It stood at that. No one ever knew whether Akeepee belonged to or was loaned to Denman. She was always only Akeepee and continued to accept Rogier's and Denman's common fealty as her rightful due.

To give up her last lingering hope of moving into a mansion in the North End was for Mrs. Rogier a feat of renunciation accomplished without bitterness or regret. She sat rocking in front of the window, counting off on her fingers the ragtag and bobtail of town who had struck it rich in Cripple Creek. George and Sam Bernard the grocers, the druggists Jones and Miller, the butcher Stark, Peck the cigar store man and Sam Strong the roustabout, the carpenters Stratton and Altman, Burns the plumber, Doyle the handyman, Reed, whose father ran a livery stable — more than forty who had become millionaires and were now the cream of North End society! Why it was that Lady Luck had led these men to fame and fortune instead of Rogier, so much smarter and more deserving, she could not imagine unless the Lord in His divine wisdom had taken a hand in the matter. Mrs. Rogier did not question it. She was content to sit rocking within that gaunt old house haunted by the Kadles which to her now had become a fortress of faith she meant to defend at all costs.

Rogier wandered about town, wondering where he could find a job of work to do. Never a good mixer, he went to the courthouse and the city hall, more diffident inwardly and more crusty of manner than ever before. Rumors of a projected large downtown building, a new steel bridge, threw him into a turmoil. He was profoundly relieved when nothing came of either. In the park he found himself scanning the construction news for small store buildings and residences which once he had refused to bother with. There was no doubt about it; he was out of touch with the times. Even Little London had changed so much he could hardly recognize it, with all its new large buildings and streetcars whizzing by full of people.

Late one afternoon he fetched up on the Busy Corner, leaning against a lamp post and staring at the Peak rising above the Antlers Hotel at the end of Pike's Peak Avenue. It was no longer a clear-cut living entity. It had subtly withdrawn into itself and floated remote and nebulous as a cloud in the sky—as he had first seen it more than a quarter of a century ago from out on the plains. As if he had never known the divinity of its everlasting promise of fulfillment, the diabolic cruelty with which it had blocked his every attempt to plumb its mystery!

Yet never for an instant, even now, did it occur to him to give up his search. Dazed and discouraged as he was, he still dimly knew that there comes to every man in that one long evolutionary life no more interrupted by death than by sleep the time when he must fight through to the life of his own inner being and so make the turn into the greater life of which he was an ultimate part. For him that time had come. Everything else — the whizzing streetcars, the passing people, his own financial worries — seemed a fantastic illusion of insubstantial reality.

"Rogier, Old Man! Where've you been all this time?"

Almost knocked down by the slap on his back, Rogier spun around to stare at an apparition in brown derby and spats and sporting a carnation in his buttonhole. Timothy: that was the name. But where he had seen him Rogier could not remember. On the school board, at the racing association?

Timothy seemed to have no doubt of his long familiarity.

"Anybody gone as long as you up in the district must have something up his sleeve. Come along now. Just time for a drink before dinner. Right out of George's new shipment from London, he told me yesterday."

Rogier, still in a daze, let himself be propelled up the street to the Ruxton Club. As the frosted glass doors swung behind them he felt immediately soothed by the quiet gentility of the place. He was conscious of the paneled woodwork and heavy beams, felt the balance of joists and pillars, was comforted by the gleams of light palely spotting the mellow ripeness of the room. Timothy at the bar, still loquacious, recommended both him and the Scotch in the same breath, then led him into the lounge to wait for their drinks. In a corner two men were playing chess; on the window seat two others sat watching as if asleep. The game ended as Rogier and Timothy walked up, the players pushing aside the small mahogany table as they stood up to shake hands. Drinks arrived and they all sat listening to Timothy animatedly talking about nothing at all. None of them seemed to mind him; and to Rogier he now appeared harmless as a buzzing fly.

"Been trying to get Rogier to tell me what's going on up in the district now that the strike's over. He must have something up his sleeve, being gone so long."

"Don't know a thing!" insisted Rogier. "I've wound up my small affairs up there."

"Righto!" applauded a heavy set man named Nelson, polishing his nose glasses. "The place is on its last legs."

"I'm not so sure about that," said the man called McHugh. "What about going deeper? They've struck four-ounce ore in the American Eagles at fifteen hundred feet. You can't expect to dig it up with shovels forever."

"The eternal optimist!" Nelson winked at Rogier. "Even at the Wild Horse the oxidation goes down only one thousand feet. Why spend good money to bring up dirt. Like you, I'm keeping out."

Rogier frowned. "I'm keeping out myself, as I said. But I'm not giving anybody else the same advice. I wouldn't be surprised to see the best discoveries made at depth — if you've got the money to go down."

Apparently few people made it a habit to contradict Nelson,

and Timothy kept his eye on Rogier as he continued talking. In his broadcloth, out of style but well cut, with his white hair and diamond collar-button both catching the light from the wall bracket, Rogier seemed quite assured. "Yes, by Jove! Nelson, you're a corporation lawyer and you've got the figures pat. You can block out ore on paper, but it's never anywhere for certain till it's at the end of a pick. So with all your facts and precedents, you're always a jump behind — a mathematical historian!"

Somebody let out a laugh. "Put that on your door, Nelson!"

During the chafing a tall sandy-haired man had come up and sat down. Timothy leaned over, presented Rogier. "This is the one I told you about, Mr. Andrews. Mr. Rogier, one of the oldest architects and builders in town. The first courthouse, the old college academy, Gazette building, churches, schools — "

"And many an outhouse you can add to that, Timothy!" interrupted Rogier.

Andrews smiled and drew him aside. "Perhaps you're just the man I should see. I'm thinking of building a summer home here. A Queen Ann cottage. Twelve rooms. Do you think you might look over the plans? They're upstairs."

"Don't mind me!" said Timothy. "Must dress for dinner. The McBurney's. She can't abide a moment's tardiness. Last time, she kept me waiting till the rest were through souping. Must off, really. Drop in again, Rogier!"

"Jackass!" somebody flung after him. "Don't know why I like him — and everybody else!"

Rogier followed Andrew up to his room and looked at his plans.

"I'm really thick on it, sir," explained Andrews, "but with building so expensive these days it's a little too dear for me. Still, with a few changes, perhaps — will you look them over?"

Rogier rolled up the blueprints and stuck them under his arm. "I'll let you know, Mr. Andrews."

Arriving back home, he chucked the roll on the sofa and wearily sat down before the fire beside Mrs. Rogier. "A lead on a job, Daddy?"

"A house for a man named Andres. Maybe."

"The Englishman? Why, he's a rich man come out here to get well. There was an article about him in the paper. He's staying at the

Ruxton Club."

"That's where I ran into him. I was up there wasting my time with that fop Timothy and a lawyer Nelson, an obstinate encyclopedia."

"Mr. Nelson—the biggest and smartest lawyer in town! And Mr. Andrews wants you to build for him, really?"

Rogier snorted. "A Queen Anne cottage speckled with gables and dormers thick as warts. Another dome bit of superficiality to disfigure a landscape that any fool could see was meant for native sandstone. Why, before I stoop to the level of contractors who kiss the behind of the North End for a living, I'll build outhouses for mill workers at Colorado City!"

She jumped up, eyes blazing. "Yes, you would! With twenty Charlie Geyslings waiting to grab such a chance!"

He grabbed up the blueprints and stalked out to the shop.

Mrs. Rogier sat trying to rock to sleep her awakened mistrust of this blunt and obstinate, proud and humble paradox of unpremeditated decisions. She knew him insecurely enough to fear the implications of his visit to the club. The fashionable Ruxton too, with its marble statuary, painting, and its monogram on all window panes, silver, linens, and stationery; the sanctum of North End society. All his life he had been independent, aloof, solitary as a relic of a vanished generation. To what end! — that now, broke and in debt, he should casually stroll inside, pick up a job with the right people, and make himself at home. Clasping her hands, she recognized it as a miracle. This was the turn! She was profoundly relieved that he had had on his best suit, and she was profoundly dubious that nothing untoward had happened — he was that careless of what he said. She could only sit rocking before the fire the hope that Rogier at last had awakened to the world about him.

R takes the North End job, but is bored by it. Abe & Jake Zebbelin show up to ask for job. He takes them up to one of his old claims, saying "It's a poor bet."

9

Mr. Andrews was comfortably settled in the card room of the club when Rogier entered promptly at ten o'clock. "I felt so chipper yesterday I took a ride, Mr. Rogier. Had my man drive past some of your buildings. Hope you don't mind my looking at your credentials?"

"All public, Mr. Andrews. You saw I don't do much fancy work."

"Solid construction. Simple taste. I liked them."

He rang for coffee and cigars while Rogier unrolled the blueprints and got out a pencil. In coarse tweeds that did not hide the bony structure on which they hung, he leaned forward.

"I took these to an architect — a boy who used to work for me as a draughtsman. Then I did some figuring. You might knock off these two dormers, eliminate a room, and straighten the lines." Rogier marked the print. "That'll cut the cost down considerably."

"You don't like those—outcrops, as one might say here? Do you, Mr. Rogier?" He smiled.

Rogier looked up. "Look. You're overhanging the creek, set against the rise of the mesa and the mountains. Why not blend in the lines of your place with the background?"

Andrews coughed, then laughed discreetly. "You have me there, man! The architect did draw up these plans for a greensward back east. But this cough. Had to change sites. What will the change in plans amount to financially?"

Rogier drew out from his pocket a sheaf of figures.

So it continued: a new sketch submitted to Andrews, his inventory and estimate to prepare, a building permit obtained, the lien taken on the property to protect his work, and finally a trip down to Sawyer's Lumber Company to see about a collateral assignment. It was that or crawling to a bank for a heavy bond.

One would never have known from his manner when he stood in the doorway of Thompson's office that the very cigars in his pocket had been borrowed from Mrs. Rogier's sugar bowl. Thompson, full cheeked as a squirrel, looked up from the invoices for the first order Rogier had placed with the foreman. "Sit down. Let's talk things over. You've been away a long time."

Rogier pushed back his hat an inch. "No time to talk today. I've got a crew starting work."

Thompson leaned back and put one thumb in his vest. "Seven or eight thousand dollars this might run. Without any security — the Old Man — you know — "

"No, I don't," drawled Rogier. "All I know is that for over twenty-five years I've been giving Sawyer my business when at times any Denver mill would have done better. Now here's another job. You can have all but the plumbing. But I want a good competitive price. And Thompson, no beatin' around the bush."

Despite — or due to — his high-handed manner, the thing went through. Teamsters and a crew, stone and brick had been secured; subcontracts let, excavation begun under Rawlings. All these details were no longer incidentals. They were worms of worry that ate inside him, leaving him depleted each night. They bored him so! The whole job, the work itself, no longer held for him a meaning.

He took to dropping in the Ruxton to which he had been given a guest card, thanks to that fop Timothy. It was usually in the afternoon before most of the members gathered for drinks. For if the quiet luxury of the club rooms always appeased him, its members too often riled him to a nervous pitch. Indeed, he had come to be regarded as agreeable and well liked, but an eccentric old-timer who could be baited.

"Well, Rogier," Nelson would greet him cheerfully, "what do you say to the Golden CycleMill in Colorado City burning down?"

"It'll be built up again," Rogier would answer.

"What for? Everybody knows the district's on the downgrade!"

Or Nelson would saunter in and shout for the boy to bring the cigar tray. "Get a good one, boys. The First Chance on Mineral Hill has finally closed down. A good hundred-thousand sunk in that hole. Did they ever get anything out, Rogier?"

"The First Chance you say?" Rogier paused. "Met Perrault once — Louis, I think. Seemed to know what he was doing. Sank three shafts and got some forty-dollar ore, but never enough to ship. Well —" And he would launch out in defense, not of the unfortunate Perrault, but of those hills so full of tragic holes.

"A jolly queer one!" one would exclaim when he left in a huff. "But on my soul I do believe he knows minin'."

"Sure," Nelson would answer. "Had a couple of good ones, too. Don't know why he let them go. There's a story, though, that he blew up one for another worthless hole. But a smart man on building. None better."

Rogier, for his part, had grown to dislike the fat and jovial lawyer who had given up his mining clients to manage estates of the retired wealthy. And he resented the growing attitude toward Cripple Creek. Sitting there in the comfortable lounge he could hear the declamations against the strike, the workers, the mines themselves. Usually they were politely hushed, well bred, bitter voices, always with an expression of aloofness from contact with the thing itself. Insulated — they, voices and men, against the very earth whose richness had brought them hence.

Nor did the town itself assuage his sense of exile. It had been conceived at the start by a Philadelphian born with the strange compulsion to ape English life and manners; and as Little London it had grown up as a genteel English spa in the midst of the crude American West. Its architecture, life, and thought showed no homogeneity with the land. The outpouring of native gold from its signal peak had increased not its culture but its vulgarity. And now substituting scenic attractions for natural beauty, luxurious accommodations for simple hospitality, petty chicanery for honesty, it was becoming a prostitute pampering to rich visitors, one which did not have even the brazen honesty of her calling, a tourist town.

Yet, he thought, trudging home, his town had always had a life of which it was now ashamed, to keep it breathing today. It had had men like Tom who dreamed and were defeated; men crazed with the same avarice that made heroes of their more lucky neighbors; men who swarmed up the mountains and died a hundred deaths. Men hardworking, simple, and unsung, the great average of men every-where whose lives like reefs of coral build up only for others to build upon. And among all of Little London's ladies there had been women in faded gingham standing at their kitchen sinks and reading the clouds above the Peak; women like Sister Molly watching the Pass day after day with hopeless incertitude; mothers grown old upon the trail with nothing but memories of an unremitting bondage for their faithfulness; women courageous and vulgar, the indolent and the damned, like women everywhere. And there must still be children in whom all this beauty roused inquietude and unrest, and disturbed with dreams impossible, as it had the children who bore them. Children tinged with the bitterness of the wealth and luxury at their hands' reach but forever beyond their grasp, and touched by its splendor too. Children of that soil who hated it and yet were bound to it forever. Who loved it and were driven from it by the same blind fury that had brought their fathers. Men, women, and children all—they were the voiceless, and their expressive silence would confound the ears long after all others' words had died away and were forgotten. They were the poor and their lives would enrich the earth. They achieved no dreams, but the dreams they made possible for others would confute the most fantastic. In their anguish and despair and folly were nourished all seeds of truth, their exulta-tion, and their moment of success. They were Little London's only hard-rock integrity.

So Rogier, irritated with his work, bored by the club, and out of step with the town itself, trudged home to sit brooding in his shop. It was all a fantasy, like a child's game he had long outgrown. The reality lay deep within him, as if locked in hard granite to which he had no key.

One fall morning before he had left the shop, the two raw-boned

Zebbelins came swinging down the back walk and pounded on the door. They were in trouble. The last bunch of strikers was being rounded up and the mines were being reopened. But for some reason Abe had been unable to get a new work card from the Association and both men were afraid they might be posted for deportation. "Durn it, Colonel! We got to stay in the district. We ain't harvest hands. We're hard-rock men. And they ain't nowhere else to go if we had money to get there. Ain't you got somethin' in mind? Just beans and bacon is all we ask. And if there's an ounce of color we'll hit it for you!"

It was a magnificent appeal. Rogier had never suspected there were that many words in the two of them. "Now boys," he began resolutely, then stopped. Their clear gray-blue eyes, set in faces brown and rugged as the hills, stared at him with an appeal at once childish and profound. In their insistence he still had something in mind, he lost all qualms that they might be foisting themselves on him again like a couple of no-account loafers. For an instant he believed they had seen into him from the day he met them. It was inexplicable, profound, weirdly prophetic that they called up now from the hidden recesses within him that one thought he believed buried and locked. The spark they struck inflamed him, swept through him with a roar. He controlled himself, turning away his face and gripping the seat of his stool. Finally he turned around, jamming his trembling hands into his coat pockets.

"Now listen here, you boys. I haven't a thing for you. I'm broke and out of the district. There's only one thing I've got left. Straight off and no fooling. You can take it or leave it."

Jake grinned at Abe. "Ain't I told you!"

Rogier continued. "A long time ago I had papers on an old working up there. Got down a level, inclined shaft, hand tramming and burros. A showing of sylvanite, but not enough to ship. So I left her."

Abe was watching Rogier's face. "She wasn't that bad, was she? They ain't no mine plumb bad, if you know what's ailing her."

"It's a poor bet," Rogier said resolutely. "It would have to be refiled. There's not been any work done to hold it. You'd have to put up a cabin and get along on a grubstake. The only good thing about it is that you could lay low up there through the winter. It might be the

end of the world as far as everybody else is concerned. Then by
spring this trouble should be over and you can get a regular job."

Jake was jubilant. "When we know a man that's got the looks
of somebody and says out fair and square, 'Boys, here's a proposition,' we're for him. Ain't it so, Abe?"

Again Abe asked, "What was so cantankerous about her,
Colonel, you not doin' enough work to see she really was a mine?"

Rogier jerked erect. "What do you reckon I was throwing
money into her for if not to find that out!"

Abe grinned knowingly. "What do you say we have a look at
her, Colonel?"

As Rogier walked out the door with them, he met Ona coming
to work on his books. "Tell Martha I'll not be home tonight. Back
tomorrow."

She looked over the Zebbelins coldly, then gave him a level
stare. "Daddy, you're not — it's not Cripple Creek!"

"I'm tryin' to find two men work!" He turned on his heel and
walked up the alley with Abe and Jake.

By late that afternoon the three men on horseback were behind
the Calf and skirting the base of the Cow. Before them rose the
gulch as it had always been and would be always. The ruts in the
road were overgrown with weeds. Not a soul had passed since that
day, when touching match to fuse, he had walked resolutely away
forever. There to the left lay what was left of the Silver Heels:
strewn planks, decaying scraps of bedding, rusty pieces of iron, a
few splintered timbers, all half-covered by the sheered-off side of the
hill. Reynolds' unmarked tomb.

Callously they rode on without stopping. The canyon grew
darker, narrower. The little stream, blocked by beavers, murmured
at the bulwark of logs, trickled over the rocks. Jake nudged Abe,
pointing to an old dump, yellow with oxidation, and a gaping
shaft — the Gloriana. Aspens appeared, the quaking brittle leaves
already turned yellow. A red-tailed hawk shot up from the cliffs,
hung a moment at the tip of its flight, and floated across another
abandoned working — the Magpie. The two men looked inquiringly
at Rogier, but he gave no sign of having noticed it. The wagon road
ended here. From now on, climbing still higher, there was only a
faint trail. Beside it bristled a porcupine, immovable as bunch grass.

After a time Rogier reined up his mare. "Whoa-up! Whoa, girl!" He took off his hat and ran his fingers through his white hair. Straight ahead and upward the gulch ended in a narrow slit in the bare, frost-shattered, granite slope on whose lofty summit fat white cloud-stallions were lazily nibbling. A great stone face that looked down with neither compassion nor defiance, with no sign of recognition.

"There she is, boys. You get what I mean, don't you?"

There was little to see. A landslide had covered the old portal. Only the outline of a corral remained, the thin aspen poles turned grayish-black. Jake and Abe did not reply. They noted the growth of spruce and pine that could be cut for cabin logs, stulls, and props; reckoned the length of haul for aspen poles for a new corral; pointed to the changing formation of the cliffs. They dismounted, tied up their horses, and began to prowl around; then climbed up the ridge and chipped off samples at different points directed by Rogier below.

"See how we followed this ridge around hunting for values? Then this outcrop. Not a speck of color—even the dullest, in that oxidized streak. It was the unoxidized stuff we went down on. Sylvanite. Not a bad showing, but it didn't last."

"You and Reynolds didn't hunt long enough for the right lead," Abe said tersely.

This was the first time Reynolds' name had been mentioned. Rogier flinched. "That was long ago and this was a long way to bring a woman!" he said irritably. "I told you this was no picnic ground!"

Abe continued to peck around, finally coming back with a piece of gangue which he held up in the fading sunlight. "Maybe it is and maybe it ain't. But if they's a thing here, we'll find it."

Rogier drew a deep breath. "I've got no promises to make. As I say, it's a poor bet."

"Gold is where you find it." Abe quoted the saying with an air of incontrovertible wisdom.

They rode back to Victor in silence. But as Rogier got on the train next day they wrung his hand till the knuckles cracked; their blue eyes gleamed; they ran beside the coach, brown faces uplifted, their long muscular arms clumsily waving in the air as if knotting anew the threads that bound him to them.

Rogier staking the Zebbelins, taking construct" jobs. Mary Ann & Ona have baby girls. Mrs White dies. Rogier in a pleasant interregnum, w/ remarkable things on the horizon.

10

There was no keeping it a secret that Rogier was grubstaking those two giant rawbones on another wild goose chase in Cripple Creek. Mrs. Rogier wearily acknowledged it in her prayers: "Dear Lord, keep Daddy from getting back into it again!" Ona, thin lipped, made out the monthly checks for the Zebbelins' supplies without a word. But she needed a name under which to list the account in her books; and Rogier, required to supply one when he filed relocation papers on the old working, had simply filled in the name of the ore — sylvanite.

So as the Sylvanite it became known even to doddering old Mrs. White. She was sitting in her corner, chewing on her wart, when Denman came in from his ranch. He could no longer wait for a name under which to register Akeepee's last colt. "Silvah Night would be a fetchin' name. Ain't that what Joe calls that theah new mine of his?" Mrs. White suggested.

"Suits her fine!" Denman agreed and hurried off.

That evening when Rogier went out to the ranch, Denman showed him the papers made out in the name of Silver Night. Rogier frowned. "Sylvanite's the name. God Almighty, man, can't you spell?"

Denman blinked his eyes, then slapped his leg and let out a roar of laughter. "God Almighty yourself, Joe! With a Confederate veteran in the house with a Southern brogue thicker'n cotton, how do you folks keep anything straight!"

Silver Night, however, fitted the filly exactly. Even Rogier agreed. Possibly there was something intangibly connecting her to the Sylvanite, as there had been between Silver Heels and the mine named after her. Rogier went out to the stall with Denman to see her for the last time. Certainly she was Akeepee's colt with every toss of her head. But where Akeepee was small and compact, with round hips, perfectly shaped as a picture horse, Silver Night was certain to be over sixteen hands high and always lean. One might suppose that with her big feet and a heavy head carried almost even with her withers she would be only a fair to middling pacer. Rogier recognized her as the epitome of his, Denman's, and Akeepee's combined efforts. As a horseman he saw how well she was let down behind, with a deep chest though light in the body. He observed how closely she was coupled, the long sloping shoulders, the sinewy legs. And he knew that if she had a heart as strong as her body they had produced a horse.

"Sure you want to sell her?" asked Denman.

"She's the last one. Let her go," Rogier said imperturbably.

But as he watched her being led away, and ever after, he maintained that Silver Night would be the fastest horse he had ever owned.

All winter, despite himself, he was kept busy. He worried, fretted, fumed; he dreamed of failures and rejected bids; he imagined himself forgotten, ignored, tolerated at best. There was always another job before him—a small residence, a hotel annex, another schoolhouse. The only one in which he took an interest was a mill job in Colorado City. Cripple Creek ore reduction had been a problem since the first stamp mill had been built along Cripple Creek, posing the difficulties of amalgamation. A chlorination plant had been built later at Gillette, but most of the ore had been shipped to the two mills in Florence. Colorado City then had put in its bid for the thousands of tons of rich ore ripped from the grass roots by erecting two chlorination plants, the Portland and the Standard.

These were followed by the Telluride, using bromide instead of chlorine as the solvent for gold. This had been taken over by the Golden Cycle, putting in a roast amalgamation — cyanide plant instead of using bromide and hot chlorine. Despite its fire, the mill was now running three shifts and expanding. The strike was over, mines were reopening, and long trains of ore were coming down. Vast new bins were needed, and Rogier was building them. This was his one touch with the district. What the Zebbelins were doing he didn't know. A monthly postcard, scrawled in a handwriting he sometimes couldn't read, was his only news.

Family events too ensnared his casual interest, if only temporarily. Although Mrs. Rogier hardly admitted it to herself, Mary Ann's baby had been born after an unusually short pregnancy. Now it was quite apparent that she and young Durgess were not wholly compatible. They both worked in the elder Durgess' catering shop where Mary Ann was avidly learning to make candy, dip chocolates, decorate cakes, make English-style muffins and other arts of the trade, as well as the value of money. All this came out during the frequent occasions Mary Ann brought down the baby, a girl named Nancy, to stay for a few days or a week at a time.

"I simply can't stand a man all day and night too!" she would complain. So leaving the baby at home, she would go to the store to work with him all day and return at night. It was obvious that trouble of a disgraceful sort was in the making, as well as blueberry muffins.

Ona had a new baby too, a girl named Leona. Once again she moved down into the old house on Shook's Run so the baby could be born "at home" like March. During the month she was there, Cable stayed too, more grim of manner than the first time. So with two daughters back home temporarily, and with three grandchildren, Mrs. Rogier was delighted. Rogier seemed too busy to do more than take their presence for granted.

Divine Providence, having supplied two new additions to the family, now exercised its prerogative of subtraction. Late in January, during a severe blizzard, Mrs. White died. They all trudged knee deep in snow from the waiting carriages to her grave in the pine-grown cemetery southeast of town. The Red Niggah, to whom she had not spoken one direct word since the midnight March was born, helped to carry her coffin.

Her death did not upset Rogier; the indomitable old lady had been ready to go for some time. But seeing her lowered into the grave beside Sister Molly under the big pine gave him a bad turn. Those two women, so alike, and caught in the same pattern of helpless futility as if it had been ordained for them from birth! Indeed the whole Hines family seemed woven from the same tribal propensities. Tom, after all these years, had never been heard of. Hiney too had vanished. Bob had moved to San Francisco and while there had been informed by an insurance company examiner that Hiney and Margaret had been traced to Shanghai, China where his trail had been lost. Bob also had visited Boné. Lockhardt had died, leaving him his money. Boné was quite a gay dog, playing the piano down on the Barbary Coast and writing popular songs. Enclosed in Bob's letter was a sample piece of sheet music, "Ching, Ching, Chinaman."

Ona, when Mary Ann played it, was shocked. "That awful bang, bang! That tin-panny ragtime song! Stop it! I hate it!"

"Hold on!" Rogier had said. "You're getting yourself all riled up for nothing. Like as not Boné's got to make a living like the rest of us."

Yet there was something infinitely repugnant to them all in the thought of Boné living in that sinister area of San Francisco's waterfront known as the Barbary Coast. Mrs. Rogier more than once had echoed the preacher's prophecy that the Lord would destroy it in its wickedness as He had Sodom and Gomorrah.

Meanwhile Rogier, who had sat brooding in the shop day and night, showed signs of rejuvenated life and interest. He had three crews working. Money was coming in: not enough to pay off all his monstrous debt, but to re-open his accounts, re-establish his credit, replenish Mrs. Rogier's sugar bowl, and to keep the Zebbelins in bacon and beans and a few unspecified items. What they were doing he didn't know; it had been two months now since he had received their last postcard. This did not worry him. Something was happening he was not fully aware of and which he could not account for. It was as if something deep inside him was rising to surface, just as the Peak once more was slowly emerging with all the clarity of its first purity and promise. He felt himself becalmed in an interregnum that could not be broken or shortened, a period of gestation for immeasurable and unpredictable events.

Jake & Abe find some gold in the
Sylvanite mine. Rogier vows to drill all the
way down to the granite of the mtn
itself.— below grass roots.

11

Calendar pages kept turning. Events outcropped above the sensory horizon and sank back down. Buildings were going up; bills were being paid. But time stayed still. Rogier, however else anyone knew him, was a man for whom time had stopped. The flowing linear stream of time—what an illusion it really was! Time was a great still pool, an element as basic as earth and air, water and fire, in which life developed at its own immeasurable pace to its own degree of fulfillment. Time! What did it mean to him now! In that invisible, immeasurable, impalpable pool both he and the Peak had been rooted for aeons to confront at last the meaning of their inner selves. Rogier kept staring at it in moonlight and in sunlight, at its dual faces of benign motherliness and masculine malignity, combined into an enigmatic mask which now he recognized for what it was. In geologic time it had stood there, a monstrous volcano belching fire and smoke upon a world that had sunk beneath forgotten seas. It had stood there in orogenic time, a lofty snow-crowned peak looking down upon a virgin continent yet unraped by greedy man. Through the quick gasp of a century it had remained inviolable while lesser prophets, robed in silver, had been gutted of their riches. And now it had come to its moment of revelation. He could see it at dawn when the rising sun flushed its snowcap pale gold, when the setting sun brought out the pinkish-red glow of its granite walls, when its dark red porphyry stood purple as blood against the melting snowpack. Gold, in all its shades and tints! And what was that? Let other greedy fools scratch the grass roots of its rocky epidermis for a modicum of pay dirt to make them rich and famous! Not he! For he also was a growth within that immovable, immeasurable, deep still pool of time, as old as the Peak itself. And now at last in their moment of truth and fruition they faced each other like two adversaries bound together in a common selfhood. Over them both a common golden sun rose and set. Through both their flesh ran the veins of liquid golden life, pulsating to the same diastolic and systolic beat. And in each of them glowed the reflection of the one great sun, the golden sun that was the heart of all. Gold! A great gold heart embodied in the depths of that extinct volcano whose remnant was the puny Peak. A heart whose beat was in rhythm with his own; whose meaning, if he could but fathom it, would illumine for him the secret of his existence which had seemed so alien to this mortal earth. Of course he would reach it, if he had to blast the whole dom top off the Peak and dig by hand down to the convergence of its golden veins in the heart that lay beneath! For time, the human illusion of flowing time, no longer existed. He had been born for this, geological eras, biological ages ago. Born as an incipient mammal to grow into an individual egohood only to seek and to find at last that universal self which combined within it both himself and the massive Peak whose granite armor he was meant to pierce.

To even the rational shell of the man who sat staring at that numinous specter it was evident that its future lay in depth. The disastrous strike was over. The population of the Cripple Creek district had been reduced from 43,237 to 28,050; the number of shipping mines had decreased from 475 to 200. Never again was their annual production to equal the high peak of $19,000,000. Still, $15,000,000 worth of ore a year was being taken out — 99½% gold to only ½% silver. And to date more than $153,000,000 had been produced from an area of only six square miles.

The statistics reassured Rogier. For all its setbacks, Cripple Creek was doing better than the Mother Lode of California, the Klondike in Alaska, the Comstock Lode in Nevada, and the gold camps of Kalgoorlie, Australia, Kolar, British India, and the Yenisei region of Siberia. What was wrong with that!

Underground water still posed a problem. The mile-long El Paso drainage tunnel had punctured the gold-filled granite bowl at 8,800 feet, releasing the water into Cripple Creek and allowing the mines to go deeper than 800 feet without pumping. Now work was beginning to drive another, the Roosevelt deep drainage tunnel, into the Peak at 8,000 feet altitude. This would drain off all water above the 2,100 foot depth reached by the deepest mine, the American Eagles, whose portal was just over 10,000 feet high, permitting other large producers to sink their shafts still deeper. Gold would be found at depth; it was not restricted to the volcanic porphyry, but lay in the granite below, as well.

To Rogier this had been a momentous discovery. It had given him a perspective of the vast subterranean world whose life went on unceasing and unhurried beneath his feet. An earth that like the sea flowed in rhythm to the moon and stars, obeying the same universal laws that kept the sun in place, maintaining an isotatic equilibrium by which mountains crumbled and washed away, old sea floors subsided under the weight of their conglomerate ooze, and new mountain peaks arose with sea shells on their summits. He could almost feel beneath him that great arterial fountain bursting from the hot, mysterious heart of the Peak.

Many pools of eruption had broken through the granite and left their gold deposits near the surface, at the very grass roots. No wonder they had been so easily found and were now being exhausted. The last and greatest pool of all still lay beneath the solid granite it had not been able to break through. For this it would be necessary to sink to depth. The fact substantiated Rogier's wildest dreams, and left him with a mind cold and clear as ice. It seemed inconceivable no one had thought of it years before. For of all that superimposed granite where was it thicker, deeper, and more resistant than the culminating point; the highest and only remnant of that ancient volcano which had towered even higher in the skies! The height that counter-balanced the depth of its hidden pool.

Instinct, intuition, foreknowledge — something, whatever it was, had pointed the way long ago. Now the light of cold reason thrown on factual statistics was substantiating it. He could feel the opposite polarities within himself coming to a verge; every thought and feeling converging, like the veins in the Peak, to a center. There was no hastening it nor retarding it; it would come when it would.

It came late one afternoon when Rogier in the shop glanced out the window to see the Zebbelins plodding down the driveway. They opened the gate, crossed the barnyard, and knocked on the door. Rogier unlatched it. "Well! Thought I told you to come in the back!"

Neither answered. They walked in, grinning like apes. Abe took off his battered hat, revealing a head brown and smooth as an acorn. Jake stood in overalls, that bulged from both pockets.

"You ain't taken up with business, are you, Colonel?" he asked.

"No," answered Rogier. "Not till you boys give an account of yourselves. Haven't got one of those postcards from you for three months."

Jake's grin spread over his face. "We was running short of money so we worked in the Mary McKinney and saved part of our wages."

Abe nudged his brother. "We ain't forgot you. We got somethin' for you." Again he poked Jake who hauled a specimen out of his pocket. Another came out of the second pocket. Two pieces of grayish ore the size of both fists, which he laid in Rogier's lap.

"Workin' in the McKinney we found out what forms the tellurides took. And lookin' for it we run into this sylvanite," Abe said slowly.

"Not a hundred yards from the old tunnel!" shouted Jake. "It was there all the time, covered up by a slide."

"A defined vein, Colonel. We followed it. The assays say it's shipping ore. What you were lookin' for."

What could be more natural? The old abandoned working had been a name and a mine to all the family for months, worthless as it might have proved to be. He thought of those other false hopes and abandoned workings—the Garnet and Fleur-de-Lis, the Silver Heels, Gloriana, and the Magpie. But now here it was, sylvanite from the Sylvanite.

"Look at that stuff! Look at it, man! We got somethin', sure as Moses!"

Rogier sat, a specimen in each hand, listening with an inscrutable face to the alternately rising voices of Abe and Jake driving like iron into the granite recesses of his being where lay the hope hidden from all but his secret self. He spun around on his stool, swept papers aside, and laid the specimens on the board. With a glass he examined minutely the fine silver-clear crystals imbedded in the rock. This was it! It was! The old voice that had shouted to him years ago when Reynolds first had run into the formation now again began to cry out.

"Crystals? Hummn. Crystals!" he muttered softly.

"One piece ran thirty-two dollars!" Jake was at his elbow, poking his finger under the glass. "We told you we'd find out if it was a mine or not!"

Rogier turned around at Abe's slow voice.

"It won't all be this good. But I figure there's enough to go down on if you've a mind to, Colonel. It'll take a piece of money to sink a shaft. Do you reckon you want to – "

"Want to!" He tried to control his voice. "There'll be money to go down! Way down!" He trembled like the last brittle leaf on a tree; and his nervous hand running through his thin white hair left wisps sticking up as though blown upright by the tempest within him. It had come at last, at the end of a lifetime of mocking toil, at the end of a boredom which had almost driven him mad. There had been other strikes before. Each time the Peak had defeated him – through the chicanery of rich men's greed, by organized labor's demand for a living wage, by the elements themselves – earth, air, and water. Now only the Peak itself offered the last barrier. He swept off a high shelf and on it placed the specimens to catch the light from the window. "Look at 'em boys! That's what we're after. We're going to drive a shaft through country rock and gangue, through breccia and sylvanite, into the granite of the old Peak herself!"

Perhaps for an instant his impassioned intensity of purpose illumined in awful splendor the depths within him. "It's just a mine, Colonel," said Abe quietly, "and she ain't even that yet. And we can only go as far as shipping ore holds out."

"A mine!" Rogier shouted irritably. "God Almighty!" He pointed out over the roof of the shed at the lofty white peak rising palely above the rampart of blue mountains. "There's your mine! We're going down into her rock bottom if we have to blow off her whole top! I won't be stopped again. Not by God or granite or human flesh. We're going down below grass roots this time. Way down!"

Rogier tries to involve Cable in mining.
Ona resists. It comes between them.

PART II

ADOBE

1

It was late Sunday morning, and Ona, washing the breakfast dishes, parted the muslin curtains with a soapy hand to stare past Mrs. Cullen's apple trees at the blue mountains beyond. The October day was clear and bright, not a cloud hanging over the Peak. There was something about Sundays that made them all alike. An intangible sense of laxity seemed to permeate the very air. Cable had got out of bed, thrown off his pajama top, and stood breathing deeply at the open widow. Tall and thin but muscular, his smooth brown skin glowed in the sunlight. The outline of his Roman nose reminded her of a laughable occurrence shortly after their marriage. He had been walking down the street when a visiting Rabbi had silently taken his arm and turned him into a nearby house to attend a Jewish wake. Cable, simple as he was, had not suspected that he had been taken for a Jew and had sat through the affair without comment.

Now he was sitting out on the porch with March on his lap. The boy as usual was bitterly disappointed because there was no funny paper to read. The preachers of Little London, bent on making it a "City of Churches," had been successful in forcing the *Gazette* to discontinue the weekly comic page because it kept the children from studying their Sunday School lessons. Cable had laid aside his paper to make up stories about bears and Indians for the boy.

In a little while he came in the kitchen. "What! Through already? Why didn't you call?"

"It's such a nice day for a picnic I thought we'd go by home and all of us go up Cheyenne Canyon."

"We'll do it some other time. I've already ordered a buggy so we can drive out and look at the lot."

Ona bit her lip, then blurted out, "It'll still be there!"

While Cable and March walked to the livery stable, she dressed and got the baby ready. Neither March nor Leona had their father's coarse black hair. But if March had his father's build and high cheek bones, little Leona had his dark skin. She was a great favorite with Mrs. Rogier who always hugged her, exclaiming, "The only Rogier in the bunch!" To this she always added, "The stork didn't bring you, honey. An old Nigger man left you on the doorstep." And she would hold up a dark leg or arm in proof.

When Cable and March returned with the buggy, they all drove out on the prairie past Nob Hill to look at the few acres Cable had bought with his savings. Waiting in the buggy, she watched him pace off a patch of tall grass and tumbleweeds, bending down to see that the stakes were set. "It'll be a fine place someday!" he said, coming back. "Look! Not a house for miles around!"

Ona nodded. She could see well enough the dry prairies stretching eastward, brown and unfenced; the rough dirt road crawling so far back to town; the glimmer of sunlight on white alkalai patches.

"We'll have us a house of our own out here," he promised. "Not a fancy place like those in the North End with an iron fence all around and statues on the lawn. But open to the wind."

Ona covered her mouth with a handkerchief and snuggled Leona against her breast to protect her from a dust devil that came whirling across the plains. "You'll get plenty of it, all right," she said when it had passed. "But I should think, Jonathan, we ought to be in town, closer to water and trees and where the children can get to school. I want March to make something of himself."

Cable slapped the boy on the back. "Ah! A line of cottonwoods will stop that little wind, all right. And how'd you like a horse to ride to school on, eh March?"

All the way back he prattled on. Only that stretch of desolate prairie aroused in him such enthusiasm. Hardly a week passed that he did not have to drive out to see it—as if, like a patch of kelp, it might float away on that vast pelagic plain. He was so simple and straightforward, so easily satisfied with her and the children, naive as a child. He seemed to live by feeling instead of by reasoning. A sensuous and sensitive man, the kindest she had ever known, and also the most violent when aroused. From the vĕry first he had accepted her wholly and irrationally; and this was exactly what still held her to him. Yet she found herself beginning to resent his mindless absorption in their simple life.

Early that evening she suggested casually, "If we're going to church we ought to get started, so we can go by home."

"Home?" Cable paused. "I didn't borrow you from the family, you know. I married you."

"Oh Jonathan!"

She loved him, their children, their home. Yet it was that ramshackle óld domain on Shook's Run she still unconsciously called home. A family worm-eaten with false pride, an aristocratic plant gone to seed, a box full of trinkets covered by a Confederate flag, a ghost-ridden house—whatever it was, no member of the family ever permanently left it; sometime he always snapped back. Ona, like Mary Ann, could return, take her accustomed place at table and go to bed upstairs as if she had never been away. And she did so often, every holiday and birthday, whenever anything unusual came up.

So of course they went, Cable pushing Leona in her baby-buggy: past Mrs. Cullen's apple orchard, following the creek west, passing under the railway trestle, and thence a quarter-mile up Bijou to the old bridge over Shook's Run. The big house was empty. Apparently Rogier was up in Cripple Creek and Mary Ann had taken Mrs. Rogier to church.

The small Southern Methodist Church was full when they arrived, the first hymn resounding from rafter to rafter. They were lucky to get seats in the back row. Up in a front pew sat Mary Ann and Mrs. Rogier, head turned to one side to favor her poor ear. During the sermon Ona noticed a man to her left staring intently at her. He nudged his wife and she too turned to stare. Ona lifted her head disdainfully but began to figit, wondering if her collar was askew or her hair messed.

Cable, with March asleep on his lap, leaned over. "What's that fellow Bennett staring at you for?" he whispered.

Ona shook her head, her eyes fixed steadily at the shouting preacher. Cable sat quietly, his dark face immobile, but keeping watch on Bennett. Ona began to worry. There was no telling what Cable might do when the services were over. She rose immediately after the last hymn, hurrying him out ahead of the crowd without stopping to see her mother and Mary Ann.

The walk home seemed long. The night was beginning to get cold; wind rattled the dry leaves on the trees. March grew tired and Cable lifted him into the buggy with his little sister. Then as Ona and Cable walked down the narrow sidewalk in front of the house next door to their own, their figures obscuring the faint glimmer of the arc-light on the corner behind them, it happened: a sudden bump and crash, a frightened scream from March, and a wail from awakened Leona. Cable, pushing the baby carriage in the darkness, had run into the iron front gate of the Franklin house. The childless, middle-aged couple was always leaving it open, blocking the sidewalk. Cable had barked his shins on it before, and several times had requested Franklin to keep it closed at night. Ona, annoyed at the mishap blurted out, "Those durn Franklins!"

Cable did not reply. In deathly silence he pushed the buggy to one side. Then in the darkness he wrenched the iron-lattice gate from its hinges, lifted it over his head, and walked deliberately down the front walk to the porch of Franklin's house. Here, with a heave of his muscular shoulders, he threw the gate at the front door. There was the sound of shattering glass and splintering wood, the crash of the gate on the floor of the porch, a woman's screams from inside. The lights flicked on and Mr. and Mrs. Franklin rushed out to confront Cable standing wordlessly in front of them.

Something in his quiet, expectant, and challenging appearance held Franklin silent and immobile. Cable turned, walked slowly back to the sidewalk, and pushing the baby carriage went on to his own house, followed by Ona.

The next evening Cable returned home from work in good

humor. "This morning first thing I stopped in Bennett's real estate office — you know, the man who kept staring at you in church last night."

Ona sat down on a chair beside the kitchen stove, entwined her fingers, and slowly looked up into his dark face. She suspected by his voice and manner what a disgraceful scene had occurred. Cable went on.

"Before I could say a word, Bennett stepped back of the counter and put up his hand. 'Please, Mr. Cable! Do you have a silver dollar in your pocket? Lay it down on the counter and look at it.' I thought he was crazy but I did it. 'Take a good look at that woman's face on it. Mrs. Bennett and I say it's an exact outline of your wife's. We couldn't help staring at her all evening. Perhaps you both noticed it. We apologize, but you must show it to your wife.' "

Cable dug out a silver dollar and passed it to Ona. "Bennett said a funny thing to me just before I left. 'If you ever leave your haberdashery store, Cable, come over and see me. I think we could get along.' Now how the devil did he know we were just about broke and ready to close doors?"

"Oh but you're not, Jonathan!"

"The store kept the New Moon going too long. We ought to have closed up that old mine long ago. Now the mortgages on the store are weighing us down. If we can get rid of it we figure we'll each have a little left to start over fresh and not be saddled with debts and heavy interest. That's why Bennett gave me an idea."

"It might be", said Ona thoughtfully, getting up and putting supper on the table. There was always something incongruous about Cable selling neckties and colored waistcoats in a haberdashery store — although, for that matter, she was never comfortable thinking of him mucking ore up in Cripple Creek. Sitting down at table she resumed the conversation. "All along I've been hoping you could get into something where you'd be happier and better known. If you could get to selling property in the North End to all the retired Easterners coming out it might be all right. But — " she paused. "Mr. Bennett might like my profile, but I don't think much of his. It's too sly and cunning. You couldn't keep up with him, Jonathan."

"I'll think about it," he said quietly.

A few evenings later when they went down for supper with the

Rogiers it was evident to Ona that Cable and his two partners, the Grimes, had been doing more thinking about their store. Rogier had returned from Cripple Creek. As if none of them knew what he was up to, he said casually, "Yes, the boys struck a lead in the old Sylvanite. Wouldn't be surprised if we opened her up — if it isn't too expensive. That's why I want those specifications, Ona. I had them all laid out."

"After supper," Ona said firmly.

Rogier reached for a spoon. "Tapioca and pineapple again. Humm. Oh say, Cable. I ran into Johnny Grimes up there. Said you were finally giving up that old hole of yours on Big Bull and trying to salvage something. I looked at the machinery, thinking I might help you out, but it wasn't worth a song. What's going on?"

Cable grinned. "The strike finished the New Moon. But we've just decided what to do at a directors' meeting of the President, Vice-President, and Secretary-Treasurer — me and the two Grimes. The current price for our one-dollar par value shares was one cent, and our last sale was four dollars for one thousand shares. So we decided to empty the treasury of its fifty-seven dollars cash and split the shares — a trunk load apiece to paper our houses!"

Rogier's eyes twinkled. "A wise move, you directors. But say!" He thrust his tapioca aside and leaned forward. "If you all quit, you might throw in with us on a real mine. We've got something. There's no telling how big it'll be. But I'll say this: we're going down. Below grass roots this time!" His booming voice lowered. He leaned back and lit a cigar. "Cable, you come out to the shop and talk with me. You won't regret it."

"No!" Ona said decisively. "Jonathan will have no time to work with you on another mine. He didn't have a chance to tell you he and the Grimes are closing down the store too. Jonathan is going in with Mr. Bennett — real estate. A fine thing for him, too."

Cable sat back, his long brown fingers toying with his silver.

Rogier got up. "Well, I'll give you the chance anyway. I'm finishing up things here, myself. Now Ona, I want those specifications. You're always hiding my papers where even a pack rat couldn't find them." Still grumbling, he walked out to the shop.

"Daddy's in it again, for sure!" Mary Ann said lightly. "We're likely to be praying even for tapioca!"

"You take March upstairs, and see if the two girls are sleeping," ordered Mrs. Rogier sternly. "Your father can take care of himself — and us — without your criticism."

Ona, still stiff and upright in her chair, watched Cable fill his pipe. His long fingers swept the cloth clean of a few flakes of tobacco, pressed them firmly into the bowl; his face was dark and expressionless as a wooden Indian's. Then she got up and followed Rogier out to the shop.

It took her but a few moments to find the papers. Now she stood with them clasped to her breast.

"Here. Give 'em here," Rogier demanded, looking up from his stool at the drafting table.

Ona did not move or reply. Her face was pale; there was an unnatural gleam in her clear eyes.

Rogier stood up. "What's the matter, girl?" he asked kindly.

The matter — dear God! The simple question illuminated the enormity of his folly and held her spellbound. How well she knew him now, this man who always had been more than her father; with whom she had worked for years; her one confidant, as she was his. He didn't know what he was doing. And to tell him would be to betray him for the first time in her life, and forever.

"Out with it, Ona!"

She stepped back a pace, clutching the sheaf of papers as if it were a treasure to be bargained between them. "You're getting back into mining again," she stated weakly.

"Dom! Haven't we been in it for years? What's itching you?"

"You're trying to pull Jonathan into the hole too!"

It was out! There was no more to be said. In that one simple statement was implied her distrust of his power, her loyalty to Cable. She could see the almost imperceptible change in his face. It struck at her heart; she knew that henceforth it was always to be between them.

In the awkward silence neither spoke. Both peas in a pod, with Rogier undemonstrativeness, they fought to get back to the casual.

"Now Daddy," she went on, "we know your luck might change. But mining is a risky and expensive venture. I really wish you'd keep out of it. What I do mean is that Jonathan hasn't any business in it, even with you. He knows nothing about it. He's got me and the children to look after. He can't afford to take any chances."

"Fol-de-rol, girl! You're getting worse than your mother. You don't have to worry. I'm letting him in just for your sake."

She could tell that now he too was merely talking.

"Come on, the papers now," he demanded. "And stop your worrying."

Ona clasped them tighter. "Daddy," she said with a resolute voice, "I don't want Jonathan mixed up with your mining."

Two chips off the same granite, they stood eyeing each other.

"Ona! A man's a man, whether he's your husband or not. Don't you try to run Cable's life."

"Or you!"

He turned abruptly and flung himself on his stool. They understood each other. The tears jumped to her eyes. But oh, if he would only remember that she meant what she had said!

"Here're your papers," she said softly, laying them down before him. "I'm going to help you all I can, like I always have. But please, Daddy! Don't bring Jonathan into it. Promise!"

He did not reply. And in his silence she felt impending a disaster that would rend her apart. It was to be a long, hard fight; to it she would have to give her best.

2

Already by five o'clock it was almost dark — these cold fall days when the trees were stark skeletons and the withered squash vines glistened with rime, when the brittle corn stalks crackled faintly in the wind and the little creek flowing into Shook's Run was covered each morning with paper ice. Ona, sitting at the window, watched for Cable. When he first appeared, emerging from under the railway trestle into the glow of the arc-light, she would get up and put the biscuits in the oven. Then she would return to her seat and watch his lanky body striding up the road. Now, with Leona in bed and March whining for supper, she still waited patiently. The tea kettle began to sing.

"Is there a genie in the kettle, Mother — like the picture in the book?"

"No, Sonny. That's just a fairy tale."

"Tell me a story about Indians. And bears and wolves. I like them better."

"Those are all fairy tales too. But I'll tell you a true story about Indians and your uncle Boné — the one who writes nice music for people to play and sing."

The boy climbed into her lap and snuggled against her shoulder.

"March! You're not going to sleep? Here, let's go get some supper if you don't want to wait for Daddy. Then you can go to bed."

Again she sat alone in front of the window. Seven o'clock and still Jonathan had not come home. Since he had started working for Bennett there was no telling how late he'd be. Out in his buggy all day and at his desk later every evening—a shame, the way Bennett treated him! She'd known from his coyote-sharp face that Bennett wouldn't stick to his promise and let Cable handle the North End properties. It was only the prairie land east of town and down along the Fontaine-qui-Bouille that had been given him. Not that Cable minded. He was like the land he sold—not barren but devoid of artificialities; not wild but forever to remain untamable completely; and whose subtle charm, once known, could never be replaced with a softer or more striking beauty.

One afternoon Ona had driven out with him and a manufacturer from New Jersey to look at a tract east of his own little piece. "Yes, sir!" said Cable, reining the horse to point out his own property. "I bought it long before I started selling land. My wife and I are going to build pretty soon. People are coming in fast, like yourself, Mr. Hichens."

"Hadn't we better drive on?" suggested Ona. "Mr. Hichens would rather see the tract. And it's getting late."

The fall rains were over; now the warm air suggested snow. The mountain tops were obscured by clouds that looked like a canopy let down from the sky. Ona could see Mr. Hichens flashing an apprehensive look back from time to time. Still the road crawled ahead into what seemed a vast brown undulating sea. Cable had taken off his hat. The wind never ruffled his straight black hair. She could see his dark face in gentle repose, knew he was thinking of his years on the plains. Again a quick momentary vision of his birthright came to her. For an instant she seemed to see it all through his eyes: the long stalk of a lone sunflower, the tumbleweeds rolling and bounding, the imperceptible movement of the wind through the grass, like breath blown over fur.

"Here we are!" said Cable, reining up the horse. "Get down so you can see exactly what we're talking about."

Mr. Hichens face betrayed what he thought about it. Indeed, how anyone could have distinguished it from any other spot in any direction was to Ona a mystery. Nevertheless he got out, stretched his legs while looking back disconsolately toward town, and politely offered her his arm.

Cable began pacing off his steps, hunting dutifully for a stake. The sod was damp and sticky; between humps of bunch grass and tumbleweed there were patches of alkalai and an occasional streak of water. Suddenly Mr. Hichens bogged down over his ankles. Ona, grabbing his arm, found herself mired. The mud was slippery, reddish adobe; the more they struggled the deeper they became entrenched. Water began to soak in over their shoetops.

"Quicksand!" yelled Mr. Hichens with the vision of sinking over his head. His legs began to work like pump handles; his feet never left the ground. Ona, herself stuck, quieted him and called for Cable. He came up behind them with an arm-load of tumbleweeds and without a word threw them at their feet. In a moment they were out: Mr. Hichens red-faced and angry, and Ona plodding to the buggy in a pair of ruined shoes and stockings.

"Adobe. Nothin' but a bit of adobe," said Cable quietly, bending down to scrape off her shoes and partially dry her feet with his handkerchief. "It don't look like much, but it takes a hold."

The episode had spoiled a sale as well as Mr. Hichens' new boots, trousers, and temper. He had sat pouting in the buggy all the way home. Too, it had occasioned a lively quarrel between her and Cable. And though all this already had almost faded from her mind, she remembered Cable's head bent before her as he methodically scraped with long gentle fingers the thick reddish adobe from her shoes. He didn't look like much either, simple and taciturn Jonathan; but dear God, she did love him so!

It was too dark now to see him from the window. Nor did she hear his light step on the porch until he flung open the door. "Jonathan! I was getting worried. Never mind. I'll put the biscuits in right now."

"Do we have to wait till you make biscuits? I'm hungry!"

"It won't take a minute. Hot biscuits and honey! How late you are. March is in bed already."

Not until they had eaten did he venture the cause of his delay.

Then, leaning back to fill his pipe, he remarked casually, "That prairie tract east of Nob Hill — it isn't going at all. Bennett's about ready to give it up. Says he's twenty years too soon." He scratched a match, lit his pipe. "It's too far out for a residential district, and the city doesn't want any manufacturing out there. In fact, Bennett's going to given up his option on it tomorrow morning."

"So you get to handle the North End properties?"

"No. I told him that didn't appeal to me. Chasing after the coattails of stuck-up toads and waiting in hotel lobbies for fat old dowagers is more than I can stand. He wants to give me some property south to get rid of. Why anybody wouldn't jump at the chance to get hold of that prairie land is beyond me!"

Unable to restrain her disappointment, Ona burst out, "I thought you had more sense! The big chance you've been waiting for, and you turn it down. The opportunity to meet important business men, to handle the most expensive property at handsome commissions, and to make something of yourself — something March can be proud of. For what! To ride outdoors in a buggy and look at barren prairie land that hardly supports jack rabbits and prairie dogs, to get stuck in adobe —"

"My mother's people always found enough there for their needs," he replied softly.

This direct acknowledgment of his Indian heritage made her bite her lip. It abruptly tumbled to a common level the imagined magnificent structure of the Rogiers. For the moment she unconsciously admitted the unconquerable force and proud humility of a race too secure in its heritage of strength and pride to defame it by casual boasts.

"But Jonathan," she said in a subdued tone, "you've outgrown that. Times have changed. And this new deal of Bennett's won't last through the winter at best."

His big brown eyes grew bigger, softer. He took out his pipe and grinned. "That's what I thought — As a matter of fact, I stopped by Shook's Run on the way home and Joe cornered me in the shop. That's where I was for two hours."

Ona drew a deep breath.

"He wants me to go in with him on the Sylvanite. The two Zebbelins won't be enough. They'll be underground and I'll be top man. Joe will have to be down here part time — till we get to shipping regularly. It'll be opened early next spring. Your father knows mining, Ona."

"If he knows mining why didn't he make a go of it years ago, when Cripple Creek was first discovered? Why did he lose the opportunity of becoming one of Stratton's partners when he developed the American Eagles, Number One and Number Two? Why did he allow himself to be cheated out of the Garnet and the Fleur-de-Lis? Sunk his downtown store buildings in the Gloriana and the Magpie? And the Silver Heels! You watched him blow it up with dynamite after Reynolds was killed in it. And look what those cursed mines did to Daddy, to Mother, to all of us. They took his business, his downtown properties and residential lots, most of the land around Shook's Run, his stable of horses, the home up in the North End he'd promised Mother, his children's chances for success!"

Her voice had risen to a shriek of outraged injustice that carried in it the frustrations of all the Rogiers. Gulping another breath, she continued. "Yes! They made an old man out of Daddy. He is! Look at his hair. Hear him talk. I know how much trouble he has with his accounts and ledgers. With buildings, with Rawlings. And now he wants to drag you into another damned mine. I won't let him ruin you and March, Jonathan. I tell you, I won't! My boy's going to have all he ought to have — a nice home, a good education, all that. You're not going in on the Sylvanite. You're not!"

Cable had laid down his pipe and arm on the table and sat watching her with an impassive face. She had learned long ago that against any emotional displays he was resistant as slick adobe. Like an Indian, he did not fight against the unbeautiful; he simply ignored it as if it did not exist. "You're getting yourself all riled up," he said shortly, rising and walking into the front room. "You better get to bed."

She lay there, restless and tormented. How easily in her outburst it all had come out — the secret, stifled resentment of the family that Rogier had not gained for them the wealth and acclaim they deserved. In a sane moment she realized its untruth. Born and brought up during those years of the great unrest, familiar with mines since childhood, she knew the vagaries of chance that led fools

and tenderfeet to the great discoveries more often than the deserving. In those days luck had dealt out fortunes impartially to all. She
had been her father's secretary, clerk, banker; she knew the sane
judgment on which he, the methodical, had based his decisions and
suspected the hazy motive that inspired his decisions.

Until now she had condoned his faults, excused his idiocyncrasies. Herself a Rogier and his daughter, she found him flawless.
But now, a mother, she awoke to a life apart from his. His weak-
nesses, his peculiarities and appearance presented to her with
preternatural clearness a loved but pathetic figure with whom she
could no longer stand undivided. For the first time she was stunned
by the appalling uniqueness of her marriage outside the family ties.
Lying there, tossing on the bed or staring dully at the dim pattern of
light on the ceiling, she realized that nothing could stop Rogier now.
Neither she nor Mrs. Rogier, the consensus of many old-timers in
Cripple Creek that the Sylvanite was out of the producing area, nor
the joshing at the Ruxton Club, could deter him from his purpose.

From the other room came the faint rustle of Cable's newspaper, the dull clack of his pipe against his shoe. The homely sounds
roused a phantom within her mind. She loved her father, but to him
and the Sylvanite she would never give as hostages Jonathan and her
boy. She gritted her teeth and lay waiting for Cable to come in.

"Jonathan, you won't go?" she asked from the darkness as he
stood unbuttoning his collar.

"Aren't you asleep yet?" he asked quietly. "I'm going down to
stoke the furnace."

Boné comes home. Timothy throws a party.

3

Rogier was still in the shop where Cable had left him. Musing for an hour or more, he had let the stove fire go out. With cold hands he rebuilt it. On a chair lay a plate of sandwiches Mary Ann had brought out when he did not come in to supper. Munching on one of these, he backed up to the stove, waiting for it to warm up a pot of stale coffee. Before it came to a boil he poured a cup and sat down.

With the heat from the crackling stove and the black sugarless coffee, Rogier began to come to life. His mind, deadened by prolonged concentration, awoke like a sleeping conscience. Unable to remember just how much he had done of all that had to be done, he quickly ran through his work: specifications for hoist and cable; cost estimates for shaft sinking per foot through different rock; preliminary sketches for two level workings; the timbering required for gallows frame, cribbing, and stulls; figures on tramming, assays, and ore treatment — all to be done and checked this winter while Abe and Jake were putting down another shaft and cutting timber for the shaft house and two bridges across the creek . . . And on top of all this, a revision of his bid for a new group of school buildings, an annoying interruption. But it would all be done, by Jove!

Again he added up in his mind the astounding costs, tried to balance the amount against his accounts. The profits from his current and next job, with a few thousand dollars from somewhere else, would get him started. None of this capitalizing and issuing shares at a par value of a dollar and getting one cent for them, like the Butcher Boy and the Nameless mines. Too much publicity, too much red tape, and too many stockholders coming up to see "their" mine. Damn the expense! He knew what he wanted: the Sylvanite, unknown and stuck up in a remote canyon where he and the Zebbelins could work as they pleased, safe from prying eyes.

But what was wrong with Cable? Given the chance of a lifetime, he had sat there dark-faced and noncommittal as a wooden Indian. His own son-in-law, to thus refuse him. But he would win him over from this crazy real estate business, stepping off the surface of the earth, unmindful of the dark profundity, the unceasing hidden life below. A little more persuasion and Cable would sell his prairie land. The proceeds, with the $1,000 he had realized from dissolving partnership with the Grimes, would come in handy for running expenses. And he needed Cable's help — a man in the family who could stay up at the Sylvanite and keep his mouth shut. And Ona! What had got into her, of all persons? Patience! A little patience!

It was a word whose meaning he had forgotten; a sluggish drag that the fire in his veins had consumed utterly. His mind jumped the months of work ahead to the completed plant: the big shaft house, the rapid unrolling of the hoist drums, the spinning cable letting him down, down below grass roots, down into granite, down into the great Peak whose inner life he meant to make his. Let Abe and Jake worry about following the vein. Let Cable worry about ore shipments and treatment charges. Let Ona worry about paying the bills. But for him alone the quest he meant this time to follow to the end.

He ambled around the room, looking at his shelves of ore specimens and reading the clippings tacked up everywhere.

> Whence cometh the highest mountains? So
> did I once ask. Then did I learn that they came
> out of the sea. That testimony is inscribed on
> their stones and on the walls of their summits.
> Out of the deepest must the highest come to

its height.
The gold, however, and the laughter—these
doth he take out of the heart of the earth: for
that thou mayest know it—the heart of the
earth is of gold.

Worn out at last, he turned off the light and trudged through the
yard to the house. Long after he had climbed the stairs to bed the
sound of the Kadles' steps followed him, squeaking in the cold eerie
silence. Rogier, as usual, had kept those faithful family ghosts up
late.

Next morning he was awakened by Mrs. Rogier, Mary Ann,
and Ona trooping in with a cup of coffee and the *Gazette*. "Boné's
coming home," announced Mrs. Rogier. "It is in the newspaper!"

It was true. The eminent composer of several piano sonatas but
better known for his popular songs was expected for a brief visit.
"Late of San Francisco, but evicted since the burning of his studio
during the great earthquake, he has been on a successful tour of the
East, where he appeared on many concert stages. It was reported he
is on the verge of a nervous breakdown, and may choose to linger on
the scene of his boyhood days. His first published piece, 'The Red
Rock Garden March,' was written here; and 'The Song of the
Willows' from his 'Indian Suite,' the piece which brought him
success, was composed shortly after his leaving for the Territory of
New Mexico. In addition to his family, the Joseph Rogiers of this
city, his many friends and members of musical circles —"

This, then, was the small, saucy boy Mrs. Rogier had reared
from childhood; the eminent composer whose hands she had continually slapped for fooling with the piano; the pianist she had yanked
by the ear down to Rogier's office for refusing to go to school. No
wonder he hadn't let them know he was coming.

He was still a Rogier, however, for an hour later a telegram
came from him. It read simply: "Inform the Kadles to stop by the
third floor cot on their rounds tonight. Arriving two o'clock."

Ona went alone to the station that afternoon to meet him,
leaving March and Leona and Mary Ann's Nancy with Mrs. Rogier.
Waiting on the platform as the train whistled round the bend, she
remembered the last time she had seen him: down in New Mexico,

standing in the stirrups on Lew's old bay nag, right arm aloft in a graceful melodramatic gesture of farewell. And there in the vestibule as the train swept in, he stood again, right arm raised in greeting, as if the years between had never been. She gulped down a catch in her throat, rushed to the coach, and was caught in his hearty hug.

"Boné! After all this time! We've missed you so!"

Tipping the porter, turning over his bags to a hack driver, suggesting they walk home—he was still the same, nervous and changeable as light on water. Still there were slight changes. He seemed a trifle shorter and his black hair showed faintly gray at the temples. With a woman's eyes she noticed the excellent cut of his soft gray worsted, the careless knot of his tie, the expensive fresh-shined shoes.

"A damned nuisance jumping around the country and hopping up and down stage platforms," he was saying, plunging along beside her. "I'm not an acrobat. I'm a composer and I can't do any work trying to show off. Besides my nose isn't built right and my shanks are too thin. But you should see New York! 'Member Shiprock sticking up out of the desert at sunup? That's Manhattan from the harbor — a pin cushion of Shiprocks!"

Ona stole a look at his face. It was a little too pale and drawn, and his talk showed he was keyed up higher than an E-string. "But Boné — the paper said you were about to have a nervous breakdown."

"Why, look!" He stopped in his tracks. "A new bridge over Shook's Run. Iron girders, too. No, that nervous breakdown story is a good excuse. It gets me a good night's sleep right often. I tell you, Ona, it wouldn't be so bad if they liked my best. That Sonata in B, now. But all they seem to like are my songs, the worse the better. My God, and haven't I written some awful ones! Ah, that lovely, lyrical 'Ching, Ching, Chinaman!' " He put his thumbs in his ears, wriggled his fingers. And Ona, still laughing, followed him across the street.

Throwing open the front door, Boné gave Mrs. Rogier no time for a hesitant though warm reception. He lifted her up for a kiss that took her breath, set her down, and was out prowling in the pantry before she could utter a word. He came back with his mouth and hands full of cookies. "The same old piano and the same old cookies!" he mumbled, spilling crumbs all over the carpet. "Dear Aunt Marthy! The loveliest mother a boy ever had even if you did used to drive me away from the piano. Still I gained in cookies. And I know you made these just for me this morning!"

Mrs. Rogier listened to him running up the stairs to wash. Then she slowly walked into the kitchen pantry. In the darkness she removed the lid from the cookie jar and felt within. It was empty. Boné had eaten the last of the batch she had baked, not this morning, but three days ago. Then, folding her hands on top, she bent her head and wept.

For two weeks Boné was hardly ever home. A second article in the *Gazette* embroidered his career, claimed him as the town's, and heralded his arrival like important news. It did not take "the members of our own musical circles" long to launch their attack. Feminine, flattering notes on scented stationery were followed by their writers. They needed no introduction nor invitation. At any afternoon hour one might descend from her carriage, adjust her hat and muff, and trip daintily to the door.

"My dear Mrs. Rogier! It has been so long since we have seen you! How lovely — oh, can I come in a minute, just a teeny, weeny minute! — to have the composer of 'Ching, Ching, Chinaman' home again. Don't you love that tune? So truly Oriental! Is he home?"

Mrs. Rogier, exceedingly polite, would seat the caller with a cup of tea and call Boné. Or the visitor, on being informed Boné was absent, would gulp her tea, get up and exclaim, "Such a disappointment! I just wanted to remind him of the twenty-eighth. Eight o'clock. We have so many guests coming only to hear him play. We won't let him forget, will we, you and I?" And pinching Mrs. Rogier on the arm, she would trip back out to her carriage.

Boné, with astounding cheerfulness, complied with every request. He went to afternoon teas and late suppers, "kindly obliged" at private parties, and played for all three musical clubs. As often as possible he took Mrs. Rogier. She enjoyed getting out, but was no longer impressed by these estimable ladies who a month before had not known her from a lamp post — and would not, a month hence.

In all the hullabaloo Boné had not yet met Professor Dearson. Mrs. Rogier, Mary Ann, and Ona recognized the need. What the

Professor would think of this young man so widely heralded, they trembled to contemplate, he was such a bear on the classics. But Boné too had a mind of his own behind his pleasant, jumpy manner. In many respects they were appallingly alike — not quite normal — and to arrange a formal meeting seemed impossible.

As might have been expected, the meeting came about quite naturally, too naturally, it seemed to Mrs. Rogier and Ona who happened to see it out the window. It was early afternoon; snow had fallen all morning and Boné was cleaning off the walk when the familiar pop! pop! of Professor Dearson's motorcycle was heard coming down Bijou Hill. Boné, head swathed in a muffler, paid no attention to the visitor who turned into the driveway and cut across the lawn. When Dearson was not a half-dozen steps away Boné gave a lusty heave. The shovelful of snow splattered the Professor from head to foot.

"You young blatherskite! Why don't you look what you're doing!"

Boné looked up, leaning on his shovel. "And why don't you tie up that gasoline nag of yours at the Nigger Boy and walk in from the front!"

Dan had stopped barking and now crouched growling at Boné's feet. Boné took off his glove and without hesitation reached down to scratch the airedale behind the ears. Dan immediately stopped growling and began a delighted whimpering, rubbing against his leg.

Prefessor Dearson snorted and stamped into the house, follow-ed by Boné. Ona, horrified, managed an embarrassed introduction. "Professor Dearson, this is Boné. You know —"

"Why shouldn't I know! I read the newspapers!" growled Dearson. "And from his music I can tell he doesn't use his left hand enough!"

"Haven't learned to use my right yet!" Boné answered cheer-fully.

Over his tea the Professor began to berate the weather. He had lost his umbrella from the motorcycle and —

"Professor Dearson would like a glass of port instead of tea," suggested Boné. "At least I would."

An hour or more later they had reached the subject of music. "Damn Wagner!" exclaimed Dearson. "A sensualist if ever a butcher was one!"

"And if he had changed a note in those first fourteen bars — "

At this moment they both looked up to see standing in the hall doorway an apparition wrapped in an ankle-length fur coat from which protruded a rosy benign countenance. It was Mr. Timothy who had unaccountably driven up in a carriage and had been admitted by a confused Mrs. Rogier.

"You, sir," greeted Professor Dearson, "are interrupting a conference between myself and my young friend here — who despite some talent and an indisputably better left hand than he is given credit for — yet persists in claiming for Wagner — "

Timothy was not intimidated. He strode in, clapped Boné on the shoulder, "Been after Joe to bring you around, Boné!" Then he reached over to grip Professor Dearson's arm. "You yourself, sir. Have you ever got rid of me till I was satisfied? You incorrigible genius!" Turning to Mrs. Rogier he said, "Madame, this is a great honor to be admitted to your home for the first time. I came only to inquire of Mr. Rogier about this notice in the *Cripple Creek Times* of a new mine he is opening."

Ona, who had come up behind her, answered quickly, "Mines are unpredictable, Mr. Timothy."

"That's why they fascinate us — both Mr. Rogier and myself," he answered quickly. Stripping off his coat to hand to Lida Peck, he added, "A Scotch and soda will do."

"Scotch after port?" Mrs. Rogier was confused. "Lida, is there any Scotch in the house?"

"In the cellar, for them as has a mind to drink it," answered Lida.

"I'll have one," said Boné.

"Me too!" added Professor Dearson.

By five o'clock Mr. Timothy had come to the point. "I'm going to give a party in honor of the sharps and flats. Been left out of everything since Boné's been in town. Won't have it! Friday night when Joe returns from Cripple Creek. The Ruxton Club. Eight o'clock.

"Count me out!" said the Professor. "I haven't entered the portals of that *sanctum sanctorum* of conservatism for years."

"This is my home. My mother would be honored to have you all," said Boné.

"Nonsense! The Deer Horn Lodge then."

"Every time you come around it means fuss and dinner," growled the Professor.

"I shall call for each of you promptly at six," added Timothy imperturbably.

The party was something to be remembered by everyone who went: all the Rogiers, including Mary Ann's part-time husband, Professor Dearson, and a host of Timothy's friends. It had snowed for two days, blanketing the mountains under a flocculent whiteness and almost blocking the North Cheyenne Canyon road. Timothy was equal to the occasion. From out of dusty storage sheds, carriage houses, and livery stables he evoked every old-fashioned sleigh in town, hung them with bells, and lined the seats with mothy buffalo robes and Navajo blankets.

How beautiful it was, thought Ona, watching the snowy cliff-walls open and close behind them, hearing the jingle of the bells and the songs drifting back from the sleigh of young people in front. And the Lodge! She caught her breath with delight as it leapt at her from the darkness, aglow with lights. The huge, rustic, log structure was festooned with spruce boughs and kinnikinnick; a huge fire in the stone fireplace lit up the polished pine floor; candles gleamed from the big table and piano. A bartender from the Ruxton Club stood behind an enormous bowl of hot punch, bottles of liquor and wine. In the kitchen a white-hatted chef was presiding over a steaming venison haunch, a browning turkey, and everything to go with them.

There was no denying the warmth of the liquor, the high humor that molded them into a friendly group. Timothy was his urbane self; Professor Dearson pungent; Boné keyed to a pitch that left little to be desired from one so royally received. Even Rogier was drawn out of his morose brooding.

Dinner over, they moved to the end of the big hall. Cigars were passed around; the ladies were prevailed upon to sip more wine. Boné, of course, was asked to play. Courteously he deferred to Professor Dearson who snorted an indignant refusal.

"Why, you two sticks!" exclaimed Mary Ann. "I'll play!"

She flounced over to the baby grand and launched into her favorite ragtime. Everyone applauded but Professor Dearson who pushed her off the stool so he could give his own famous version of the "Black Hand Rag." Boné played and then after conversing lowly with the Professor gave up his seat. Professor Dearson sat down, laid his fingers lightly on the keys, and looked up at Boné. The boy nodded. With all the force of wrist and fingers the old man crashed down in a loud chord, began a wild rhythm strange to all but Ona.

"The Corn Dance! I remember!" she shouted.

Boné did not reply. Slowly he began to circle round the room, head down and back bent, lifting his knees high, bringing his feet down with a powerful stamp. Once again, after all these years, Ona saw and felt him as she had when he had practiced the steps in Bert Bruce's trading post. Finished, Boné came over and patted her hand. "I thought I'd forgotten, but it all comes back."

The party was growing serious now. They pulled their chairs up to the fire and quietly listened to both Professor Dearson and Boné who gave their best. Ona grew annoyed; somebody in the corner was whispering interminably. She looked around. Rogier was emphatically shaking his head and Timothy was scrawling on a scratchpad balanced on his knee. She thought it rather strange that a man like Timothy would go to such trouble and expense to give a party like this to a family with whom he had no social connections whatever, poor as they were. Now remembering his allusion to the *Cripple Creek Times* report of the Sylvanite, a quick suspicion jumped into her mind. Certainly they weren't talking about a building contract. Resolutely she dismissed it and tried to concentrate on the playing.

It was after midnight before they left. On the way home the snow stopped falling. The moon came out. The drivers had taken off the straps of bells, and through the eerie blue light the sleighs sped home swiftly and silently as ghosts.

Rogier invited Boné to join in the Silvane't mine venture. B gives him $5K & goes to the Navajo Reservation. Cable is working on the mine. Rogier drives Cable, the Zebbelins, & other workers hard, hauling machinery up to the mine.

4.

For two days Boné stayed in bed upstairs in the barny third floor. Only for supper each night did he come down in brocaded slippers and a black silk dressing gown emblazoned with a golden dragon. He was tired out, he said.

On the third morning Mrs. Rogier sent for Dr. Beverly. He sat talking for a half-hour, then got up and casually announced that Boné was not tired out; he was on the verge of a nervous breakdown. Two weeks rest in bed and no excitement, he prescribed, and after that a good three months' rest from work in quiet, agreeable surroundings. Boné pooh-poohed the verdict, but stayed in bed; it was the easiest way to avoid all engagements. His cheerfulness gave way to a sullen apathy that withstood all interference. He tore dinner invitations to bits, shouted down the stairs that he was out whenever the doorbell rang, and refused curtly to see again the people whom he had greeted so cordially the week before.

In the darkness they all passed in parade before him: the plump-breasted dowagers who had used him to further their social ambitions, the bejewelled hangers-on of the exclusive rich, vapid wives and yawning husbands, music club members repeating technical phrases from their textbooks—the whole tribe who had sung his praises, lauded his meager accomplishments, and by their extravagant flattery insulted his integrity beyond repair.

Suffering under his own accusations, he saw himself charmingly accepting their ovations, gracefully acceding to every request, and passing for what he knew he was not—a composer of national stature. True enough, his work was known over all the country. His tour had been successful. In Cleveland, Pittsburgh, Philadelphia, Boston, Chicago, even New York, his audiences had been receptive, the press notices kind. But it was his songs, those light melodious airs and ragtimes dashed off in San Francisco that had recalled him to their minds. Not the solid composition of his "Indian Suite" that had cost him so much sweat and worry. Never his two piano sonatas to which he had given the best of his talent and skill. Here at home these were hardly known. Humbled by the work of masters to whom he had always bent in obeisance, shamed by the standards of an art to which he meant to give his own best, he felt himself a poseur, a charlatan, for accepting the unwarranted praise. And those who gave it he despised.

Songs, songs, songs! They had grown to be the bane of his life. Melodic fragments that came to him from every possible source and that once built upon still leapt at him derisively from a piano in an obscure Barbary Coast saloon, from a boy's whistle, or from a shop girl humming on her way to work. If he could just quit writing songs and get down to honest composition!

There was a sudden creak. He sat up, realizing it was only the Kadles on their nocturnal rounds. He could hear the regular, intermittent squeak of the deliberate steps coming up the stairs, pausing at every door. Mechanically, with a nervous hand, he began to mark a beat. A crazy, simple tune tried to jump into his head. He flung down, ear to pillow, and swathed his head with covers.

Matie Vrain, who was in town for the first time in two years, came to see him. The very sight of her dark wrinkled face brought back those days when life was sharp and simple as the smell of sage, colorful as the cliffs flaming red under the turquoise sky. Matie was still working on the Reservation, and thinking of moving to the hospital near the new Navajo Indian Mission sponsored by the Women's Home Missionary Society.

"You remember the old mission in Jewett Valley, near the Hogback? Well, it was sold to the Presbyterians, and the Society moved to its new site, up the San Juan about twenty-two miles. It's across the river, near the La Plata suspension bridge west of Farmington. Miss Tripp, who started the school for Navajo children, is the one. And you remember Mrs. Aldridge, the field matron? Oh yes! There's a big trading post at Shiprock, and another one started."

Matie sighed. "That's the reason I'm going to move. Lew's getting queer, Boné. Seems like she's more Indian than white. Says the country's getting too civilized for her, and keeps talking of going off alone, way downriver."

"And Bruce?"

"Oh, Bert's all right except for his leg. It keeps going numb on him. He has to lie on a bed behind the counter most of the time. He kind of liked you, you know. Always figured you'd be coming back."

Boné lay staring at the lumpy, weather-beaten face before him. "Before you go back, Matie, I want to see you," he said at last, with a flicker of hope in his eyes.

As the winter wore on Rogier spent an hour with him every day, usually late in the afternoon when no one else was around. He would stamp up the stairs, sink into a chair, and after the barest greeting launch into his talk. Things looked fine up at Cripple Creek. The mines were being drained in great shape by new drainage tunnels. Freight and treatment charges had been reduced considerably; $5 ore could be shipped at a profit.

With this as a background, he began to elucidate the excellent prospects of the Sylvanite. One afternoon he brought up the results of the latest assays and pulled out of his pocket two new samples and a magnifying glass. On another he explained in detail the planned development workings. On still another he cheerfully imparted the news that the Zebbelins had finished their cabin and built two bridges across the creek.

Boné was quite aware of the intent of this continued harangue and tried to forestall it. "Sounds like it's going to be a great mine. I'll be so glad for you and Aunt Martha. After all these years! But it's not my line, mining. Frankly, I'm at a crucial turning point in my own career — if you can call it that. I —"

"You're right, my boy! Wait'll the snows melt. Then we'll go down. On the best working you ever laid eyes on, son!"

An equal measure of compassionate pity and extravagant admiration infused Boné as he listened to him talk. An old white-headed man, eyes bright with an almost unendurable gleam. But still the man who had loved and raised him as a father, who had understood and condoned his own dream, and whose monthly checks for years had enabled him to preserve a sense of independence against Lockhart's munificent hospitality. How indomitable he was, as if possessed of inexhaustible energy! Still Boné refused to ride up to Cripple Creek with him, although more and more often he was helplessly drawn out to the shop where Rogier could talk without fear of interruption.

It was on one of these days, early in March, that Rogier finally and outrightly came to the point. "I'd sure be willing to take you in with me, boy. It's just a family affair, Cable and me, and Abe and Jake. No outsiders if we can raise the money to go down."

"Wish I could," answered Boné slowly. "If I were only sure of some money coming in, so I wouldn't have to stop work to go on tour and write these everlasting ragtimes!"

"If the Sylvanite runs into a blanket vein you won't ever have to worry, any more than Cable and Ona. You'll be independent for life!"

Boné stared out the window, unable to face him.

"As a matter of fact, son, I'm in something of a pinch," Rogier went on. "I'd counted on a little money to cover the invoices for some machinery I ordered. It's at the freight depot now. How long they'll hold it I don't know. But — Well, it's a problem that has me worried."

Boné flung around. "I've got about five thousand dollars to carry me through a siege of serious work. I have the feeling that if I don't make it now, I never will. There's no telling when I'll have another chance." He hesitated. "You can have it. I'm going back to the Navajo Reservation where I won't be disturbed and expenses will be low. So if you want, put me down for a share in the Sylvanite."

Rogier nodded his head, but the sudden gleam in his eyes betrayed him. "I'll take it! It's not much you understand, considering the cost of mining these days. But it will get that machinery off the depot platform. What about that, eh?" He slapped Boné on the shoulder. "Son, you've got yourself a share in a good mine! It's going to pull us both out of a hole! Don't you worry!"

Boné laughed. "You know, Uncle Joe, we're both after the same thing. If we hit it, we hit it. If we don't, it won't be our fault!"

Two weeks later Boné left home as he had left years before, sick and worn out. He was off to the Reservation with Matie Vrain,

Early that April, Rogier began packing hoist and boiler up the canyon from Bull Hill junction east of Victor. Jake had written that they had better start moving before the spring freshets and while the snow was still hard enough to support a sled.

It was the news Rogier had been waiting for. He hired four laborers in town to help — to avoid talk in Cripple Creek — and took the train next day. With them went Cable. The real estate deal, as Ona had foreseen, had petered out; for the present he was out of a job and could spare the time.

The men worked swiftly in the cold clear morning. Abe and Jake had built two sleds and engaged two spans of mules. On the stoutest of the sleds the heavy steel drum was loaded and buckled to the iron supporting bolts; on the other was lashed the cable reel. "Where's those jackasses I told you to get?" demanded Rogier. The burros were driven up. "Pack those boxes on 'em. No need of wasting time. Here, don't you know how to throw a hitch?" He set his foot against the shaggy ribs, heaved on the ropes. "Cable, you and Jake take a couple of men and go ahead with the burros to break trail. Mind you, now: a level route where the sled can't topple. Watch the bridges and keep out of the swamps. It's liable to be wet along the base of that aspen grove."

They started out, crossed Grassy Gulch shimmering white with snow, pulled around the base of the Calf. For two hours they labored up the pass behind Cow Mountain, finally reaching the mouth of the canyon. In the cold dry air the breaths of men and beasts puffed out like smoke against the somber blue-clad mountains. The aspens were grey along the creek bottom, the cliffs tall and frosted white. In the eerie silence the men plodded on with an occasional curse, a snap of rawhide echoing like the report of a forty-five and arousing the chatter of a flock of magpies in the grove.

A deer leapt out of a thicket, stood quivering, then turned and bounded up the slope.

Late that afternoon Cable, wiping the sweat from his face, stood looking up the slope at the Sylvanite. There was the last bridge of rough hewn pines over the stream, the big new cabin, and the shaft and tool house ready to receive the machinery. Even the corral was shiny new with unpeeled green aspens.

"You sure have done your work," he said quietly to Jake.

"You know the Colonel!" Jake replied shortly. "He's goin' after it, no mistake. And we'd better be gettin' back to help him."

It was early evening before drum and reel were unloaded from the sleds, the miscellaneous boxes stacked in place. "Let's close up now, boys, and get back after the other load. We'd better be fetchin' that boiler up while we got easy going," Rogier called.

The men did not move except to congregate at the door of the cabin. "What the hell!" expostulated one. "We been at this all day long on nothin' but a dinner of bacon and beans. What's the all-fired rush?"

Rogier pointed at the sky. "Look for yourselves: clear as a bell. The sun will be comin' out in the mornin' and melting the trail. You know how much that boiler weighs. We'll be sloggin' down in slush, gettin' stuck at every crossing."

"It's gettin' dark. We want to eat," the men began to mutter.

"What's the difference whether you work two days or a day and night?" Rogier demanded. "We've got to get this job done. Double time for the night, boys! What do you say?"

"We say we don't want to. We'll do it tomorrow."

"I'm tired out as the men," Cable remonstrated. "We can't work in the dark anyway. A good night's sleep is the thing for all of us."

"Dom lazy jackasses — every one of you!" Rogier grumbled, turning away.

Abe already had built a fire in the cabin and was busy mixing biscuit dough.

The hearty meal put the men back in good humor. They lit their pipes and lounged before the fire, picking spots for their blankets. Betweentimes they warily cracked jokes at Rogier for being in such a goldarned hurry — he having walked up the hill with a torch to inspect the machinery and see that none of the boxes had been lost. A half-hour later he returned, threw open the door and stood looking out at the patch of star-stung sky flung like a banner over the opposite canyon wall.

"You boys better be rollin' up in your blankets. It's goin' to be a good day and we've got to hit the trail early."

True to his word, he roused them out at the first faint streak of dawn above the cliffs. It was still dark in the cabin; and the men got up grumbling at the cold, at the icy water, at Rogier. Aspens, pines, cliff, and stream emerged slowly but distinctly in the break of day; the stars still shone, but without luster. Abe, man-wise, took his time at the stove; he kept heaping the platter with pancakes until every man was stuffed. Rogier, idling at the fireplace with a cigar, could restrain his impatience no longer.

"Abe, I've never seen you so slow. What's ailing you, man?"

Abe took off from the stove a fresh bucket of coffee and set it on the table without answering.

One of the men let out a goodnatured laugh. "What's the rush, Mr. Rogier? Them gold nuggets will be here when we get back!"

Rogier angrily flung out the door. The sun was just showing over the pine-tips.

A half hour later they were on their way, mules and burros fresh and frisky as an early squirrel in a nearby spruce-top, the men laughingly taking turns riding the empty, ungainly sleds.

By mid-morning they presented a different appearance. They were wet to the knees, splattered with slush and mud until they were hardly recognizable. One stopped to wipe his face with his hat; another straighteded up stiffly, his hand to his back.

"Dom it! I told you men that sun was comin' out to raise hell. Cable! Get these burros off the trail. They've tracked up too much already. What're you tryin' to do — get us stuck in slush?" Inflexible, merciless, and unwearied, Rogier drove them on.

It had been a fight from the first. The cylindrical, slippery boiler kept springing the ropes as if they were made of rubber. Cleat after cleat it broke on the sides. Heavy, cumbersome, too long for the sled, its back end bumped the ground at every rise. They were continually cutting a new trail through snow. But now the warm April sun was melting the crust and the frozen stream.

By noon they had made it up the difficult grade and down the other side. Somber, wordless, and worn out, the men flung themselves down in the wet. Cable pleaded their unspoken need for food and rest. Rogier, grim-lipped and indomitable, shook his head. He stood facing the small meadow threaded by the stream over which they must pass. The snow field, lit by the sun, gave back a dazzling brightness. Only for yards on each side of the stream was there a patch of dirty gray. The men rose to their feet, knowing what it meant: the snow was melting and in the soft wet marsh grass underneath the heavy sled was likely to bog down. An hour's wait would never do.

The quarter-mile stretch took them over two hours to cross, with every jack-man of them heaving beside the mules at every step. Rogier was triumphant; like a victorious general he was all for pushing forward immediately before luck turned against him. Despite him the men scattered for wood, built a fire, boiled coffee, and ate.

The trail leading off the meadow into the mouth of the narrow forested canyon, made a sharp turn to the right along a thick grove of aspens. Just above it the stream had been blocked by beavers and the sudden thaw had sent it pouring over the dam and spreading a thin flood almost to the edge of the grove. Not until they were in it, did any of them realize how deep it was.

"Look out! Whoa-up! Whoa, boy!" shouted Jake, digging in his heels and throwing himself backward with the reins wrapped round his fists.

"Dom it to hell!" growled Rogier, running up. "Now, we've done it! Just like I told you. Stoppin' to eat, eat, eat. That water wasn't up an hour ago."

The left runner of the sled had sunk almost out of sight; the heavy boiler, listing precariously, looked likely to go over.

The men worked fast and furiously. New ropes were slung from the boiler and half-hitched to the nearest aspens to hold it in place. All four mules were again strung out to pull at the sled — the ropes to be tightened at every step. Aspen trunks were cut and trimmed of branches, laid corduroy fashion in front of the sled runner. All the men bent backs to the downoff-side. Finally the mules were whipped up. The sled did not budge.

Again and once again they made futile efforts. Rogier shut his mouth in a straight, grim line and began walking slowly over the ground, scrutinizing every foot. The mouth of the canyon rising upward into the blue shadows of pine and spruce was so tantalizingly close.

"If we could just get up there on that gravel slide where the snow ain't melted yet we'd be plumb outa trouble fer all the rest of the way." The remark came wearily from one of the men leaning against a panting mule.

Rogier walked up to him. "And just how do you propose to do that?" he demanded.

The fellow flushed and moved off with an apprehensive look over his shoulder.

Two of the burros were hitched with the mules. They were able to stir the sled an inch, but the minute they let up it settled back again.

"If we could get them other two on we might do somethin'," Jake said quietly.

"Well, why don't we?" cut in Rogier.

"Ain't no traces, no straps, no nothin'. All we got's up in the tool house."

"I'll go after them," spoke up Cable, motioning for another man to follow him.

It was a long stiff hike, and loaded down with their heavy burden they took over two hours to make the trip. For still another hour the men sat around clumsily fashioning traces and harness from ropes and straps.

The eight animals and eight men, working together now, made another effort. The sled jerked out of its clutch, but the back end of the boiler snapping two of the ropes slid off into the mud.

Of cool, calm Rogier, master builder and contractor for $100,000 jobs, there was now no semblance left. The back end of a boiler resting in mud — no more than that! — made him out a madman. He stood there on the edge of that white virginal valley faced by the dark slope of immemorial pines, and heedless of the knot of men and beasts around him, raised his face to that of the great icy Peak rising above him. For a moment he was silent. Then he took off his hat, ruffling his white hair, and threw it on the ground. He beat his fist into the palm of his left hand. Suddenly he began to swear. It was an epithetic denouncement of valley, canyon, Peak, the snow, men, and the weather—and it frightened a mule which shied from the impassioned intensity of his voice with a sudden squeal. The men backed away, silent and embarrassed, as if taking upon themselves the unwarranted guilt for the unfortunate mishap. Cable alone seemed to remain untouched. Dark and taciturn, he sat down on a log and calmly lit his pipe.

When Rogier finally quieted and backed away, Jake picked up the fallen hat and began in a shame-faced manner to beat off the snow and muck with a cold, bare hand.

"I reckon they ain't nothin' to do but wait till evenin' when it freezes up again," muttered one of the crew.

"And the sled and boiler too? Hell, we'll never get it out then," replied another.

Abe walked over to Cable. They talked, finally went over to Rogier. "We figure there's only one thing to do," Cable told him decisively. "Send the men back to the Sylvanite. Cut off cable from the reel and use it instead of rope. It's the only thing that'll hold her."

Rogier stared at them as if they had proposed to violate his own personal integrity. "Use that cable?" he shouted. "You must be mad! That's hoisting cable, you fools. I figured it to fifty feet. Just what we need to get down to where we're goin'."

"Order more if you need it—which you won't. That shaft's not goin' clear through to China."

"And be delayed weeks—never!" Rogier flung around, shouted to the men. "The man who lays hand on that steel cable is responsible to me for destruction of personal property. Do you hear, men? You stay here, understand? We're goin' to get this out tonight. Now, by Jove!"

He began to give orders. Two pines were felled, stripped of branches. The logs, slantwise, were driven into the ground to keep the boiler from rolling off. Mules, burros, and men laboriously snaked the front end of the sled around to face the aspen grove. By dark the back end of the boiler had been raised on the sled again.

"Jesus, where we goin' now?" swore a voice from the deep dusk. "We can't go through no grove of aspens."

"That," answered Rogier quietly, "is exactly where we're goin'."

And now began the heartbreaking task of chopping a pathway through a hundred yards or more of thickly growing trees to get back on the trail. Foot by foot sled and boiler were snaked ahead, and finally slid upon the hard packed snow and gravel base of the canyon trail.

Torches were lit, the flames rousing from the dark canyon the cry of a wolf; in the flickering red light the men resumed their march. The night was cold, a bitter biting cold that froze the wet boots and leggings of the men and formed a thin white fringe on the shaggy hair of mules and burros. It was long after midnight when they at last pulled into the clearing where sat the cabin and big corral of the Sylvanite.

Abe worked up a hasty meal, put on a pail of coffee. The men, worn out, ate and flopped on the floor in their blankets, feet to fire. A half hour later Rogier came in; it was he who had remained outside to unhitch and feed the animals, to break the ice at the creek and carry back and forth buckets of water, to carefully hang up their harness and throw the bars on the corral gate. He sat down at the deserted table, poured out the dregs of the coffee and dug a single scrap of bacon from the cold grease in the pan.

"Dom fine work, men! Double time for both days. Every one of you. Hey?"

No one answered. Already asleep, they were stretched out like stiff corpses on the floor before him.

Rogier got up slowly, ran his hand through his tousled white hair before putting on his hat; he figured there had better be some wood split to build the morning fire before he turned in.

5

When Cable returned to town, it was with news that all the machinery had been set in place despite a new fall of snow and that work sinking the shaft had commenced. Rogier, he said, would remain at the Sylvanite for yet awhile, but would soon be down again to see about his building work.

Ona, sitting with her mother when Cable returned, said nothing. Throughout supper and all the way home she maintained the same heavy, negative silence. She put the children to bed, waited quietly until Cable had finished his few chores. "Jonathan," she said then, "you can't do this to me."

"What?"

"You know what, Jonathan. Going up to help Daddy for a few days and staying more than two weeks. But it isn't the work or time that really matters. You know what it is. I could tell it the minute you walked in the door. 'Our mine!'—'When we get the shaft down!' After we had ironed it all out once, for good, that you weren't going in on the Sylvanite."

"I agreed to nothing of the kind. If I did, that time has passed. Last fall. What do you want me to do?"

"Do?" She looked at him with an ironic smile that did not hide her anger. "So you have to be told that your precious prairie land turned out to be a miserable deal Bennett tried to palm off on you! That he didn't even own it—just held a short option. That you wouldn't get into first class real estate, and now you're out of work at all. Do you have to be reminded that we, myself and children, must be considered too? Or are you planning to move us home?"

This last brought a slow flush to his swarthy cheeks. "You wouldn't be so hoity-toity if the Sylvanite came in a boomer! It would be a different story then. You'd be Rogier enough to share in the profits. Why the independence now — for the first time in your life?"

She rose, crossed the room to sit down beside him where she could lay her hand on his. "Let's don't quarrel, Jonathan. You know how afraid of the Sylvanite I am. And Daddy too. All my life I've been plagued with mines, mines, mines! They're all alike, good ones and poor ones. They ruin a man every time. I want you to keep out of such risky ventures. Daddy's too old to change. It's in him for good. But you—you're still young, Jonathan."

He withdrew his hand from under hers, deliberately filled and lighted his pipe. "Now that you've begun it, let's see the thing through. First of all, I married you and expect to take care of you and the children. I'm not a Rogier, nor am I a waif picked up and added to the family, expecting to be provided for out of the Sylvanite. I stand on my own feet."

"What are you doing wasting your time on the Sylvanite for, then, when you could be about your own business?"

"Because," he said simply, "I've put in part of my bank account on the Sylvanite."

Ona had risen, let down her hair. The news caught her, hands under the tresses. She sank back down with shocked amazement, flung back her hair, tried to speak. The long brown hair, soft and fluffy from washing, crept over her face as she leaned back and turned her head. "You couldn't! Oh, you couldn't be so foolish. Not if you loved me—or thought of the children."

"But I did," he said quietly. "All of you."

It was midnight when they finally went to bed, worn out and sleepless from a quarrel whose end neither could foresee. It dragged through summer and fall into winter—a futile wrangle whose objective both seemed to have forgotten.

Cable kept returning to Cripple Creek, a week, two weeks or more at a time. Between trips he studied and tried to sell insurance; Ona was still bent on his being a businessman, and fought his moving permanently up to the mine. The arrangement kept them all on edge: Rogier who was after him continually, Ona who resumed her quarrelsome pleas the day he returned, and Cable who each day drew more closely into himself.

Work on the Sylvanite progressed steadily. The shaft was down a hundred feet, commonly assumed the proper depth for a level, but Rogier was insisting on another forty feet before cutting a station. Cross-cutting would then be commenced to tap the vein traversing the property. Overhand stoping, working up on a raise instead of down on a winze, he had figured would be a good thirty percent cheaper; they could take advantage of gravity instead of having to install a small lift. He already had bought an old iron bucket of 900 pounds capacity to use instead of a cage, a supply of drills and hand tools, and enough dynamite for the winter—box after box buried halfway up the hill in back of the cabin. He was well satisfied with the assays and counted on shipping ore soon.

But it cost so much—the dom hard country rock! He had to spend half his time in town, not daring to let his business drop; it was the only source of income to carry the mine. Hence his frequent calls for Cable to take his place with Abe and Jake.

Rogier's current contract called for a two-story annex to one of the schools; it amounted to comparatively little money, but upon it hinged his bid for a new group of schools for the West Side.

"It doesn't amount to an awful lot, Rawlings," he told his old foreman, going over the plans. "You can do most of it yourself. You know how rushed I am up on the hill—and where to find me."

Rawlings assented to boss the job after taking a few days off, Rogier digging the foundations while he was gone. Returning to the job, Rawlings methodically and carefully checked the work done. The foundations had been dug three feet too deep. He sent a man for Rogier, catching him just as he was leaving for Cripple Creek.

"Doggone it, Joe! Look what you went and done. You know we can't have that."

"Shoot!" growled Rogier, winding up his steel tape. "How the devil did I let that happen? And so all-fired deep."

"Exactly three feet to the inch. We can't fill in with dirt, it'll settle. And if you pour cement, it's goin' to cost too much."

Rogier got out his pencil. "Right you are, Rawlings! You do have a head on your shoulders. We'll fill it in with coarse gravel from the west pits and add water. It'll set hard enough to bottom the concrete."

In a few days Rogier's mistake had been rectified; and leaving Rawlings in charge to begin pouring cement, he left for Cripple Creek.

There were no mistakes made at the Sylvanite. He went over every detail a dozen times, sat up half the night figuring and brooding over his plans. Two months later, on the 140-foot level, Abe struck the vein. It was solidly filled with gangues and tellurides which assayed a sylvanite ore running, at best, almost $30 to the ton.

Cable at home was elated at the news, and got ready to join Rogier at the mine. Ona watched him pack with a frown. "Don't get too excited. Mines are like prostitutes. They all promise more than they give."

"What do you know about prostitutes?" demanded Cable.

"And what do you?" she countered in a level voice.

She kissed him goodbye warmly enough, but when he had gone compressed her lips in a stubborn line. Rogier, for the time, had won. But it was not the end. She knew men and mines too well.

That month by month regular shipments of ore were made changed little the consensus regarding the Sylvanite. A few old-timers straying up the gulch held it to be a freak pocket. Timothy and his group of club members speculated on its actual existence; the mine was not listed and they could obtain no information from Rogier who had stopped coming to the Ruxton. Even the family, oppressed by the specters of previous failures, regarded it with awe tinctured by a spot of fear and wondered where all the money went.

To be sure, Mrs. Rogier was given a generous contribution for her sugar bowl. Jonathan and Ona, with new furniture, moved up the street to a bigger house. Boné was sent a little money as a cheering token, and a case of books. Such were the visible dividends from Rogier's investment. Every other cent he was putting back into the mine, determined to go down another ninety feet to a second level.

"We're out of money again," Ona told Cable one morning.

"I'll get another check from Joe. Forgot it last time I was up there," he answered casually.

"It's awfully embarrassing, this having to ask you for money all the time. And you having to go to Daddy. I don't see why you can't be paid your share at a certain time every month. Then I'd know what to count on."

"Oh, that's all right. You know how it is. We don't have enough ore for a carload yet. When we do get a check from the mill we'll have our money, and you can pay off the bills."

Ona bit her lip. "No, it isn't all right, Jonathan! It's wrong all the way around. You know how Daddy is. So bound to put everything back in the Sylvanite, he forgets we have to live. It just gives me the feeling we're living off him. And we're not! We've put our bank account and all our savings into it, and you give him most of your time. I do wish you'd stop and go on with your insurance. Something substantial to fall back on when the Sylvanite peters out. Let Daddy hire a man."

"What makes you talk like that?" he asked irritably, walking into the kitchen and pouring himself a cup of coffee.

She followed him, and disregarding March who was playing with a wooden pistol on the table, continued her tirade. "From knowing a hundred mines! They're all alike as soiled women. Entrancing for awhile and then poof!—they've eaten up all your money and the best years of your life, and vanished. Look at Hartsel. Famous Hartsel! When I was little, he was worth a hundred thousand dollars from his Bluebell. And now, look!" She jerked up from the back of a chair where it was hanging a bit of blue ribbon. "Where did I get this band for Leona's hair? At Pelta's Dry Goods Store. From the little clerk at the ribbon counter. Hartsel!" She lowered her voice. "Jonathan, I'm afraid of the Sylvanite. It's playing us a trick. It won't last."

His brown inexpressive face might have warned her. He was usually so kind, so gentle—gentle as an Indian's cupped hands replacing a baby trout in a stream. She had seen him, in a hurry to catch a train, stopping to unknot the laces of March's shoes; and watched his patient brown hands untangling Leona's hair. A slow rhythmical man careful of insignificant details and content to let the big things take care of themselves — yet likely for no reason at all to erupt like volcano.

What he said now was inconsequential; it was as if his voice carried a spectrum of tone audible only to the boy hacking at his wooden pistol with a butcher knife.

March jumped up from the table, pointing his pistol at his father. "Don't you be mean to my mother! I'll shoot you!"

With unbelievable swiftness, and without a word, Cable turned on him. Grasping the boy by the collar and the seat of his pants, he flung him through the screen door and over the back porch railing. It was a good six foot drop, but fortunately the earth of the garden was soft from recent spading. The boy lit flat on his belly, legs and arms outspread. By the time Ona reached him he had regained his breath, unhurt, white-faced, but too scared to cry. It was the first time his father ever had lain hands on him. Cable, without waiting to see whether the boy had been hurt, had flung off to town.

That afternoon Cable was strolling up Tejon Street and happened to glimpse March walking downstreet toward him. The boy saw him at the same time. He halted with the look of a scared rabbit about to hide behind a lamp post or dodge into the crowd of passers-by. Before he could move, Cable crooked his finger. The boy obediently followed him into the drugstore.

"About time for a dish of ice cream, eh?" said Cable. "How about a nut sundae?"

March grinned sheepishly as they sat down at the long counter flanked by big red and blue glass jars, and in back of which hung the large Red Raven sign he liked so well. Cable watched him eat. Then taking out his pipe, he said casually, "Too bad about that business this morning, March. But the first thing a man's got to learn is not to mix in other people's affairs. Nobody's. Just what concerns you. I guess you'll remember that, won't you, son?"

March licked off his spoon, glancing up at his father. A quick, shy smile passed over Cable's face. March grinned. "Yes, sir!"

"I see Buffalo Bill's Wild West Show is coming early this summer. The posters are already up. A lot of Utes'll be here too. Reckon we ought to take it all in. I'll make it a point to come down from Cripple Creek. What do you say?"

"Ohh! Will they attack the stagecoach and scalp the soldiers and burn the women at the stake and all?" March sat up, talking garrulously.

"The whole bloody business, I reckon," Cable assented complacently.

They walked out of the door hand in hand —

Buffalo Bill's Wild West Show! To the boy of those years it was always to stand out with a preternatural clearness and tragic intensity undimmed by time, like something not seen but recalled by a memory hidden deep within him. Not the mock heroic figure with long yellow hair leading the morning parade on his white horse and shooting his clay balls with less markmanship than birdshot. Not those who followed him, sitting limply in their saddles and swaying unconsciously as reeds in the wind: the hunters in broad hats and buckskins, the silent mountain men, the prospectors in red flannel shirts, the masked badmen and those who brought them to dust, the chiefs regal in paint and warbonnets, the braves naked but for a clout and a single eagle feather, the squaws with papooses lashed to cradle boards on their backs. Never just these, framed by the colored posters with the melodramatic Buntline touch, the shouting crowds filling the grandstands with the drunken loafers below, the dust, the flies, the war paint dripping from a warrior's chin upon a copy of the *Denver Post* spread across his knees, a lounging chief noisily sucking ice cream shortly after his demise, a squaw begging pennies.

Not the sorry form he saw, but the splendid substance of a life, an unbelievable century drawing to a close, through whose still-open gate rushed at him sight, sound, and smell of something he could almost touch. A story without plot and without end, music without melody, a kaleidoscopic panorama still too new to be confined in a frame. The vast sunlit plaines, the slow red rivers, the heaving blue walls of the great male Rockies — what horizons could hem in these backgrounds of America's only true legends? Tomorrow their tales would stand beside those of Arthur of Pendragon and the Knights of the Round Table. The hazy picturebook figures of Launcelot and Sir Galahad faded at the crack of a forty-five. Toward him galloped the warrior horsemen of the Great Plains, lances up, feathers streaming in the ceaseless wind, in phalanxes that would have put Ghenghis Kahn to rout. What names these heroes bore, so earthy and commonplace they sent a tingle up his spine! Sitting Bull and Roman Nose, Red Cloud, Rain-in-the-Face, Kicking Bear. Crazy Horse shouting his battle-cry, "It's a good day to die!" Old and unarmed White Antelope calmly singing his death song on the dawn when he was massacred with a whole village of women and children not far east. Siegfried and the dragon, Jason and his Golden Fleece, the journeys of Ulysses had nothing to compare with these epics of grassroots America. Still their cadence was not yet measured, their tones not yet suave and polished. The veil of time had not yet blurred their sharp outlines. They unfolded here, close and touchable, they moved here before him truthfully, formless, and without fault. They were a part of him who needed not to be told they were the priceless and unmeasured substance of his birthright, so completely did he respond as he sat spellbound upon his plank seat while the sun rode from south to west and dipped behind the mountains that had seen it all an incalculable number of times.

And now the long procession of covered wagons came crawling slowly over the plains. The creaking wooden wheels, the ceaseless jolting that churned butter, the canvas wagon sheets drawn tight over the bows. The patient weary women sitting limply under their starched sunbonnets, the wail of a child, the men plodding behind with a cow whose teats had been chewed off by wolves.

But now, so suddenly, that single, eerie, high-pitched cry! Almighty God! Who could ever forget that long, loping crescent of Cheyennes! The thunder of their hooves, their sea of feathers breaking over the crest of hills. A single shot. The chiefs swerving to the right and left, riding in a circle about the wagon train, the warriors bent low over their spotted ponies and shooting arrows under their necks. Gracefully the feathered shafts tore through the canvas wagon sheets. Men with rifles knelt patiently behind the wagon wheels, shot steadily and deliberately, and spat on their hot breeches. A woman handed one a supply of fresh bullets. An Indian fell headlong; the riderless pony trotted off and started eating grass. And now a band of brave cowboys dashed up, in the nick of time. The Indians withdrew. And then over the horizon galloped a troop of Dragoons! Bluecoats! The wagon train had survived the attack, but it must go on to water. It slowly unwound and passed out of sight over the plain —

The show was over. Buffalo Bill rode out on his white horse and took off his hat. He raised his right hand aloft, palm outward. Then with a quick turn, he galloped off. The hard plank seats emptied. Boy, man, and crowd trickled between Indians washing the war-paint from their cheeks. Dead white men had come to life, brushing dust from their clothes. The beautiful cowgirls were selling their photographs. The corrosive shadow of the mountains obscured all these imperfections. Only the vision of beauty persisted because seen with an inner eye.

Mama and Leona were probably waiting at home with a hot supper. But upon March the spell still held. "Daddy, did you ever kill Indians?"

Cable brought up short. His swarthy brown face set; his big Indian nose jutted out like Pike's Peak; his soft black eyes seemed to grow hard and shiny as flint. He strode to the buckboard and said curtly, "Get in."

They drove silently out of town to the encampment along the creek. In the darkness the pale gray tepees loomed up against the willows. They got out, and March followed his father up the long lane. In the red glow of small cooking fires dark taciturn faces leapt at him. The shadows of blanketed figures writhed on the stretched skins and canvas. A tepee flap yawned open into the mysterious blackness within. A dog barked. Somewhere there sounded the soft beat of a drum.

Cable did not pause. With March at his heels, he picked his way between moccasined feet that did not move to let them pass. At the end of the lane a big fire was burning down into a bed of coals. Around a carcass spitted over it sat a circle of men loosely wrapped in blankets that revealed their naked breasts. Cable stopped but said nothing. Then one of the men looked up and grunted; he had on a red shirt with some colored porcupine quills worked on it. Cable nodded, pushed his way into the circle of eating men, and squatted down cross-legged as they.

How funny he looked among them, it seemed to March standing behind him. His suit was neatly pressed, his high collar was white and stiff in the flamelight, his shined boots tucked under his haunches. And yet March sensed in him something he had never felt before. A strange solidarity with the blanketed figures around him, as if he felt completely at home. One of them said something to him in a gutteral tongue. Cable for reply made a queer sign with his hand. The rest of them grunted or laughed.

Cable reached down with his delicate brown hands and tore off a chunk of bread to put on a tin plate at his feet. Then he got out the toad-sticker with its long razor-sharp blade which he always carried. Leaning over the carcass spitted on the coals, he deftly laid back a flap of thick fat and cut off a slab of lean meat underneath.

March stirred uneasily at his shoulder, expecting his father to pass the filled plate to him. But Cable seemed oblivious of his presence. Holding up the slab of meat to his mouth with one hand, he cut off a bite with the knife in his other hand, and continued eating. When he was through, he wiped his fingers on his straight black hair. Then picking up a tin cup he raised it to his shoulder. "Water!" he said curtly.

A wave of hot resentment flooded March as he took the cup. His father had known he was there all the time, but he hadn't given him anything to eat, and now he was ordering him to go get water. Just like a maid or servant girl or something. For the first time he noticed the squaws and children hanging around the outside of the circle. They hadn't been given anything to eat either. And now suddenly he was oppressed by a feeling of male domination exuded by this circle of lazy, lordly, and impolite men over all those who stood patiently waiting outside. It magnified his own helpless childhood, increasing his resentment, and at the same time its force compelled him to step back into the darkness.

Water! Where was he to get it? Down at the creek. Through the lane of lodges and dark hairless faces with strings of braided hair tied with strips of red flannel, the greasy store-pants and stretched-out moccasins. Into the frightening darkness, the thickets of willows. His heart pounding, he filled the cup and hurried back to hand it to his father. Cable took it without thanks and without turning around.

For another hour now the men sat there smoking and talking about the show. Then as the circle broke up and the women came in, Cable filled a plate with meat and bread for March. "Good meat, son. Eat that juicy strip of fat. Indian candy!"

And now at last, in pale moonlight, they drove silently home to a world March had almost forgotten.

Cable & Ona fight over March's summer plans —
to Cripple Creek w/ Cable or home w/ O? Cable
ends up taking him to NM reservation to
Boné, but doesn't return. Sylvanite stops paying,
Rogier gets $2,000 for Boné & $2,500 fr. Timothy,
Give T. a share in the mine,

6

  The long day they had spent together at Buffalo Bill's Wild
West Show somehow had established an intimate relationship between March and his father that had been lacking before. Ona
realized this one evening when, cuddling him on her lap, she waited
for Cable to come for supper. She had been talking of his growing
up into a big boy, maybe going to college, and becoming a famous
man like his uncle Boné.

  "Daddy's more fun!" March interrupted. "He takes me everywhere and let's me do what I want. He doesn't keep sayin' 'don't do
this' and 'don't do that.' That's why I like him. And guess what.
When school's out he's going to take me with him up to Cripple
Creek. To stay with him and Grandad and learn all about the mine in
the ground. What do you think of that?"

  Her body stiffened, then slowly relaxed. She put him down and
led him into the kitchen, her face strangely grave. "I'll give your
supper now, March, so you can go to bed. And get that idea out of
your head. Your father knows you're too small yet to go up to the
mine. You're going to stay down here and have a nice summer
helping Mother. Now ssh! No talking back, mind!"

Disappointed, the boy soon crept off to bed. Ona tucked him in, kissed him, and went back to her seat at the window to stare silently into the darkness. At the sound of Cable's steps, she rose and slowly opened the door; her face was pale and set.

"What's the trouble?" he asked. "Either of the kids sick?"

"No. I want to talk with you. But come have your supper first."

Cable ate silently but deliberately, then put down his napkin and slowly filled his pipe. "A good supper, Ona. Now do you want to go into the other room?"

Ona ignored the remark, pushing aside his plate and leaning forward. "March tells me you're planning on taking him up to the Sylvanite when school is over."

"We're great chums now. It'll be good for him."

"Jonathan, you know I'd never stand for that. Never! If it were the last thing in my life."

He leaned back without replying, his face dark and expressionless.

"No!" she went on, her voice thickening. "I remember how Tom and Sister Molly's lives were ruined. I've done what I could with Mother to keep Daddy out of Cripple Creek, until now I know nobody can help him. I've tried to encourage you to make a success in business—real estate, insurance, anything to keep you out of mining. All of you are alike. Cursed by a damned mine—whatever name it's called."

Cable, elbows on table, drawn tight into himself, let her continue.

"And now you want to take March up there and get the thing started in his blood too. To make it seem so natural to him that when he grows up he won't know he's accursed like the rest of you. Jonathan, you're a fool if you think I'll let my boy go like that!" She drew a deep breath; her voice grew quieter, more resolute. "He's my boy, a Rogier to the marrow of his bones, and he's going to have his chance. He's going to get an education, do something, be somebody, He's never going to see a mine! My foot's down now to stay, Jonathan. I'm not fooling. My boy stays with me if I have to take in washing. You can do what you please, but you leave him alone. Understand?"

It was the climax of that quarrel which long had been beating them apart as with ceaseless waves upon the shore. And it resolved into an open fight for the possession of a boy who still saw them undivided. Only for a time did they maintain in his presence a commendable behavior. Cable was quiet, taciturn. Ona was quiet, reserved. Then gradually they broke out into sudden eruptions at any cause. Twice Ona spanked March for innocently asking when his father was going to take him up to the mine. To atone for the unjust chastising, she began to coddle him like an infant child. Her maternal poses, arms around the boy at every opportunity, aroused in Cable a sullen resentment.

"What do you think he is, a little tin Jesus? Let the boy alone. He can live his own life and form his own ideas without so much harping on the subject by a doting mother."

The last week of school dragged by. Rogier, surprisingly, came up to the house. "Where you been?" he demanded of Cable without prelude. "Don't you know with this good weather we've got to make hay while the sun shines! Thought you were coming up for the summer to help us on the Sylvanite!"

"I might," said Cable quietly. "Been thinkin' of bringing up March for company. Then again I might not. I like to see the rest of my family too, you know."

"Move them all up to the district. I'll get you a house in Victor."

The suggestion roused Ona to justifiable fury.

"Dom it!" growled Rogier. "Minin's minin'. It's no picnic. But there's no call for you to get so riled up." And mystified by the unbearable tension in the room, he strode out without an answer.

The quarrel, now that a decision was at hand, came to a head. Ona, on her knees with her arms around March, was a she-animal defying anyone to take away her cub. The posture was so silly and melodramatic that Cable flung out the door. When he came back from town that evening, Ona was waiting for him with March on her lap.

"Jonathan," she said in a quiet, resolute voice, "this can't go on. We both know that. So I've settled it for good. I telegraphed Boné that I was sending March down to the Reservation to spend the summer. He'll live at Bruce's trading post — Bert is lame and never gets out. Boné is there most of the time. And Lew will get up there often, so it won't be like he won't have a woman to look after him."

She bent down, brushing the boy's hair from his forehead. "You'll like it, Sonny. Remember the story of the rug beside your bed? And there'll be lots of Indians like your father tells you about, only kind and friendly. Won't that be nice?"

"Ohh yes," the boy muttered, too excited to talk.

"Now get to bed and go right to sleep. When you wake up I'll have your suitcase all packed to take to the train right after breakfast."

When he had gone, she turned a pale stern face to Cable. "I'm sorry if you don't approve, Jonathan, or if I've hurt your feelings. But it's the only thing left for me to do. And if you insist on going up to the Sylvanite, I'll miss you both and pray for the time we can all be together for good."

"So you'd send the boy to strangers, a hundred miles from a railroad, just to keep him from being with me?" Cable asked quietly.

"No! To keep him away from the Sylvanite!"

Cable, without answer, walked out of the room.

The next morning they rose early. Ona had packed March's suitcase the night before. Now while he ate breakfast, she sewed a $10 bill with his name and address in the waist of his pantaloons. Meanwhile she kept calling Cable for breakfast. After a time he came out with a suitcase and a dufflebag which he set down beside March's in the hall.

Cable poured himself a cup of coffee and, ignoring the bacon and eggs, stood munching a piece of toast. "The trip is too much for a boy alone. I'm going to take him down there myself."

Ona stood biting her lip, her hands clenched together at her breast. Neither seemed aware of March's excited chatter about having his father for company. There was an awkward silence, broken when a neighbor girl came in to mind Leona.

They walked in silence to the depot, stood waiting for the train. There seemed nothing either could put in words. When the train pulled in, Cable boosted up boy and bags and waited beside Ona until the conductor called, "All aboard!" They kissed.

"Take good care of yourself," he said calmly.

"And you, Jonathan," she answered, too proud to confess her fears and longings.

He swung aboard and without a backward glance strode through the vestibule into the coach.

Ona stood watching the train until it vanished around the bend. Then, the tears beginning at last to fall, she plunged sobbing up the tracks to home.

A week passed and then another before a postcard came from March in Cable's handwriting:

"Tell Mama this is a big country a long way off. I got wet when the wagon swum the river. There are lots of Indians. They ride horses and mostly wagons. They wear bracelets like girls and ain't the scalping kind. They ain't no post office or even town so maybe you won't get this. But we're here anyway with love."

There was no postscript from Cable, but she expected him to return any day. When he did not come, she began to worry. Rogier did little to ease her anxiety. He demanded to know why Cable hadn't returned to work in the Sylvanite as he had promised.

"I expect him soon," she said. "Probably he's taking a short vacation first."

Rogier returned to the Sylvanite in a devil of a temper. Abe and Jake had lost the vein and were piling up non-shipping ore on the dump. "No more drifts!" he ordered. "Just fooling around, you are. We'll go down some more. Another level, two if necessary, by Jove! I tell you boys, you've got to keep going down. What became of those men I sent you?"

"Just one, Colonel," said Jake mildly. "When we stopped shippin' ore we let the other go. You can't pay a man outa nothin'. We figured that."

"Bah! Leave that to me. I'll get the money and see you get help for that shaft work. Cable. He's long overdue."

There was no doubt about it; he was feeling a squeeze. Cable had not returned to help Abe and Jake, and it was necessary to call back the mucker they had let out. To pay his wages Rogier gave Ona only half the monthly allowance she had been receiving as a return on Cable's investment in the mine. This seemed quite reasonable, for with Cable and March away, the family had been reduced by half.

To sink the shaft would be expensive. He had turned in a bid for the group of six west-side schools in Little London to pay for it, but the contract had not yet been awarded and the money would not be forthcoming for several months. Rogier could not wait. He wrote Boné . The Sylvanite, he asserted, looked better than ever despite the fact that the present stope had been exhausted. They were in hopes of sinking the shaft still deeper when money from a forthcoming building contract became available. Meanwhile they were losing time. There was no doubt Boné would receive a substantial return from his investment so greatly appreciated. He hoped the lad was writing good music and his health was improved. He must remember to let nothing, nothing, come between him and the dictates of his inner self.

An answer came in due time — a draft for another two thousand dollars. Enclosed with it was a letter stating how sorry Boné was that it was no more, but not to hesitate a moment in applying it to the further development of the mine. He had finished his long orchestration and was leaving for another winter's concert tour back east.

Rogier, disappointed by the amount, did not let Mrs. Rogier read the letter. He simply told her of Boné's success. "They won't let the boy alone, Marthy! He's got to go on another piano playing expedition to keep them satisfied." Nor did he mention the money he had received; he was too busy estimating how many feet down it would sink the Sylvanite shaft.

A week later he received an unexpected windfall. He had stopped in the Ruxton for a cigar, the first time in months. It was a dull cloudy afternoon and a group of men sat talking over a small corner table in the barroom. There was nothing for it but to stop and pay his respects.

"By George, boys! The old prospector has returned. How's that hidden mine coming, Rogier?"

His mine was hardly more than a rumor to them; their sallies were extravagant and preposterous. They accused him of boring under Bull Hill and tapping the Portland and Independence. They demanded he empty his pockets of gold nuggets, suggested that at least he let them in on his secret. They meant to be kind and friendly, but their witless jokes were barbs which stung Rogier to the quick.

"Fools, the whole pack of you!" He lit his cigar and stalked into the lounge.

The group set up a delighted cheer. For the first time they had got under his skin; he seemed really human.

Rogier in the lounge bent down over a paper covered with figures. So absorbed was he in his ever-present problem—how far down he could get with Boné's money, how far down the profit from his school contract would carry him, how far down he must get sometime, somehow—that he did not at first notice the elegant figure of Timothy seated beside him, his creased trouser leg thrown over the arm of his chair.

"Well!" he looked up startled.

Timothy negligently lit a cigarette. "Those esteemed friends of ours don't believe you have a mine."

"So they sent you to find out, hey?"

"No indeed, Mr. Rogier. I came myself. As you might remember, I'm interested."

Dom! He had forgotten completely the $2500 Timothy and Pearson each had invested in the mine during Boné's visit! His forgetfulness or his remembrance of it now irked him beyond measure. "Timothy, when I permitted you to participate to a small extent in my mining venture, I gave you to understand that it was strictly a family affair. It is not listed on the Exchange. I have no fancy printed share certificates and no fool stockholders calling for reports and worrying about their money. I allow no one on the premises. My mine is my mine! I own it, run it, and am not under obligation to reassure you that you'll make a fortune out of your modest investment. On the contrary, you may lose it!"

Timothy unwrapped his leg from the arm of his chair. He sat up straight and slapped Rogier on the shoulder. "Old man, you do me a rank injustice! You underestimate me! Don't think for one minute I came here to ask for a confidential report on its development, to plague you with a single question about it. No sir! From the day I first heard about it, I had a hunch you had something tremendous in mind. You're too good a businessman not to have something sound. And what is good enough for Boné and Pearson and your son-in-law is good enough for me!"

Rogier unbent. "It's a good mine, Timothy. No mistake about that. But whether it'll pay off is another matter."

Timothy unbuttoned his coat and turned back the satin-lined flap. From his waistcoat pocket he drew a blank check from an

English-leather wallet calling for a pen from the desk, he filled it in for another $2500, and slid it toward Rogier.

"Understood, Mr. Rogier. I shall never interfere or ask questions. I ask merely to let me take a sporting chance. You know I'm rich enough. I've never worked a day in my life and never will. Why, man, I've wagered that much on a horse! Win, lose, or draw, this five thousand means nothing to me. I want the fun. And to pay for it, I can keep my mouth shut — about some things!"

Rogier grinned. He folded the check and stuffed it in his trousers pocket. "You're a lazy dom fool, Timothy. Don't know what kind of an agreement to give you."

Timothy stood up and airily buttoned his coat. "Such things never interest me. But mind — however it turns out, I would like a gold nugget to hang on my watch chain."

"You shall have it if it takes all the gold in the workings!" Rogiér scrawled on the side of the paper not already filled with figures a briefly worded receipt, giving Timothy a share in the Sylvanite. Timothy thrust it into his flowered waistcoat, and breezily walked out to the barroom. His cronies were still joking about Rogier's mythical mine; and as Rogier left, he could hear Timothy's voice raised louder than the rest.

7

The queer retentiveness of the human mind that blanks out the significantly important only to grasp the trivial! Sunlight on water, shadows of clouds upon the plain, the smell of father's pipe — of such things, evanescent and enduring, may be woven a boy's memory.

Sitting small and still upon his plank seat, he watched beyond the ears of the team the illimitable desert keep spreading out, cut by deep arroyos and shallow washes. A vast emptiness without a frame, a monotone never monotonous. He remembered the swirling brown river at the ford, lit red by the setting sun; the streaming horses and the muddy water clutching at his knees; the two braids of greasy black hair before him and the pattern of the blanket they hung upon. He remembered the smell of sage. The gray ghostly wash of the Gallegos under the rising moon. Then the long, low adobe trading post squatting in the draw. A fire glowed outside. About it lounged blanketed figures with dark and somber faces, tinctured with a strange racial smell. He was carried inside, stiff and sleepy, past a hawk-faced man sitting silently in lamplight. In ten minutes he was asleep in his shoes. This is all he remembered of a tiresome three-day journey, fragments of a dream of time; for he had made an interplanetary transition from a known world to the unknown — to "a big country a long ways off," isolated in time, whose rhythm and meaning like the beat of a drum erased from his mind all that had gone before.

In the morning when March awoke, the post leapt out at him in the cruel clarity of sunlight. A great adobe fortress with walls almost four feet thick and windows latticed with iron bars. Shaped like a cross, its trading room or bull pen was almost forty feet long. The walls were flanked with shelves of staples and canned goods; *ahzay* — patent medicines, iodine, cough syrup, castor oil. Sloan's Liniment, colored shirts, and Levis. On the floor were stacked bags of flour, salt, sugar, pinto beans, bushel baskets of onions, and huge sacks of raw wool beside a pair of scales. Around a huge wood stove were boxes of sand to spit in. On wooden posts hung saddles, bridles, bits, cinches, and harness. From the *vigas* overhead hung slabs of mutton ribs, strings of jerky, a *ristra* of dried chiles. A glass candy case boasted licorice sticks, jelly beans, gum drops, and Christmas candy. At one counter were displayed bolts of rich, solid-color velveteen and lengths of flowered gingham; and in another case pawn jewelry; glowing silver, mellow turquoise, rings, bracelets, eardrops, huge squash blossom necklaces, and heavy concho belts.

The focal point of this vast marketplace was the long wooden counter which extended down one side of the room. Behind it, on a raised couch covered with a Navajo blanket, lay Bert Bruce, the trader, the master of a wilderness domain. Partially paralyzed, his hair turning white, he looked out like a reclining emperor upon the room crowded from sunrise to sunset with the slim-hipped Navajo men with their dark arrogant faces, the scrawny and the fat women in their flounced skirts and numerous petticoats and richly colored velveteen blouses slithering around in fawn-pink moccasins twinkling with silver buttons, and the children rubbing dirty noses against the candy case.

Off from this trading room lay the windowless rug room behind a massive locked door. Here, stacked from floor to ceiling, were the blankets for which The People exchanged the necessities for their primitive existence. Rare old *bayetas*, brilliant Germantown weaves, fine, striped Chief blankets. Soft glowing red, deep indigo blue, simple white, natural brown and gray; in stripes or in intricate patterns; with simple bold designs whose origin could be identified at first glance; tight enough to hold water, to outwear a century. A minimum $50,000 worth maintained at all times; Bruce had never been known to buy or sell a blanket of spurious weave or dye.

In the other wings of the post were his kitchen, always cluttered with dirty dishes, and his own bedroom; and the rooms he had added to accomodate his two helpers, a stray missionary or government agent, the Vrain Girls, Boné, Cable, and March.

This was Hon-Not-Klee, Shallow Water, the trading center for a 3,000 square-mile patch of desert, the hub of all the life that revolved around it.

Far west across the sandy Gallegos stood Shiprock. To the south and east stretched the sage-studded desert broken by Canyon Blanco and El Huerfano, the sacred peak. To the north the muddy San Juan marked the boundary of the world March had left. Here squatted the little towns of Farmington and Bloomfield, the hospital and Navajo Methodist Mission. Even these seemed far away and as unreal as the railroad junction seventy miles farther north across the Colorado line.

If the desert around March seemed like a sea, life at the post was conducted with shipboard routine. At sunrise the great doors were unlocked, the windows opened behind their bars. March could see the squeaking, springless wagons of the Navajos rising on the swells and drifting in to the courtyard. All day the trading went on. There was no hurry. The tall, slim-waisted men would stand around smoking, spitting, talking. The women in their voluminous petticoats and brilliant velveteen blouses would pick lice from their hair. The children would nose the glass candy case. Then a man would lug in a Pendleton of wool — some forty pounds sewed in a Pendleton blanket with yucca strips — and inquire how much the trader was paying. Bruce would open a can of tomatoes, the great delicacy, or put on a pot of Arbuckle coffee. Then came the great nine-foot-long regulation wool sacks holding some 300 pounds of wool to be weighed on the scales.

Bruce would remember how much the man owed him that his pawn silver did not cover. The amount of the debt he would jot down, subtracting it from the trade slip which he handed to one of his clerks. Then the women would step up with the man to trade out the remaining sum for flour and sugar, a new coffee pot, yard goods, and a Pendleton blanket. To conclude the trade, a little candy in a striped-paper sack would be given to each child.

There was no transaction too small to escape Bruce's attention. His Navajo speech was equal to theirs. He knew their superstitions, traits, and customs; he had worked with their medicine men in preparing for their ceremonial Sings. He met their haughty arrogance with bland self-assurance, their cunning with shrewdness, their stubborness with tact. Hard, practical, and wise, he proved himself every day the recumbent master of Shallow Water.

At sunset the great doors would be closed, the windows drawn behind their bars. All inside would gather at the table for the evening meal, and March would be sent off to bed.

Famous Uncle Boné was not much fun, really. There was no doubt he was Bruce's pet. For when Bruce had given up his post in town he had built here a little one-room adobe just like the one Boné had stayed in there a long time ago. Moreover, he had moved into it the piano Boné and Lockhardt had used. It was a good thing Bruce had put him away from the post, thought Boné, for the Navajos, hearing the tinkle of his piano far down the draw, would shake their heads as if the *Belicana* were crazy.

March wandered down there often. In the morning Boné was grouchy, and during his spells of work untouchable. He would be at the piano, touching a key at a time and then turning around to make a funny dot with a twisted tail on a sheet of paper ruled with lines. On the table sat a square box with a tin arm sticking out. It swung back and forth, tick-tock, like a clock.

"Is this how you make music, Boné?"

He spun around. "What the devil you doing here, boy? Haven't I told you to keep out of here this time of day?"

And when March backed to the door, Boné was likely to jump up. "Well, as long as you're here, go make the bed. Not that anybody cares, but see you tuck the covers under the foot better this time. And don't bother stirring up dust with that broom again today."

Something was bothering Boné. Worn out, worried, and irritable from his nervous breakdown, he acted like a man no one dared approach — like Lockhardt, whose place he had subtly usurped. Goodnaturedly, Cable would take him out a hot lunch. In the afternoon Boné would take a nap. Then, near sundown, he would dress up and come to the post wide-awake and cheerful.

One night he asked Cable abruptly, "Jonathan, is that Sylvanite Mine all right?"

Cable turned around, giving him a sharp look. "Boné, how do I know? I put all I had in it, and it was doing all right when I left."

Boné jumped up, strode around the room. "Every week I've been getting letters from Daddy. He must think I'm made of money! I've sent him all I have. I'd counted on a couple of years — a long rest and time for good work. But now I can't finish this long orchestration. I'm facing another long concert tour, with just two new songs between me and starvation. Lord man, what'll I do? Be honest. What do you think my chances are?"

Cable spread his hands. "Boné, you know Rogier better than I do. Why ask me?"

A couple of weeks later Boné left the Reservation.

March missed him, but a few days later he got a horse. A small pinto, just his size, that an old Navajo was holding in the courtyard of the post. "That's the one I'm going to ride, Daddy!" he exclaimed at once.

Cable walked up to the horse, lifted a foot, swatted him on the flank, watched his ears go back. "We'll get you a horse, sonny. No hurry."

"This one! I'm going to ride him now!" March insisted.

The old Navajo, whose graying thin hair was tied in a chignon in back, said something in a low gutteral voice. Cable shrugged and lifted the boy into the crude saddle, shortened the buckskin stirrups to his short legs, and stepped back. The nice little pinto laid his ears back again. He crow-hopped a few steps, broke out into a short run. Then he plowed up short, arched his back, and March flew off into the sand, scraping the skin off his nose and cheekbones.

When he got up, ready to cry, the Navajo was holding the pinto by the bridle. Cable was looking at him with a stare which gave him that feeling the boy had experienced the night after Buffalo Bill's show. "You said you were goin' to ride him. Then do it," Cable said coldly.

It was the Navajo this time who boosted March back on the pinto, loosening the reins. With a swat on the rump, the pinto broke away. March gripped the saddle with both hands, shut his eyes. Unchecked, the pinto ran through the sage, plowed through a dry wash, whirled round a clump of chamisa. March clung on desperately, bouncing around like a cork in a heavy sea, and staring at the tossing horizon. After a time the pinto trotted back and let himself be caught by the old Navajo.

The boy could not stand up when Cable took him off the saddle; his legs were numb and there was a terrible pain in his crotch. Cable laid him down on the sand and wiped the blood off his face. "Well son, you did what you said you were going to do," he said kindly. "Just take it easy awhile; you'll be all right." Then he walked off with the old man to dicker for the horse.

During the next couple of days he gentled the pinto. He sure did! March watched him ride him from hell to breakfast, slap him with a saddleblanket, and jingle the bridle in front of him until he wouldn't spook no matter what you did. Then, of course, they had to go on a long ride together with their blankets and saddlebags.

Maybe it was the last of the three nightcamps of the *Entah* ceremony, ending with the Squaw Dance, they were sleeping in their blankets, feet to fire, when across the boy's mind, or rather across that mysterious narrow plain which separates the sleeping and the conscious minds, there was traced the path of a new and wonderful sound. An abrupt, shrill piercing yell soaring to the midnight sky, then breaking like a rocket into a parabola of eerie song. How it splayed out across the naked stars, those clear male voices with their strange and wild intensity! Indians singing! No other sound could ever hold for him the indescribable power and freshness and haunting strangeness of that song gushing forth into the soundless desert night.

Now wide awake, he heard the faint splashing of horses' hoofs at the ford. The singing stopped. Cable was already on his feet, stirring the coals awake. Little fire-tongues licked at his lean brown hands propping up the blackened coffee pot with stones. The flickers became flames, their glow filling the clearing in the brush.

"I'm awake!" March called out.

"Lie still," his father answered without looking up.

Abruptly a yelp thrust at the boy like a lance from the darkness. He could feel his scalp tingle, as if his hair had jerked up stiff as the quills of porcupine. The brush crackled. Raising his head, he saw them behind his father: three somber figures sitting on their horses.

Cable, squatting on his haunches, back toward them, did not turn around. Deliberately he set out on the ground three tin cups and a small stew pan. They reflected an accurate gauge of the mixed-up clatter of four horses up the gravelled slope, subtly betraying his seeming unconcern. The three horsemen knew it. They dismounted and strode into the flamelight without greeting. They were Navajos in dirty Levis, their ragged black hair bound by headbands of red and green cloth.

The silence was oppressive. No one moved or spoke. About each was the wild sanctity of aloneness, a sense of guarded self-effacement. Above all, the boy felt their terrifying awareness: the gathered-in strength, the easy casual grace fortified by a thousand quivering nerve ends. So it was with Cable. He stared indifferently into the fire without a look at his visitors. And yet March could feel his own awareness, sounding to the full all that moved and did not move at the edge of the circle of which he was the vibrating center. Terrible really, this silent, guarded sense-appraisal between the three men and the one.

Then the fourth Navajo strutted in and yelped once beside the fire, cruelly and derisively. He was plainly full of whiskey. Cable filled the three cups and stew-pan with coffee.

"I want some white man's thin meat!" the drunken one demanded.

"Bacon can be bought at the post," Cable said quietly. Gently but decisively he waved his hand toward the cups

All began to drink, smacking their lips over the black, twice-boiled Arbuckle. The sugar tin went around and was emptied.

"He is from the Gallegos," said one.

"The tall dark man at Shallow Water."

"This is the one," Cable assented listlessly.

"It is said a pony was stolen from the white man's ranch up by Red Rocks."

This was common gossip; a native policeman had come to the post a week ago, trying to trace the thief, the drunken son of Mrs. Black Kettle. "Who knows?" asked Cable softly.

There was no answer. He took out his black stub pipe. And now March sensed a subtle change. It was his father now, not the strange dark man who could so instantly and effortlessly slip away from his son. The others sat rolling cigarettes.

"I want tobacco!" arrogantly demanded the drunken one.

Cable carelessly tossed out his pouch. The drunken Indian filled his brown Wheatstraw, then slyly hid the pouch under his blanket. Cable appeared not to notice. "The *Entah*. Is it over?"

"Three camps. Three nights, as is proper. It is finished."

Suddenly, without moving his feet, Cable rose. He thrust out his long arm toward the drunken Navajo who jerked back. Then he opened his hand, palm up, sternly but silently demanding. The pouch fell at his feet. As he stooped to pick it up, a snicker sounded. The men stood up.

"I shall walk with you to your horses," said Cable easily. "Our two might stray off with yours. That would cause us trouble."

The sky toward the east was beginning to pale. March could hear the receding hoofbeats of four horses. Cable came back with their two mounts, picketing them nearby, then flung himself down on his blanket without speaking. March snuggled in his own blanket, knowing that their horses would not be run off like the rancher's pony by the drunken son of Mrs. Black Kettle.

There weren't many of these trips; Cable was too busy. Quiet, somber, and unsmiling, he stood all day beside the recumbent master of Shallow Water. In his faded denim shirt and Levis, his dark face burned darker and his straight black hair grown longer, he seemed to have been there always. He got down cans from the shelves, bundled up sheep and goat hides, prepared blankets for shipment, sorted silver, kept accounts, rode to the bank in Farmington. Like the other store clerks, no task was too menial for him. But as he spoke Navajo more fluently every day, Bruce relied on him more and more. Cable had a way with The People. He knew their idiocyncrasies and their tricks. For all their barbaric splendor, they were to him just like himself: alive with human passions, cursed with fraility and folly, blessed with the gifts of the inscrutable Most High—men alone and lonely under the same unchanging stars as he, confronting the encroachments of an alien civilization.

Hosteen Day-u-gi, a giant and rich man whose wives owned a great flock, brought in a load of wool packed in the regulation sacks holding 300 pounds or more, and opened negotiations with Bruce. The trader, with a slight gesture, surprisingly referred him to Cable beside him. The two men began to dicker, comparing prices offered at other posts, and the length of the haul. After a time they agreed on a price, and a bag was thrown on the scales. Cable figured the amount on a scrap of wrapping paper. Hosteen Day-u-gi, smarter than he appeared, indignantly pointed at the marker on the scales and accused Cable of short-changing him thirty pounds. It was true, but Cable stood firm on his offer.

The argument brought a crowd of Navajos around them, all protesting with shocked looks at Bruce. Bruce, resting on one elbow, refused to arbitrate. Hosteen Day-u-gi threatened to reload his wagon and go to another post. Still Bruce said nothing. Finally he shrugged and called to Cable. "Open her up then!"

The floor was cleared, the bag emptied, and the wool shaken out — revealing a big heap of sand. A titter of restrained amusement ran through the bull pen. Hosteen Day-u-gi, six feet tall under his high-crowned Stetson, was not at all embarrassed. He leaned back his head and roared with laughter. Bruce, lying behind the counter, enjoyed the joke as much. He clapped for a clerk to open a case of canned tomatoes and to put on a big pot of Arbuckle. Cable grinned his great relief.

It seemed so obvious that Cable belonged here, March did not notice that his father never mentioned going home. When he received a letter from mother, he read it out loud but avoided all talk about it afterward. One day March was talking about the rug Bruce had given her years ago. He had picked out another for her, his very own present. Although he didn't know it, it wasn't a hand-woven Navajo blanket but a Pendleton woven of pure wool in gorgeous colors in Pendleton, Oregon for the Indian trade — superlative weaves beloved by all Navajos, those with fringes being called shawls, and those without, robes. Cable said nothing; it was expensive, more than he could afford. But Bruce simply folded it up and threw it at the boy as a gift.

"We'll take it home with us, won't we Daddy? And wrap sage and cedar inside it to make it smell nice?"

"Might as well send it, son," Cable answered tersely. And he wrapped it up next day for the boy to address.

Matie Vrain came to spend a couple of days. The first thing she noticed were a couple of blankets hung up on the wall in Bruce's room. "Humm. How in the world you get these?"

"Come in yesterday. Cable got 'em."

"Humm," Not in twenty years had she known Bruce to allow anyone in the post to appraise and buy a ceremonial blanket. "He must be pretty good."

Bruce shrugged; Cable was standing at his shoulder.

Matie turned around to Cable. "It's a good thing you're here to help out. Bruce isn't getting any better. He needs a good man to rely on. Why don't you move Ona down and settle in?"

Bruce and Cable glanced at each other for an instant, then Cable turned away.

During supper Matie talked continuously; it had been a week since she had spoken English. "Lew left yesterday with a man and two pack horses. Clear down the San Juan. You know there's nothing there. Guess she's just turned Indian."

"Don't blame her. Times are changin' too fast," said Bruce.

Matie, over sixty years old, withered and brown as a frost-bitten pumpkin, still was strong with the Spirit. "Our Navajo Methodist Mission is all set to open school this year. The one about four miles west of Farmington, right on the San Juan near the La Plata suspension bridge. Buildings fixed up. And a new superintendent coming, Mr. Timmons. Come down and see it sometime."

That evening after supper Bruce drew Cable aside. "Matie mentioned something that's been on my mind. There's plenty of room here for all your family if you want to bring 'em down. Fact is", he finished lamely, "with this leg I could do with a partner."

A sudden warmth lit up Cable's eyes. There was no chance to reply. Somebody was beating on the locked door; he went to see who it was.

A little bit later when he was putting March to bed, the boy asked sleepily, "Daddy, are you going to take me down the mine this summer too?"

Cable laughed. "What do you mean, this summer? Don't you see the chamisa turning yellow? Summer's almost over. Now into bed!"

But, the boy thought as he dropped off to sleep, his Daddy hadn't even mentioned going home.

Cable not coming home. Ona devastated,
March sent to mission school.

8

No! Never did he mention returning home; and sitting with his letter in her lap, Ona stared with dull eyes out the window at the cottonwoods beginning to turn yellow along the creek.

One, two, three months, and in not a single letter had Cable said he was coming home. With his first letter she had got over her resentment and assumed that he would soon return. Day after day she had listened for the train whistling around the bend and waited for his step on the porch. He did not come. And then he had written again. The letter was kind in tone and informative of content, but between the lines she could read that he was stubbornly entrenched at Shallow Water.

The surprise and the injustice of his action stunned her. To leave her so, on the pretext of taking March to the post, was an inexcusable and petty revenge she could never forgive. And facing the long summer, alone with her pride and hurt, she wrote him a long letter that betrayed nothing of her feelings. Nor did her manner; she acted as if he might be spying on her every move.

She kept the house spotless, maintained a cheerful composure. Occasionally she took Leona and Mary Ann's Nancy on a picnic to the park. She worked on Rogier's books and went to church with her mother. Yet as the weeks dragged by she found herself gritting her teeth on the way to spend the customary Sunday evening in the big old house on Shook's Run.

Mrs. Rogier, catching up Leona in her arms, would exclaim, "The only Rogier in the bunch! And what do you hear of that brother of yours, child?"

Rogier, worried and restless, was always grumbling. "What's Cable mean, loafing down there! When is he coming back to help me? By Jove, Ona! I told you to write him a week ago."

And then over their teacups Mrs. Rogier would say in a confidential tone that had become almost unbearable, "Ona, I do declare it seems strange how he can stand being among those dirty heathen so long — him so neat and clean all the time. What in the world's he doing?"

"He's tending to business!" snapped Ona. "Jonathan's a grown man and quite capable of deciding his own affairs. It's all right with me if he stays all winter!"

And then each morning toward ten o'clock her heart would begin pounding and she would stand peeping through the curtains at the postman coming down the street.

"A letter from the Territory today, Mrs. Cable," he would say — so infrequently, for all her watching.

"Well!" she would answer with a smile. "I hardly expected one today, the boys are so busy down there!"

Inside the house she would read it through hurriedly, and with a dull stab of pain and resentment resume her work. The afternoons and evenings were hard enough to bear. But the nights! Dear God! Then she knew what he'd done to her. A Rogier whose passions were enclosed within the sound shell of self-restraint. Ona could never have been swept off her feet. Nor had he taken her thus. But quietly firm, gently insistent, he had insinuated himself into her life. There was no prolonged love making, but the passion was there. An engulfing fire that, once they had come together, seemed to consume her utterly. What became of her then when she seemed to resolve into an unholy flame that fused with him! The memory made her flush. And then by day he left her as completely as he had come. This was the Indian in him, without constant endearments and caresses. And she had grown content to feel him slip away, knowing he would always come again.

So she lay there, realizing that in the husband she had the lover too. It was as if for the first time she had awakened to her woman's need. Why didn't he come back? She loved him! She had to have him! Didn't he need her too? She flung over in bed with the hot blood staining her cheeks in the darkness. Yes! No man could come to her as he did, enshrouded in the mindless passion that made them one, without the same deep need.

But his letters! She could have torn them into bits, these only letters she had ever received from him, yet she read them again and again. They were terse and impersonal; they mentioned the weather, the trading, the occupants of the post — everyone but himself. Like his love making and his quarreling, they were subtle and deep-felt. Yet, taciturn and matter-of-fact, he betrayed himself by the very medium with which he thought to cloak his thoughts. The astounding communicativeness of the written word, that no man can ever hide behind.

She saw it so clearly—the squat adobe post, the well and the willow, The People coming in their squeaky wagons—as she remembered the even tenor of her own early days at Shallow Water. Him too she saw quietly working as if in rhythm to something within himself alone. She loved him so! Simple, subtle Jonathan, slippery as the adobe banks of the Gallegos, whom she could never hold against his will.

Looking forward to the opening of school, Ona bought March a new little corduroy suit with brass buttons on coat and pantaloons, drawing him a picture of it in her letter. His childish answer almost broke her heart. He thanked his mother, but wouldn't she send it to him in case Daddy didn't bring him home? Enclosed was an unembroidered statement from Cable that Bruce had offered him a share in the post at Shallow Water if he would stay. It was more than Ona could bear. She went into the bedroom and flung herself down beside the scorned little blue suit and wept.

It was thus Rogier found her when he stalked into the house in a devil of a temper. "When in the name of Almighty God is that man comin' to help me out? He ought to know Abe and Jake can't manage things while I'm away! He —"

Ona waved Cable's note in front of him. "He's been offered a share in the trading post, Daddy! Oh, I'd give anything if he'd come back. Even let him go to Cripple Creek. We miss him so!"

Rogier frowned. "A share in a backwoods grocery store selling canned peas to Indians? When he's got a share in one of the greatest gold mines on Pike's Peak? No, he's not that crazy. Don't you worry. I'll get him back!"

Rogier returned to his shop, composing with all his craft and skill a lengthy letter to Cable. The Sylvanite had been developed to the point where Cable's help was imperative. Four men were needed to run it — Jake and Abe below, a man at the dump above, and somebody to run the hoist and take charge. In Rogier's own absence. Cable would be relied upon to keep things going. The value of the ore was increasing so steadily there could be no delay.

Hardly had he mailed this than he was struck by the obvious fact that these youngsters of his were having a family squabble. So he wrote again that Ona, dear girl, was wasting away with worry over her husband and boy. This would never do! Reassured by this appeal to the emotions of a family man, Rogier mailed his letter that night. Only in the cold light of morning to have another practical thought. That dom Indian trader would be paying him actual money for his work. What did he, Rogier, have to counter that? Belatedly he realized he had cut down Ona's allowance from Cable's investment to the point where she was having a hard time making ends meet. Was this what was worrying Cable? Ah, he knew how to fix that! He scribbled out a check to Ona for five hundred dollars, writing Cable he had advanced this on Cable's salary, adding that the ore from the Sylvanite amply justified the payment. This, he was sure, would win over his son-in-law; and he could borrow it back when Cable returned.

September came and school opened—without March. And now Ona plumbed the depths of a loneliness she had never dreamed existed. The Rogiers, rooted in the passionless stability of the old house on Shook's Run, were no longer a refuge. She stood alone and separate, but incomplete. Dear God! why wouldn't he come home? Because he was a man and thus possessed the inherent right to pursue his own folly, forcing her to admit at last that it is a woman's lot to love blindly or clearly but without pride or shame. It was a bitter lesson and she learned it well, these long weary evenings as she rocked alone in an empty house.

She began to write him honestly and clearly. He answered kindly, but the steel was there behind his words. He had no job at home; the Sylvanite was not a dependable future. But Bruce, laid up and getting old, had offered to take him in as a partner. Besides, here at Shallow Water he felt in touch with things. There would be plenty of room for them all in the post if she ever thought of coming down. "In touch with things" — "a dependable future!" The phrases opened before her a chasm she could not cross. She could see him, like Bruce, spending a lifetime in a remote Indian trading post, becoming with his own Indian blood more untouchable than ever; and herself, with never a soul to talk to except an occasional government agent or wool dealer. For now, a woman and a Rogier, she no longer saw with a romantic eye that symphonic summer spent with the Vrain Girls..She saw only those two old women, burned black by the sun and wrinkled by the wind, who had given their lives to a nomadic tribe of Indians only at last, like Lew, to ride away forever into a wilderness still more empty. No! She wanted a home and schooling for the children. She wanted him back with March, to resume their normal life together.

Hurrying to the corner to drop her letter in the box, she knew her appeal was vain. Heaven itself would have to send him back. As if in answer a single drop of rain fell on her hand as she posted her letter —

The rain traveled from the high Colorado peaks south down the Continental Divide and kept spreading over the vast upland desert: from the Brazos west to Black Mesa, as far south as Hosta Butte and the Zuni ridge. One could watch from Shallow Water the ominous thunderheads changing from white to dirty wool-gray, the mist blanketing the late September chamisa, the interminable showers. The Gallegos swelled, burst its banks, and flooded sparse cornfields and squash patches. There was nothing to do in the post but sit and listen to the driving rain.

Briefly the weather cleared; and Matie, marooned at the post by muddy roads, insisted on driving March to the Mission. "We'd better go now while I have the wagon," she told Cable. "If it rains once more, we'll never make it. After all, what's here for him to do? He'll enjoy being in school, even for a short time."

Her proposal to put March in the Navajo Methodist Mission

brought to a head the impasse that had faced Cable and Bruce all summer. Bruce, old and ailing as he was, was too wise to ask questions, to push Cable. But his generous and flattering offer had perturbed Cable as much as Ona's and Rogier's letters. He had a deep-rooted, atavistic desire for the simplicity and subtlety of life at Shallow Water; something about the solitary post, the vast sweep of unbroken desert around it, The People themselves, recalled the Great Plains of earlier years. With Ona there, and a school for his children not more than twenty-five miles away, he knew he could face life with equanimity and gratitude all the rest of his days. So until he could think things out, he assented to March's enrollment in the Navajo Methodist Mission School.

Early Monday morning Matie and March drove away in a light spring wagon. By noon it was beginning to rain again. Soaked to the skin and worn out from the long drive through slippery adobe, they stayed in Farmington overnight. The little town lay some sixty miles south of Durango, at the base of the Colorado mountains, and on the northern edge of the immense upland desert of the Navajos. The San Juan River was the natural boundary. Draining the high mountains, it swung down in a great curve to its confluence with the Animas River not far from town. Two miles west it received another tributary, the La Plata. From here it swept westward between high clay banks through the sandhills past Shiprock toward its junction with the mighty Colorado.

Farmington's straggle of houses and apple orchards lay a mile back of the river between the junctions of the Animas and La Plata. It had nothing to recommend it to March save a warm fire and supper in the house of a friend of Matie's. He was glad when next morning she again lashed over the wagon the heavy tarpaulin, bundled up March on the plank seat beside her, and drove off. The horses plodded deep in mud; the wagon slid from side to side in the slimy adobe. The boy, huddled in blanket and greasy canvas, sat staring at the great brown river rolling past. From the bottomlands to the clay banks on the other side the muddy flood was choked with debris and cottonwoods torn loose from its banks.

When they reached the suspension bridge Matie pulled up the team. In good weather the bridge hung high above the river. Now it seemed to have sagged until the floor boards were almost level with the water. Even the approach to it was obscured by the muddy wash. Matie compressed her lips. "Bet we get our feet wet!" she said cheerfully. One of the horses balked, setting up a frightened neighing. The woman lashed out with her whip, and gingerly the horses stepped upon the bridge.

For an instant March was terrified by the feeling of being set afloat; the wagon had depressed the bridge the few inches necessary to bring it to the level of the river, and now a thin wash obliterated the planks. He had the sensation of walking, like a Sunday-school picture of Jesus, upon the swirling stream. He closed his eyes; the sweep of water made him dizzy. When next he opened them the team was halfway across. And now they were lost indeed. The opposite bank seemed miles away. From upstream the river, a half-mile wide, poured down upon them with a force that made him huddle close against the woman as if for protection.

"Sure, boy, you're not scared?" Matie demanded, warily watching out for floating debris.

"No, Ma'am," he answered, drawing an inch away. His hands were cold and stiff from clenching the wagon seat, his feet numb. Scared solemn, he fixed his gaze upon the building that now loomed up across the river.

"Thank goodness!" ejaculated Matie, once again on firm but slippery land. "Those horses sure were scared, weren't they?"

At any other time the small hospital she and Mrs. Mary Aldridge had established might have seemed a cheerful refuge. Yet the minute they stepped into the waiting room, March was oppressed by the crowd of Navajos squatting around the walls. Water trickled from their hair and oozed from the corners of their blankets, making puddles on the bare floor on which they sat, patient and enduring. On all their faces was the same look of helpless incertitude.

Matie opened the door to the inner room, then swiftly closed it. His one quick glimpse inside at two bloody, recumbent figures was enough for March. Matie took him into the kitchen.

Mrs. Aldridge was boiling water and laying out shiny instruments on a clean towel. "Oh, you're back, Matie? Just in time." She nodded toward the next room. "Horses bolted at the bluff. Hosteen Tso got his leg caught in the traces when he jumped for the reins. Almost off — we've got to finish it. Don't know where the doctor from town is, this weather, but we can't wait. Oh yes, the wagon went clear over. The others in a bad mess. Look 'em over while I get ready. You brought the anesthetics with the supplies?"

Matie pulled off her coat, rolled up her sleeves. "There's been an accident, March. I'm going to be too busy to take you to the Mission. I'll find somebody else. But here's a cup of coffee and a piece of bread while you're waiting. Tell Mr. Timmons I'll see him later."

March couldn't eat his bread for the sight of the bloody figures he caught every time the door was opened, and a sweetish sickening smell coming from the table at which Mrs. Aldridge was working. But a Navajo man came to drive him in the wagon to the Mission two miles downriver.

The Navajo Methodist Mission compound of three buildings and corrals and sheds for stock and chickens looked imposing in the rain. But once inside the two-story adobe, March found the room in which he had been left cheerless and cold for all the heat of the stove. It was a half-hour before Mr. Timmons came in. The superintendent was tall and lean, with a cadaverous face and a big Adam's apple on which, like a ball bearing, his small head revolved within a high starched collar. He wore a black bow tie, vest and coat, his boots alone deferring to the country and the weather. Entering the room, slicking his wet and fresh-combed hair, he stopped short at sight of the bedraggled boy standing at the stove.

"Well! What is the meaning of this? What are you doing here?"

"The Indian brought me."

"What Indian? Where are your papers? Bless my soul! Speak up, boy!"

"Aunt Matie's Indian. He brought me here to go to school."

Mr. Timmons stealthily approached the boy who backed away; then shot out his cuffs and began warming his hands at the stove. "Matie — Matie Vrain. Oh, yes. She'll have to fill out papers. You're not a Navajo. But this is indeed a house of refuge. No favors and God's loving kindness to all." He turned to a woman who had just come in. "Miss White, another member to join our happy family. Take him to the dormitory, and see that he marches down with the rest for supper. Six o'clock sharp, mind!"

⑨

How repellently and frigidly repressive it was, this primitive outpost on the Jesus Way. Confined indoors by the rain, March exhausted its meaning on his first day.

The "happy family" of six adults and twenty-seven Navajo children marched into breakfast promptly at seven o'clock, standing at the table for Mr. Timmons' morning prayer. " — and the blessings of our Holy Father, Jesus Christ, Merciful Provider, be upon this our daily bread, Amen." He pulled back his chair, shot his cuffs over his plate, and sat down. Beside him sat Mrs. Timmons. At the other end of the table sat Miss White, a teacher. To her right, neat in collar and tie, was Mr. Pike. He was new to the country and kept talking about "conditions back east" and "conditions out west," particularly the "condition" of the San Juan roaring by outside.

"It ain't no bad condition a'tall!" boomed out the hearty voice of Mr. Monta, perhaps seventy-five years old, who boarded at the Mission. "No, sir! I been in this here country since the year One, and seen rains worse'n this by a long shot. The river ain't never been within a stone's throw of this here ground!"

"But Mr. Monta, it's already up to the foundation of the

laundry." Mrs. Timmons' weak voice carried no conviction and her husband silenced her with an upraised hand.

"It is my opinion," he stated loudly, "that we are in no danger of being discommoded by an overflow. Moreover I would remind you we are safe in His sacred palm, as sparrows one and all. Miss White, there will be no deviation from the day's schedule."

At her signal, March and the Navajo children filed out of the room behind Frankie Damon, the half-breed interpreter. From the start March liked Frankie. Middle-aged, he was human, kind, and attentive to the needs of every child. His eyes were peculiar though: smoky gray and expressionless behind dropping eyelids. Suddenly the boy realized Frankie was blind. Yet so well did he know the whole compound of the Mission, he could walk unhesitantly from room to room, and building to building.

Lessons were conducted in the downstairs portion of this large two-story adobe, whose upstairs served as a dormitory. The twenty-seven Navajo children ranged in age from eight to fifteen years. Many of them had left their *hogans* for the first time, their brown little faces stolid but still expressing their terrified amazement at this new world of the Mission. All were dressed exactly alike: the girls in white pancake hats, starched white slip-ons over their gingham dresses, and high-buttoned shoes; the boys in denim shirts and pantaloons, their hair cut short and thoroughly deloused. To contribute to their loss of individuality, Mr. Timmons, who could not understand Navajo, had peremptorily assigned them English names: Abigail, Alice, Hortense, Geraldine, Percy, John, Joseph, Ira —

Mr. Timmons was present with Miss White to begin the first lesson with a hymn:

> Jesus a-yo a-so, 'nih,
> Bi nal-tsos yeh sil, hal-ne,
> Al-cin-i-gi-a-nis-t' eh
> Co si-dzil dah, Ei bidzil —

Mr. Timmons stopped the singing with an upthrust arm. "Now we have the tune! In English now!"

> Jesus loves me,
> This I know —

Again he stopped the singing with a protesting arm.

"What is this I hear? Somebody is singing native pagan words! English now, everybody! Hear me, Frankie?"

So inch by inch, hour by hour, they plodded on the Jesus Way towards Salvation.

At noon they ate, rested, and went back to study the colored lithographs and stories of Jesus. After supper they were all marched upstairs to sleep. There were two rows of beds for male and female, separated by a thin wooden partition at whose end slept Frankie Damon. How terrible these nights were to the sole white boy! For now, after a day of repression among the Belicanas, the Navajo children were free to talk in their own language, of their own families, customs, and traditions. An alien in a strange new world, March would listen to their sibilant whispers.

Only Frankie Damon tried to bridge the gap. He told the children about Shallow Water and March's two aunts whom their parents knew; and March the place names of the children's homes. Through him March learned the real names of his companions, and began to get acquainted with them. His favorite among the girls was spunky Kigpah, "On the Warpath;" and his closest friend among the boys was Yabatya, "Brave," who had earned his name because as Frankie said he always "dared to do right." Then the light would be turned off, talk ceased, and in the darkness he would lie sleeplessly listening to the lash of rain outside . . .

Matie, after sending March to the Mission and helping Mrs. Aldridge to hack off Hosteen Tso's leg before gangrene set in, stubbornly walked back across the suspension bridge with an empty saddlebag to fill with crucial medical supplies. Now, marooned in town for a week she found it still impossible to return to the Mission. It was still raining.

Messages from Colorado expressed fear that the Rockwood Dam above Durango was weakening, and warned people in the lowlands to move to safety. Knots of townspeople, ranchers, and traders stood on the corners oblivious of the rain, watching the steady rise of the river. The floor boards of the bridge were under water — if they still held; only the suspension cables were visible, cluttered with debris, and likely to snap at any moment.

"I've got to get this stuff to Mary!" Matie kept muttering forlornly as she wandered from group to group.

"Forget it!" a man answered gruffly. "If that one-legged Navajo dies — and they never do! — what's one dead Indian? The hospital's on high ground. Do your worryin' about that Mission. All those kids ain't got a chance down there on the bottoms."

His remark eased Matie's obsessive concern over the crude hospital so short of supplies. "Warn Mr. Timmons! He's got a telephone. Tell him to move everybody to the vacant homestead a half mile back up on the ridge."

The man did not budge. "That damn fool Timmons! He's been called like everybody else. Says his buildings are safe. What do you expect from a greenhorn?"

Matie grabbed up her saddlebag and hurried to the telephone office. After a long line of people, her own turn came. She called the Mission; no one answered. She called the government Indian agent at his home and office; Mr. Shelly could not be found. There was nothing to do but spend a sleepless night, hoping that the rain would stop and the river go down.

In the morning more news came in. The railroad tracks from Durango had been washed out by another cloudburst in the mountains, and a flood was expected that night. At Shiprock the Agency buildings were already flooded, and hundreds of Navajo gathered for a Sing had fled to higher ground. Many of them on their way home had made it to the La Plata only to find they could not cross. They were still huddled under their wagons on the high bluff above the San Juan.

Worn out and desperate, Matie found in a trading post two Indians she had known from boyhood. To one of them she gave the saddlebag stuffed with medicines and a message to her co-worker, Mrs. Aldridge: she was to send word to Timmons that the Mission was to be emptied immediately. To the other she gave a packet of letters and a telegram that had lain waiting a week for Cable, and a hastily scrawled note of her own. She minced no words. A flood was expected down the San Juan that night; March was in the Mission which was expected to be washed away; and that whatever happened, Cable should be on hand.

The two Navajos rode away, slimly erect under their dripping stovepipe Stetsons, both headed upriver where there was another bridge beyond the Animas' junction with the San Juan: the one to ride back on the opposite side of the river to the hospital and the Mission, and the other to ride down the Gallegos to Shallow Water. Matie watched them fade into the mist, praying that the bridge would hold, and computing wearily the twelve or fifteen hours it would be before Cable reached the Mission. If Timmons would only move!

It was noon when she finally got a call through to the Mission, but Timmons refused to talk. Imperiously she demanded Frankie Damon and talked to him for five minutes in Navajo in case Timmons might be listening at Frankie's shoulder.

Late that afternoon a report came from high country: they were to expect the first rise about 2:00 a.m. and the second — the rise from both rivers — between 3:30 and 4:00 a.m.

Not until evening did she locate the Agent, Mr. Shelly. He was in his office, splattered with mud, and still supperless. He listened patiently to her as he waited at the telephone. "We've all been as worried as you about the Mission. It's no use to call again. They've all gone to bed on schedule, and Timmons as usual has given orders the telephone is not to be answered."

"Try!"

"Of course! Don't you see me ringing?"

There was an answer.

"Frankie," Matie whispered. "Thank God!"

Shelly demanded the superintendent and was informed Timmons refused to talk.

"You tell Timmons I demand that he vacate the Mission immediately with all the wards of the government. Do you understand, Frankie?"

Damon promised to deliver the message and went to bring Timmons to the telephone. Neither returned or if they did, could not talk. The line had suddenly gone out.

There was nothing more Matie could do. Sick with fear, she stumbled home to spend another sleepless night listening to the increasing roar of the river —

That noon, when Matie had called the Mission, the happy family had been gathered at table for the midday meal. Miss White had answered and called Mr. Timmons, who refused to answer. Before she could hang up, Frankie Damon quietly took the receiver.

March saw Mr. Timmons jump up from the table and rush toward him. "You know I don't allow any such interference! You —"

Frankie silently handed him the receiver spouting Navajo.

"We speak English here!" shouted Mr. Timmons.

Frankie calmly took back the receiver and listened for a long time. When he finally put it back on the hook, Mr. Timmons, hands on hips, demanded, "And what was that about, if I may ask?"

"The river will flood tonight. We must move out to high ground right away," answered Frankie.

"We will not move! God will protect us! Take your seat at the table!"

Mr. Pike smirked. "I'm an expert swimmer."

The meal ended in silence. Lessons resumed. At three o'clock came the playtime recess. Mr. and Mrs. Timmons went back to the separate adobe house in which they lived. For the children there was no play outside in the rain. They sat on the floor listening to the patter on the roof and the roar of the river. Frankie sat with them, head against the window, listening. In a little while he rose, fumbled for his coat, and called for Yabatya to go outside with him.

"Frankie, please can't I go too?" begged March.

The three of them left the building, March hanging to the blind man's hand, Yabatya holding his other arm. To March it seemed that Frankie had eyes as they began a circuit of the buildings and corral. Then suddenly they stopped; water was swirling over their ankles. Frankie and Yabatya talked in Navajo for awhile, and they went back indoors.

Mr. Timmons didn't come back until suppertime. Then he and Frankie had a terrible row in front of everybody. Mr. Timmons was real mean, though he talked like God's prophet. Frankie, usually so good-natured, talked right back. He insisted they all move out, before it got too dark, to that old homesteader's place, a big adobe of four rooms, all vacant. The livestock too.

"Never!" roared Mr. Timmons, forgetting his oratory. "I'm not going to have all the people in town running my business and I'm not going to be dictated to by a blind interpreter on my payroll who can't see his hand in front of his face, let alone hear God's command. I'm not answering that telephone anymore or listening to another word from you!"

No one ate much. Mrs. Timmons and Miss White were frightened. Mr. Pike kept grinning at the hearty reassuring boom of Mr. Monta's voice. The children sat still, oppressed by the restless undercurrent that swept the room. Foxy, the little terrier the children loved, scampered in.

"Get that dog out of here!" shouted Mr. Timmons. "Lock him up in the laundry!"

Frankie took him out. Evening prayers were said early and the children were marched upstairs. March didn't feel like going to bed. A vast inquietude, a nameless fear, filled the room. The other children too sat stiffly on their beds, peering out the window. Frankie began to talk in Navajo. After a long time, he turned to March. "I've been telling every boy in the room not to undress, but get in bed. Keep on your clothes and don't talk." Then he went into the other room and told the girls the same thing. The lights were put out. March sat on his bed, listening to the stealthy sound of blankets being pulled off the beds around him. The air was charged with excitement, with fear. He could only sit there, trembling, waiting, and wondering where Frankie had gone.

Miss White's steps and the light of her lamp appeared on the landing. From the girls' room he heard her shouting through the partition. "Frankie! What did you tell my girls, I want to know? The very idea! They won't undress or go to bed. When I undress one she puts her clothes back on the minute I go to the next. I demand to know the meaning of this rank insubordination!"

The next minute she stalked into the room with her lamp. Frankie wasn't there, but every boy was sitting on his bed fully dressed and with a blanket wrapped around his shoulders. "Oh, you too!" she screamed. "I shall report him to Mr. Timmons this instant. And you and you." She pattered downstairs and they could see her lamp bobbing across the courtyard.

Then Frankie called and they all trooped down, boys and girls. Yabatya lit a lantern. In its light they saw that Frankie had hitched the horses to the wagon and opened the corral gate, letting loose horses and cows and chickens. By the time the Timmons had dressed and come out, followed by the two men and Miss White, they were ready to pull out: Frankie holding the reins on the plank seat with Yabatya beside him to serve as his eyes; the little children crowded in the box; the bigger children, who were to walk behind, hanging to ropes. And now it was all a nightmare in the pouring rain. The stock milling around, Foxy barking in the laundry, lamps and lanterns flashing, Mr. Timmons yelling. "I forbid you to leave! Hear! Get out of that wagonbox!"

Instead, Mrs. Timmons climbed up on the seat beside Yabatya, weeping bitterly. "I've got to go. I'm afraid. Please go with us!"

"That team and wagon is Mission property!" screamed Mr. Timmons. "Pike, you see that it's brought back here!"

Miss White began to show signs of hysteria. Adding to the rank insubordination of Mrs. Timmons and the rest, she waded through the water in her pearl button shoes, grasped the end of a wagon rope with one hand, and hoisted an umbrella with the other.

Frankie could wait no longer. He laid the whip on the horses and the wagon moved off. March looked back behind the children and Miss White plodding through the rising water to glimpse the three men in the light of a lantern. Timmons was still shouting. "Go, then! Go! I shall put my trust in the Lord!"

And now all was dark save for the lantern lights bobbing up and down in the water lapping against the wheels and the legs of the plodding children. It was too late to reach the abandoned homestead only a half-mile away; the approach was under water. Frankie drove on. March could think of nothing save Foxy barking in the laundry.

Eventually a light appeared ahead, then the hospital loomed up. It was as crowded as when he had left it a long, long time ago. But Matie wasn't there, Mrs. Aldridge couldn't tell him from the other children, and he could no longer see the bloody recumbent figures in the inside room. There was no space left in the reception room for all the people from the Mission. Frankie took some of them into the storage room. March, with Yabatya and Kigpah, squeezed into the kitchen between the Navajos huddled about the stove. He was wet and cold and hungry, scared and miserable. Worn out, he wriggled into a corner and slid down against the broad haunch of a squaw. It was warm and soft as the flank of a horse. In this cramped position he went to sleep.

Flood. Cable rides thru rainy night, March safe. Cable decides to go home.

10

Cable at Shallow Water had just stood up and yawned, stretching his long arms above the pot-bellied stove in the bull pen. "Might as well turn in, Bert!"

On the floor, propped against the walls and stacks of pelts, lay a dozen Navajos sleepily swathed in their blankets despite the stuffy room. They had been there for a week or more, and if it kept on raining confidently expected to stay another spell. Bruce got up on his crutches and hobbled off to his room as if they were not there, leaving Cable to see the post through another night.

Cable turned down the lamp on the counter, took off his shoes, and lay down on Bruce's narrow cot. He slept soundly but lightly, back to the faint glow of the lamp, a hidden revolver within easy reach for emergency.

Minutes or hours later — which, he never knew — he was awakened by the slosh of a horse's hoofs outside, the click of the door latch, and a gust of cold air. They were almost simultaneous, so swiftly had the messenger leaped from his horse and opened the door — and before he had reached the stove, Cable was on his feet and turning up the lamp. The Navajo, sopping wet, stood silently watching Cable put on his shoes. Then, without greeting, he handed his message to Cable.

"When did you leave?" asked Cable. It was his only question. He roused Bruce, got into warm clothes and boots. The letters and telegram from Ona and Rogier he thrust into his pocket without opening.

Bruce came out, read Matie's note, and talked with the messenger. "I'm sorry, man," he said simply turning to Cable. "If you can get across the Gallegos, follow up the bluffs to Two Trees, then turn due west. But mind the alkalai flats. Hear?"

Cable nodded, threw on a torn slicker. The master of Shallow Water turned to the Navajos on the floor. It was not what he said, but his inflexible commanding spirit that roused them to their feet as if he had cracked a whip. There was no need to flatter them with his friendship, to remind them of the coffee and food they had been gorging for days. He simply called for their best pony and lightest saddle, and they jumped at his bidding.

To Cable he gave a light buckskin pouch containing a box of crackers and a cake of unsweetened chocolate. He grabbed from the pawn case a squash-blossom necklace of silver and turquoise, thrusting it into Cable's hands. "Don't know what he'll do with it, but the boy always fancied one of these things. Give it to him for me."

For an instant their eyes met and held. Cable thrust the useless ornament into his pocket, and flung out of the door to his horse.

It was pitch dark and still raining; for a moment, as he swung around the post, he could see nothing of the willow, the wagons, shed, and stable. Guided by the roar of the creek, he picked his way carefully downstream. At the ford he paused. The Gallegos was swirling over its bank. Suddenly, with his slap, the mare plunged into the stream. The shock of cold water as the pony went down was like a blow. Stunned and gasping, he clung to the horn with both hands. Finding footing, the pony made its way to the opposite bank. Cable came alive again. Feeling the ground firm beneath him, he headed north and swung at last into the sage.

The little mare was a good one. She lay down to the ground in an easy rhythmic lope, nose out, fighting for the reins. He let her have them; she could pick her way among chuck holes and clumps of sage better than he. Easing his weight on her by riding on the point, he settled down for the long ride.

The rain began to let up. He could make out the dark floor of the desert extending to the sand hills along the river. So close! And yet hours, miles away! Resolutely he tried to fasten his mind upon the mare, Shallow Water, any trivial remembrance, only to find himself a moment later staring across those miles of sage that separated him from the endangered Mission and his boy.

He remembered the compound well: the three adobe buildings, the corral and sheds, the big cottonwoods flanking the road, the flowered bluffs behind. Yet its pleasant aspect in summer when he had seen it kept fading into the new and terrifying vision before him. He knew the dry, sandy Gallegos too well after a rain not to be able to imagine the San Juan in flood. The Mission was on bottomlands, on the west bank of the river where it made its turn — at the one spot where the buildings would receive the full force of the flood. Again and again he saw the children, the teachers, March! caught like rats in a trap. Why didn't they move? There was no answer to his ceaseless conjectures. He kept riding. And with him rode a dragging sense of guilt that slowed his pony's pace and kept whispering with those voices he had long ignored — Ona's letters asking for her boy, Rogier's blunt requests to return, and Matie's suggestion that March would enjoy school after so many months. Most clearly it spoke to him with phrases of the boy himself: "Aren't you going to show me the mine this summer, Daddy?" — "Are we going home?" Nothing could shut out the thin boyish voice. Cable could only tighten his lips in a straighter line and dig spurs in the laboring mare.

The junipers of Two Trees appeared against the horizon; warped and twisted, they looked in the mist like weeds at the bottom of the sea. He knew then the rain had stopped and the night was on its wane. He swung to the left and was caught in the soggy alkalai patch. It was necessary for him to retrack and detour with fury in his heart for the delay.

It was almost dawn; the inky blackness had paled to a thin purple against which the far sand hills flanking the river stood out almost imperceptibly. He became aware of other lone horsemen and lumbering wagons, all heading with him toward the growing rise of hills. One by one he passed the wagons, seeing without noting the soggy figures huddled in their blankets, the drawn but immobile faces that never looked around as he galloped by.

Reaching the crest of the hills, Cable reined up the panting mare. It was lined for a quarter of a mile with horses and wagons as if the desert night had spewed up all its human life. Some of the people were squatting on the ground, others sat their ponies like cardboard figures against the horizon, still others mounted and on foot were crawling and slipping down the slope. There was no talk, no noise, no confusion. All, like him, seemed withdrawn inside their impenetrable shells.

It was dawn, a dirty woolen skein blanketing both earth and sky. From far down below, still too dark to see, came a sullen ominous roar. Cable knew what it was. He sat fighting back the insane desire to ride madly down the slope before he could get his directions. Only a minute, a minute more, and it would be light!

At no other time in his life did he show more clearly the inner texture of his obscure breeding. That inexhaustible Indian patience! Covered with muck to the crown of his hat, muddy hands crossed over the saddle horn, he sat immobile as a figure modeled from mud.

It was light. The opposite bank emerged, dotted with people. Then the valley and the river. Two miles upstream a thin column of smoke was rising from the shadowy-gray outline of a building on the high river bank. Then suddenly and without warning the sight burst before him.

Below and a little to the left of him, the river swung past the site of the Mission. The buildings were gone. Only the floor of the laundry, to which was bolted the machinery, remained on its foundations. On this stood a man waving his hands frantically, and a dog going through the contortions of barking. Behind it the river was tearing out the big cottonwoods. As he watched, one of them slowly went over. For an instant it seemed suspended in air, roots upward with a ton of dirt, then it vanished to come up stripped of branches. Farther behind in a quiet eddy a pig and a dozen chickens swept round and round with a scatter of debris. Still the great brown river swirled down with inconceivable force, rising in a high wall, then breaking away, leaving a hole gouged out bigger than a house.

Cable did not flinch. Slowly he gathered in the reins. And with a dull glance upstream at what he knew now was Mrs. Aldridge's and

Matie's hospital, he urged his tired mare down the sandy slope —

That night at the hospital no one had been able to sleep for the roar of the river. March couldn't even hear Mrs. Timmon's blubbering in the next room. He had been awakened from his short nap of an hour or more by a muffled crack and snap when the first rise of the river took out the suspension bridge. The warm fat haunch underneath him stirred. He sat up. All the Navajos were sitting up, wide awake too. He could sense running through them, like animals, a curious awareness and nervous expectancy. What they were waiting for, he didn't know; but he kept waiting too.

Finally it came: a roar like that of a train over the crossing near Shook's Run back home followed by a loud crash. Mrs. Timmons screamed and dashed outside. Mrs. Aldridge, Miss White, March, and all the Navajo refugees followed her as she ran toward the edge of the rise.

The rain had stopped; the sky was clearing. Across the river the bank was black with people from town. On the high bluffs above the La Plata was another group. The first rise had taken out the suspension bridge. Now the second rise was pulling out the east anchorage; girders, spans, and cable work were swept loose and whirled away like string. But it was not at this the watchers were staring. They were watching the flood take out the last of the Mission buildings farther off. One adobe wall after another crumpled like wet paper and vanished in the waves of muddy water. To March it was incomprehensible; he could not relate the sight to the Mission of last night. But Mrs. Timmons lay on the ground hysterically screaming.

Then suddenly Mission, bridge, and river were replaced by another drama more compelling because human. One of the Navajos who had slid his horse down the slope of the sand hills and was riding slowly upstream, stopped and gave a shrill cry. Then lashing his mount forward he rode into the crowd from the hospital. He had spotted the Mission children.

As if it had been a signal for an attack, the horizon like a bow string shot forward horsemen, wagons, running men, and waddling squaws. March watched them plunging down from the crest, rushing toward him — whooping, yelling, waving arms and blankets, lashing horses. It was like a charge in the Wild West Show. Like a spring roundup when branded cows are loosed to hunt their calves. From around him the twenty-seven children of those fathers, mothers, brothers, and sisters who had believed them washed away with the Mission acted themselves like dead who had returned to life. Soggy new shoes flew over the sand, quilts and store blankets dropped on the ground, and from bedraggled gingham dresses and buttoned little coats, from beneath round hats and floppy bows, brown stoical little faces burst into bloom as they rushed to meet the charge.

March stood watching a fat mother kneeling on the ground before her girl, pinching her legs, stroking her arms, her hair, her face. Then he turned around to see something that he would never forget to the slightest detail — the sight of Cable who had slowly ridden up to see, without warning, his own son standing safe before him. He was sitting loosely on his mare, his hands clutching the saddle horn. From his high cheek bones down, his dark face might have been hewn of rock. His jaw was clenched until the knotted muscles stood out, his lips a thin straight line. The rest of the face the boy could not see for his father's eyes. Always black and big, they were now like caves into which he fell headlong. Suddenly he saw that tears were gushing down his dirty cheeks, leaving streaks through the mud. Cable sitting there on his mare, unmoving, un-speaking, but weeping in the early morning light!

"Daddy! Is that you?"

Cable, loose-jointed as a sack of meal, seemed to fall out of his saddle and on his knees. His long arms swept the boy to him, head on his shoulder. His whiskers scratched, his tears splashed down the back of the boy's neck. He didn't say a word.

All morning they watched the man and dog marooned on the laundry floor. Mr. Pike kept waving his hands for help, but poor little Foxy didn't know what to do. He'd take a step one way and peer down into the raging torrent, then turn around to look down on the other side. Some cowboys on shore were waiting with lariats to lasso the machinery when the river went down, but the floor rose and topped them both into the river. Mr. Pike disappeared instantly, his body to be recovered twelve miles downstream three days later. Foxy was washed toward shore and lassoed by the cowboys.

About noon a crowd of Navajos came, bringing a bedraggled and unconscious old man. It was Mr. Monta who had jumped from the roof and had been washed to a mud bank. For a long time Mrs. Aldridge worked over him. He was still alive but he had lost his mind.

That afternoon they all rushed out of the hospital again. The river was going down, revealing a black clump stationary in its flow. It was Mr. Timmons clinging to the top of a tree, somebody said, looking through field glasses. Not until next morning could the men lasso and yank him ashore, more dead than alive.

Matie was in the first boat to cross the river after the flood had receded. She brought food and coffee for all — and a big hug for Frankie Damon who had saved the lives of the Mission children. "I don't have a single pinch of tobacco for you, Frankie! But you'll get more than that when I tell Mr. Shelly and everybody else at the Agency what you've done! We'll find a better place for you, with good pay too!"

Cable, holding March on his lap, looked up. "I know a place you'll like, Frankie — mine, at Shallow Water," he said quietly. "Once there, you'll never want to leave. Can I take you down?"

Matie stared at him a long time. "I - I thought you were staying, Jonathan, and Ona might be coming down, and March would stay with me while he went to school in town. I wish you would, Jonathan — on account of Bruce. Shallow Water needs you, and Frankie too."

Cable looked out into the desert. The sky was clear; the outline of a distant mesa was etched against the horizon; stars were coming out bright as silver buttons. He hugged March more tightly. "I reckon not," he said with a slow smile. "Son and I — Mother needs us both, and we need her, don't we, March? We're going home, Matie."

And yet on that first morning home, when he rose and looked out the window, it was with a feeling he had turned his back upon something that would haunt him always.

Henceforth that high Peak gleaming pale silver with early snow was to encompass his life and hopes: its bare frost-shattered granite slopes cutting him off night and day from the world below; the clank of machinery and the creak of the cable the only sounds penetrating the cloying darkness within; and the cold slimy walls of the stopes, resistant and enduring, mocking the futile expenditure of his

strength. There would be Jake and Abe, simple-minded orphans
without roots in fertile earth, hard-rock men in every sinew. And
Rogier, warped and unpredictable—a man, he knew now, who
would stop at nothing until he had plumbed the utmost depths of his
folly.

Behind him lay Shallow Water, a flowering of something atavistic and dormant within him. For there did exist, always, that one
earth whose unique place-rhythm found an echo and an answer in
every man, as if the soul of each race and tribe had been fecundated
with the mystery of its own earthly womb. And he who had been
long away or returned for the first time to the earth of his flesh felt
then the deep and wordless but triumphant cry of his inner self,
"Home! At last I am come to home!"

He felt like Cable the fierce proud morning break open the eyes
of his soul that had never seen before. He saw the lofty amphitheatre
of sage-gray desert tilting upward to the pine-studded foothills and
hemmed by the immense wall of the Rockies in their curve: blue as
smoke, blue as chalcedony, blue as turquoise. In the splendid terror,
in the wild silence, in the cruel and magnificent clarity of the day,
everything stood out pure, serene, virginal. So new! And yet so
immeasurably old that it was as if he had known it all long, long
before. In the house made of evening twilight, in the house made of
dark cloud—in summer sun and winter snow, he remembered it all,
all like a wordless voice, like the voice of an inner consciousness.

For what had he forsaken this manifested outer form of his
secret inner self, this land and its people whose blood-beat was
tuned to his? Not for the cold sweaty darkness of the Sylvanite or
for the petulant, driving Rogier. He had left it and willingly, with all
that it contained of him, for that single moment when he had stood
again on the threshold of his home. When Ona had opened the door
and into his wife's arms he had gently pushed his son, alive and safe
from harm. Never, never! could he have faced her or himself, had he
stood there alone.

And so late that October he picked up his duffle bag and strode
off toward that high snowy Peak—strode off like Sister Molly's
Tom, Rogier, a thousand others, all loved by someone like her who
sat behind uneasy and troubled by disquieting dreams but powerless
to do aught save smile and hope and wait.

PART III

SYLVANITE

1

Now, late in the afternoon of a sunny spring day, Rogier sat on a rickety chair in front of the Sylvanite hoist. The wooden shanty, cluttered with tools and muck-smeared overalls hanging on the walls, and rank with the smell of an open carbide can, was cold as an ice box. The door was open and across the greasy planks of the threshold the western sun lay thin and yellow. Rogier stamped his feet, slapped his gloved hands, and continued staring fixedly at the big hoisting drum before him.

At the sound of a bell he jerked erect and let out the big lever to his right. The huge drum began to revolve. He watched the black steel cable swiftly unwinding, layer after layer of coils slipping off smoothly from right to left. The old cheap hoist was without an indicator; he watched instead for a bright mark chiselled on the greasy steel rope indicating the layers unwound. When it flashed into sight he drew the lever toward him for half-speed and stood up to look over the high reel.

The window glass of the shanty was cracked open. Through it the long line of cable inclined upward to the top of the gallows frame outside, revolved in the pulleys, and stretched tautly down into the open shaft. In a moment the rusty half-ton iron bucket rose into sight above the shaft collar. Rogier jerked and locked the reel lever, dutifully pushing a wooden peg in his punchboard to indicate the bucket was up.

Now, after maneuvering the bucket to the wooden ore chute, he pulled on the catch and listened to the dull rumble of more than a thousand pounds of ore sliding down to the sorting dump. Outside he could see Cable, bundled against the wind, standing on the runway behind his empty little tram car.

"Hey!" Rogier shouted through the window. "You keepin' track of all these buckets?"

Cable nodded curtly.

"How's it sorting?" he yelled again. "I want some good samples!"

Cable nodded again; and scraping out the chute, went on with his work.

Rogier swung the bucket free again, and ringing his bells, lowered it to Abe and Jake working below. Then marking his punchboard, he relapsed into another cold half-hour's wait. Up the trail he could glimpse the stout log cabin and the neat corral of green aspen poles for the shaggy burros used to pack in supplies. Compared to these works of axemen's skill the surface plant in which Rogier sat was not much to look at, but it was sound. Sound as a bottom dollar! The timbers of the gallows frame were of well-seasoned pine; the shaft was cribbed for the first fifty feet; the dump was held on the slope below with heavy log baffles.

Little it mattered to Rogier that the plank shaft house and tool shanty looked like backhouses in Poverty Gulch, that everything was covered with muck and dust. He had not installed a single line of electric lights; the men were compelled to use carbide lamps. Nor had he put in a compartment shaft or cage. The men had to be lowered in the empty ore bucket, coats over their heads to keep out the drip of water. The huge iron boiler that had been so laboriously hauled up the trail still sat unused on its frame. Rogier had been in too much of a hurry to install a hoist engine. He had brought up a light gasoline engine to run the hoist; it would require less time than for the men to cut wood.

No, nothing mattered to him if the plant was good enough to

pass inspection. His one concern was to go down, down below grass roots. And so he had. Abe had found the new lead perhaps a hundred yards from the old outcropping which had petered out. The vein dipped downward at a steep angle. Abe had proposed another inclined shaft along the plane of the vein, but Rogier held out for a vertical shaft. Dom the expense! It would give him the greatest vertical depth for the least footage. And measuring the dip of the vein he had stepped off the site of the shaft house and gallows frame.

Sinking the shaft vertically, they had established station levels at 150 and at 250 feet, making crosscuts eastward to intersect the vein. For a time they had taken out shipping ore—a fair grade of sylvanite. When this gave out Rogier had sunk the shaft still deeper and repeated the process: establishing levels every hundred feet and cross-cutting into the inclined vein again. Anything to get down, down! Thirty to forty dollars a foot through solid granite meant nothing to him if only he could feel himself sinking, sinking down into the depths of that resistant and enigmatic Peak which forever plagued him.

The windfalls of money from Cable, Boné, and Timothy had given him the means; he was down now to below 450 feet, and figuring how to go down another hundred feet. But to get money for it, to keep Abe and Jake from grumbling, and to appease Cable and the family, he had to strike more shipping ore. And for that he was dependent not only on the Sylvanite, but on the whole Cripple Creek District.

Abruptly he picked up the binoculars from the floor beside him. Adjusting the screws again, he stared once more out the open door and down the gulch toward the far rise of Battle Mountain.

Cripple Creek, the "$200,000 Cow Pasture," in its first decade had produced with its 475 mines more than $100,000,000 worth of gold from an area of scarcely six square miles. In those ten years Rogier had watched the annual production jump from $200,000 to the stupendous amount of $18,149,645—and that barely scratched from under the grass roots.

Then had come the turn of the century and the turn of the tide for Cripple Creek. What now in the last ten years had happened to the district?

The labor strike had called the turn. During the disorders, with mines closed and mills shut down, the production had been cut almost in half. Gradually the mines had opened up again, new ore discoveries were made, and mills were running overtime. But still production kept dropping: to $14,000,000; $12,000,000; and last year to $10,562,653. And worse: to get $10,000,000 worth of gold now it was necessary to treat 756,900 short tons of ore as compared to only 451,082 four years ago, so greatly was the value of the ore decreasing.

If to the decreasing population of the greatest gold camp on earth this was indubitable warning that the gold was petering out, it only confirmed the secret and unalterable conviction of the white-haired, erratic, and cranky old man who now sat in the rickety hoist house of a temperamental mine staring through his binoculars at the imposing surface plants on Battle Mountain.

His former carpenter Winfield Scott Stratton, the late and world-renowned Midas of the Rockies, had believed that all the gold veins in the district converged under Gold and Globe Hill. To monopolize this center he had spent $7,000,000 of the $10,000,000 he had received from the sale of his Independence in buying up more than one hundred claims and control of eight mining companies, practically one-fifth of the whole district.

How wrong and foolish he had been! Now, scarcely ten years since his death and the collapse of his stupendous scheme, his theory had been proved false. Why, his multi-million dollar properties on Gold Hill were producing less than eight percent of the district's output! The greatest producers were still the Independence, being gutted of another $10,000,000 by its British owners, and the fabulous Portland. These and the other mines on Battle Mountain were producing almost forty-three percent of Cripple Creek's gold. And Battle Mountain rose directly across the grassy valley down which Rogier looked from his lofty perch; a signal mountain located on the shaft of that arrow whose point struck deep into the high gulch on the slope of Pike's Peak where he now sat!

Years ago he had divined the goal of his impassioned quest. There had not been one vast upheaval through the granite walls of the ancient volcano. There had been several different blow-offs; and of the many pools of eruption, that on Battle Mountain and Bull Hill was only one. The last and greatest pool of all still lay hidden beneath the solid granite where the eruption had not been able to break through. And where was all that superimposed granite thicker, deeper, more resistant than on Pike's Peak itself? Pike's Peak, the culminating point, the highest stub remaining of the great extinct volcano which had towered so high in the skies!

If it seemed inconceivable that no one had thought of it, it had revealed to him with cosmic perspective the vast subterranean world whose life went on unceasing and unhurried beneath his feet. A life that in turn gave life to plant and bird, beast and man. An earth that like the sea flowed in rhythm with the moon and stars, obeying the same unknown universal laws that kept the sun in place, maintaining an isotatic equilibrium under which mountains crumbled and washed away, old sea floors subsided under the weight of their conglomerate ooze, and new mountain peaks rose with sea shells on their summits. It was a revelation. He could almost feel beneath him that great arterial fountain bursting from the mysterious hot center of his earth. And he—he only!—was boring down, down through it to the living heart of the Peak itself.

Occasionally an old-timer would stray up the gulch to the Sylvanite. "God A'mighty, man! Don't you know this here workin's too far north? Granite, plumb hard-rock granite. You won't find no gold here!"

Rogier, imperturbably chewing on his cigar, refused to answer a single question. With a face indomitable and serene as one of granite, he pulled the lever which again released the ore bucket from the chute. It caught on the shaft cribbing; he stood up and yanked at the chain until it was free and dropping swiftly down the shaft. "Get down! You!" he muttered masterfully, throwing the lever to high speed.

Punctually now at four-thirty, as every afternoon, sounded the three-bell signal which meant passengers coming up the shaft. Rogier, with a slight frown, slid the hoist lever to slow speed and watched for the ore bucket to rise above the shaft collar. The rusty iron bucket was of half-ton capacity suspended on steel cable capable of lifting forty tons in compliance with the safety factor required by law. It was nevertheless too small in size for two men. Jake squatted in the bucket, arms in and head down. Abe stood on the rim, one hand holding the supporting cable, the other gently pushing against the cribbing of the shaft to prevent the bucket from revolving and crushing him against the timbers. Hoisting them was a slow process. One saw first the bent head of Abe with his metal hat dripping slime, then slowly his spread legs and between them the muddy face of Jake blinking eyes at the sunlight. Cable, up from the dump, was on hand to steady the bucket while they climbed out.

"Kind of early, ain't you, boys? It's still the middle of the afternoon," said Rogier.

"We've always quit at four-thirty and we ain't goin' to stop now. It's regular," answered Jake, putting out his lamp. Neither of them reminded Rogier that since early morning they had been working down below in cold and damp and darkness, drilling, mucking, tramming — doing the work of four men; he wouldn't have been satisified with a twenty-four hour shift. Both crawled out of their jumpers, kicked off their boots and stood rubbing their hands.

There sounded underground a sudden dull rumble, followed by another. The last thing before coming up each night, Jake set the blasts; the dust would be settled before work next morning. The four men continued talking. Standing before a long plank shelf, they inspected the ore Cable had brought in — a chunk from every bucketful that had come up the shaft. They selected samples to thrust in Cable's small canvas sack. Carrying this, Cable walked to the corral and straddled a burro. It was his last job each night to ride down the gulch to a box nailed on a fence post. Scattered throughout the district were hundreds like it. They were the boxes in which were left the day's samples from the mines for the assayer to pick up on his rounds.

Arriving at the Sylvanite box, Cable drew out the limp sack used the day before. In its place he stuffed the laden sack brought with him and jogged back up the gulch. The sun, just sinking below the mountains, flooded the high open meadow and lit up the tips of the highest peaks. Below in the canyons it was already dark. Only the snow patches among the pines gleamed palely as shards of moonlight. Wondering what the previous day's run had assayed, Cable stopped the burro and drew out of the sack a slip of paper. The flare of a match lit up the figures on it.

"Doggone!" he said to the burro. "The Old Man will be glad to hear that. It might give him an appetite bigger'n a canary's."

Thrusting paper and sack into his pocket, he dug his heels into the little one's ribs. The burro continued mincing along. Cable leaned to one side, tore off a willow switch. "Now you get along! Jack!"

Under the switching the burro pattered quickly and daintily up the trail, Cable's long legs dangling almost to the ground. A fire was going in the cabin and the men were just sitting down to supper. Cable tossed the assayer's report in front of them. "It isn't high, but we can start shipping," he said, washing in the corner. "Abe, I told you you were sending me up some better looking stuff."

Abe looked at the figures. "Humph — .74 ounce ore! We had a full ounce showing on the level above. And how long did it last?"

Jake swiped his mouth from elbow to wrist and picked up the slip. Even to his slow mind the figures represented something more than intelligible news. "We git maybe $15 a ton. It cost us $8 to mine and treatment charges run close to $5. I reckon that leaves us about two bucks a ton and we got to haul it down the gulch to the siding. Slow pluggin', I say."

Rogier, at the head of the table, had been angrily and impatiently listening to Jake's long monologue, watching him scratching his head and biting his nails to aid his laborious calculations. He could restrain himself no longer.

"Give me that paper!" he shouted, leaning forward to sweep it with an eager glance. "Three-quarter ounce ore! The average of every ton shipped to the mills from the whole district. What in Sam Hill's wrong with you fellows? A man would think you were sittin' at a wake."

Abe gave him a curious glance from his mild blue eyes. Then opening a half-dozen biscuits on his plate, he began covering them with a stream of black molasses. In the lamplight his bald head glistened like a billiard ball. His shirt front was open; under his beard his massive chest was white and hairless as a baby's. The muscles of his arms moved like ropes as he wiped the rim of the can with his forefinger, set it down, and went on eating in a passive silence that gently rebuked Rogier's noisy exhortations.

"Yes!" Rogier was yelling at Jake. "I told you it costs about $8 a ton to mine. But that's the total cost of mining development, sorting, and every other dom thing. Now that we've got our shaft and plant it costs us only $3 stoping to get it out. That's why half-ounce ore has always been good to mine."

"Maybe Jake's hit the nail on the head," interrupted Cable. "All that money for development has been paid out and ought to be included, raising the cost to $13 a ton milled, easy. This is a business we've got to make pay."

Rogier's face flushed under his white hair. He brought down his fist on the table so forcefully that the plates and saucers rattled. "Business! Who told you this was a business? This is a mine, and more too. It's a shaft to Hell if I can get her there! There's going to be no fool business cluttering up the Sylvanite. Get that through your head."

The silent, shocked surprise that greeted this heresy made him pause a moment. "It beats me how you boys could figure such a thing," he continued in a lower voice. "All that development is paid for. Way behind us. We can't let the past drag at our coattails. We've got to look ahead. See? A good sound plant, and hundreds of tons of three-quarter ounce sylvanite costing only $3 to stope and $5 for treatment, leaving us a tidy little profit of $7 a ton. Money all the way around, eh boys?"

Cable pushed back his plate and lit his pipe. With a dark expressionless face he listened to Rogier with incredulous amazement. By no effort of his will could he make himself believe this was the man who, when he had come to Colorado, was leasing two of the biggest mines in the district for $10,000 a year apiece. Mines with miles of underground workings and double-compartment cages taking crews below in three shifts. Mines he had given up for this erratic and remote working that at best produced ore that might bring a dollar or two profit on the ton.

"Yes, sir!" Rogier was saying, jabbing at Jake with his fork.

"You don't say, Colonel!" Jake was muttering, his eyes wide with childish amazement. "I'll swan! Wouldn't it beat the band?"

"I'll stake my bottom dollar on it, Jake. A thousand feet or more down. Then one day you'll lift your pick and break into a stope that'll make Aladdin's Cave look like a junk shop, that'll blind you with a radiance brighter than a May sunrise. Ore, Jake, the world has never seen. In crystal formation. Glimmering like glass prisms. Stuck to the walls like frozen drops of water. Hanging from the ceiling in icicles of solid gold. Glistening on the floor like sands of crushed jewels. So precious you'll get down on your knees and scrape it up into little canvas bags. Not by the ton. By the ounce! By precious little pinches between your fingers. God Almighty, man! Can't you see it?"

Suddenly aware of the deep silence becalming the room, he turned around. Cable, dish towel in hand, was standing motionless at his shoulder. Behind him Abe had stopped trying to unscrew the cap from a bottle of horse liniment. No trace of a smile lurked at the corners of their mouths; no echo of disbelief was reflected from their eyes. Rogier stood up and faced all three men.

"Have you ever known me to deliberately falsify?" he asked in a calm voice resonant with that fey quality which imbued his profound conviction. "What I have just said is not idle fancy. How I know it I don't know, save that I already see it and feel it within the touch of a pick. Here in Cripple Creek will yet be found the greatest ore deposit that the world has ever known. A treasure greater than Croesus ever took from the sands of the Pactolus or Solomon from the mines of Ophir." He stared deliberately at each of the three men. "And it will be here in the Sylvanite. Under our very feet."

With an abrupt snort he broke out, "Jake! For two nights running you've forgotten to lock that tool house. Good God, man! We just got through layin' in a supply of hand tools."

"Yes sir, but nobody ever comes up here and the coyotes can't eat picks, Colonel. I — "

He went out the door followed by Rogier.

Cable finished his dishes. Smoothing out the wrinkles, he neatly draped the wet cloth over a chair. Abe was standing in front of the fire in his long underwear and massaging his leg with liniment.

"What's the matter, Abe?" Cable asked quietly. "Aren't things up here going all right for you?"

Abe nodded his bald head. "The Colonel ain't so steady as he used to be, is he?" He squinted at his knotty muscled leg, then with horny hands resumed his patient rubbing.

Cable did not reply.

2

With Cable up at the Sylvanite most of the time, Mrs. Rogier besought Ona to move down with her. Ona demurred; she wanted her own home. But she did move closer to the old house on Shook's Run in an old-fashioned clapboard shaded by cottonwoods. It was set on the street parallel to the high railroad embankment through which was cut an underpass leading down Bijou Street to Shook's Run.

The location had its disadvantages. Passing trains marked off the hours. One heard first the shrill blast of the whistle at the grade crossing two blocks north. Then with a rush and roar the train swept by, shaking the house until the very dishes rattled, raining cinders on the roof and stripping the cottonwood branches of the last clinging leaves. A minute later came the piercing scream of brakes as it slowed down at the station. If it were a northbound train, the agony of its passing was more acute and prolonged. Heavy freights required a helper on the grade; and the two engines, belching smoke and buckling the cars back and forth as they tried to get under way with a full head of steam, seemed trying to jerk the train in two. On rainy days they let out a steady stream of sand on the slippery rails, the spinning wheels grinding it to a shower of sparks that could be seen a block away. Most of the neighbors were railroad people. Under their influence March and Leona were soon calling out, "10-5! Number 6 right on the dot!" when the train went by.

Yet all this sound and movement was muted for March by that snowy Peak rising at the end of Bijou. "Is that where Daddy's working, way up there in the sky?" he would ask his mother.

"On the left side, just a little way down the south slope from the top, son."

"Ain't I ever goin' to get to see his mine?"

Ona ruffled his tousled hair. "When school is out, if he'll take you, maybe you can go."

And sure enough he went; and until his dust had given up its share of native granite it would still be there unchanged, not so much a landscape as a state of mind that opened in full bloom at his first look: the high bare hills seamed with gulches, hirsute with gallows frames, smokestakes, and shaft houses, corroded by glory holes and splotched with ore dumps; the shabby little towns cluttering the gulches with squalid shanties and whose stubby streets were blocked by canyon walls or mountainous tailing dumps; the refuse-laden gullies below and the dizzily winding roads and railroad spurs above; the pale sparse aspen groves and dark patches of pines, the clouds filling the canyons; and rising above all, the snowy summit of the Peak itself. He heard the snorts of the 2-8-0 iron ponies clawing their way up from Phantom Canyon on the Florence and Cripple Creek narrow-gauge and the puffing of a bigger 4-6-0 Ten-Wheeler on a spur; the dull, resonant roars of underground blasts; the tinkle of a honky-tonk piano. He smelled the yeasty buckwheat cake batter working in the buckets on the back stoops, the smell of raw whiskey spilled on a bar. Stark of outline, shamelessly blatant, and always crude, the district still carried inexplicably something of the romantic and unreal; and like the memory of a loved face it was always to reflect the unchanged vision of a boy of those years who saw neither its beauty nor its sordidness, but only its ever tragic freshness.

When he finally arrived at the Sylvanite, Jake and Abe had just come up the shaft. Besmired and unshaven, in boots and overalls, they stood blinking in the bright sunlight at the brass-buttoned little cowboy Cable held by the hand. "My boy, the one I been telling you about!" he said proudly. "Reckon you can put him to work?"

They nodded stiffly, without speaking. Rogier came out of the shaft house. He walked around the boy, looking at the thin leather chaps, the shiny tin buttons, the colored kerchief around his throat. "Great God! What's this?"

"My new cowboy suit," said March. "Mother bought it for me so I could ride the burros."

Rogier scowled. "Don't expect to wear that fol-de-rol around here. You'll get those chamois skin pants wet and freeze your little bottom off. And those boots — where's your rubbers, boy?" He snatched the hat off March's head, slapped it on again. "The first time you go down the shaft the wind'll take care of that. Humph! Mad as March, like I always said."

That evening after supper Rogier retired to his own corner of the cabin. His bunk was along the east wall, and at its head in the corner was a small table covered with papers. Here he spent his evenings puffing on a cigar and figuring. Cable washed the dishes and March wiped them. Jake sat at the big center table reading his newspaper with moving lips and forefinger. Abe, shirt and shoes off as usual, squatted on a chair close to the fire. Across his lap lay an old pair of dungarees gone through the knees. These he was reworking with a solemnity as forbidding as Rogier's absorption. From time to time he threaded his needle, squinting through the eye like a marksman taking aim at a difficult target.

Cable and March sat down and played checkers. No one spoke. The flames crackled, a coyote howled. Every once in awhile Cable let out a tiny, irritating cough. And sitting there in the silence the boy was reminded of the trading post at Shallow Water. There too had been solitude and silence, the kind but blunt companionship of only men. But everything there had seemed so vibrantly alive and resilient, so subtle and rhythmic. Here he sensed an ungiving hardness, a tautness in the very air. What this difference was, as between adobe and granite, he didn't know. "It's kind of like Shallow Water, isn't it Daddy, but different."

"I reckon so," Cable replied carelessly, with a tiny cough.

Later, when March crawled into his bunk, he whispered to his father, "I don't think Jake and Abe like me. Abe hasn't said a word or even looked at me."

But in the morning when he rose, there on a chair beside his bunk lay a little pair of dungarees. Abe, sitting up half the night, had cut down his old pair to fit him.

In these he went down the Sylvanite.

Those big resplendent surface plants, the great steaming boilers and electric dynamos, the hoist operator sitting enthroned before his double drums with their indicator dials and winking signal lights, the two-compartment shafts and cages filled with men, the electrically lighted level stations and miles of tidy drifting— "Why, Granddad, your mine's not as big and nice as the Mary McKinney, is it? Daddy took me down it with all the tourists when the train stopped, and it had electric lights and everything."

Rogier slammed back the hoist lever, stood up to see over the greasy cable reel, and rang his bells with a frown. "No, by Jove! We're not runnin' a tourist excursion. When you go down this hole keep your head down or you'll get some sense knocked in it."

March watched his father scoop up a handful of carbide for his lamp and add water, saw the narrow pencil of flame spurt out and hold steady when he applied a match. "Come on, son." The ore bucket was lowered to the shaft collar. Cable lifted the boy in and stood on the rim holding to the cable.

Slowly the bucket began to descend, sliding down the slimy cribbing to straighten out into a vertical drop. Crouched in an inch of water at the bottom of the rusty iron bucket, March stared upward at the fading light. He could barely see his father. The jagged rock walls dripped water, seemed to bump against the bucket, and oozed a cloying coldness that penetrated his thin jacket. He shut his eyes, still feeling earth and darkness rushing upward. "Level Number One!" called Cable's reassuring voice. The boy opened his eyes to see a blank hole shoot upward. At the fifth hole the bucket stopped.

Jake came pushing a little iron car down the narrow tracks. March stood back against the wall, watching the two men load the ore into the bucket. Then he followed them through a long dark hall into a slope almost as big as the bedroom at home, where Abe was mucking.

"What keeps the roof from falling down?" he asked apprehensively.

"Hard rock," said Jake. "It don't need no timbering."

"Where's the gold?" he asked again, looking vainly for chunks of glittering metal hanging from the walls.

Cable and Abe were on their knees, tracing downward a thin

grayish blue streak in the wall. Cable took his pick and broke off a piece that crumbled between his palms. "Heavily oxidized, isn't it?"

"Never know what we'll run into," said Abe, "As crazy a workin' as he ever said it was."

Cable frowned, then turned to March with a smile. "There's the gold vein, Sonny. Jake and Abe follow it wherever it goes. See those holes they've drilled there? That's where they'll put the dynamite tonight. Tomorrow they'll shovel all the blasted rock into the bucket to send it up to me. I'll sort out the ore that holds the gold to send to the mill. The rest I'll throw on the dump. See now what makes dumps?"

"But don't it get all mixed up, Daddy?"

"Oh, sure. That's why your granddad needs me to sort it, even though Abe and Jake do all the work! Now come on. Let's don't interfere."

Even as they turned away there began the deafening sound of the drills. Dust filled the stope. March began to cough. Just as they reached the level station there was the sound of bells. Jake and Abe came running.

"What's the trouble?" they demanded. "It's not noon yet!"

Cable and March went up first and waited for Abe and Jake, then all four walked into the hoist house. "What's up, Colonel? Ain't nothin' wrong?"

Rogier locked the hoist, picked up his binoculars, and walked out to the dump. Here he squatted with the others gathered around him, staring fixedly through the glasses at the bald summit of Pike's Peak. Even with the naked eye one could see the tiny jet of smoke from the cog-train crawling up the slope.

Rogier passed his glasses around. "It's June 17th and near high noon, isn't it? Well, if the Maharajah can realize the significance of the Peak, I reckon we can knock off work a little early and meditate with him. We need it, so close to our work we forget our real purpose."

All three men knew what he meant, remembering the article in the paper. The Gaekwar of Baroda, illustrious Maharajah of India, was stopping in Little London with his retinue on his trip around the world. Today he had chartered the cog-train to the summit of Pike's Peak, one of the famous sacred mountains of the world. He had requested the officials to prohibit anyone else on top for the duration of his visit. For at high noon he was going to kneel for a half-hour on a golden rug and — so close to Heaven — commend himself and followers to the mercy of Allah.

Yes! That mighty potentate of the East was not too humble to render obeisance to the divine will on this great manifestation of its living power. They themselves could not do less, Rogier had declaimed; they who also vibrated in unison with the pulse of that mighty heart into which they were driving so relentlessly.

Nor now at the appointed hour had he forgotten. Jake and Abe walked off to eat and rest an extra half-hour, followed by Cable and March, leaving Rogier alone to meditate in undisturbed silence with the Maharajah above him.

This then was all there was to the Sylvanite — cabin, corral, tool shanty, hoist house, and a vertical shaft; and March fitted unobtrusively into the hard and simple life constrained by the routine the mine enforced. By night Rogier sat figuring how to go down still deeper. By day he sat at the hoist, an inexorable taskmaster. Abe and Jake worked down below, blasting, mucking, drifting. Cable above sorted at the dump, and occasionally spelled off Abe or Jake. Upon March fell the disagreeable, homely chores: washing dishes, sweeping the cabin floor, sunning blankets, tending the burros, and running errands. Infequently he sat at the hoist, providing a helpless and unargumentative target for Rogier's vehement mutterings.

The men now selected their assay samples earlier in the day so March could ride down the gulch with the sack. How lovely were those June afternoons when jolting slowly along on his flop-eared Pike's Peak Canary, the boy gave himself to the wild and serene beauty of the long narrow canyon. The aspens had leaved, new grass was sprouting among the old. Everywhere were flowers: wild sweet peas and yellow wall flowers, anemones and fragile columbines among the pines, tall penstamons along the rutted trail, and in the flats blankets of wild orchids. Color everywhere, rich and full. Only the thistleberries white as snow remained to tell of winter. The little creek poured merrily over the beaver dam; a red-tailed hawk launched itself with a scream from the cliffs; a porcupine waddled up the slope. Everything awoke and moved with delicious abandon to transient summer, and March could feel it rush through him without restraint.

On Saturdays there came a break. Abe and Jake after work dressed up and went to town. "What do you do there?" March asked them. Neither answered and strode off stiffly in squeaking boots.

"Don't ever ask them that again," Cable said sharply. "This is the one day they can live private lives. It's nobody's business."

Sometimes they staggered home shouting at dawn. Mostly they didn't return until Sunday afternoon, morose and sullen, to lie snoring on their bunks. On alternate weekends Rogier, and then Cable and March, went down to Little London. The train rides back and forth were exciting. There were two standard-gauge lines into the district besides the narrow-gauge from Florence. The Midland Terminal crept up Ute Pass from Manitou to Divide, the summit of the continental watershed, passing the little resorts of Cascade and Green Mountain Falls with their ornate hotels. Entering the district from the north, the train detoured around Battle Mountain to Victor, and cut over Raven and Gold Hill to the brick depot in Cripple Creek at the head of Bennett Avenue. Sitting on his green plush seat, nose pressed against the window, March could hear the big Mogul puffing up the grade, the thunder of the exhaust against the blackened cliffs. He could see the smoke shooting high at every stroke of the pistons when the engine swung round the horseshoe curves, crept across the high, spidery trestles. Then entering a tunnel, the coach was suddenly enveloped in darkness and smoke and a rain of cinders.

For one of the Midland's locomotives he developed a strong attachment that began one Sunday when he was down in Little London. Cable had taken the family to Manitou for a day's outing, and they were walking up to the Iron Springs Pavilion to fill their water bottles and to buy some of its famous salt water taffy in all colors. Shortly after they had passed under the high wooden trestle by which the train spanned the narrow canyon, they were halted by the sound of a tremendous crash. Running back, they confronted a terrible sight. A number of boxcars and flats in a freight had plunged off the high trestle and were dragging down more after them. One car after another was derailed, toppled over, and plunged down to crash into kindling on the great boulders below.

"Oh my God! Why don't they jump!" exclaimed Ona.

March knew who she meant — the engineer and the fireman in the locomotive. He identified it at once: Number 60, one of the 2-8-0 mountain-climbing Moguls he had ridden behind often. "Look!" he shouted. "Old Sixty's hangin' on!"

The Mogul was indeed. Her eight drivers were clawing at the rails like a mountain cat, pistons shooting fire and smoke pouring from her straight stack. The engineer had his throttle wide open, and the fireman was sweating in a frenzy on the apron. All the cars but one had been dragged down now; and as he watched, it toppled over.

"Don't look!" shouted Ona, grabbing Leona and turning her back.

Old Sixty was still hanging on. And as he watched, the coupling parted with a loud snap. The car plunged down, leaving the locomotive alone on the rails high above.

Always thereafter March boarded the Midland with fervent praise. "It's Old Sixty, Daddy. She'll get us there!"

The Short Line was different but just as exciting. It followed the old stage road from Little London, climbing up the steep canyons behind Cheyenne Mountain. No resorts, just scenery along the way. A trip that bankrupted the English language, President Teddy Roosevelt had asserted when he visited the district. And the scenery was easy to see, for the train carried an open observation platform on the back coach where March always insisted on sitting. Here he could hear the clickety-clack of the wheels on the rail joints below him, the squealing of the flanges on the sharp curves. Far ahead he could see the sleek-boilered Consolidation engine rounding the bend, hear the mournful wail of the whistle from the quill. High above him loomed cliffwall and mountainside. And down below on a siding in an open meadow the Wild Flower Special, a train of roofless coaches, waited for its picknicking tourists to gather armfuls of wild flowers. They were always jerked up by roots, March knew, and so wilted in the sun by the time the Special got back to Little London that the picknickers dumped them in the trash cans; but there were always plenty with more. And now again, out of this serene and yet brooding mountain wilderness, he climbed into that high granite domain swarming with human ants.

He was becoming bolder now, riding throughout the district on its interurban system during the long summer afternoons. It had two tracks between Victor and Cripple Creek: the Low Line and the High Line which on Bull Hill near Midway reached an altitude of 10,487 feet, the highest trolley point in the country, Cable told him. It was a fine ride for a nickle. He learned the hills, towns, camps, and mines; the great producers like the Independence, Portland, Ajax, Pharmacist, and Gold Coin, and those with funny names like the Pocohontas, Butcher Boy, Red Umbrella, The Ore or No Go, the Lulu, Lizzie May, and the Nameless. Like other urchins he partitioned empty cigar boxes to hold samples labelled "Native Ores of Cripple Creek". These he hawked to tourists on the railroad platform at Cripple Creek.

One afternoon there he ran into a gang of boys from Poverty Gulch, the slum of the Tenderloin. The leader, a sturdy miner's son, stalked up to him. "Where you come from?"

"The Sylvanite!" March boasted. "We own it!"

"That ain't no mine!" shouted one of the boys. "Everybody knows old man Rogier is crazy!"

"And it's over by Victor!"

This was enough for the big bully. For if the main producing area was around Victor, the "City of Mines," Cripple Creek was the oldest camp and largest town, giving its name to the district. And so between them had grown up a rivalry that extended from the most influential mineowner to the sorriest mucker. "Ain't nobody from Victor goin' to steal our customers! Let's run him out!" Knocking the cigar box of samples from March's hand, the leader attacked with flying fists. In an instant the platform erupted into a melee of fighting urchins that was broken up only by the station agent and two brawny bystanders. The boys took to their heels.

March found himself slinking down Myers Avenue. Looking back to make sure he wasn't followed, he sat down on the curb to wipe the blood and mud off his face and clothes. Behind him stood a long row of big houses with funny names: "The Homestead," "Ol, Faithful," "The Library," and "Sunnyrest." Huddling there, muddy, bruised, and miserable, he watched the ladies coming back from their afternoon drives or walking down the street. They weren't dressed in drab clothes like the miners' wives, but in bright taffeta from which daintily protruded little slippers. A plumed hat ruffled in the wind, a parasol glowed with color in the sun.

Suddenly he felt a hand clapped on his shoulder. "What's the matter, Sonny? Lost your last friend or a nickel down the gutter?"

March spun around, looking up at a slim young girl, kind of pretty but pale, and wearing a flowered dress.

"Here, you come with me," she said, taking his hand and leading him into the house behind them. The parlor was more like one in a hotel, with a red carpet, three sofas, and a potted rubber plant. In it several more ladies were sitting. One of them stood up, an older woman with sharp features who looked bossy. Immediately March took off his hat.

"What's he here for?" she demanded of the girl.

"I'm going to clean off the boy's jacket and pants a little so he can go home without gettin' the tar beat out of him."

She took him down the hall to a small bedroom and was right nice about it too. She didn't look when he took off his pants until he was in bed, and she gave him a magazine to look at while she was gone.

"There!" she said, coming back. "I scrubbed off the mud slick as a whistle. They're still a little damp but they'll dry out in no time when you get into them. 'Course your shoes are still muddy, but so are every boy's."

The older woman came in and the three of them talked a long time. "My name's Charlotte," the tall girl said. "Now what's yours?" March told her; and impulsively told her also about his father and grandfather, Abe and Jake, and the Sylvanite. He liked the way Charlotte laughed; it made him forget her pale face. And she had the funniest little wrinkles at the corner of one eye — just two of them. "And what's your name?" he asked the older woman abruptly.

"Madame — Madame Jones," the woman answered with a frown. "But you better be running along. Here's a quarter. Keep out of the mud."

March stood up. "I sure am much obliged, Madame Jones. And maybe I'll bring you some flowers, Charlotte. Daddy would sure like you too!"

The girl laughed, but Madame Jone's face got thundery. "Now boy. I don't want you bringing your menfolks here a'tall. I won't have it! And if you don't want a licking, you won't say anything about coming here."

Charlotte smiled. "Let's keep this to ourselves, just for fun. And sometime if you don't forget you can bring me two flowers, a big one for my room and a little one to wear!"

March did not forget his promise. The following week he came back with an armload of wild flowers. The Madame met him at the door with no recognition on her face. "What do you want, boy?"

"Why, it's me, Madame Jones. You remember me. I brought Charlotte the flowers."

She stared at him queerly. "Charlotte's busy." Then seeing his face quiver with disappointment, she pulled him inside the parlor. "Oh, I remember now! What was I thinking of?"

In back of the parlor was a short bar. A few men, half-drunk, were wrangling with some of the ladies. To escape the noise, said Madame Jones, March could wait down the hall in another small sitting room. Shortly afterward Charlotte came in, her pale and fragile face lighting up at the sight of March waiting stiffly in his chair with an armful of wild flowers.

Every week thereafter March stopped at Madame Jones' to see Charlotte. Sometimes she was busy and he had to wait almost an hour. There were times when they talked for only a minute before she sent him away with a quarter to spend. On other days they spent nearly the whole afternoon together. Once they were interrupted by a hoarse voice shouting down the hall, "Goddamn it! I know who I want! Where's Charlotte?" Then the boy could hear Madame Jones' hard voice calmly telling him to close his trap before she rammed his tongue down his gullet with a poker. "It's my uncle," said Charlotte, her brown eyes clouding. "He's such a noisy one!"

There were other girls living at Madame Jones': Lulu, Belle, Flora — many whose names he could never recall on seeing them in the parlor. But invariably he took off his hat, grinned shyly, and was answered with kind and hungry greetings, good-natured jokes, or by a polite civility in which he detected a hurt resentment because his loyalty never wavered from Charlotte. Madame Jones, he knew, did not approve of him; but she was always polite and whisked him in and out as if he might soil the red carpet with a speck of dust.

What held them together, March never knew. At each visit he

found in Charlotte something new. She was changeable as a chameleon: somber, tired, and listless, abnormally cheerful, or burning with a quiet vitality whose depth or origin he could never fathom. Only her pale girlish face and the astounding contrast of her dark hair and big brown eyes never changed. If her lips were violently red some days, they were hardly pink on others, and one day they were almost cold blue. She was very young, but to March at times she seemed old and weary-wise as his grandmother. He liked her best when she was a child with him, remembering familiar fairy tales. But at all times, whatever her mood, they met as friends should always meet — two lonely souls stripped of age and sex, caring little of the paths behind them and grasping the precious moment of contact from which sometime, and forever, they would be withdrawn by the mysterious and irrevocable power which swings each man and each star into an orbit which is his alone.

3

Early in June the old house on Shook's Run began to fill again. Matters between Mary Ann and her husband Cecil Durgess finally had come to a head. A divorce had not yet mantled them with disgrace, but Mary Ann had traipsed off to start a delicatessen store of her own somewhere, leaving Nancy in Mrs. Rogier's care. She was a fair-haired, light complexioned girl about the age of dark-skinned Leona who came down every day to play with her.

Two weeks later Sally Lee arrived to spend the summer. In her entourage were a beribboned baby who went by the name of Sugar Lump, a fat and pouty Negro nurse named Josephine, and a tall slim girl who was introduced as Miss Evelina, one of Sally Lee's rich neighbors. Getting out of the carriage, Miss Evelina stood with folded hands staring at the Negro boy hitching post while Sally Lee embraced her mother.

"Oh, he does need a new coat of paint! And the old house too!" exclaimed Sally Lee, noticing the look. "You know, Mother, Miss Evelina and I just wracked our poor brains wondering where to spend the summer. No one, simply no one, stays in Memphis. Then I thought, 'Miss Evelina must see Pike's Peak and Sugar Lump will adore cool Colorado.' She has a little heat rash already, our drawing room was so stuffy. Josephine, you must bathe and powder her immediately."

Mrs. Rogier watched her carelessly pass a crumpled bill to the driver. "Oh, keep the change. I do detest these silver Colorado dollars; they're so heavy to carry in my purse."

Still talking, they walked inside and sat down in the front room. "You received my telegram?" asked Sally Lee.

"All three of them," answered Mrs. Rogier. "The last two really weren't necessary. It made no difference whether the train was late. For your first visit home we'd have stayed up all night to welcome you."

"It's so much easier to send telegrams than writing letters. Why, you don't even have to write them. Just tell the porter what to say."

Miss Evelina spoke up. "Sally Lee has promised to show me the Garden of the Gods, Seven Falls, and all the sights. Says I shall like cool Colorado better than Canada and the other places where one usually summers, you know. Too, she has been telling me of Colonel Rogier and his gold mine and charming idiocyncrasies."

"Just Mr. Rogier would be better than Colonel, I think, my dear," remonstrated Mrs. Rogier. "He was never an officer, not even a soldier, and he detests all the military. And our mine isn't really a treasure chest. But we will do our best to make you comfortable." She turned to Sally Lee. "How about Sister Molly's big room for you and the baby? Josephine can sleep in the alcove where she'll be handy at night. Nancy will move her things upstairs so Miss Evelina can have the middle room next to yours."

"Of course, Mother. And see that the big redwood closet is cleaned out for our furs."

"Furs?"

"Now, Mother! You know we can't be driving up the canyons without wraps, after just coming from the South."

Mrs. Rogier did not blink an eye. She was staring at visions of Sally Lee in a skimpy gingham dress galloping by on one of Rogier's horses or climbing barefooted up the cliffs after wild raspberries.

"Josephine, you come along with the baby. I'll show you where you can bathe her." Her tone and manner showed Josephine instantly a woman who knew how to handle Negroes.

"Yas'm," she said obediently, and followed Mrs. Rogier upstairs.

A moment later Mrs. Rogier stuck her head in the middle room. Nancy was pouting on the bed. "I won't give up my room to *her!*"

"You will be very quick about it, honey. The Third Floor. And don't leave a single finger-mark on the bedrail either."

Something of her calm, decisive manner remained after she had gone downstairs and was left alone with Sally Lee. "You haven't changed a bit, Mother, but the house has," Sally Lee said defensively. "Why don't you make Daddy paint it and the Blackamoor, and re-gravel the driveway?"

"Oh, I wouldn't pester him about such little things."

Sally Lee felt suddenly abashed, as if her mother's smiling look had stripped her to her silver shoe-buckles, sheer hose, and lace-trimmed lingerie — handmade and imported from France, Aurand the darling! "But I can't understand. After all your wishing and waiting for a big house in the North End and a pair of matched bays. And teaching us always to demand the best. Nothing but the best!"

"I'm sure you will always have it, Sally Lee. And what a nice start with a husband like Aurand and your baby. I can't tell you how glad I am."

Sally Lee gave her mother a hug and backed away. She expected now, at last, a sniffle and then a deluge. There was no sign of either. Mrs. Rogier stood before her, small and slim and straight — all steel. Her eyes were clear and untroubled; and in a firm voice she said casually, "And now dear, you'd better run up for your bath. Miss Evelina probably finished ages ago."

Now alone and rocking in her chair, Mrs. Rogier looked back upon a past that would have seemed unbelievable had she not seen it preserved and reflected in Sally Lee. It was all there: her craving for a mansion in the North End and a position of social prominence, the ostentatious display to flaunt before her neighbors, her false pride and foolish vanity, the old Rogier attitude of divine superiority before man, God, and the Devil, and the placid assurance that no plum hung too high on the tree of this world's approbation for her to pick at will. Sally Lee, of all persons! Penned up in that gaunt house on Shook's Run, deprived of friends because they were too "common," and nurtured with the outmoded traditions of a vanished aristocracy, Sally Lee in every act now betrayed the pathetic snobbishness that once had been her mother's.

Mrs. Rogier, being a mother, did not condone Sally Lee's manner and aspirations; she simply ignored them as one from whom all these same foolish trivialities had been burned away. And rocking in the warm June sun, frail and indomitable, she never realized that now, stripped of pretense and faced with certain failure, she was at last a real lady.

Every day she showed it. Alert, courteous, resourceful, she began the battle, knowing the inevitable end. For Sally Lee had learned her lesson well — the insidious corruption of wealth that blinds the most sincere. Two or three times a week she hired a carriage for the day. With Miss Evelina beside her in the back seat and Josephine up front with Sugar Lump, she drove to Seven Falls, Garden of the Gods, Cave of the Winds, and up both Cheyenne Canyons. She came home laden with souvenirs: Indian moccasins and bows and arrows manufactured in Chicago, carved gypsum bookends, polished agate paper weights, spoons, little boxes of Cripple Creek ore specimens, and views of the region by the stack. That she had no use for this tourist fodder made no difference; it seemed the thing to do. She attended shows and concerts as a matter of course, usually leaving in the middle of the program. She bought clothes that hung in the closet yet unworn months after her departure. And when she needed still more money it was only necessary, after an apologetic "Dear me! How frightfully expensive this town has become!" to send a telegram to dear Aurand.

This careless extravagance she carried on at home in a delightful manner that impressed Miss Evelina with the indubitable fact that she was indeed the daughter of the owner of a gold mine in fabulous Cripple Creek. Every day she took a notion for some rare or unseasonable delicacy that was ordered by telephone and sent down in a hurry before she changed her mind. That all this bulged Mrs. Rogier's accounts to astounding proportions seldom entered her head. When it did, Rogier's gruff delight at the new dishes dispelled any qualms.

He came down from Cripple Creek every other weekend. Because Josephine was fat and black, he assumed she could cook.

After sixty years he was determined to taste corn pone that embodied all the memories of his childhood.

"I'se a nuss-maid," objected Josephine. "Ah ain't no cookin' Negra."

"Oh, go ahead and try," urged Sally Lee. "We'll all help."

They made a day of it – Sally Lee, Miss Evelina, and Josephine. Mrs. Rogier was forbidden to enter the kitchen and ordered to rest. This rest was punctuated from early morning till supper time by falling pots and clanging pans, by Miss Evelina daintily emptying the closet in search of the egg beater hanging over the dripboard, by Josephine prying into every nook and cranny with the insatiable curiosity of the black, and by Sally Lee wasting a week's groceries in cooking a miserable meal.

For of all gathered around the table, including Ona and Jonathan, no one save Rogier but acknowledged the truth of the old maxim that too many cooks spoiled the pie. Despite two quarts of champagne the ham was dry and tasteless; the candied yams were too sweet and soggy; the asparagus tips were scorched; and the whipped cream on the glazed strawberry tarts had been allowed to turn.

But Rogier, engrossed in the memory of a boy of ten eating corn pone taken off an open fire, chewed happily on his crumbling square and kept up a long harangue on Negro cooking that left no word for anyone else. Through it all Mrs. Rogier sat at the end of the table with a pleasant smile and politely sipped her half glass of wine.

Not until next morning did she have a word to say. She took only one look at the kitchen. The stove was covered with dried batter; the sink piled high with unwashed dishes; every pot and pan was dirty and the room completely disordered. At nine o'clock the carriage drove up outside. Sally Lee and Miss Evelina, with Josephine carrying Sugar Lump, came down for their drive.

"Goodby, Mother. Don't know when we'll be back. Be sure and save my letters!" Sally Lee called cheerfully.

"Just a minute!" said Mrs. Rogier quietly. Nancy behind her, almost in tears, was slumped down at the dinner table waiting for the inevitable summons to clean up the mess. "Josephine! You don't think you're going out driving and leave that kitchen the same way you left it last night, do you? If you're going to play at being a cook you're going to finish the job. Now you get upstairs and into some old clothes. I want every pot and pan scoured till it shines, the silver polished, and the floor scrubbed!"

The woman's fat pink lips pouted; she glanced at Sally Lee for help.

"You heard me!" said Mrs. Rogier. "I'm not going to tell you a second time. Now git!" She turned around. "Nancy! Put on your hat and wrap. You're going out riding with the folks to mind the baby. And see that you do mind her." Without a look at Sally Lee, she walked back to her rocking chair and picked up the morning newspaper.

Sally Lee and Miss Evelina, a little shamefacedly, slid out the door with Sugar Lump to wait in the carriage for Nancy.

Thus Mrs. Rogier began to wage that heroic and womanly battle of which she only was aware. Never once did she utter a word against Sally Lee's and Miss Evelina's extravagance, giving them her best as if it were not quite sufficient for their needs. And when in return they brought her a bag of candy or a foolish bauble she accepted it gratefully. Yet all the time she was checking her bills for the slightest error, wracking her head for ways to utilize every scrap of food so no one would realize she had used it. And alone with Rogier, she was sharp and grasping as a miser.

"Just half enough, Daddy," she would tell him, counting the generous allowance he gave her. "It's a downright cryin' shame you have to feed so many extra mouths with all your other expenses. I've made up my mind to tell Sally Lee she must do her share."

"What? And make a boardin' house of the girls' own home? The first time she's been back?"

"Well, I shall let them give up some of their running around. There's no reason for setting such a table every day. We shall all get sick with so much rich food."

"By Jove! You'll be wanting next to feed them sowbelly and beans. Never do get anything to eat in this house 'less they order it!"

"Well, Daddy, I can't pay the bills on this."

And staring at her with incredulous eyes, Rogier would storm about the vast sums he was pouring into her lap, threaten to hire a cook who knew her business, berate her for her extravagance — and end by giving her another hundred dollars; a hundred precious dollars that he might have used in the Sylvanite.

Embarrassing scene as Rogier, a little drunk, leaves the Ruxton club w/ a porter's coat on. Sally Lee mortified in front of her friend & then remorseful & unable to sleep at night. She's still a Rogier.

4

It was a hot sultry afternoon that now, just past three o'clock, was cooling off for the daily shower. Summer was ending and Sally Lee and Miss Evelina were leaving next morning. Watching the sweating Josephine strapping the last of the overloaded trunks, Sally Lee looked up at her mother. "There! I'm tired enough to drop. All I can think of is a breath of fresh air."

"It's going to rain," said Mrs. Rogier. "You'd better lie down instead."

"No! I'll tell you what. We'll order the carriage for five o'clock. That'll give us an hour to drive around. We'll stop by the Ruxton to pick up Daddy, then take dinner out. Mother, you do the calling while I take my bath. Be sure and tell the club to tell Daddy to wait for us."

"I don't believe I would," protested Mrs. Rogier. "Daddy hates to have anyone come after him, anyplace, and this is a men's club."

Sally Lee laughed. "We won't compromise him!"

Promptly at six o'clock the carriage swung round the corner and stopped outside the club. Rain was coming down in a steady drizzle. The three women waited patiently: fifteen minutes, a half-hour, and still Rogier did not come out. "I won't go in after him, Daddy or not!" Sally Lee declared with sudden vehemence. In dreary silence they continued to wait.

Of a sudden Miss Evelina drew up erect, and with a tense embarrassed face stared at the club entrance. Sally Lee looked out. As she did so there began a loud and prolonged guffaw from a dozen men standing in the doorway —

Rogier, some time before, had entered the club and asked for Timothy. He was told that Mr. Timothy had not come in yet, and that Mr. Rogier's own family would call for him there. Snorting with impatience, he flung into a far corner of the lounge and ordered a drink.

Dom it! He wanted to see Timothy now, only for a minute, and get home before his family traipsed in. Fishing out of his pocket the token he had promised Timothy, he laid it beside his glass of whiskey. They were both the same color, and both stimulants to his imagination.

The solid was a large burnished gold nugget looped by a fine gold wire whose clasp could be attached to Timothy's watch chain. Naturally it wasn't a nugget of free gold, nor was it exclusively of gold mined from the Sylvanite. How could it be! A mill didn't work that way, reducing the ore from each mine separately. Nevertheless the nugget was of gold minted from the run in which had been included a shipment of ore from the Sylvanite. There was no use explaining all this to Timothy. But he would be pleased. The thing cost enough, what with shaping, burnishing, and mounting; and it did look fetching, glowing soft and dark yellow beside the coppery gold whiskey. For that matter, wasn't it congealed liquid itself, bled from the veins of the breathing earth? Lost in his reverie before it, Rogier was startled by a hand clapped on his shoulder.

He looked up. It was Timothy who had come up with a group of his cronies. Rogier rose to his feet. There was no use thrusting the nugget back into his pocket; they all had caught sight of it. "Here. Put this on your watch chain," he said gruffly, handing it to Timothy. "And my compliments go with it."

Timothy let out a yell of delight and snapped it on his chain to dangle against his showy waistcoat. "A tear-drop of pure unalloyed beauty, man! A radiant smile from eternal darkness! It deserves a drink and toast from all of us!"

None of his companions knew of his investment in the venture, but for Rogier the cat was out of the bag. The men set up a chorus of unmerciful joshing.

"A gold nugget! Just like that, boys!"

"Where's mine? You heard me say I wanted one too!"

"Why, he has got a gold mine, men!"

To all their quips and sallies Rogier was immune, affable and good-natured. Then, as usual, somebody threw at him a serious question. Rogier answered thoughtfully, but was indignantly refuted; the man's wink to his cronies he did not catch. And now Rogier was led into a long harangue on the subject ever in his mind — the auriferous structure of the Cripple Creek volcano, its history, geology, and philosophical significance. With sly grins his listeners settled down in their chairs. The room was gray; the rain drizzled persistently down the window panes. Across the thick carpet the boy trod lightly back and forth from the bar with more drinks. The hour passed, the chimes in the lobby tinkled the half-hour. Still Rogier talked, stimulated by the whiskey and brooking no opposition.

Abruptly, his glass halfway to his lips, he happened to look out the window. Setting down the glass, he rose to his feet. "Well!" he muttered, a little thickly. "My girls have come to fetch me!"

Without more ado he hurriedly strode out of the room. Flinging on a coat and hat from the rack in the hall, he swung open the door. Behind him trooped all his listeners. At the door they stopped and set up a guffaw that could have been heard to the corner and which aroused the three women in the carriage in front.

Sally Lee, looking out, stared transfixed at the ludicrous figure of her father stumbling down the front steps in a strange hat and coat. The hat was an old derby that, as he hit the bottom step stifflegged, jolted down over his ears and eyes. He stopped to push it back. His hand caught in the torn lining of a black-and-white raincoat, several sizes too large and flopping around him like a blanket, the tail dragging on the wet sidewalk.

" 'Where did you get that hat?' " sang out one of the men in the words of the popular ditty.

"Throw her, cowboy!" yelled another. "She's gettin' you

down!"

Then a howl of glee went up as somebody recognized the clothes. "He's tryin' to steal the porter's hat and coat!"

Sally Lee reared back in her carriage with a mortified face that suddenly went white. Was this her father—this ludicrous and pathetic old Ichabod struggling in a greasy old coat like a netted hawk! Her own father acting like a fool in front of the Ruxton, and with her in plain view of all those men! Never — never! — would she be able to hold her head up in town. And to face Miss Evelina — Then she did gasp.

Mrs. Rogier was out of the carriage and swiftly walking to Rogier. She gave one level glance up the steps at Timothy bent over and howling with laughter like the rest. Then she said quietly to Rogier, "Here, Daddy, let me help you." In a minute she had disentangled him and handed the coat and hat to an attendant who had come out with Rogier's own.

He dug in his pocket for a dollar and handed it to the boy with a grin. Then putting on his own coat and hat, he waved good-naturedly to the crowd and walked out to the carriage with Mrs. Rogier.

"You'd better drive straight home, Jim," Mrs. Rogier told the driver in an even, unexcited tone.

"By Jove!" exclaimed Rogier with an amused grin. "That was the domdest fittin' coat you ever got me out of, Marthy. I figured I was caught in my shroud."

Mrs. Rogier patted his hand, and the carriage drove on in a silence unbroken by the water splashing against the wheels. Miss Evelina leaned back languidly, looking straight ahead. Sally Lee did likewise but with every muscle tense. She was biting her lip; and she too considered it quite expedient to forget the farewell supper uptown promised them all.

Now, just past midnight, she lay sleepless in her bed. Something in the familiar squeak of the Kadles' steps that she would not hear again remorselessly cracked her heart at every step. For a moment they stopped outside in the hall. Sally Lee dug her face into the pillow. She could feel upon her, even through the closed door, the condemnation of those two faithful family ghosts. They alone saw through her, knew her for the child of that old house she would be always.

She had the wild desire to fling out of bed and confess her shame to them who had known all her childhood worries, hopes, and trespasses. The clear thought of how she would look standing in the empty hall held her back. Sugar Lump would be awakened. Josephine would be angry and sulky. And Miss Evelina in the middle room — Sally Lee, clenching her hands, lay listening to the Kadles' footsteps retreating down the stairs.

Too late! For tomorrow morning she was going home. And not until now, with that devastating picture of the afternoon before her, had she realized how much she loved her father. Roll and toss as she might, she could not shut out the vision. But strangely it was not his ludicrous appearance she saw now. It was the calm, unembarrassed manner with which he had met a perfectly normal and amusing incident. Even then, jeered at and a little confused by liquor, he had maintained, without effort and without being conscious of it, an easy dignity too sound to be affronted. And her mother — she too had acted impulsively, thoroughly right.

Nor could Sally Lee escape the memory of her own actions and the frigid manner successfully maintained all evening in front of Miss Evelina. Her last evening home!

"Oh, God," she breathed into her pillow, "Why didn't I laugh and shriek at Daddy, and jump out and fling my arms around him in a big hug, and josh him for cutting up so? Why didn't I take them all to the Antlers for a jolly farewell supper?"

She knew too well; and she could have rushed to Miss Evelina's room to rend that stuck-up nitwit tooth and nail. And all the time she knew that in the morning she would be casual and polite, and that for months after they reached home the subject would never be mentioned.

Oh, she was a coward and a fool, fool, fool! She was the same little girl in gingham who in the "poor days" had eaten little but biscuits and molasses, the freckled young woman who alone had been permitted to work out Rogier's horses on the track. What had happened to her to make her act as if her mother had all kinds of money? Not once all summer long had she taken the family out for supper, or offered her mother a dollar for expenses. But tomorrow morning she would thrust a roll of bills into her hands — and get it back with a gentle smile whose ironic meaning only Mrs. Rogier could manage! Sally Lee knew she couldn't even send a check from home. That would be worse; Rogier wasn't a man to be paid off like an inn-keeper.

Oh, she knew now how much she loved them both. When she got home she'd write often, send them expensive presents, and see that they would always have plenty of money. And the small, still voice of the Kadles' silent condemnation whispered the lie back to her heart. Back home she would drift again into the easy, forgetful life made possible by Aurand's success. She would relapse into that habit of mind which believes everyone must have as much as she because, "Dear me, how can one possibly get along on less!"

No, not then or tomorrow morning was the time to make amends. Now! This instant she would tiptoe into her mother's room and light the lamp. She would smooth back the hair from her forehead, kiss the loved lips that had scolded her so many times, and sit there with her, hand in hand, for one long talk at last.

Then, so quietly, she would sneak down the hall to her father's room. The instant she laid a hand on the door knob he would awake and grumble, "Who the devil is this, this time of night?"

"Your own ornery and contrary Sally Lee, of course! Came in to tell you I still love you and to ask when in the Sam Hill you're going to buy some new fast pacers and a trotter or two."

And he would sit up with a twinkle in his eyes. "Dom me, girl! You know the track's all gone. But, by Jove! We sent Aralee around, didn't we? And if Silver Night — Sally Lee, you go on back to bed and don't be givin' me none of those smacky kisses you give that man of yours!"

Sally Lee lay motionless on her bed. She wanted to get up and she couldn't. Dear God, she couldn't and she didn't know why. And torn between her two bitter selves, wracked by an anguish greater than she ever had known, she finally burst into blessed tears.

A half-hour later she lay quiet and limp as a wrung-out towel. For now at last she knew as a mother herself that nothing in this world could sever the bonds that held her to this gaunt old house on Shook's Run and those within it. In pride and shame, in all the misery of success and the comfort of false hopes, she was still a Rogier.

March learns the seemier side of mining —
suicides, murders, failures, & the disrespect w/
which the locals view his grandfather.
Charlotte, his prostitute friend, dies. He
goes to the funeral.

5

They were all familiar to March now as he whizzed past them
on the Low and the High Line, those great mines that had made
Cripple Creek the most famous gold camp in the world. Not only the
fabulous Independence, Portland, and Gold Coin, but the Dr. Jack
Pot, Mary McKinney, Elkton and Ajax, Strong, El Paso, Granite
and Golden Cycle, dozens of others whose tales of discovery and
production almost rivaled his grandfather's ranting prophecies of
still greater wealth to be found. Why, in the Cardinal on Globe Hill
had been discovered wire gold assaying 800 fine or $500,000 to the
ton! And only thirty-seven pounds of highgrade from the Pike's
Peak Lode had brought $11,840!

But now in the last weeks of summer March learned a new side
of Cripple Creek. It began that Saturday afternoon in Victor when
his father took him into a saloon with a long, polished mahogany bar,
a spotless mirror behind it and a glittering array of glasses. Even the
brass rail and the hour-glass spittoons were shiny as gold. Then at
the end of the bar he saw an array of food that made his eyes pop:
crisp green onions, radishes, and olives on ice, a whole baked ham
stuck full of cloves and a steaming roast beef oozing pink juice,

butter cut into little squares, rye bread and hard crispy rolls, all kinds of pickles, and slices of white or yellow cheese, and — "Sandwich, Sonny? Free lunch, you know!"

Cable had two drinks while waiting for March to finish his heaped plate. When he paid for them with a $20 bill, the bartender gave him back all his change except a $10 bill which he passed to March with the terse remark, "Here's a souvenir for you!"

On the margin of the bill, scribbled in ink, the boy read: "The last of £10,000."

Cable explained what a "pound sterling" meant on their way home, telling him about the young man who had come from England to make his fortune in Cripple Creek. Here he had spent all his patrimony except this ten-dollar bill without making a strike. With it he had bought a bottle of whiskey in the saloon, walked to Arequa Gulch and blown his brains out.

"The last of £10,000" — it was a refrain that now continually sounded in the ears of a boy who for the first time perceived that not every venture, every man, is unavoidably marked for success. He learned of the solid foundation of lost hopes and abysmal failures upon which Cripple Creek, as every other success, had been built.

There was the First Chance on Mineral Hill into which Louis Perrault had sunk three different shafts and spent £10,000 without obtaining enough ore to make a single shipment.

He heard of the death of a poverty-stricken, ninety-year old man in a cheap lodging house on Larimer Street, Denver. He was Hall A. Premo, who had just refused a settlement of more than a quarter-million dollars for his share of the C.K. & N. on Beacon Hill. Premo in the early days of the Cripple Creek rush had been rich, respected, and generous. One day he had grubstaked a down-at-the-heels prospector named Horace A. Granfield for one-half interest in any strike he made. Granfield made a rich strike on Beacon Hill, and Premo footed the bills for development. The C.K. & N. was a boomer. But Granfield, dressed up like a Thanksgiving turkey and swinging a cane, passed Premo on the street without a nod. Shortly afterward he sold the mine and went to New York to become a financier on the profits. Premo smiled wryly; it was the same old story of rank ingratitude. Yet he was still rich and consoled himself with the thought he had helped the fellow out. Then his own mines petered out, his investments crashed, and the labor strike finished him. He found himself as destitute and forlorn as Granfield had been. Granfield! He wrote Granfield in New York, reminding him of his agreement to share in the mine, begged at least a grubstake from the man he had once grubstaked. Granfield refused. Premo finally obtained a law firm which instituted suit against Granfield. Year after year dragged by. Premo was ninety years old and living in poverty when the lawyers came to him with the news he had at last been awarded $265,000 by judgment in favor of his suit. "It's not big enough — appeal the case!" he quavered. There was no time. He died penniless in his lodging house.

Often March stared wonderingly at a heap of rubbish on Crystal Hill — all that remained of the magnificent gesture of J. Maurice Finn, an unscrupulous lawyer who had served Stratton, and who had wrung a fortune from the Mountain Beauty and the Caledonia on Gold Hill. Again and again March tried to envision Finn's Folly as it had been when President Teddy Roosevelt had addressed the miners from its front steps. A three-story mansion it had been, with twenty-six rooms, and surmounted by four towers each flaunting an American flag. The grand staircase in the reception hall was elaborately carved. On the wall behind it was painted a mural of the Mount of the Holy Cross, and from one of its gulches spurted a real stream of water into a circular pool filled with mountain trout. But Finn's mines had petered out, his law practice failed. He became an alcoholic, and of all his preposterous dreams and hopes there remained only this pile of rubble.

How many stories like this there were of failure and betrayal, how many deserted mines and glory holes gaping on the hillsides like graves empty now of even foolish hopes. Yet how perversely strange it seemed to March that men pointed out these great failures with the same curious pride they directed attention to the notable successes.

The most heartbreaking failure of all, and of which Cripple Creek was inordinately proud, was the Coates Prospect Hole, owned by the St. Patrick Syndicate of Scotland. It boasted a shaft 700 feet down, and 3,500 feet of lateral work. The plant had been almost totally destroyed by fire three times. One million dollars had been expended for development. And not one ounce of pay ore had been taken out. "Not a damned speck of color, mind you!" — a statement told visitors with consumate pride.

This negative aspect of the district lent a new and disturbing significance to the Sylvanite. March began to be aware of chance phrases he heard about it and his grandfather. They were confirmed by more and more visitors coming up the gulch to see the crazy venture located so far outside the producing area. Most of them were hardy old pioneers with time heavy on their hands who had left their saloons and rooming house chairs. They were followed by a few curious townspeople expecting to see in Rogier an Acherontic, white-bearded maniac. They found him morose and untalkative, but undeniably in full possession of a blunt wit that flayed their hides whenever they managed to goad him into an argument. When towards the last of the summer a few tourists began to ride up the gulch upon hearing exaggerated tales, Rogier could stand it no longer. At the first sight of a stranger approaching he would shout out of the cracked window of the hoist house for Cable to throw rocks at them from the dump.

Cable instead erected a "Keep Out — Private Property" sign at the turning. This, for the time at least, stopped the flow of visitors. The mere appearance of brawny Abe and Jake at their Saturday night orgies was enough to halt the talk in town. Work on the Sylvanite went on as usual. If March was infected by a doubt that the Sylvanite might not be all that Rogier promised, he did not show it.

Perhaps he was dreading his last visit to Charlotte. It came as it had to come. Madame Jones let him in, nodding toward the back sitting room. When Charlotte came in, he was still standing beside the taboret, his face flushed, a distressed look in his eyes.

"Charlotte!" he blurted out at once. "I'm goin'. I can't be comin' back no more."

"But March. School doesn't start for another week. You can come two more times."

"No. Daddy's taking me down tomorrow."

The girl stood still, smiled, bit her pale blue lips. One of her thin hands gently caressed her throat in a pathetic gesture of re-signation. The boy's brown eyes clouded, filled with tears; and at sight of these, the girl's face took on an expression of unendurable hunger. Still she did not move.

"Good-bye, Charlotte. I like you — I — " Suddenly, one foot in the doorway, he blurted out with a sob, "Charlotte. You never have — aren't you going to kiss me good-bye?"

The girl, in one stride and with a face suddenly transfigured, was on him like a panther. Frail, light, and all nerves, she lifted him off his feet with unbelievable strength and kissed him with rapacious ferocity.

When finally she loosed him, the boy backed hastily away and stood looking at her with an astonishment sharpened by an edge of fear. He lifted a hand to his burning lips; one of them was slightly cut and bleeding. "I never knew you were so strong, Charlotte. You hurt my lip."

Charlotte backed to a chair and sat down stiffly. Her two hands raised to clasp her head; the long loose sleeves of her dress fell down to reveal, in the thin white sunlight filtering through the curtains, her frail white wrists through which could be seen the tracery of blue veins. Her face, from the color of wet cement, changed to a white marble. Then, giving way to the pressure of a flood of some long damned up desire, it broke into a horrible grimace of pain and guilt that disfigured forever the boy's memory of her girlish smile. "God forgive me!" she whispered. "Not you, March. Not you!"

The boy could endure it no longer. "I don't care," he shouted hoarsely with a frightened sob. "I like you better than ever!" Flinging open the door, he fled down the hall to the street outside without stopping to tell Madame Jones good-bye.

Charlotte never saw him again.

But the boy saw her once more. It came about through one of those inexplicable juxtapositions of time and place that men are wont to call coincidences, but which in long perspective sometimes reveal a deep intent. The occurence was rationally simple. Cable up at the mine had been sick, and Ona was worried. "Oh, if I only could be sure he saw a doctor or took medicines or something. He just won't buy them, I know!"

The difficulty was solved simply enough when March offered to ride up to the mine Saturday morning, promising to return Sunday afternoon. So he had taken the train with a bulky package of cough medicine, liniment, a hot water bag, and a miscellany of cold remedies.

It was late October. The bare hillsides had lost the yellow scarlet, and russet cloaks flung over them by aspen, scrub oak, and ivy. The Peak was white, the mountains marine blue — a cold, clear background against which the unpainted timbers of the frames and the shanties of the camps stood out as desolate refugees from approaching winter. March got off the train at Cripple Creek, intending to take the Low Line to Victor. Abe or Jake was to meet him there with a burro so that he would not have to walk up the gulch to the Sylvanite. The cold wind whipping down Poverty Gulch rustled the paper package under his arm. His cheeks were red as apples. He was smiling as he turned down Myers Avenue; there was just time to say hello to Charlotte.

He was too wrapped up in his anticipations to surprise her to notice the black crepe hung on the door, and the solemn row of girls sitting in the parlor. Madame Jones appeared. She was wearing a stiff black taffeta dress, long silver earrings, and a cold officious manner that set off her sharp, frigid face.

"Boy, what are you doing here now?" she demanded.

"Can I see Charlotte — just a minute, Madame Jones?" he asked, frightened a little.

"She's not here. Still over at Fairley and Lampman's. Maybe they'll let you see her," she said harshly.

The boy backed out, feeling a chill premonition congealing all thought. Slowly, as if on wooden legs, he edged around the corner, down the street. There it was, inescapable: Fairley Bros. and Lampman's Undertaking Parlors.

Somehow he managed to walk inside. The parlor for the moment was empty. A big fern hung down from a stand at the window. Several chairs stood on the plush green carpet. Then on a table he noticed a large glass case. It was filled with relics of notable people who had been laid out at the mortuary: a lock of red hair from famous Pearl De Vere of the Old Homestead, the combs of Two-Go Ruby who had swallowed strychnine, the pistol of a gambler who had shot himself through the mouth. "The last of £10,000!" flashed through March's mind.

Abruptly there exploded behind him the voice of a man who

had walked out of the morgue. "A pretty collection of doodads, hey!"

March spun around, all his insides suddenly melted. "Charlotte! Is she here? I mean — "

The man let out a guffaw. "If it don't beat all hell! Kids in knee pants, old codgers with canes, muckers, and gents. What that skinny slip of a girl had to draw'em all is beyond me!" When the boy did not answer, he added gruffly, "Sure. Till the funeral this afternoon at three. Want a look?"

March followed him to the morgue in back. He had never seen a corpse; but under the compulsion of a horror whose meaning he had not yet fully accepted, he looked into the coffin. It was Charlotte and yet it wasn't Charlotte. Her head, framed by her dark brown hair, rested on a small silk pillow; her bony fragile hands were crossed over her breast; she appeared at first to be sleeping a sleep profound and restful. It was her face that appalled him: white with a whiteness no rouge and powder could color; immobile with a frigidity that forebade anything to open eyes or lips, to crinkle those two tiny wrinkles at the corner of one eyelid. Something was gone — a mysterious something he had never thought about till now, when he first noticed its absence; the one mysterious something no man has ever fully defined.

With one wail, "Charlotte, she's dead!" he flung out the door.

Cable was waiting for him with two burros at Victor, and during their long jog up the gulch March sobbed out at last the story of his meetings with Charlotte all summer. It was a confession, for it was impacted somehow by a sense of guilt he could not quite define. "Myers Avenue? Madame Jones' place, eh?" murmured Cable gently. "I don't recollect the name. The third house from the corner, you say? Well, anyway, I reckon we better go to the funeral, son."

Dinner was on the table in the cabin when they arrived. It was a miserable meal. Abe and Jake had shaved and were dressed up in their Sunday suits of black and bulldog-toed shoes, ready to leave for Cripple Creek. Rogier was grouchy because they were taking off so early. And March couldn't eat.

Abe and Jake kept squirming on their bench. Finally Jake broke out, "Don't say nothin' more about her! It's disrespectful to keep harpin' on the dead! If we're goin', let's go!"

Cable gave them a quick penetrating look. "Is that what you're headin' for?"

"We done sent the Madame our contribution," Abe said defiantly.

They straggled down the gulch: March and Cable, still a little weak from spending several days in bed, on burros; Abe and Jake. grim-faced, striding beside them without speaking. The funeral services had begun when they arrived at Fairley and Lampman's. The small parlor was full, forcing them to stand in back for the sermon, prayer, and hymns. Not until they stepped outside did they realize the loyalty death engendered. The coffin was being loaded in an open hearse. Along the walk and behind it in the street a crowd had gathered: all the girls in Madame Jones' establishment, inmates from the other houses on Myers Avenue, people of the Tenderloin, miners and muckers and children from the shanties of Poverty Gulch.

Abe, who had bought a nosegay of flowers, thrust it into Jake's hands. He, just as abashed, edged up to the hearse where Madame Jones was standing. She gave him one withering look, and another to Jake and March and Cable.

"Well, I'll be Goddamned." she muttered, but with no other sign of recognition. "Put 'em on the hearse, you fool! They ain't for me, are they?"

Slowly the hearse moved away, followed by a dozen rigs and buggies, and people on foot. As the procession headed up Bennett, men lounging along the street, too ashamed to attend the funeral, accelerated their pace until they caught up with the crowd. Others loafing in the saloons drank up and hurriedly left the bars. March trudged along silently with Cable, Abe, and Jake. The sun was gone; a raw wind whipped coat tails and scarfs. The grade was steep. He could hear the squeak of wagon wheels in the dreary silence. Utterly miserable, he kept blowing his cold nose every few steps. Up the hill he looked back. Gray clouds were beginning to droop over the tops of Mineral and Tenderfoot Hill, and Gold and Globe Hill were hazy in the mist. Cripple Creek below him looked like a jumbled mass of toy brick buildings and wooden shanties that had been let down from the sky in a handkerchief. It was all so desolate, so dreary and cold; the boy shivered in the wind, remembering the flowered hillsides of summer. The Mt. Pisgah cemetery they now entered was more desolate still.

It lay on the slope, sparsely covered with withered brown grass. The graves were dug in the frost shattered granite, many of them blasted out of the solid rock. Each was surrounded by a picket fence to keep out wolves and coyotes. The wooden headboards which still resisted wind, rain, and snow were gaudily covered with scrolls and sentimental epitaphs.

> Here lies Richard Dunn
> Who was killed by a gun
> His real name was Pryme,
> But that wouldn't rhyme.

Nearby stood a great granite boulder with no other marking save the simple statement. "Here lies the only man who called Bill Smith a liar."

The cemetery was divided into two sections: the lower half for good, respectable folk; the upper half, on the high saddle of the hill, for the unknown and poverty stricken, the denizens of the Tender-loin. Here the procession stopped and grouped about an empty grave. The coffin was lowered. The preacher, the long tail of his frock coat flapping about his legs, finished speaking and praying. Now a group of girls began singing a hymn. One of them turned to mumble in another's ear. The Madame in front whirled around. "You there! Shut up!"

Across from them miners, gamblers, workmen and parasites, pimps and prostitutes, storekeepers and druggists appreciating the Madame's trade — they all stood there in the profound silence of the hills, attesting by their own silence the solidarity of mankind, bound together for the moment by her whose fraility was at once their weakness and their strength, the invincible bond of final brotherhood.

March, for the life of him, could not reconcile his memory of Charlotte with the body in the grave being sealed in the granite slope of Mt. Pisgah. Frail Charlotte, who with her short and awry life, her folly, grace, and alloted wisdom, was yet among the applauded and successful, the dissolute and the damned, the failures and forgotten, who had lent their lives in the desolate region for uncounted others to build upon.

The ragged hymn stopped. The grave was filled in and a few bunches of flowers placed on top. And now March saw a bare-headed scarecrow stagger up toward the preacher. From the pocket of his long coat protruded the neck of a bottle, and in his arms he bore a wooden headboard lettered in black. The sharpened end of the stick on which it was nailed he stuck into the head of the mound. March recognized him from the purple sash worn around the outside of his coat, and the brass horn stuck inside it — Joe Dobbs, the Poet Laureate of Cripple Creek.

Turning around, Mr. Dobbs pulled the bugle out of his sash, blew "Taps" upon it. Then pointing to the epitaph on the headboard, he recited:

> Here lies the body of sweet Charlotte,
> Born a virgin, died a harlot
> For fifteen years she kept her virginity;
> A damn good record for this vicinity.

The preacher intoned a sonorous "Amen!" Madame Jones with a curt, "Let's get going, girls!", herded her flock into their hired rig. And behind it, in the bitter dusk, March trudged back to town with Cable, Abe, and Jake.

Rogier worried. Sylvanite & Cripple Cr not
doing well. Takes mystical comfort in going
down into mine. Gets big construct'n job
& promises to send proceeds up to Abe
& Jake to enable them to keep digging
down. Appears Rogier wants to go to
center of earth.

6

Rogier was worried. There was no doubt the world was beginning to turn against him. He was equally convinced the world was
wrong. Julian Street, a journalist of great repute, had come to cover
the Pike's Peak region for *Collier's Weekly*. Rogier read his write-up
after he was feted and dined by the elite of Broadmoor and the
North End. To his bread-and-butter compliments, his superficial
appraisal of Little London, Rogier paid no heed. But when Street
referred to the Garden of the Gods as "a pale pink joke," he began
to smile. Rogier continued reading:

"Houses elaborate as the Grand Trianon — lend themselves
best to formal, park-like country which is flat; while Elizabethan and
adopted Tudor houses seem to cry out for English lawns and great
lush growing trees to soften the hard lines of roof and gable. Such
houses may be set in rolling country with good effect, but in the face
of the vast mountain range which dominates this neighborhood the
most elaborate architecture is so completely dwarfed as to seem
almost ridiculous. Architecture cannot compete with the Rocky
Mountains; the best thing it can do is to submit to them: to blend
itself into the picture as unostentatiously as possible."

Rogier leaned back, slapped his leg, and roared — his only laugh in months. "By Jove! The same thing I told that Mr. Andrews years ago! Thank God for one honest newspaper scribbler!" He immediately rushed out for an armload of more copies. The clippings he pasted to his own lettered stationery and mailed out to all his potential clients.

A few days later Julian Street rode up to Cripple Creek and got off at the Short Line depot. Walking up Third Street, he turned east on Myers Avenue, and was invited into a crib by a Madame Leo. He talked with her possibly an hour, then rushed back to catch his train on its return trip to Little London. Rogier, with all the district, anxiously awaited his reportage on world-famous Cripple Creek.

His article appeared that November. Of the town itself, which he hadn't seen, Street had little to say save that it was "one of the most depressing places in the world. Its buildings run from shabbiness to downright ruin; its streets are ill-paved, and its outlying districts are a horror of smokestacks, ore dumps, shaft houses, reduction plants, gallows frames, and squalid shanties situated in the mud." The Madame's remarks he reported at length, including her request to send her up some "nice boys" from Little London for business was poor. Street also casually mentioned that Cripple Creek was above "cat-line" as well as timber-line, as domestic cats couldn't live at such high altitude.

At this view of itself as seen by the unprejudiced eye of the world below, Cripple Creek set up a furious howl. Housewives and whores had cats by the hundreds sent up from Little London to prove Street's assertion false. Indignation meetings were held in churches and parlors. Protests were wired to *Collier's Weekly,* demanding refutation of the article. When nothing availed, the City Council formally passed a resolution changing the name of Myers Avenue to Julian Street.

Rogier, deeply hurt, sulked through the excitement. The world was contemptuous of Cripple Creek. The district was on the wane; everybody knew it. Production was still falling, the population decreasing. Electric cars over both the Low and High Line were more infrequent. Two men were overcome by gas in the Star of Bethlehem.

Up at the Sylvanite things were worse. Rogier was quite aware that insidious gossip was calling the mine the Pike's Peak Bubble. Even Abe and Jake kept talking of giving it up and finding a better one for him to lease. And Cable had a bad chest, coughing for hours after drilling down below with the Zebbelins, and writhing in agony each night with pleurisy. Moreover, there was no money to pay him to meet the expenses of Ona and the children. Reluctantly Rogier sent him back down to Little London for the winter.

"Just for the winter, mind!" he insisted. "We'll hit shipping ore again by spring, and need your help!"

With Cable gone, Rogier himself carried the weekly samples to the assayer's office. Grim, aloof, and dignified, he would mount a shaggy little burro and ride down the gulch, his legs dangling, his white head swathed and bent in contemplation. The errand took all day; for he no longer trusted the assayer's report, and insisted on watching the handling of his precious samples.

The assays were cheap, being simple fire assays for gold in low-grade ore instead of expensive and complete chemical analyses. Too, the assayer was an old, mild, tobacco-chewer whom Rogier could bully without rousing a frown of resentment on his placid homely face. His office was a dilapidated brick building from which one end had been torn out to make a great furnace. He usually ran through twenty to thirty assays at a firing. Rogier stuck with him to the end, shivering with cold in the outer room where the ore was crushed; sweating in front of the great furnace as he waited for the small bone-ash cups to be removed with long tongs. But never in his own cup a globule of gold and silver bigger than a pin head.

"No!" he would exclaim. "Sure you didn't get my sample mixed up with one of these others, Simms?"

The old assayer did not reply. He only sat there spitting tobacco and gazing mildly out of his rheumy blue eyes at one of a thousand men who had read their success or failure from the work of his hands. Then, with a benign glance he continued his work, weighing the infinitesmal speck and computing its contents.

"Less than a quarter ounce! Good God, man!" Rogier would snort. Then throwing down a dollar, he would stride out into the bitter dusk, straddle his mousy burro, and jog slowly back to the Sylvanite.

Supper was waiting. Rogier announced the assay, and sat down to eat in silence. In a few moments he pushed back his plate. It was time for the usual before-bedtime argument. "Dom that old fool Simms!" he began. "Reckon he's trying to pull the wool over our eyes?"

"Told you that sample wasn't no good," said Abe gently.

"You watched him run it," added Jake.

"I tell you we've got gold here!" boomed Rogier. "What I want to know now is why we're not gettin' any place?"

"It ain't you, Colonel. You're a smart man, like I always said. And it ain't us either; we do our work. What I think" — Jake looked around with a solemn expression of deep wisdom — "is that it's the Sylvanite. She's just played out. Now I was a-talkin' the other day," he continued swiftly, "and found out we could lease the Paint Brush real cheap. Just givin' up the Sylvanite for a spell."

At this Rogier's fist came down on the table with a bang. The Zebbelins had anticipated it, merely raising their refilled coffee cups. "No, by Jove! Never! You boys are stickin' to the Sylvanite till Hell freezes over! There'll be no more such talk!"

Jake, always scared half out of his trousers by the demoniacal fury in Rogier's eyes, scraped back his chair an inch. Abe dropped his glance, stroked his whiskers, and took a long swig from his coffee cup.

Rogier changed his tactics by reiterating his prophecy that here someday would be found treasures greater than Croesus ever took from the sands of the Pactolus or Solomon from the mines of Ophir. Right here!

"Ain't never heard of them fellers or mines either, and I asked about them," grumbled the sulky Jake.

"Exceeding the amount of gold Cecil Rhodes took from the mountains of South Africa, then," went on Rogier. "Deposits that will make the fortunes of Tom Walsh, Tabor, and Stratton look like a poor man's bread tax. You've heard of them, hey? Not gold *ore*, Jake, you dom fool, that has to be shipped to the mill in carloads. You remember what I told you about breaking into a stope floored with grains of gold sand you can scrape up in sacks, whose walls and ceilings are hung with gold crystals? Glistening, glittering like an Aladdin's Cave! It's here under our feet somewhere. No, boys, I won't let you leave me now. You've been too faithful and suffered

too many disappointments for that. You've got to stay and get your
share!"

At night he could not sleep, so vivid were these images he had
evoked. Tossing in his bunk, he would grit his teeth, compose
himself, and command his tense body to relax. And through the
planks of the bunk, through floor and earth and granite, from the
deep heart below, would come the measured rhythmic beat of the
cosmic pulse of the Peak. With it throbbing in his aching head, he
would get up, wrapped in his blankets, and stare out the window.

It was winter now, clear and bitter cold, the mountains white
and blue — a deep marine blue from which foamed like crested
choppy waves the snowy peaks. Hemmed in on three sides, the
little cabin looked down upon the pale and pitiless world of frozen
white. Now at night and in moonlight the long narrow gulch took
on the pale violet aspect of a frozen arm of the sea or the greenish
cold glitter of an alkaline river bed. From his window Rogier could
see the formless shadows of deer trafficking like ghosts to the corral
for scraps of hay. An owl hooted dismally from the top of the gallows frame; the faint howl of gaunt cruising timber wolves carried
over the ridge; a dead pine cracked with the cold; a cougar screamed like a frightened child; — and all these sounds seemed woven
from the same warp and weft as the eerie silence.

What made him so sure of what lay deep below? Instinct was
not enough. Nor was reason, the strata above it. But superseding
both existed that mysterious realm of intuition to which Rogier gave
full allegiance. For if the one was the perception of the bodily
senses, and the other that of the calculating mind, this was the
apperception of the spirit transcending both. A consciousness time-
less and spaceless, so limitless that it informed every drop in the sea,
every grain of the earth, every breath of air, every cell in the tiny
organism of man. Formless and unproven, denied and refuted as it
might be, he knew it for the one ground fact underlying all lesser
facts reflected from it. Yes, by Jove! It told him, over and over, what
he had always known without knowing that he knew. It told him all
he wanted to know. And every trip down into the Sylvanite confirmed it.

Getting into his boots and overalls, he would crawl into the
rusty iron bucket with his sputtering carbide lamp. As he began to

slide slowly down the shaft his troubles and worries flitted upward like the faint splotches of daylight on the cribbing. Now, dropping swiftly down, he gathered to himself the consoling mystery of the deep velvety blackness rushing up to engulf him. He took no heed of the rude jolts as the bucket knocked against the sides of the shaft, the dull somber ring of iron against stone, a flurry of sparks, the quick spin of the bucket. Crouched inside, Rogier watched over the rim the roughhewn rock glimmering in the faint light of the lamp held on his knee. He could see a micaceous glitter in the granite like that of artificial snow sprinkled on a child's Christmas tree. In the glint of pearls in the cracks he imagined that he could hear and see the slow musical drip of water from above in a silence thick, cloying and profound.

At the first level Rogier would get out and walk the length of the drift, exulting like a man returning to his native haunts. Quick, sharp, and hollow, the sound of his steps echoed along the abandoned passages, his lamp crawling through the eternal dusk like a phosphorescent bug. Always he could have flung his arms aloft with joy, feeling above him the solid mass of rock. He was below the horizon of mankind's eyes; the wrinkled crust of the earth men trod so lightly, heedless of what lay beneath; below the tides of river and sea, ever contracting and expanding under the influence of moon and sun; the dreary surface of an earth stained by men's blood and tears, fought over and furrowed—below grass roots at last! And staring upward, he fancied he saw the ends of those mortal roots of a life he had escaped at last. On top of him stood the mighty Peak—a reassuring weight that gave him comfort.

But still on the sheer sides of winze and stope he saw evidence of surface life: brown streaked rock oxidized by the carbolic acid contained in seepage water from melting snows. And he would walk back to the level station and impatiently ring the bell. Then he would go down to the second level, to the third and fourth in turn, prowling alone through abandoned drifts, stopes, and cross-cuts. And the deeper he descended, the more secure he felt. Often he hooked his lamp to the wall and stood staring into the unfathomable gloom of a cavernous stope. The darkness and silence were thick, impenetrable; they merged into what seemed a new element. Then suddenly it congealed about him as if frozen into the resistant immobility of solid rock. Now he stood motionless. The old queer sensation came upon him that he too was of that stony flesh which pressed against his own, that it too lived and breathed and echoed to the pulse of a hidden heart. He could feel its rhythmic beat, feel it close around him and adhere with the familiar and comforting illusion of adding to him another strata of being.

And now for an instant he lost his sense of balance, direction, and gravity. It was as if he were metamorphosed into a creature who, like a fly, could walk and stand head down. He faced only the earth's depths which so intrigued him: the hundred miles or less of the upper crust from which had been thrust the Peak and its shoulder mountains; the underlying 2,000-mile-thick mantle; and the vast hollow core at whose center, 4,000 miles down, lay the fiery heart which radiated solar energy throughout the arterial structure of the earth's stony flesh with a temperature of perhaps $6,000°$ Fahrenheit under a pressure of some 3,000,000 tons per square foot. The conjectured measurements meant nothing at all to him. His own divinations, like X-rays, cut through distance, pressure, and temperature without rational impedance. Rogier, dizzy with the vision that suddenly possessed him, sank down on his haunches, bent over, and held his head in his hands. It was as if he were on the verge of a vast abyss, at the perimeter of the aura of an undiscovered sun in the center of his planet, fixed and immutable within a universe duplicating the one outside.

The vision,, with all the force of indisputable truth, vehemently refuted the unsubstantiated theories that the interior of his planet was solid, molten, or gaseous. What need had his earth of another sun millions of miles away in outer space? Here it had its own. Was not every soul, mineral, plant, animal, and man answerable alone to one immutable law, and sufficient unto itself? Was there not a living world constructed within a drop of water, a grain of sand, a microscopic cell invisible to the naked eye? Let men stand alone then, self-reliant and serene in their own completeness, admitting the universality within their own earth as within themselves, and ceasing their scientific prattle of other alien worlds far off in space.

Here beneath their feet was the one disregarded mystery of all time: a vast subterranean universe upon whose surface they trod without a thought for what lay below. Where, oh where, were the intrepid explorers of modern scientific thought? Diving like frogs into the shallow seas, ballooning aloft into the air; thoughtless fools to whom the subterranean core of their own earth was so mysteriously unknown that they ignored it to conquer others! Thousands of years behind the intuitive ancients, they did not yet know that at the center of their own earth lay the golden sun of life, surrounded by its galaxies and constellations.

And crouching there in the abysmal darkness until his spell wore off, Rogier felt rise within him the power of his unalterable conviction. He would get down yet, through porphyry, through granite, to that golden heart.

Abe, working in one end of the drift, caught the tiny flicker of Rogier's lamp and glimpsed his shadowy figure staring off into the invisible depths. He walked up quietly. Rogier straightened up, and they glanced into each other's eyes.

"Quittin' time, Colonel. Let's go up."

And ringing the bell for Jake at the hoist, they rose again to surface. Suppertime came when they could not escape the inevitable.

"What we goin' to do now, Colonel?" asked Jake. "We finished cross-cuttin' like you said, and there's no more sign of a lead than of a jack rabbit in heavy brush."

"Go down another level. You'll find it," answered Rogier promptly.

"Shaft sinking costs money and you ain't got it," Abe said tersely.

Rogier jumped to his feet. "I know you haven't been paid for a month! Why don't you say so!" he screamed.

Said Abe quietly, "We ain't said nothin' about that, Colonel. We said shaft sinking costs a might of money. That's all."

Rogier sat down. "I'll get the money. I don't know how. But I do know there's an almighty power in which I trust completely. Whatever you call it, whatever it is, it won't let the Sylvanite down."

Four days later the letter came. Rogier's bid for the construction of two big additions to the high school in Little London had been accepted — a job running to almost $90,000.

Rogier was jubilant as he left to board the train. "Keep goin' down. The money will keep comin' up. Hey? I'll see you come spring!"

Cable back, but not himself. Mary Ann
back, w/ a candy shop business scheme.

7

When Cable came down from the Sylvanite, Ona was shocked
at his appearance. He was gaunt, hollow cheeked, and coughed
continually. Shaved and cleaned up, he looked worse. His high
Indian cheek bones seemed ready to protrude from a skin that had
lost its dark swarthiness and was now an unhealthy yellow. His big
dark eyes were somber and without luster. At night as he lay
wrapped in her arms, she could feel his ribs, hear his labored
breathing, feel the damp cold exuding from his pores in a per-
spiration that left his pajamas wet next morning. Only after a stiff
drink of whiskey upon arising was he warm at all.

"Jonathan, you're sick. Really sick. Please see a doctor."

"Just a cold and that pleurisy," he answered. "Nothing to worry
about."

And yet she did worry tremendously. He was not like himself
— alert and rhythmically alive, though silent, to everything about
him. He was dull, tired, apathetic. Not even their long guarded talks
of what to buy the children for Christmas aroused him.

"We haven't got much money, as you know," he said with a
quiet smile, "but buy them just what they want. Let the rest of the

folks slide; they don't matter."

How he loved his children! Always his patient smile rested upon them like a benediction; his long brown hands, once smooth and tender as a woman's but now hard, calloused, chapped, and split open, were forever finding excuses to touch them — tying hair-ribbons, lacing shoes, brushing tousled hair back from their smooth foreheads.

For days he was content to sit at home by the fire, warming, resting. Oh no! This was not her Jonathan! What business had he being confined in a cold dark mine high up in the snowy mountains? He belonged to the wide wind-swept plains he loved so well.

That Saturday, a warm and sunny one, Indian Poe, the vegetable huckster, came by as usual with his rickety wagon. He was an old Cheyenne, dark, wrinkled, with long greasy black hair. Because he and Cable long had been friends, Ona always patronized him — although, too, his vegetables were always fresh and cheap. Cable walked out to the street with Ona to see him, giving him the tribal sign. Indian Poe for answer merely laid his dark hand on Cable's arm. For a minute they talked in Cheyenne while Ona looked at lettuce and radishes. Then Poe asked in English, "Long time. Where you been?"

Cable replied that he had been up in the mountains hunting for gold. "Gold. Big nuggets, see?" Grinning, he marked the size of a marble in the air with his thumb and forefinger.

The old Indian gave him a penetrating stare and grunted. Then he reached into his wagon and brought out a clump of unwashed beets. From it he picked a lump of dirt the size of a marble and handed it to Cable. "Gold no good for Indian. This more better."

Cable laughed. Slowly his face changed as he crumpled the dirt between his fingers. "No, no good for Indian."

When Ona had filled her apron with vegetables, Cable climbed up on the plank seat to ride with Indian Poe on his rounds. Ona watched them drive off. The old Indian in his ragged coat was humped over the reins, head down. Cable beside him, in his tidy coat and shined boots, duplicated the posture. Like blood-brothers bowed under the same insupportable weight, they sat mutely staring at the plodding feet of the broomtail team.

Every Saturday it was the same. Cable made the rounds with

Indian Poe: up and down the streets, ringing a little brass bell, stopping to let housewives inspect the trays of vegetables in the decrepit wagon. Ona, upon seeing them, bit her lip. The ride was getting Cable out into the sun, of course. But God had made her a Rogier, and she could not restrain an involuntary shudder at the thought people might think Jonathan was a vegetable huckster with that ragged old Indian.

He finally got a job, but it did not deter him from making his Saturday rounds with Indian Poe. His position was that of a salesman for a life insurance company. The opening was fortuitous. The incumbent had died suddenly, leaving a section of town to be covered, weekly collections to be made, and new policies to be written. A man who could be trusted was needed at once; and that man was the son-in-law of the builder Rogier, whose work crew the company wanted to insure.

The opportunities seemed boundless. Cable was representing a fine company, associating with businessmen, and making new friends throughout a fast growing town. Ona and Cable were both delighted. So every morning he would stride off to work in his neatly pressed suit and freshly shined handmade boots. But every night it seemed he came home later. There had been a sales meeting he had to attend after work, or a prospect to talk to in the evening, or something else.

One morning the head of the office, Mr. Perkins, dropped in to invite Ona to the sales meeting that evening. It was the policy of the company, he said, to enlist the support of the wives of the representatives in the great effort being made to insure the welfare of the community. "We're all one big family, you know. We want you with us."

Ona was glad to go with Cable, and took along March. The small office uptown was crowded with the "one big family" of twelve salesmen, their wives, and a few children. Mr. Perkins, big-boned and florid, with a gold-mounted elk's tooth swinging from his watch chain, was in his element. He stood before them, making a speech like that of a football coach urging his team into battle. He expounded the prime importance of life insurance in the health, wealth, and happiness of the entire country, and the recalcitrant Pike's Peak Region. He revealed the necessity of bringing this divine message to every man and woman in the community. It could only be accomplished, he reminded them, by the constant, unremitting, and devoted work of those chosen twelve representatives who, like the chosen twelve disciples of another cause whose name he did not need to mention, were dedicated to this task.

"Every minute of the day," he thundered, "they must carry this sense of obligation to duty. Every person they meet must be regarded as a possible candidate for a policy. And when they go to bed at night, they must review in detail their accomplishments and how to better them next day. And to aid them, they need the whole-hearted, unstinted support of their wives and children — this one big family.

"The reward will be great," he continued. "We are making a sixty-day drive, and the family of the winning salesman — the one who writes the largest dollar amount of life insurance — will be given a free, all-expense-paid trip to Denver with accommodations in the world-famous Brown Palace Hotel!" He paused a moment. "Now, for the results to date!"

Mr. Perkins wheeled out from behind him a large blackboard and turned it around to face his audience. On it was chalked the names of the twelve chosen salesman with the dollar amounts of the insurance they had written up to date. Cable's name was at the bottom of the list.

Ona glanced at Cable. He sat there stiffly upright, his face impassive above his high white collar.

Mr. Perkins expostulated the virtues of Mr. Devoe at the head of the list. He reviewed the eminent qualifications of Number Two and Number Three. He kindly pointed out the methods and means by which Numbers Four to Eleven could improve their lagging records. "And now, Number Twelve, our Mr. Jonathan Cable. He is new to us. His feet are not yet solidly rooted in the ground of insurance, of life insurance. He needs our support, the support of his family who are with him tonight. And let me postulate the hope, let me prophecy, that with their whole-hearted endeavor, their un-stinted devotion to the cause, they well may rise step by step, and perhaps win three whole days, magnificent days, at the Brown Palace in Denver!"

Cable, Ona, and March trudged slowly back home. Cable went

down to stoke up the furnace while Ona put March to bed. "Was Mr. Perkins makin' fun of Daddy in front of all those people?" asked March. "Why didn't he get up and hit him?"

"On no," answered Ona. "That's business, son."

Next week Cable bought a bicycle. Having no buggy or automobile, he had found that it was too tedious walking to make his rounds. The bicycle was a short, squat one, with the paint peeling off its rusty iron, and it had no brakes. Cable had leather toe-clips installed on the pedals; in these he thrust his handmade boots — the foot fetish of every Indian. The seat was small, the handlebars high. Often March saw him peddling past school, a long, lank Ichabod from whose coat pocket protruded his long stiff-covered account book.

"He looks like an Indian who oughta be ridin' a horse!" shouted his schoolmates. "Why don't you tell your Dad he needs a haircut!"

March had nothing to say. He remembered the father he had known at Shallow Water, the dark and taciturn horseman who had faced down Black Kettle's son. He remembered the strong and gentle man who had sorted ore on the Sylvanite dump at Cripple Creek, and cooked suppers for Abe and Jake and Rogier in the cabin at Cripple Creek. And he couldn't reconcile them with the man he saw now. Cable on his bicycle and on the plank seat with Indian Poe had become another strange character in town. But when Cable arrived home at night, jumped off his bicycle, and clasped him, heart to heart, in a quick and close embrace, then he knew this was his father, his only father, the guiding hand at Shallow Water, at the Sylvanite, the strange and wonderful man who was his father whatever he seemed now.

That winter Mary Ann returned home to the old house on Shook's Run for the first time since she had left town. There was no doubt she expected to stay, for her trunk and bags arrived with her. Nancy took one look at them and let out a scream of joy. "Mother! You're back! Oh, I've been so lonesome!"

Mary Ann gave her a hasty kiss. "Lonesome? With your grandmother and grandfather here, Ona and Jonathan coming down, and March and Leona to go to school with? Why don't you run up to their house now and tell them all to come down to supper tonight? Tell them I'm back and I've got somebody I want them to meet."

When Nancy had gone, she settled down in the parlor with Mrs. Rogier for a short preliminary talk before the rest of the family arrived. The need for it was soon obvious. Mary Ann during her absence had been divorced at last from her husband Cecil Durgess. Mrs. Rogier shuddered. She had been spared the disgrace of a public court hearing, with hundreds of persons flocking in to witness the severing of bonds of holy matrimony between a member of the Rogier family and a husband to whom she had sworn to be faithful till death did them part. There had not even been an announcement in the *Gazette*; it had been simply a matter of signing some papers sent to Mary Ann by mail, or something. Still it was a blow.

"Now, Mother," said Mary Ann pertly. "It's nothing to be sorry about. Cecil was a no-account bum, and you know it. I was glad to get rid of him. And besides, divorces are dime-a-dozen these days."

She then led up to another subject just as delicate. She had brought back with her a fine gentleman, a firm friend, to stay with her until they found another and better business opportunity. "Jim's a dear. You'll love him. I met him in Salida while I was in business there — but I'll tell you all about that this evening. Anyway there's a possibility, a distinct possibility, that Jim and I may establish a closer relationship than one of business associates, if you know what I mean. That's why I think he should stay here with me, so we can all get acquainted."

"Here? Living in this house? Mary Ann!"

"A roomer, Mother. Just like Jonathan before he and Ona got married. Certainly you have no objection to that!" she said sharply.

"But wouldn't it be more circumspect if he found accommodations elsewhere?" murmured Mrs. Rogier.

"Rats! Neither one of us has much money left after settling up our business. We'll take the two middle rooms on the second floor. Nancy can move up to the third floor."

"But — "

"Good, It's all settled then. I'll have our trunk moved up there before Jim comes."

Supper that evening was something of a strain. Not that Jim wasn't a big, simple, likeable fellow. But Nancy was jealous of the attention her newly restored mother gave him, and resented giving up her room to him. And Mary Ann dominated the table with talk of her new business career. Having been married to Cecil Durgess, she had obtained from the famous Durgess catering firm many fine recipes, formulas, and trade secrets, and she had become an excellent candy maker and chocolate dipper. Resolving on a career for herself, she had opened a "Cande Shoppe" of her own in Salida. Here she had met Jim, temporarily out of work, and began teaching him the trade. Unfortunately, Salida, in the Rockies south of Leadville, was a rough and backward town that did not appreciate high quality candy and delicatessens.

"Chocolate creams with pure fruit centers, real butter instead of glucose, they could not appreciate at all," she indignantly proclaimed. "Of course I had to price them at seventy-five cents a pound. But they preferred peanut brittle at a quarter, sloppy fudge made out of cocoa instead of Swiss milk chocolate, which they could buy at any counter. And I simply refused to lower my high standards. No! Salida was not the place for me. So we simply closed up our Cande Shoppe and came here to stay until we can select the proper town."

She was a pert little woman with a face that seemed to have become sharpened of late; and Rogier, listening to her decisive voice, felt doubts that she was the shrewd businesswoman she fancied herself to be. For like most of the Rogier girls, brought up in the passionless stability and holy confines of the old house on Shook's Run, she had never betrayed any sense of business whatever. She had never been able to add up a row of figures, in fact. And this big fellow, Jim, likeable as he was, probably was no great help. Certainly Rogier would never have put him on his own payroll.

Still he viewed Mary Ann's return with something like a philosophical objectiveness. To him, high above human frailty and men's follies, she was like ore that the world had not assayed as pay dirt and had been returned home like a useless tailing. Yet he knew that a tailing thrown out on a dump might contain valuable minerals that would pay for extraction when the market price of the metal was high. So that what today was regarded as a tailing may not be such at another time.

Mary Ann and Jim settled down in the big house. Impractical and feisty as she was, Mary Ann was generous. She had brought

Nancy, Leona, and March handsome presents, and Jim could always be depended upon for a stick of licorice or a chocolate bar. That they soon quit paying Mrs. Rogier money for their board and room was not too much of a hardship. Mrs. Rogier simply kept drawing more from Rogier's advances on the High School Annex he was building. And from these large demands for household expenses, she always extracted a little to add to her sugar bowl. The time would come, she knew, when it would be their only bulwark against disaster.

8

Rogier's finally amended contract of $87,000 for the High
School Annex called for one large classroom building adjoining the
present structure and another to house the manual arts shops.
Because the grounds were located within view of North Park, the
plans had been drawn with an eye not only toward utility but also a
pleasant appearance to offset the old tower-like school. Rogier
understood it was one of his most important jobs. He was getting
old—just turned seventy—and competition from younger builders
had been very keen. Only his reputation as the town's oldest and
most reliable contractor had won him the job.

Pressed to obtain money for the Sylvanite, he jumped into the
job with abandon, letting sub-contracts as quickly as possible.
Never in his life had he gone into partnership without losing money,
and Ona warned him against doing so.

"Lighting and heating and plumbing are all very well, Daddy.
But this concrete work is different. It's pure construction work
you've always done yourself. And this man Deere you want to
sub-contract — what do you know about him?"

"Nothing except he's in the business and you're not!" replied

Rogier irritably. "Besides, I'm in a hurry and can't do everything myself!"

So he signed. The work got under way with Rogier's large construction force managed by his old foreman Rawlings, a plumbing crew, and Deere's concrete men. Deere was a fat, jovial man with small, shoebutton eyes. Neither Rogier nor Rawlings liked him and kept out of his way as much as possible. The excavations were completed; concrete was poured; stone masons and brick layers were brought in; the walls went up quickly.

As the work advanced, Deere became more and more over-bearing, stalking about the job, criticizing and applauding, over-harsh with some men and unduly familiar with others — acting in general like the lord and master of them all. This familiarity was unbearable to Rogier. He grew to abhor the sight of Deere, stalking away with contemptuous indifference whenever he saw the man approaching.

Rawlings, usually so mild and uncomplaining, remonstrated to Rogier about something Deere had done. "Why, the other night an hour before quittin' time two two-ton trucks pulled up there at the side. And there was that gosh-blamed Deere having the day laborers collect scrap lumber for him to take home! It ain't his wood. They wasn't his men neither; they were on our time."

Rogier blinked at the petty trick. Always it had been understood that on all his jobs the waste lumber was to be given to his men to haul home for kindling.

"Now, Rawlings," he said, holding his temper down, "you tell the men personally that after quittin' time they can gather up all the scrap lumber. Every jack-man can make his own pile to carry home or save until he gets a truck load. Then he can pay his own fifty cents to haul it away. That'll keep the place cleaned up. But no squabbling, mind!"

Rawlings noticed more incidents. Whenever Deere's concrete mixers needed moving on the job or in the town, it was always Rogier's teams or trucks which were called to do the work. And it was Rogier's carpenters whom Deere used to construct his forms. He was running a skeleton crew augmented by a vast amount of work done by Rogier's men which was not provided for in his sub-contract. Rawlings also noticed Deere hanging around the desk of the timekeeper Moody whenever Rogier was out of the office.

Rawlings said nothing of his suspicions to Rogier. His employer always had been a man for facts. Too, he had a stiff-necked pride so rooted in his own integral honesty that he could never believe in baseness from any man he once had accepted. Even in his few squabbles with Deere he had been courteous enough to lead the man out of ear-shot from all employees. And invariably he addressed him as "Mr. Deere," a formality that Deere never reciprocated.

But what was wrong with Rogier, to be so blind to the obvious? Rogier, he observed, was more nervous and erratic than ever before. And forgetful! In his office, half the time, he was staring at a sketch of a mining shaft instead of his own blueprints. And what was worse, he was gone days at a stretch — up to his blessed mine in the mountains.

Patient, faithful Rawlings! He could — and did — cuss Rogier daily with mild ejaculations of extreme annoyance. But for the man he had served for years beyond recall, whose family accepted him as an integrated part of Rogier's professional life, Rawlings had a deep affection and loyalty which never wavered. Unknown to anyone and long after hours, he began to feed his suspicions with fruitful observations.

One night just past eight o'clock when Rogier was in his shop, engrossed in a schematic of the Sylvanite, a knock sounded on the door. Thinking it was Mrs. Rogier or Ona come to disturb him, he did not even raise his head. Again the knock sounded, louder, more insistent. Rogier impatiently let down his legs from the high stool, and flung open the door to see Rawlings.

"Come in, man, come in!" he said gruffly.

"No sir. You come with me. I've got something to show you!"

There was that in Rawlings' sharp and obstinate voice which Rogier obeyed without question. The two men walked swiftly and in silence to the unfinished job. Rawlings produced a flashlight and led his employer into the tunnel connecting the two buildings. Here on a bench, his lantern and a half-empty pint of whiskey beside him, dozed the night watchman. With a kick Rogier sent the bottle splattering against the brick wall. At the sound of the shattering glass the watchman sat up, blinking his eyes. Before he could utter a word Rogier swung around, grabbed up a water pail, and drenched the man from head to toe.

"Where'd you get that bottle?" demanded Rogier.

"Mr. Deere give it to me," he whined, sputtering. "He said a little drop don't do a man no harm."

"Get off this property and get your time in the morning! If I see you hangin' around and whinin' to Deere, I'll have you arrested. Git!"

Then turning to Rawlings as the man vanished down the tunnel, Rogier demanded irritably, "Doggone it, man! Why can't you tend to things like this instead of bothering me?"

For answer Rawlings led Rogier out of the tunnel and pointed to the lighted window of Rogier's small wooden construction office across the lot. "Two or three nights a week they're in there, both of them."

The two men cautiously approached the shanty and peeked through the window. Moody the timekeeper was pointing to an entry in his big ledger. Deere, seated on top of Rogier's desk, threw back his head and let out a roar of laughter. Then, awkwardly bending forward, he patted Moody's arm.

Rogier, followed by Rawlings, yanked open the door and stepped inside. His sudden appearance snapped off Deere's laughter like an electric switch; the man's jaw dropped and hung as if caught by the fold of fat under his chin, his eyes opening wide with fright. Moody pushed back his chair, nervously closing the ledger and hugging it to his vest, his face red as a radish.

"You conniving yellow-livered poultroon!" thundered Rogier in the deathly silence. "And you, Moody — what are you doing here in my office this time of night? You and your tricks! Why, you ignorant little pen-pusher — I was in this business when you were in diapers. You can't fool me. If you can't keep up those books in the daytime there's a dozen others who can. You're keeping them for me, understand? Not Deere here. And the next time I catch you conflabbin' with him I'm going to kick you off this property so hard your pants are going to burn your back-side. Get out of here now!"

Nor could he wait for the frightened timekeeper to rise and crawl around his desk. He reached out a hand, grasped the man's high celluloid collar, and flung him out the door. For a moment he stood staring at Deere sprawled across the top of his desk.

"And you. By God! If I ever saw an unprincipled fat skunk, you're it. Struttin' around here like Mr. Jesus H. Christ himself. The Big Boss of the Whole Works. Tellin' Moody how to keep my books. Using my men. I told you once, like a gentleman, you were nothin' but a concrete pourer hired to do your work and keep out of my way. Are you deaf? Well, I'm tellin' you again you're workin' for me just like any hod carrier. Who told you to come in my office and lounge on my desk like a whore on a sofa? Get off!" He lunged forward, banging his hand down on the desk.

At the resounding slap beside him, Deere scrambled off and backed against the wall. His face was white; the muscles of his heavy jowls trembled; his small eyes blazed with fright and anger.

And still Rogier kept shouting with magnificent vituperation. He had jerked off his hat. His thin white hair was touseled, his face red, his body trembling with rage. He called Deere every name he could think of, insulted him beyond the endurance of any other man —and began again as if his insults and epithets were inexhaustible. Deere edged forward, intending to brush past and leave the shanty. Rogier stepped in front of him. "No, you don't, Deere! You're going to stay right here till I'm good and finished. And by God, man, if I have to thrash you within an inch of your life, it won't be here. I'll do it in front of every jack-man on the job!"

Deere slunk back.

Rawlings interposed. "Now that's settled! Mr. Rogier —" He was utterly shocked; and staring with unbelieving eyes at Rogier, he nervously began to pull his ears with hands that itched to shut out the astounding outburst. He could see so clearly the Rogier of years ago: walking in quietly and divining the truth of the situation at a glance; could hear him tersely ordering both men out with a cold merciless voice that forestalled talk; envisioned him swiftly going through the books, putting his finger on any discrepancies, and replacing both men at once — all without a trace of visible perturbation. Why, scarce half-dozen years ago he would never have forgotten himself thus. He simply would have called in an expert accountant and acted on the facts. But now! Rawlings kept pulling his ears with trepidation.

He suddenly noticed the ugly leer creeping into Deere's face. With a start he realized that Rogier had overstepped himself. A minute ago he could have walked out leaving Deere and Moody scared to death that he knew perfectly all their machinations. Now it was too late. Rawlings knew that Rogier did not realize the truths he had spoken. His anger was simply derived from his own injured pride and personal animosity against a man whom he could not help but instinctively hating — an outburst occasioned by perhaps no more than the sight of Deere sprawled across his own desk. And by the sneer on Deere's face, Rawlings knew that he too suspected as much. Rogier had only made an implacable enemy of the man who with Moody would resume his scheming more adroitly, now that he had been forewarned. And nothing that Rawlings could ever say would convince Rogier of his folly.

He turned suddenly as Rogier stopped talking and stood glaring at Deere. The concrete man returned his glare with a frightened but contemptuous sneer, grabbed up his hat and strode toward the door.

Rogier stepped back to let him pass. After a minute he slouched down at his desk and carefully smoothed out the rumpled blueprints. "There, by Jove!" he said finally. "That ought to teach him to behave himself!"

Rawlings, with a long sad face, sat pulling the lobes of his ears. He surmised correctly that this was to be Rogier's last big job.

Cable goes back to mine, w/o hope. Dying of despair

9

Boné had written another immensely popular tune. He sent home a music sheet on whose cover was imprinted a picture of nebulous ghosts, and on whose margin was scribbled in pencil, "With apologies to 435 and the Kadles. Love. Boné." Mary Ann and Ona spread it out on the piano that evening; and sitting down on the bench, sang and played it to the family:

> They squeak, they creep
> And yowl and prowl,
> Whoo — whoo — whoo?
> *Our old family ghosts!*

Ending it with a crash of chords, Mary Ann spun around laughing. "Can you imagine a crazy thing like that! One of the best selling pieces in the country. Boné's done it again. Just like 'Ching, Ching, Chinaman'!"

"Nonesense!" ejaculated Rogier. "From a grown man, too. What about that symphony or something he was supposed to be doing?"

"His letter says it's going to be published in Vienna. But he's on another tour back East. When it's over he's going back to San

Francisco," answered Ona quietly.

"I do think he could have restrained himself from being so publicly facetious about our own home," added Mrs. Rogier.

Nancy scowled. "There's nothing funny about it. There's something I been meaning to tell you." She hesitated. "You know that bed I've sleeping in on the Third Floor. Facing the door of the little south room at the head of the steps. There's where it happens just after midnight."

"What?" asked Ona.

"A light. A pale round sort of light. It shines on the wall at the head of the steps for a long time. Then, just as slow, it slides along the wall and stops on the door of the little room on the landing." At the look on Rogier's face she raised her voice. "Granddad, I'm not fooling! I'm not a fraidy-cat either! It happens when the moon's shining and when it's dark. I pulled down the window blind so there wasn't any shine from the arc-light outside, I hollered once and I threw my shoe once. I tell you, it wasn't anybody and that light isn't natural. It's spooky."

Rogier's reaction was immediate and decisive. "Dom those Kadles! They've been keeping up this tomfoolery long enough. Their everlastin' squeakin' is bad enough without any more nonsense. I won't have it!"

He moved Nancy downstairs and hammered into place a big plank across the Third Floor stairs.

"Daddy, see what you've done!" said Ona testily. "Driven nails into the polished redwood bannister. And how is Mother to get her sheets and blankets off the bed, I'd like to know!"

"What's wrong with her crawling underneath that plank, she's little enough. But I say, let them rot." Gathering up his hammer and saw, Rogier clumped noisily down the stairs.

Nancy's resentment at sleeping on a cot was soon dissipated; she got her old room back. One night Jim left the house without saying goodbye. A week later Mary Ann, murmuring vaguely of another business opportunity offered her, left to open a Sweete Shoppe in Silverton.

Early that summer Rogier's High School Annex was finished and both buildings formally accepted. When the books were balanced, all men and accounts paid, there remained for Rogier a few trifling hundred dollars. Due to his own lack of acumen, the rascality of Moody and Deere now vacationing in California, and the fact that he had been diverting his profit to the Sylvanite, he was financially little better off than when he had started.

But he had put down the shaft another eighty feet — at the drilling rate of $36 per foot through solid granite — where it had broken into a great vug or underground chamber. Rogier immediately established a new level station and ordered exploratory tunnels cut. He was jubilant as all get-out.

"Look! A forty-five foot vug. Right in solid granite. Didn't I tell you we'd be running into something?"

Jake and Abe nodded gloomily. "Sure, Colonel," said Jake. "A vug like that cave of Aladdin's or somebody. Floor and ceiling of solid gold. Crystals big as walnuts. All that. But we haven't found a single trace."

"The whole thing's clear enough now for me," added Abe. "There's been a big blow-out here. The little veins we worked were close to the surface. The farther down we come the worse they got. And now with this big poop hole it's plain there's no use goin' deeper. It's an empty air-bubble. A Pike's Peak Bubble. I'm for quittin'."

For Abe it was a long speech and a significant judgment.

Rogier was aghast. "Hold on, Abe! You can't mean what you say! Didn't I tell you we'd hit a chamber full of gold crystals in solid granite? Now you've hit a chamber. A forty-five foot vug, man. It's only a sign of another to come. Then you'll see what I told you!"

Having heard this prophecy so often before, Abe turned away. Rogier grabbed him by the arm. Abandoning his grandiloquent descriptions, he got down to brass tacks. "You're too good a minin' man to quit now, Abe. A short exploration tunnel first. Just to be sure. You wouldn't throw me down before a last look, Abe? God Almighty, man! You're my right arm!"

It was an outright, desperate appeal the faithful Zebbelins could not withstand. They firmly protested against sinking the shaft deeper, but agreed to work the new level for all possible leads. The drilling crew was released, and again Abe and Jake took up the labor of cutting laterally through hard rock. Scarcely ten feet to the northwest they blasted into another hollow chamber or poop hole.

Splayed on one wall was a thin tracery of sylvanite ore.

Rogier went wild with excitement. "It's just as I told you, boys! We're reaching the cardiacal center of the old Peak herself! The golden heart of the Rockies!" He could not be kept out of the big chambers. How vast and cavernous they were, greater than any stopes he had seen, even in the Elkton. How silent, how black! They evoked in him a sense of wonder that instantly dispelled any thought of mining. Their mystery was more profound, shrouded in that Cimmerian darkness whose velvety texture was like sable. Lost in this eternal labyrinth of time, he crawled deeper inward, oblivious of surface time. Only Abe could get him out.

"Look, Colonel. With you down here below, Jake's got to man the hoist above. That don't leave nobody to work but me, and it's more'n a one-man job."

Rogier blinked at the truth in the sunshine.

"Somethin' else," went on Abe. "The assays have come in. It's shippin' ore again. Just barely. But I say there won't be enough for a shipment. That stuff is just splayed out thin on one wall. It don't look like it goes through."

"How do you know?" shouted Rogier. "Let's go through and see!"

"Who's goin' through, with Jake up above on the hoist? And who's goin' to do the sortin'?"

"Cable of course," Rogier answered without hesitation. "Didn't I tell you last winter I'd have him up here again? Don't you worry. I'll get him up here." He rushed down to Little London.

Cable had reached the end of his tether as a life insurance salesman. Under Mr. Perkins' merciless driving he had climbed up four places on the blackboard of endeavor: riding around town on his bicycle all day, visiting prospective clients every evening, buttonholing acquaintances on streetcorners, fretting at night. The effort had worn him out. Even Ona knew that he was not cut out for a businessman. And when, bored and listless, he dropped back to the bottom of the list, they both knew he and Mr. Perkins had come to the parting of their ways.

"Jonathan, you know what I want?" Ona asked him one night, flinging her arms around him. "To build our house out on your prairie lot, and move away from everybody where we can be happy!" They had not driven out there all spring, and she was worried at his unaccountable loss of interest in it.

Cable smiled gently. "To build a house would cost a lot of money. And I won't be getting it selling insurance any more than I got it selling neckties."

"But surely there'll be some other way."

"What?"

Ona could not answer. A week later Cable quit his job before he was fired, and began hunting another job while the bills began to pile up. It was during this propitiously discouraging time that Rogier arrived with the electrifying news that he had struck pay ore in the Sylvanite and needed Cable immediately.

Cable was not impressed. Still he muttered, "Shipping ore, eh? Well, that's something."

"Something?" growled Rogier. "Steady wages to meet all household expenses. Your share when we hit it big. It's opening up now — hollow chambers that'll give way to the treasure vug I've been telling you about. Why, — "

"No!" said Ona, cutting him short. "That's the same old story I've heard all my life. Jonathan's never going up there again if we have to starve!"

And now it began again, the same old battle between her and her father. This time she knew it for the last, remembering Cable's condition when he had returned from the mine last fall. Too well she knew the danger of miners contracting phthisis from drill dust; that pneumonia was almost invariably fatal in the high altitude; and the additional dangers from falling rock, bad air and gas, a hundred other risks. She did not blame Rogier now; she knew him too well. It was only that accursed worthless mine which for years had been the bane of all their lives — draining their purses, their hopes and lives, enslaving them like a monstrous machine, warping Rogier, and now at last trying to draw Cable within its relentless greedy maw. It was no use; she'd said it all before.

She knew it that night when in her thin silk shift she flung herself upon his lap and against him. By the pressure of her breast, the demanding clasp of her warm arms, she appealed without shame to the slow fire within him to burn away her fear, to enwrap her within its passionate shroud against all else. She could feel the answer in his embrace as he ran his hand under her arm, along her bare side and up to close upon her breast. But so slowly! It was warmth, but not fire, without the swift fusing passion. Of a sudden she went cold with fear.

"Jonathan! Why don't we cut loose and go to Shallow Water? Write Bert Bruce!" she gasped, astounded at the thought which had suddenly leaped out unbidden.

He raised his head, staring out the window as if at the fleeting vision of sage and sand, the sandy Gallegos in moonlight. "Too late," he said, "I reckon I'm in the Sylvanite to the end."

Next evening he told Rogier at supper he would return with him to Cripple Creek. Ona kept pestering her father with questions: Was the cabin really warm and comfortable? — Did they have enough to eat and plenty of blankets? — Jonathan did use the hot water bag and rub his chest at night, didn't he?

The questions remained unanswered then and for months afterward. Ona could only sit at her window and wait and hope, and then get up and write another letter to Cable.

Up at the Sylvanite, he read them through slowly and dropped them into the fire. This listless release of her words of encouragement and love was not the index of his character. He was like a man whose mainspring was broken, who no longer cared to retain his hold upon a life so devoid of meaning. When a sock wore through at the heel, it too was dropped into the fireplace instead of being retained for darning. One' by one he discarded his belongings, gave up his hold on the mine. With Abe and Jake he did his work without shirking but without interest. And when he was through, he refused to discuss the mine's prospects.

Most of the summer he felt well. He sat in the sunshine upon the dump, sorting ore, the breeze hardly disturbing a thread of his coarse black hair. On infrequent weekends he went down to Little London, his healthy appearance reassuring Ona, and his listless air disturbing her. March came up, doing the chores and rushing off to spend the day rambling around the district. What was happening to him Cable did not know. But it seemed he was cut off from a vital relationship with his wife, his son, from Rogier, Abe and Jake, from the mine, life itself.

Then, unannounced, came fall. March returned to Little Lon-

don to go to school. Cold rains set in, then frost. Cable, spelled off
from work on dump and hoist, went down into the mine where he
found it even colder. In the evening he sat bowed and cross-legged
on the cabin floor in front of the fire. Jake and Abe never minded
him, so early they went to bed. And he seemed to exude a dark
repellent aloofness that forebade communion. He had begun to
cough again.

There was beginning to resolve within him the struggle which
meant the end. How often had he witnessed on the Reservation that
hopeless confusion of the Indian trying to adapt himself to the
advancing civilization of the white. Yet it was a trivial problem
compared to his own. No Vrain Girls, no government agents could
help him. For in Cable was not a racial unity of character that had
only to adapt to an outward change of conditions. Deep within
himself, the mixed-blood, was the turmoil.

It had always been so, as if his very bloodstream raced all ways
in hopeless contradiction. Educated, loving Ona and his children, he
had found himself time and again in a position to succeed to a dull
and comfortable existence. And then from somewhere within him
rose without warning a wave of black negation washing him adrift on
the other side of that vast gulf in which lay the centuries between the
red and the white.

His months at Shallow Water had marked the turn. The vast
sunlit desert of sage and sand, the dark-faced People — to these his
long submerged atavistic instincts had leaped exultantly, obliterating
all his life since childhood. Only Ona and Rogier, the one who held
him by emotion and the other who tugged at the strings of his
outward existence, had brought him back to a meaningless routine
that little by little crushed out of him all spontaneous life. Living
rhythmically, devoid of ambition and competitiveness, and with an
attitude that implied an acceptance of his oneness with the animate
universe, Cable never reasoned by analysis. He simply felt.

And now caught without escape he did not, like the white, fight
violently against the unbeautiful. Like an Indian, he refuted it as if it
did not exist. But there was nothing left. Nothing but the heaviness
of frustration settling in his heart, the stifling sense of
self-unfulfillment. So he sat there, high in the cold granite canyon,
stolid, taciturn, without hope. Sat as thousands before him had sat

wrapped in their blankets: in dwindling Reservations, in Indian schools, in jails; fed, clothed, administered to, but with the mainspring of life broken within them—a race of men never assimilated, not understood. What they lacked no one seemed to know. It was as if their whole inward existence had been geared to a rhythm that once broken could never be attuned.

So Cable, staring into the flames. He had made his fight. The turmoil had died within him. Money from the mine, a position down in town, his lot out on the prairie, even Ona and his children, meant nothing to him now. Nor did a renewal of life at Shallow Water. It was too late. He wanted nothing. He remembered an old Plains Indian shut up in jail years before who had sat for a month without speaking, and when finally released had crawled off to sit on the edge of town and die. He remembered a little Navajo boy placed in a Reservation school who had stolidly refused food, preferring to starve unless sent back to his *hogan*.

They did not grieve nor brood. He knew now what it was they felt: that black stifling sense of negation clouding his mind, gathering in the pit of his stomach, paralyzing his deep nerve centers. That impenetrable Indian stolidity against which nothing could avail. Nor did he fight against it now. He was content to give himself to it wholly. Only, growing cold, he reached to the bunk behind him for a blanket. With a gesture seemingly habitual, he wrapped this around his shoulders, and sat staring at the dying embers with a face dark and immobile as if of carven wood.

10

A week before Christmas, Rogier in Little London received a
telegram from Abe and Jake. Mrs. Rogier rushed with it up Bijou
to Ona's house. "Now don't get excited none! You know how a cold
scares people to death that high up!"

Ona grabbed the telegram. Atrociously worded, misspelled,
and unimproved by the busy railroad agent and telegraph operator
at Victor, it said simply that Cable was "more terrible sicker" and
to "blanket him conclusively" when he arrived on the afternoon
train.

All the family went to the station to meet him, but Cable did not
get off the train. Not until Rogier had asked the conductor and
turned to stride up the platform toward the engine, did Ona com-
prehend the Zebbelins' message. Ignoring the children who clam-
ored, "Where's Daddy? — I thought he was comin' on the train," she
ran swiftly behind Rogier to the baggage car.

She stopped abruptly, stuffing her handkerchief in her mouth to
stifle a scream. The big door of the car had been slid back, a hand
truck of trunks and express unloaded and wheeled away. Inside on a
collapsible canvas cot partially covered with a greasy tarpaulin, lay

Cable.

With Rogier she sprang toward the car. Rogier put a foot on the wheel hub of a second truck pulled up to the open door and tried to clamber inside. Two men, heavily armed, pushed him down and ordered him to stand back, pointing to a stack of bricks half-covered with a canvas and stacked in the car opening. Ona knew what it was: a shipment of gold bullion being sent down from the mill to the Denver mint. "Make 'em take Jonathan out first!" she screamed at Rogier.

"It won't take a minute, lady," one of the guards said gruffly. "Can't you see the stuff's all piled up and ready? It's got to catch the Denver express."

Gold, always the gold that had to come first! She stood back, breathing a wordless but anguished prayer, her gaze on the still form of Cable. Times on end she had seen men thus rushed down from Cripple Creek on the first train; pneumonia at that high altitude was swift and fatal. At last the cot was lowered to a truck and hauled down the brick platform. Ona walked beside it, holding her coat over Cable's drawn face to shield it from the stinging blasts of snow. He was awake and tried to smile. "We figured I'd better not wait," he muttered thickly. "Abe's a good horse. He carried me most of the way down the gulch."

And now began another anguishing delay inside the waiting room; they had forgotten to order an ambulance. Leona muttered plaintively, a little frightened. March, ever so sensitive, was a-shamed of his father's appearance. He kept shrinking from the rude, curious travelers gawking at the group around the cot. It was bad enough to be stretched out helpless before so many people. But his father was so dirty! His long, black, uncombed hair hung over the edge of the cot. He was unshaven, his ears brown with dust, and from beneath the tarp his half-boots stuck out caked with muck.

By the time they reached home Ona had got hold of herself. They laid Cable on the sofa in the parlor, Ona jerking down from the winuow the Christmas wreaths which collected soot and dust.

"I wish you'd taken him home and put him in Sister Molly's big front room upstairs," said Mrs. Rogier.

"This is his home and mine," Ona answered curtly.

The doctor Rogier had called arrived. "He ought to be in a

hospital," he told Ona after his examination, "but I wouldn't move him now. Not even upstairs to the bedroom. Parlor or not, this is the place for him. I want you to sleep in the dining room, close and handy, and keep the fire going. Have the children stay upstairs out of the way."

That evening, unannounced, a red-headed French nurse named Suzanne knocked at the door. She had a nice smile, was quiet and unassuming, and after one glance took charge of the house. Thus began a desperate two-day period marked off regularly by the passing trains which shook the house and rained cinders against the rattling windows, the only noise in the quiet house.

For hours at a time Mrs. Rogier sat stiffly in the dining room. Cable from the first had captured her fancy. Between them—a woman flushed with the pride of a Southern aristocracy however false it might be, and a shy swarthy stranger of Indian blood—had grown a strange attachment, if only to attest the solidarity of aristocratic humility and peasant pride, their equal strength and courageous honesty. Neither was ever only common. Rogier, helpless, restless, and erratic, stormed back and forth a dozen times a day. The children, peeking inside the parlor, ate quietly in the kitchen and crept upstairs. Suzanne was capable and indefatigable, earning forever their blessings. In her precious few moments of rest she read European war dispatches in the newspapers, admitting she was waiting for her call. And Ona every moment gave the sick man her undivided care, if only to sit uncomfortably dozing beside him but still grasping his hand.

But he, the beloved object of their unceasing attention, seemed oblivious to all but the thin streak of light, like the eastern horizon at dawn, which showed below the drawn window blind. At this, hour after hour, he stared with black unfathomable eyes. He had been shaved and washed, and yet with a swift and almost imperceptible change his foreign aspect increased; his cheek bones stood out high and gaunt, his big Roman nose became increasingly prominent, his eyes grew blacker, and as his color ebbed his swarthiness seemed ingrained to the very bone. He lay there as if impenetrably cloaked at last, not alone by the dark shadow, but by a racial fortitude summoned from a long past. He never asked for his children and took no cognizance of whether it was Ona or the nurse who administered to him.

"Is your husband a drinking man?" the doctor asked Ona the afternoon of the second day.

She drew herself up proudly. "Certainly not!"

The doctor left without comment.

Now, that evening, four days before Christmas, Cable's labored breathing developed into the faint sound of a rattle. March upstairs, wide-eyed and sleepless, had forgotten to say his prayers; an omission he tried to make up for thereafter until grown by murmuring, "Oh Jesus, help nobody dies tonight" — a terror-stricken appeal from a guilt he could not forget. He got up and crept down the stairs. The door to the parlor was closed. He knelt and peeked through the keyhole. His mother was lying on the sick-bed with her arms around his father. She had taken off her shoes, and the boy could see in her cotton stockings her toes crooking stiffly with.anguish. The nurse was sitting across the room.

The boy retreated to sit mid-way up the stairs in the cold darkness of the shabby hall, shivering in his thin nightgown. His mind was too numbed by a nameless fear to think. But against the fear he ground his teeth and clutched the wooden bannister. A strange compassion gripped and squeezed his bowels. He felt almost sick enough to vomit.

In a little while the nurse found him there. She helped him into his warm coat and boots. "Go down to your grandfather's house and stay there," she told him. "Tell him — just tell him we sent you."

March crept downstairs, past the parlor, and out the front hall door. It was snowing heavily. There was a Christmas party in the house next door. Through the window he could see the lighted candles on the tree. He crossed the road to the railroad underpass. A single light faintly illumined the sandstone blocks on either side. Through the underpass he emerged at the end of Bijou Street. There was not another arc-light between him and the bridge across Shook's Run, a half-mile west. To his left, in the vacant prairie between the railroad and the curving creek, stood a deserted wooden shanty. Two weeks past, a Negro inside had killed his wife with an axe. The following day the boy had peeked inside to see the besplattered blood and the black hair sticking to the slashed walls. So now he walked in the middle of the road.

The snow was almost up to his knees. The flakes drove down his unbuttoned collar, melted and wet his nightgown. Somewhere a dog whimpered. It sounded more lonely than a wolf at timberline. And to his side under the falling snow, as if they were the shacks and shanties of Poverty Row, a sparse row of buildings held still more people asleep and insensible to the misery, pain, sorrow, and mystery forever bestriding the lonely roads across the wide and bitter earth.

Alone in the dark snow-stung night! Alone in the glare of the midday sun, in crowds and work and worry, in the illusions of success and proverty. He would always be alone, but never more than now.

He crossed the bridge over Shook's Run, cautiously approached the gaunt old house. All three stories were dark. For awhile he stood on the steps. He was here — from back there. Why? It was all preternaturally impressed upon him, to carry always. And now the fear and pain and strange compassion made him more sick than ever. He began to shake violently. And yet he began to dread seeing anyone, as if his only wish was to hide his misery in perpetual solitude.

Finally he rang the bell, kept ringing.

A lamp appeared inside, and beside it the face of Rogier. March watched him part the curtains, set down the lamp. Unlocking the door, he stood there in his nightshirt holding open the screen.

The boy did not move or speak. He clenched his teeth in a vain effort to stop the echo of a rattle that shook his whole body. With big brown eyes he stared at the wisps of white hair sticking up above the rough-hewn face, the steady, suddenly comprehending eyes.

Then an arm reached out and gathered him against that old body already half consumed by the strange fire within. Pity and compassionate silence, they weld us together without the need for words. The door banged behind him.

Thus did he too come to his grandfather's house.

Near midnight the death rattle stopped in Cable's throat. The nurse rose, looked at him and the woman in whose arms he lay, and went out to the dining room to stare at the headlines of the newspaper spread out on the table. Then she went upstairs to sit quietly beside Leona, restlessly tossing in bed.

With the cessation of the rattle, the dying man turned slightly and fell on his back across Ona's arm. The silence was profound and oppressive; it seemed to lie in a stagnant pool filling the room. The fire had gone out, and a cloying cold seeped through the window cracks. Ona raised slightly in order to stare at the beloved but unfamiliar countenance of him who was slipping now, without effort and forever, from her love's grasp. It was less serene than implacable, a face devoid of expression save for the unfathomable black eyes which stared fixedly, without interest or indifference, into that realm which opens to all more indifferently still. Yet, unaccountably, she could still feel something within him still mortal as wet adobe. Slippery, unconstrained, it seemed to overflow that ungiving barrier over which he stared with rapt indifference — overflowed and then slipped back again.

Suddenly, and without warning, a flicker of intelligence lighted his eyes. It was as if the gates of his inmost being had swung open and shut. He smiled, the barest withdrawal of lips from his white even teeth. In reflex his hand closed upon hers. And then, passing from sight forever, all that was mortal of Cable slipped the fetters which had bound his wild freedom and elusive strength — passed effortlessly as a feathered shadow over the sunlit plains which had ever called his vagrant spirit.

A few days after the funeral Ona and the children moved down to live in the gaunt old house on Shook's Run. Mrs. Rogier had prepared Sister Molly's big redwood bedroom for them. "It's the best room in the house, like you know, and big enough for a half-dozen. March can have the alcove and the front balcony all for his own, and you and Leona can make yourself at home in the rest."

Ona, grim-lipped, shook her head. "The Third Floor will be plenty good enough."

Mrs. Rogier gave her a penetrating look. "You can't possibly feel that way, child. Of all persons, you should know best that this house is like your Mother's heart — you really have never been gone from either."

It was this incontrovertible truth that hurt the most. A woman who had returned at last to that inescapable old home, at once a womb and an oubliette, she knew now that her marriage and life with Cable had been but a brief absence during which it had been given her to experience for once and always the outside world, to taste the joys and fears, the freedom and responsibilities of one who stands alone. It was as if she had completed — so soon! — the circle of her life, only to realize now the precious independence for which Cable had stood against the Rogiers. Henceforth she was to be not an individual but a part, indistinguishable from those others who had failed to escape from their ancestral womb.

Resolutely she ripped off the plank boarding up the stairs and marched up to the barny Third Floor. In the crepuscular winter light it looked altogether forbidding. Dust covered the plank floor, the rafters, the bedsteads. Spider webs and cocoons clung to the corners. And from the ceiling, like sewed-up bodies, hung the sacks of bedclothes and pillows. After two days of washing, scrubbing, tacking down carpets, laying rugs, and hanging curtains, it still looked depressing but presentable.

March, big enough for a room of his own, was given the little south room at the head of the steps. On the floor he spread Ona's Two Gray Hills rug, and on the bed the one he had sent her from Shallow Water. On the walls he hung Cable's Plains Indian treasures: a soft buckskin shirt with a panel of crimson-dyed porcupine quills, a gorgeous war bonnet of eagle feathers tipped with red yarn that hung to his knees when he put it on, and a dozen pairs of Cheyenne and Arapaho beaded moccasins. Jewelry given him by Bert Bruce and the Vrain Girls littered dresser and bookcase: Navajo bracelets, necklaces, rings, and belt buckles of silver and chunk turquoise. The barbaric color and strangeness of the room whenever Ona walked into it, gave her a start. It seemed to her that with all these relics he was trying, unwittingly, to evoke the nebulous past of a dead father and a dying race. She was glad to see, much as she hated it, a big case of ore specimens from Cripple Creek.

The barny north room, extending two-thirds the length of the house, Ona reserved for herself, Leona, and Nancy who moved up with them for company. It was long and low, dark and cheerless even in daylight and summer. Nevertheless Ona was content in it. It forced her downstairs to work. Never could she stand the thought of sitting and brooding in Sister Molly's room. For now like one reincarnated, she found herself apeing the despair of Sister Molly whose Tom had blithely set up the Pass to Leadville to make his fortune, leaving his two boys and Sister Molly to grieve herself to death.

As the days wore on, Ona was increasingly troubled by the spector of that memory; it seemed to her that the pattern of life in this gaunt old house never changed. Tom, who had left Sister Molly and his two boys; Jonathan, who had left her with Leona and March; Cecil Burgess and Mary Ann who had abandoned Nancy here in this graveyard of lost hopes. And behind them all, the same enigmatic mountains, the same wild lust for gold or silver, the same curse that had killed Tom, old man Reynolds, and Cable.

A stray suspicion leaped into her mind. Shortly after Cable's death, remembering the doctor's question whether Cable had been a drinking man, she had asked him what he meant.

"He was sinking so rapidly I thought a drink of whiskey might rally him, but didn't know whether he could stand it," the doctor had replied. "No offense meant, of course."

"Of course."

And now she lay writhing under that question which would forever remain unanswered: did Cable's morning glass of whiskey make him a drinking man?

But what if she had encouraged him to refinance his haberdashery store, to settle on his prairie lot east of town, to remain with Bert Bruce at Shallow Water? Vain regrets, unanswered questions which, alone at night, she knew futile. She, with March, Leona, Nancy, and Mrs. Rogier were imprisoned hostages to Rogier's monomaniacal search for gold in the Sylvanite, come what might.